The New Shell Guides
Northern Scotland and the Islands

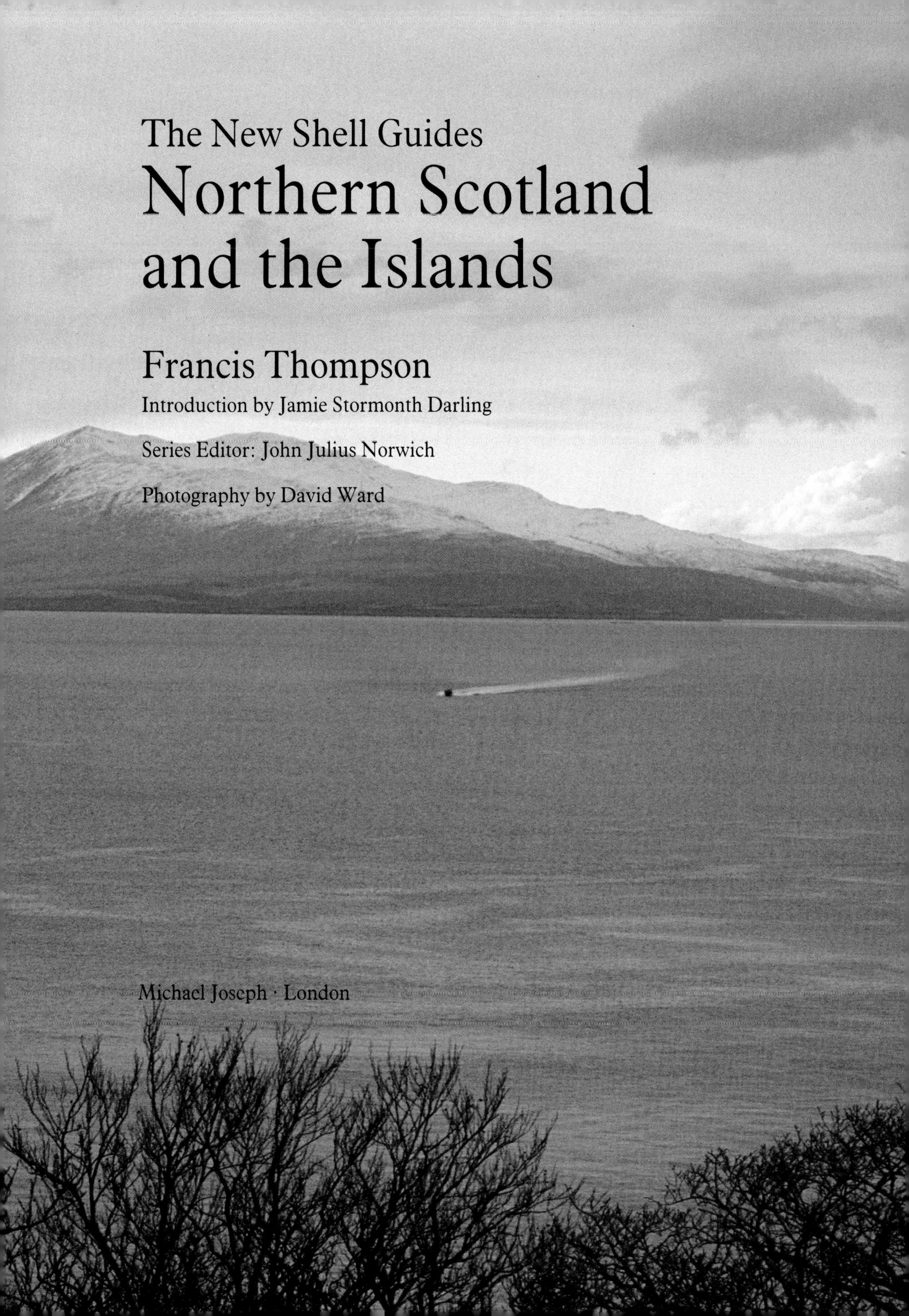

The New Shell Guides
Northern Scotland and the Islands

Francis Thompson

Introduction by Jamie Stormonth Darling

Series Editor: John Julius Norwich

Photography by David Ward

Michael Joseph · London

First published in Great Britain by
Michael Joseph Limited, 27 Wrights Lane,
London W8 5TZ 1987

This book was designed and produced by
Swallow Editions Limited, Swallow House,
11–21 Northdown Street, London N1 9BN

British Library Cataloguing in Publication Data:
Thompson, Francis, 1931–
    The new Shell guide to Northern Scotland
    and the islands.
    1. Hebrides (Scotland) — Description and
    travel — Guide-books
    1. Title
    914.11′404858   DA880.H4

Cased edition: ISBN 0 7181 2763 3
Paperback edition: ISBN 0 7181 2768 4

Editor: Raymond Kaye
Cartographer: ML Design
Production: Hugh Allan

Filmset by Wyvern Typesetting Limited, Bristol, England
Origination by Adroit Photo Litho Limited,
Cecil Street, Birmingham B19 3ST
Printed and bound by Kyodo Shing Loong Printing, Singapore

A list of Shell publications
can be obtained by writing to:

Department UOMK/60
Shell UK Oil
PO Box No. 148
Shell-Mex House
Strand
London WC2R 0DX

*Front jacket photograph: Castle Stalker, Loch Laich,
near Oban*
*Back jacket photograph: Croft, near Achiltibuie,
Inverpolly National Nature Reserve (see p. 143)*
Title page: The Mull ferry departing from Oban (see p. 169)

Contents

Editorial Note   7

Introduction *by Jamie Stormonth Darling*   9
The Scottish Clans   21
Crofting: A Way of Life   29
The Impact of North Sea Oil and Gas on Scotland *by H. F. Wickham*   37
The Gaelic Dimension: the Scots Character   43
Scotland's Wilderness   51
The West Highland Way   61

Gazetteer   67

Further Information   211
Bibliography   212
Maps   213
Index   221

John Julius Norwich was born in 1929. He read French and Russian at New College, Oxford, and in 1952 joined the Foreign Office where he served until 1964. Since then he has published two books on the medieval Norman Kingdom in Sicily, *The Normans in the South* and *The Kingdom in the Sun*; two historical travel books, *Mount Athos* (with Reresby Sitwell) and *Sahara*; an anthology of poetry and prose, *Christmas Crackers*; and two volumes on the history of Venice, *Venice, the Rise to Empire* and *Venice, the Greatness and the Fall*, now published in one volume as *A History of Venice*. He was also general editor of *Great Architecture of the World* and, more recently, author of *The Architecture of Southern England*.

In addition, he writes and presents historical documentaries for BBC television and frequently broadcasts on BBC radio. He is chairman of the Venice in Peril Fund, a Trustee of the Civic Trust, a member of the Executive and Properties Committees of the National Trust.

Francis Thompson was born in Stornoway on the Isle of Lewis and he now works there as a Lecturer in Electrical Engineering at Lews Castle College.

His second career as a freelance writer began some thirty years ago and he has since contributed to magazines, newspapers and has broadcast talks and short stories on radio. His main literary interests have centred on the Highlands and Islands of Scotland and he has written some twenty full-length books. He has been closely involved with the history and culture of the Gaelic-speaking areas of the Highlands. In 1979 he won the Hugh MacDiarmid Memorial Cup for poetry.

Sir Jamie Carlisle Stormonth Darling was born in 1918. Educated at Winchester and Christ Church, Oxford, he joined The King's Own Scottish Borderers as a Territorial Officer in 1938.

In 1949, qualifying as Writer to the Signet (Solicitor) with a law degree from Edinburgh University, he was appointed Secretary – subsequently styled Director – of the National Trust for Scotland. For 34 years he served the Trust through an active period of rapid expansion. He was knighted in 1984.

Hugh Wickham, a keen sportsman, joined Shell International Petroleum Company in 1964 from Associated Electrical Industries, where he had been Films Officer. He was appointed Public Relations Manager of Shell Thailand in 1969 and joined Shell UK on his return to England as Deputy Trade Relations Manager. In 1975 he was appointed Customer Relations manager and took up his present position as Manager of Marketing Communications in 1977.

David Ward was born in England in 1960. He graduated with an Honours Degree in Photography from the Polytechnic of Central London in 1983. In addition to his recent work he is currently working on a series of walking books – a personal passion.

Editorial Note

Entries in the Gazetteer are arranged alphabetically. If a place name begins with 'The', this follows the main element in the entry heading, i.e. **Trossachs**, **The**.

If a name within the text of an entry is printed in CAPITAL LETTERS, this indicates that it has a Gazetteer entry of its own.

Entry headings are followed by a map reference in parentheses, thus: **Aberdour**, *Fife* (5/2B). The figure 5 is the map number; 2B is the grid reference, with 2 indicating the across, and B the down reference.

Every effort has been made to ensure that information about whether buildings, estates, gardens etc. are open to the public, and at what times, as well as statements about ferry services, were as accurate and up to date as possible at the time of going to press. Such particulars are, of course, subject to alteration over the years and it may be prudent to check them locally or with the appropriate organizations or authorities.

Introduction

JAMIE STORMONTH-DARLING

With over 50 years of enjoyment in exploring, and always learning from, the Scotland that lies north and west of its 35-mile waistline, which stretches from the Forth to the Clyde estuaries, I have been most fortunate to have been constantly on the move throughout the north and west. I have also been privileged through the National Trust for Scotland to have joined in the guardianship of nearly 40 national possessions. These range from remote St Kilda and Fair Isle to Brodick Castle on Arran, with its gardens and the Goat Fell range as background, and from the wealth of magnificent castles and gardens in Aberdeenshire to the hallowed island of Iona in the west. I hope that even the mention of these magical places will whet the appetite, and cause this book to be used as an indispensable guide, and that each day spent on trek in Scotland will give the reader as much excitement, enjoyment and insight into this land of ours as it has given to me.

The timing of this new Shell Guide is perfect – indeed it is overdue. So many new developments, improvements and opportunities have occurred in recent years that it is good that information on them can now be gathered together. It is over 21 years since the last edition, and that covered the whole of Scotland. Now we are able to devote our attention to the whole of the mainland north of the Forth and Clyde, and all the islands.

Much has indeed happened. There has been a veritable revolution in attitudes towards welcoming and informing visitors. Standards of presentation and interpretation have been vastly improved, and there is an excellent spirit of cooperation among those who work together to make each visit memorable and enjoyable. There is a whole host of organizations, some of central and local government, some voluntary and independent, and an increasing number of private owners, all working towards a more integrated network of places to visit, with clear information on how to find them.

Any Introduction should of course highlight the most essential ingredient in the pleasure of any visit anywhere: the people you meet; all those there is time and opportunity to talk to on your travels. It is all too easy to dash through a country without making real contact with the people whose guest you are.

By way of encouraging you to get off the fast roads, and thus to succeed in meeting the true Scot, here are the reflections of a percipient and experienced English traveller. These comments by H.V. Morton over half a century ago are still true today; they come from his Introduction to *In Scotland Again* (1933). 'The more I know of Scotland the more certain I am that of all countries in the World it is the most kindly, the most polite, and the most considerate.' And he goes on to recollect the 'warmth of feeling, a sincerity which is purely Scottish'.

The BBC in a television series tried to answer the question 'Who are the Scots?' It is a good question, which encourages us all to go out and try to find the answer. Whatever the background history, it is fascinating today to find that many communities, areas and regions of Scotland have distinctive characteristics. The Fifer is distin-

Opposite: St John's Cross and St Columba's shrine, Iona (see also p. 144)

guishable from someone in Aberdeen. The people of Orkney and Shetland are different again from the mainland Scots, and to the west the Hebrideans are a race apart.

Contrast there certainly is in people, but it is the contrast and change in landscape and way of life that make the strongest appeal. You never have to travel far to delight in a complete change of scenery (and nowhere in Scotland is more than about 66 miles from the sea). The Kingdom of Fife is a good example in miniature, with its fertile fields dominated by the Lomonds looking down on Loch Leven, and its castle where Mary, Queen of Scots was imprisoned. To find heather, and even grouse, surrounded by such a lowland scene is typical of this variety which is repeated in Angus. There early barley and potatoes and July raspberries march alongside the Highland Boundary Fault, beyond which life and climate are very different. Indeed, the full range of experience from a coastline of sandy beaches and a rich wild flora through fertile fields and forestry to the hills and glens of Angus with their red deer and ptarmigan can be gained within 30 miles.

The places that contend for the title of 'the heart of Scotland' lie along that north–south rift where the river Garry bursts through at Killiecrankie. The attractions in that most beautiful area, which can be enjoyed over at least a nine-month season, speak for themselves: from Blair Atholl, with its white harled castle shining out against the background of Beinn a' Ghlo, the working meal mill close by, to the walk though the Pass of Killiecrankie to Pitlochry and its famous Festival Theatre. Here the Garry is joined by the river Tummel, adding to the great weight of water borne by the Tay – one of Europe's great rivers – as it flows past Dunkeld and Perth to the sea at Dundee.

Opposite: Scotland's contrasting scenery. (Above) Wheatfield, near Inverness; (below) heather and fern, Strathconon
Below: Loch Tummel, Pitlochry (see also p. 180)

The Ring of Brogar, Orkney (see also p. 175)   *(Richard Muir)*

Let this area, extending downstream to Dunkeld, be your centre for as long as you can stay. Its variety and changing beauty will never disappoint you, and you can take advantage of the excellent and skilfully landscaped A9.

Leaving this centre you might go eastwards through Strathardle and the braes of Angus towards the mudflats of the Montrose Basin, famous as a wildfowl reserve, or westwards along the Road to the Isles 'by Loch Tummel and Loch Rannoch . . .' as the famous song goes.

A few miles south of Rannoch Station, a most precious remnant of the Old Caledonian Forest survives. This is the Black Wood of Rannoch, of the greatest interest to the forester, entomologist and historian. West across Rannoch Moor, Glencoe, and west again is the sea at Ballachulish on Loch Leven: all in all an itinerary to discover the varying moods of Scotland.

The roads are now so good that you may travel from Edinburgh to Inverness in 100 minutes, and between Ullapool and London, a distance of nearly 600 miles, only Contin in Ross-shire retains its 30 mph speed limit. Roads have also replaced ferries in a number of places.

These few thoughts suggest two entirely different ways for the traveller to enjoy Scotland: either from one of at least 25 excellent centres from which to radiate at leisure; or, more energetically, to follow a trail in pursuit of all those places that have something in common. In either case the number of places to visit and sights to see is a challenge to anyone's stamina.

Many of the places to be visited are owned by, or are under the protection of, organizations that exist for the 'Benefit of the Nation'. On behalf of the Secretary of State for Scotland, the Historic Buildings and Monuments Directorate holds over 330 properties of national historical importance. The Nature Conservancy Council has declared 66 National Nature Reserves, and very many Sites of Special Scientific Interest. The Forestry Commission owns a vast acreage of woodlands within which it manages camping and caravan sites, and woodland trails; and local authorities have organized a number of Country Parks. There are also the voluntary and independent bodies such as The National Trust for Scotland, The Scottish Wildlife Trust, the Royal Society for the Protection of Birds, and many others. These look after and make available to the public more than 200 places, large and small, considered worthy of special care and attention.

The catalogue is impressive and must include the family houses and gardens open to visitors on a regular basis, as well as the more than 200 private owners who welcome visitors under Scotland's Gardens Scheme.

The second method for the visitor to explore Scotland – by tracking down those places linked together by a common theme – will involve journeys by car through interesting countryside, and also over the waves.

As a good example, let us take the prehistoric periods, the Stone, Bronze and Iron Ages. For outstanding monuments of these early times we must go primarily to Shetland, Orkney and the Outer Hebrides – starting from Shetland, where in midsummer there is twilight at midnight, so far north is it. Two of Shetland's ancient landmarks are world famous: Jarlshof, and Mousa which is one of the finest surviving broch towers. Orkney will demand as much time as Shetland – visits to Maes Howe, 'the finest megalithic tomb in the British Isles', and to Skara Brae must not be rushed. The hunt for our past could be pursued in the Outer Hebrides on the western shores of Lewis where the Standing Stones of Callanish are unique in Scotland.

Space prevents mention of such monuments on the Scottish mainland, well-endowed as it is, except in our search after these ancient brochs. There are two at Glenelg in Wester Ross that are worth visiting – additionally, and particularly, for the fine view of the peaks of The Five Sisters of Kintail at the head of Loch Duich.

There are many other subjects that can inspire such 'thematic' journeys. One might be 'the abiding heritage of Celtic art'. The remarkable Pictish sculptured stones with their unexplained symbolic formal decoration are mainly to be found in eastern Scotland. Twenty-five of them have been gathered together in the Meigle Museum near Glamis Castle in Angus. Further north, by the roadside east of Forres, is Sueno's Stone, the most remarkable of these unique stones with their mysterious messages. They reveal the transition from a heathen Pictish symbolism to designs enriched with beautiful Celtic ornamentation accompanied by Christian crosses. This naturally leads on to our next possible project, which would be to trace the work of the early Christian missionaries starting from Iona, the cradle of Christianity in Scotland. The Celtic Church has left us with many notable works of art. These include the fine Kildalton Cross on the island of Islay, and the galaxy of monuments in the Kilmartin district of mid-Argyll.

Clan histories and your own roots are another fascinating theme. At Inveraray Castle, the Duke of Argyll presents the stirring history of the powerful Clan Campbell with great skill. The Clan Donald Centre at Armadale Castle, on Skye, most generously provided by loyal American clans people, combines with great sensitivity the adaptation of the Victorian stables as well as part of the castle as a Clan Centre with a presentation of 'the great Clan Donald'. Using these two clan histories

Overleaf: Ruthven Barracks, Kingussie (see also p. 148)

Inveraray Castle (see also p. 141)

and these two bases you would cover most of the west coast, and the Hebrides. To visit Armadale, use the road from Fort William through Glenfinnan to Arisaig and Mallaig, then take the ferry to Skye: a superb way to enjoy west coast scenery.

Glenfinnan suggests another subject that links up many famous places. Tracing the Jacobite story from 1689 to 1746 would take in names that ring in Scottish history: Killicrankie, Glencoe, Kildrummy Castle, Sheriffmuir – and all those landmarks associated with the last nine-month campaign from Glenfinnan to Culloden, and the final departure of Prince Charles Edward from Loch nan Uamh, not far from Glenfinnan itself.

The Jacobite theme should also prompt visits to Ruthven Barracks at Kingussie, and to Fort George, both of which are now well cared for and so well presented to visitors.

There are other subjects that can provide itineraries to extract the maximum enjoyment from precious days in Scotland. The gardens of Scotland, mostly still in private hands, would necessitate travelling throughout the country on journeys that would show the variety due to different weather conditions. The gardens of the east coast will be late, while Inverewe near Poolewe in the west, on the same latitude as Hudson's Bay, enjoys an early spring, thanks to the Gulf Stream. Any journey north in March would be rewarding, but if time does not allow this, a visit to the gardens at

Opposite: The stillroom at Glenfiddich Distillery

Brodick on Arran, and to Crarae near Inveraray on the shores of Loch Fyne, would be well worth while. Each has a marvellous background of hill and sea and would confirm that Scotland possesses some exceptionally fine gardens, lovingly and skilfully tended, for which it is justly famous.

Those who are interested in wild flowers will find both the coastline and the 'high tops' an especially happy hunting ground. To know where to go, the Gazetteer will help, but so will that enthusiastic band of Ranger/Naturalists waiting for you at many of the Reserves of the Scottish Wildlife Trust, or at the properties of The National Trust for Scotland. Ben Lawers, lying north of Loch Tay, is perhaps the best centre of intelligence and is interesting not only for the exciting flora of the Ben itself.

Where to go in search of birds in their season is another subject on which the Gazetteer will be of help, but detailed information should also be sought from the appropriate organizations: Scotland has an exciting range of birds.

A most welcome development has been the opening up of many private estates. It is not that any law of trespass prevents us going where we will – so long as we do no damage – but it is better for everyone if we stick to recognized paths, and it helps if we can visit those estates that go out of their way to welcome us. A notable example is Rothiemurchus close to Aviemore, where a full day could easily be spent enjoying the lower ground of this famous estate, where its whole life, its farming, forestry and fishing, can be seen. Alternatively the chairlift up Cairngorm operates – wind permitting – throughout the year. But please, one word of warning from someone who proudly wore 'Mountain' on his uniform during the Second World War: *never* take the Cairngorms or any of our Scottish hills for granted. The weather can turn savage without warning. Remember, too, 'a 1000 feet up the Cairngorms is a risk of exposure equivalent to 1000 miles northwards into the Arctic regions.'

Scotland's distinctive architecture, vernacular and military, is another absorbing theme for your journeys. James VI described the villages round the coast of the Kingdom of Fife as 'a beggar's mantle fringed with gold'. Here the traveller should leave the main roads and enjoy these delightful villages on foot. The great tower houses and keeps of the north-east that rise so starkly from the ground are in marked architectural contrast. In imitation of the great craftsmanship of these military structures, the Victorians evolved the Scottish 'baronial' style. There are numbers of recent publications that are invaluable guides to this architectural heritage, and the Gazetteer is very informative on this subject.

On a less exalted note whisky is a good subject on which to end this celebration of the delights of Scotland. There is now a Whisky Trail with maps and a warm welcome at many distilleries. A whisky centre at Rothiemurchus provides all the information and one of the latest developments is the complete story of a small distillery told at Dallas Dhu, near Forres in Moray.

Scotland makes imaginative and intelligent efforts to welcome, to inform and to satisfy the varied interests and enthusiasms of all those wise people who decide to spend their holidays here. 'Haste ye back!'

Inverewe Gardens, Poolewe (see also p. 180)

The Scottish Clans

The word 'clan' is an anglicized form of the Gaelic *clann* meaning children. The use of the word in the English language is usually in the context of something Scottish, but particularly Highland. In effect, 'clan' means a tribe, a group of people with a common ancestor, which is certainly the case in Scotland, hence 'Clan Macleod', 'Clan Campbell' and 'Clan MacNab'. But, whereas a tribe is generally accepted as a primitive grouping, the clan is accorded a high degree of sophistication in its organization. Whether this is because the Highland clans formed part of British society, and therefore could not be equated with the tribes to be found in the remote corners of the erstwhile British Empire, is open to question. After all, an admission that Great Britain had tribes within its own home frontiers of civilization was something that could not be explained away with ease.

It was in the year 1822 that the great British public realized that a tribal system operated north of the border, when King George IV paid a visit to Edinburgh, the first sovereign to set foot on Scottish soil since Charles II in 1651. The royal occasion was organized by the Wizard of the North, Sir Walter Scott, whose literary outpourings had engendered in the mind of his reading public a hazy, romantic image of a people who spoke a foreign language, who possessed fierce loyalties to territorial clan chiefs, whose mountainous environment produced 'the noble savage', and who were dressed in brightly coloured costumes loaded with archaic armoury like dirks and claymores. Having produced the image, Walter Scott was forced to stage an event that went some way to consolidate the popular concept.

Thus it was that the ample girth of the sovereign, now weighing in at 20 stones, and which had once been, in slimmer times, dressed by Beau Brummel, was garbed in tartan finery to match that of his cohorts. Even the Lord Mayor of London, a Wapping biscuit manufacturer, was obliged to appear in Highland dress and grace the royal levee held in Edinburgh's Holyrood House. The royal visit was attended by swatches of Highland Chiefs accompanied by squads of their clansmen. Sir Walter Scott wrote to the Macleod chief at Dunvegan in Skye: '. . . do come and bring half-a-dozen or half-a-score of Clansmen, so as to look like an Island Chief as you are'. Other chiefs joined the parade with their tartan trail reinforcing the image of a north of Scotland populated with the noble savages Scott had fathered in his fiction.

As for the city of Edinburgh, it was blanketed in deep drifts of tartan and subjected to the continuous drones of the ubiquitous Highland bagpipe. Yet another Walter Scott fiction had been created in a pageant which must have been worth seeing and worth the experience, but hid a truth that Scott's son-in-law, J.G. Lockhart, hinted at when he wrote: 'When one reflected how miserably their numbers [the clansmen] had of late years been reduced in consequence of the selfish and hard-hearted policy of their land-lords, it almost seemed as if there was a cruel mockery in giving so much prominence to their pretensions.'

The final irony occurred at the banquet given in honour of the sovereign in Edinburgh's Parliament House, when the Macgregor chief toasted King George as

A clan grave at Culloden Moor

Back row, left to right: the late Sir Iain Moncrieffe of that Ilk (then Albany); Sir Crispin Agnew of Lochnow Bt (Unicorn Pursuivant); the late J. I. D. Pottinger Esq (then Islay Herald); front: Malcolm Innes of Edingight (Lord Lyon)   *(Scottish Field – Roderick Martine)*

'The Chief of Chiefs, the King'. It was in that very building centuries before that the Scots Parliament had proscribed the very name of Clan Gregor by statute for crimes for which they were not wholly responsible. There had never at any time been love lost between Edinburgh and the clans of the Highlands, as the experience of the Macgregors and the Macdonalds of Glencoe proved, and to which the sore and painful history of the Highlands stands as witness.

   The fact of the matter was that by 1822 the clan system as an organization of society had all but disappeared and was about to be replaced by a superficial subscription more to the idea than the reality. A vogue for tartan was started which has continued apace to present times when you can have a special tartan designed to satisfy your whim and fancy. Clan societies now flourish all over the world paying due homage to a common factor: the surname and its derivatives. A Council of Scottish Chiefs convenes at regular intervals. The astonishing fact is that what can be called the 'clan spirit' still lives and pervades all things Scottish. How did it all begin?

While the clans as such did not come into existence until round about the time of the Viking hegemony, ground rules for their organization, hierarchy, laws and societal behaviour had been laid much earlier by the Celts who had penetrated across Europe to Britain by 700 BC. The Celts were very much a tribal people who preferred to live in fluid groupings rather than settle in one place. Their distaste for fixed urban growths is still echoed in the Highlands where large towns are few and far between. What they lacked in the obvious strength derived from a central political administrative facility, they made up for in their tribal cohesion, based on an extraordinary cultural unity. Their love of colour and intricate design pervaded all of Europe in the Dark Ages. While the Huns and Vandals perpetrated atrocities, the Celts were hard at work illuminating manuscripts and shining lights of learning from their monastic centres in Ireland.

Their tribal structures were quite distinct. The aristocracy included kinglets elected by general consent, nobles, priests and warriors who had achieved distinction in battle. The second echelon included craftsmen, poets, singers and musicians, farmers and providers of services. Then came a category who were not allowed to carry weapons, who owned neither land nor goods, a class that included slaves. In Celtic society women were regarded as equals and could even be elected queen. Their laws were enshrined in the code of Brehon Laws which were humane, just and fair. These provided for education, fosterage, ownership of property, the repayment of debts, and punishment for killing – not always a death sentence for murder.

The fosterage system was one in which the son of an ordinary member of the grouping was taken into the chief's household and given the same treatment as a chief's son. This served to strengthen the bond between chief and the emergent clansmen and created a strong sense of equality within the tribal community. From the chief's point of view the system allowed him to appeal to his close relations with his men for support in times of emergency. This relationship was echoed in much later times when many of the Highland regiments were raised by clan chiefs to satisfy the Government's repeated requests for bodies of fighting men who eventually found themselves engaging in war arenas as far away as India and Malaya.

When the Vikings began to roam the seas in the 8th century they found tribal communities who laid claim to specific territories, a characteristic which eventually emerged when clans were identified by the land they occupied; as yet the use of a common surname had not come to identify the clan itself.

Once the Vikings realized that their strength allowed them to establish settlements, a new element was introduced into the older tribal society. Kinglets were set up who were invested with powers over the resident population. These often married into the local aristocracy and their children took the names of their fathers. Thus the Macleods claim descent from Liotr, son of Olaf the Black, who was King of Man and the Northern Isles. The eldest son of Somerled, who married the daughter of Olaf the Black, was called Dougall (Gaelic: 'Dark Foreigner', thus indicating that many Highland clans are neither wholly Gaelic or Celtic) from whom descended all the

The men of Lonach (Scottish Tourist Board)

Clan MacDougall. From Somerled's second son descended MacDonalds, Mac-Alisters and MacRuaries.

Other clans claimed different origins. The MacNabs (sons of the Abbot) sprang from originators who held high positions in the old monastic houses. The MacKinnons took the name of Fingon who was related to St Columba in Iona. Others took their name from important office bearers in the old Celtic tribal system, such as the bards. Where the embryo clans were too small in numbers to protect themselves, they joined a stronger neighbour, sometimes taking the same name.

By the 13th century the various clans had become well established, identified by their respective surnames and territories and with the clansmen declaring allegiance to the chief. As for the chief of the clan, he controlled the clan lands by common consent. Only in a later century was the chief given legal titles to the lands over which he held sway. When that happened, at a stroke the chief became a man apart, a landowner created by charters given in return for royal favours or for political services. His clansmen, at the same stroke, became his tenants-at-will.

The general characteristic of the clan was that of a society consisting of a chief with 'his sons, brothers, men, tenants, servants and assisters', everybody in fact who was connected to him, directly or indirectly, by kin or tenancy or contract within his jurisdiction by tribal custom, by feudal law, or by rights of property. The differentiating element was the reality or convention of blood relationship perpetuating rights such as belong to the head of a family but are not necessarily recognized by law, though enforced by the general will of the clan. In this way, backed by the common law as owners, or at least superiors, and by clan custom as fathers of their children, Highland chiefs were possessed of a power without parallel for persons of the same quality elsewhere in Britain. In fact, landed possession, tribal (that is partly real and partly conventional) relationship, jurisdiction and dependence – these or any two of them were the framework of the clan, of which the surname was the conventional benchmark.

Highland history is chock-full of incidents which set clan against clan: claims to territories, inter-clan marriages gone wrong, insults arising out of being invited to dinner and placed below the salt, and cattle raids. The more lasting clan feuds arose from disputes over land. It was such a difference that kept the MacKintoshes fighting endless feuds with the Camerons and the Keppoch MacDonalds for centuries; and the MacDonalds in general with the Campbells in general. Some passing MacDonalds stole MacLean cattle from the island of Jura, and the mistaken feud that followed sent war birlinns with armed crews flitting up and down the seas of the Inner Hebrides for many years.

One clan chief decided to create a bond between his own clan and another and agreed to marry, unseen, the daughter of his intended ally. She turned out to have only one eye; in a fit of pique he sent her back home again accompanied by a one-eyed horse, a single-eyed attendant and a one-eyed dog. Needless to say the gesture started yet another incident in internecine clan warfare.

As the centuries passed it was inevitable that those who had a more direct kinship with the clan chief would create a kind of middle class in the society, acting as a buffer between the chief and his clansmen. The chief's ownership and occupation of certain lands gave him the right, legal or assumed, to dispose of these lands among his relatives. It was this that marked the first great cleavage between the owners and the real tenants of the land, who paid the chief rents in cash, and the great mass of clansmen who were the actual cultivators and labourers. Add to the 'gentlemen' class

The clan gathering, Meadowbank (*Scottish Tourist Board*)

their officers of dignity, personal servants and other dependants, and it can be realized how huge an idle class (that is a class disdaining labour as unworthy of their standing and high birth) was imposed upon the working tenantry.

An indication of how large these retinues were is seen in the Statutes of Iona, passed in the early 17th century, which sought to impose a limit on the number of retainers a chief might have. These retainers included pipers, harpists, bards, bodyguards and the like. They were all entertained by the chief and must have been a sore burden on the working clansmen who had to feed and cater for them all.

While each clan managed to live off the land and clan chiefs had little need for actual cash, the system tended to be self-sufficient. In general, the Highlands were not always as barren as they are today. The labouring class ensured that the land was worked to its full capacity and, from early accounts, there is evidence that there were few if any periods of starvation like those that occurred all too frequently in the 19th century.

The dilution of the clan system began when Highland chiefs were legally obliged to send at least one of their male descendants 'to the south' for education. And when these educated sons returned they imported new ideas and life styles, and the suggestion that cash in the hand was better than the return in kind offered by the working tenantry. Slowly the fleshpots of the south offered attractions which could not be resisted and required money for their consumption. This development, in turn, changed the chief's whole dependence on his clansmen to his dependence on cash rents from his immediate tenants, the tacksmen, who were often directly related to him. They in turn pondered on the question of how to obtain cash from the cashless society that comprised their subtenants.

The only answer was to lease their lands to those who could pay large sums of money for sheep farms and estates devoted to sports, all of which required the clearance of the clansmen from their holdings. Though this answer is rather simplified here, it was in fact what occurred over a period of two or three centuries and was instrumental in further eroding the clan system. In some cases, clan chiefs who had amassed huge debts were forced by creditors to sell off their estates, situations which brought in new landowners who cared little or nothing for clan relationships and less for the large numbers of unsecured tenants on their new possessions. These latter were then cleared off mercilessly.

But even the chiefs themselves engineered mass emigrations, either offering free passage to America or Canada to their tenants, or else using harsher methods to clear away their erstwhile clansmen. It was the MacMillans who were among the first to arrange for systematic emigration to Canada for whole communities. In 1802 three ships were charted to take over 1000 men and their families to a new life under strange skies. In a letter dated 1805, one emigrant MacMillan wrote: 'We cannot help looking to our native spot with sympathy and feelings which cannot be described, yet I have no hesitation in saying that considering the arrangements that daily take place, and the total extinction of the ties betwixt Chief and clan, we are surely better off to be out of the reach of such unnatural tyranny.'

In other instances clan chiefs took advantage of the fact that a large labour force was readily available. This was seen when the industrial demand for alkalines was interrupted by wars in Continental Europe. The only available substitute was the seaweed kelp, from the burning of which was extracted an alkaline ash which was used in the production of soap and glass. The kelp weed was cut from around shore

A pipe band, Stirling   *(Scottish Tourist Board)*

rocks with hooks and sickles by workers standing in ice-cold sea water, often up to their waists, or else was gathered as 'drift' from the beaches.

When the wars in the Baltic interrupted supplies, followed by the problems in the Americas around 1800, the price for kelp ash went through the roof. To cash in on the kelp bonanza many chiefs required their tenants to collect, dry and burn the seaweed, paying them minimal amounts for backbreaking work. The kelp ash in turn was sold for high prices. Profits to a landlord, who had little or no capital investment in the business and no direct involvement in the manufacturing process, could run very high indeed. One clan chief, MacDonald of Clanranald, whose lands were in the Uists, was able to make some £20,000 per annum. Then, when the bubble burst and foreign imports reached Britain again, the Highland population found themselves on the high-water line, deprived of their small income. Chiefs once again found themselves encumbered with a large tenantry who could not pay rents and the vicious circle of clearing tenants off the land began once more.

If the Highland clan system was evolved through centuries of an intricate and slow maturation process, its dissolution was equally complicated by many factors which acted either severally or in concert. Sociologists might claim that the system represented a backward state of civilization. Yet it had its basis in the concept of equality among its members, from the highest to the lowest, its fair laws, its code of hospitality offered to the stranger at the gate (even if that stranger was a member of a feuding clan), its recognition of the equality of women, its right to depose an incompetent or a tyrannical chief, and that no person was a slave to anyone else. There is no word in the Gaelic language to denote slavery; when a Gaelic speaker has occasion to refer to a slave he has to borrow the word *traill* ('thrall') from the Norse. Above all the unique sense of kinship which permeated throughout the whole clan was a characteristic of coexistence that few other types of society ever attained to.

Perhaps the clan system can be summed up in a Gaelic proverb: *Theid duthchas an aghaidh na'n creig* – 'Kinship will withstand the rocks'. And even though rocks can be eroded by both weather and time, they, like the clan system, still remain.

Crofting: A Way of Life

In 1886 a new species appeared in the statute books of the British Isles: the crofter, now solidly embodied in the Croftings Holdings Act of that year and in subsequent Acts promulgated in 1955 and 1976.

A croft was once described as 'a piece of land surrounded by regulations'. That description embraces humour, fact, frustration, stoicism and an underlying hope and aspiration, to say nothing of the long painful history that was undergone to achieve the status inherent in that offhand comment on what crofting really is.

Briefly, crofting is a form of land use peculiar to certain areas of Scotland, mainly the north-west and western Highlands and the four island groups: Shetland, Orkney, and the Outer and Inner Hebrides. Much of the land involved, some 1.4 million acres, is of poor agricultural quality and thus the holdings, the crofts, are relied on mainly to provide subsistence living, with extra income derived from other work, such as fishing, weaving, crafts and tourism.

At the present time there are about 15,000 crofts, of which over half are in units of less than 10 acres of inbye land, that is land close to the croft centre and usually used for wintering sheep. In addition to the croft holding, a crofter has access to land called common grazings as a statutory right, subject to the agreement of township governing bodies called grazing committees. This land is used mainly for such purposes as sheep grazing and peat cutting. In purely agricultural terms the land is of little use; much of it is waterlogged with bogs and marshes, and ground infested with heather and bracken. That being said, it is also the right of any crofter to resume his allotted share of the common grazings for his own purposes: for instance, to reclaim his share and plough it, seed it with grass and put it to more intensive agricultural uses. However, having received his share of the common grazings, he has no further access to the larger area of common land.

Apart from its being a form of land use, crofting has social overtones, in that it has kept a residual population in many places in the Highlands and Islands that would otherwise have become depopulated and left to dereliction. Indeed, the tenacious crofting population has done much to prevent the Highlands from becoming nothing more than a beautiful, deserted wilderness. Thus, crofting is essentially a way of life. That it is little more than this is the result of a history of land use which has a special place in the memory genes of the present generation, who know full well what their forebears had to experience to become members of this unusual class of land users, which is unique in the British Isles.

Before 1886 there was no statutory legislation applicable to the crofting situation in Scotland. Even the term 'croft' came slowly into being and meant, in Gaelic where the word is *croit*, a small piece of arable land. The 'crofter' was recognized as one who held a 'croft' of land. The modern croft and crofter or small tenant seldom appears much before the beginning of the 18th century; crofters were in fact tenants-at-will, under the authority of the tacksmen and wadsetters. (These were men who had leased land from a landlord, then subleased it to tenants.) In practice their tenure of

Interior of a black house, Colbost, Isle of Lewis, c. 1955   (A. MacArthur, Stornoway)

the land was only secure so long as the tenant was industrious and paid his rent in cash, in kind, or in work service; under these terms he was allowed to occupy his house and land without fear of eviction. Seldom, in fact, did the actual proprietor of the land come into direct contact with his tenants, though this did occur in some areas, where there was a close social bond between the laird, usually a clan chief, and his people.

Before the Croftings Holdings (Scotland) Act of 1886, all the crofts, farms and agricultural holdings in the country came under the ordinary agricultural law of Scotland. Under this law, a crofter was regarded as the tenant of a piece of land owned by a landlord; the tenant's occupation of the land was on a year-to-year basis and at a mutually agreed rent. This was the extent of the crofter's legal recognition, and it made no difference whether he and his forebears had lived in the same place for generations or whether he was a new tenant of a year's standing.

The law recognized the right of a landlord to terminate a crofter's tenancy at the end of any year after issuing 40 days' notice in writing. The landlord could then recover the land, together with any buildings or improvements on it, and was under no legal obligation to offer recompense, financial or otherwise, for those improvements, even though it was the tenant who created them. The situation was, of course, different when the landlord had actually provided buildings and equipment for use by the tenant for an agreed price and for an agreed term of lease.

Although this system operated reasonably well in other parts of Scotland, in the 1870s in the Highlands and Islands the working out of a terrible history was coming to a head, with the Clearances only one of a number of successive factors that brought to public awareness the complete inadequacy and weakness of the law as it pertained to agricultural practice.

Much of the residual population of the Highlands and Islands had been shifted from their original holdings in the 18th century, a process that started soon after the Forty-five uprising, to make room for the more profitable sheep (and, later, deer) and the people were forced to cling to marginal lands next to the sea, on inferior soil, with imposed restrictions such as, for example, being forbidden to take even seaweed from the shorelands to use as fertilizer. The people had absolutely no security of tenure and lived in housing conditions which appalled even those familiar with the urban slums created by the Industrial Revolution. Perhaps the most astonishing element in the whole scenario was the forbearance of the people themselves, even in the face of the enforced Clearances that had begun in the 1820s. Like Stoics, they accepted the march of their history as inevitable, with little thought for the future. The only modern parallel that can be cited is the legion of displaced persons in the Europe of the 1940s whose nightmare was orchestrated by forces quite beyond the reaches of pity and humanity. But something had to snap, and snap it did.

No small number of Highlanders, who had previously emigrated from their native heaths to find work, education and acceptable standards of living in the Scottish Lowlands, became concerned with what was happening in the Highlands. They considered the massive contribution Highlanders had made to creating the British Empire. They had fought in the Seven Years' War when Britain gained India and Canada for her growing domain. They fought in the American War of Independence, and in the Peninsular and Napoleonic Wars that followed. They distinguished themselves with Wolfe at Quebec, with Sir John Moore at Corunna and with Wellington at Waterloo. And in the Crimea it was the Highland Brigade, and the

Croft at the Crofting Museum, Kilmuir, Skye (see also p. 193)

93rd Highlanders in particular, the 'Thin Red Line' of history, under the leadership of Sir Colin Campbell, who really saved the day at the Battle of Balaclava.

That record of service was, however, no guarantee of protection from those whom the Government now saw fit to recognize as legal *proprietors* of the land rather than as feudal superiors and agents. Against that background it was inevitable that some counteraction would be organized in an effort to obtain at least minimum rights, among which security of tenure was the most important. The counteraction that manifested itself had two main elements.

First, the ordinary people themselves had turned to the new religion of the Free Church of Scotland, formed after the Disruption in 1843, when large numbers left the established Church of Scotland. In the Free Church men, who had been ordinary members of their former congregations, found themselves appointed as elders, going through a process of selection which required a high order of articulateness. So well equipped did they become in this field that when the Napier Commission was set up to investigate the crofting problem in 1883, the Commissioners recorded their amazement that simple crofters could present their evidence and their case with both eloquence and forthrightness. By an accident of religious history the Free Church had given many crofters a training arena in which they could equip themselves with the very tools needed in the forthcoming war of words.

The exiled Highlanders in Scotland's large towns and cities formed the second important element in the battle for crofting rights. They aimed as high as they could and focused their attention on Westminster. They realized that unless the land issue became politicized, little pressure could be placed on the House of Commons to stir it into action. Some became crofter Members of Parliament. Others orchestrated campaigns through the newly formed Land League, which were highly articulate to the extent that they attracted the attention of the national Press.

While all this was progressing, the ordinary Highlanders also played significant roles. The first scene was enacted in 1874, when crofters on the island of Bernera, on the west side of Lewis, revolted against the intolerable conditions imposed by the factor of Lewis, acting on behalf of the landlord, Sir James Matheson, whose fortune had been made in the Far East. The Bernera crofters turned a minor incident, in which the sleeve of a sheriff officer's coat was torn off, into an event which resulted in three of their number being arrested and later acquitted. Though the 'Bernera Riot' was a small enough affair, it had important repercussions. It afforded the radical Press the opportunity to publicize the invidious position of crofters in the Highlands and Islands, and create a sympathetic public opinion which was to be a considerable weapon of advantage a decade later when the cause of the crofting population eventually made its overdue appearance on the floors of both Houses of Parliament.

In the decade from 1874 many astonishing incidents occurred throughout the Highlands. This was the time when the wealthy English and Scottish *nouveaux riches* vied with each other in the purchase of Highland estates, to play God over sheep, deer, salmon, grouse and human beings, albeit through the medium of their managers, the estate factors. It was the attitudes of these factors that blew into life the smouldering fires of resentment against injustice. In Skye, to quote but one area, many petty tyrannies were exercised by the factors. The common method there of dealing with arrears of rent was to issue a summons for the removal of the defaulting tenant, instead of issuing a simple notice for the recovery of a small debt. Even when a crofter was evicted, the incoming tenant was obliged to pay off his predecessor's arrears: purchasing the 'goodwill' of the croft was the term used to describe the technique.

If a debt was required to be paid off, the crofter's poor goods and chattels were impounded. There is on record an instance where a baby in a cradle was priced at sixpence. Thus crofters not only found themselves homeless and landless, but also without the domestic tools for basic living. Many petty restrictions were placed on crofters. In some areas they were not allowed to keep dogs which might put up game and deer, hunted by shooting tenants on the estates of absentee landlords. Deer were often forced down from the hills to make a dash for safety across the crofter's planted fields, with inevitable damage to crops; this had to be endured without compensation. In the island of Barra, the landlord demanded 60 days' labour for every acre of potato ground, leaving little time for the crofters to attend to their own crops in a short growing season.

By 1882 the simmering pot of crofting troubles was ready for the final boiling and it needed just one incident – perforce it had also to be violent – to make the contents spill over and create a situation where a decision, one way or the other, had to be taken to settle the issues involved.

By a fortuitous coincidence the matter was brought to a head on an estate in Skye owned by Lord MacDonald, one of a decreasing number of traditional clan chief landowners whose forebears had once been able to call on their armed clansmen to fight for the clan lands and honour. Far from being incomers, as were many of the Highland landowners, the Macdonalds had eight centuries of Highland history behind them, with many illustrious names in the family line. Yet, by the 19th century they commanded little loyalty from the crofters, many of whom bore the same surname, for the old relationships had disappeared: Lord Macdonald was just another landlord.

A number of crofters from the Braes area of Skye went to Lord MacDonald's factor, yet another MacDonald, to demand the restoration of the summer grazings

A two-storey croft house, Durness (see also p. 121)

which had been taken away from them 20 years previously. The demand was rejected out of hand and the crofters retaliated by declaring that they would withhold the payment of their rents until the grazings had been restored to them. Both the demand and its rejection were made in a fairly calm atmosphere; its violent outcome was furthest from the minds of all concerned.

But the matter was not allowed to rest. Lord MacDonald considered that he and his position had been affronted, so he went to law demanding that his tenants should be tried and evicted for criminal intimidation. In its wisdom, the law decided that there was no case to answer; but, true to its traditional form in the Highlands, it advised Lord MacDonald to evict those whom he thought might be the ringleaders among the Braes tenants.

Eviction notices were taken out against a dozen or so men, delivered by a sheriff officer and two assistants. Before the trio came in sight of the Braes townships they were met by over 100 people who burned the summonses and told the officers to go away. In this way was the final fuse lit to create the situation which was eventually to gain the crofters their long sought-after rights. It was decided to make a once-for-all example of the Braes crofters and within weeks the Sheriff of Inverness-shire asked the Government for 100 soldiers. In its cautious wisdom it sent only 50 policemen from Glasgow. With them came a battery of Press reporters, scenting blood. Though the Press presence was there to support the cause of the landlord, it unwittingly provided the crofters with the best means of publicity possible.

What is now known as the 'Battle of the Braes', between police and the crofters and their wives, came to a sore and bloody conclusion. The ringleaders were arrested, tried, and found guilty but had their fines paid for by sympathetic supporters. When they returned to Braes they witnessed the disputed summer grazings already being taken over by other crofters. This time the law could only suggest the response usually associated with British colonial administration: send a gunboat. The gunboat duly arrived but instead of the expected detachment of armed marines, there was only a Government representative, a sure sign that matters were coming to a head.

In March 1883 a Royal Warrant was issued to set up a Royal Commission, the Napier Commission, whose remit was to investigate the whole of the crofting problem in the Highlands and Islands. It was the end of the beginning. The Commissioners did their work well and quickly. They travelled all over the region, taking written and oral evidence, much of the latter being presented in Gaelic. The final Report, based on evidence contained in four hefty volumes of oral evidence, and a fifth, running to over 500 pages of written submissions, came out in favour of the crofters. Then, in 1886, the Crofters Bill was introduced to the House of Commons and in due course was placed on the Statute Book.

Subject to certain conditions of tenancy, the crofter now had security of tenure and could bequeath his croft to a member of his family. These were basic rights. In addition, any crofter who renounced his croft was entitled to be paid for any improvements created by him. Thus ended a period in Highland history which was vividly described by the members of the Napier Commission:

> From 1882 to 1887 the Highlands and Islands were in a state of unrest – in many places there was open lawlessness. Rents were withheld, lands were seized, and a reign of terror prevailed. To cope with the situation the Police Force was largely augmented and in some cases doubled. Troopships with Marines cruised about the Hebrides in order to support the Civil Authorities in their endeavour to maintain law and order. The tension and excitement of those days have passed away, and peace and tranquillity prevail where 25 or 26 years ago the Queen's writ did not run.

Over the last one hundred years, crofting has slowly improved, though in the same period some of the restrictions that continued to bind the crofter have meant that little more than a residual population has been maintained (on land that would otherwise become derelict). In recent years, however, the term 'crofting' has come to include non-agricultural activities, such as catering for tourists, that give the crofter another source of income.

It has been a long haul for the crofting population of the Highlands and Islands to achieve their present position of relative strength. The sad fact of the matter is that the land itself has not been allowed to become a significant element in the Highland economy, to provide the kind of environment which engenders a healthy social structure keen to exercise initiative and enterprise. That has yet to come.

As a way of life, crofting has much to commend it. It provides for a unique social structure in its various townships which often require the creation of a communal and self-help basis on which to survive. It has also had a significant impact on the maintenance of the linguistic (Gaelic) and cultural values that might otherwise be dispersed and disappear altogether. Crofting provides a keen edge to life which offers some route to a kind of spiritual satisfaction in which optimum ideals can be achieved. The visitor can often sense the world of difference between the picturesque villages of the English countryside and the townships of the Highland scene, which are equally picturesque but perhaps not so photogenic.

The English settlements have a long, stable history of close communal association, and also a history of regulation imposed by the local feudal manor and its lord. The

Spring digging, Ness, Isle of Lewis, 1954   *(Donald Morrison, Oban)*

surrounding countryside is witness to centuries of careful cultivation by the toiling
villein and serf, and the total encompassing atmosphere is one of slow-moving,
almost Utopian contentment: at least that is the impression the tourist receives.
Many Highland townships, on the other hand, while some are indeed of long
standing, have a much shorter history, having been created by the displacement of
populations in the last one hundred years or so.

Many of the present-day crofting townships are products of the crofters' immediate forebears, men and women who often had to make the very soil from an alchemic
mixture of seaweed and crushed stones, having been forced to settle on the most
infertile and rocky land possible. The crofting townships also have an atmosphere of
perpetual change, as dwellings, for instance, are revamped from the old vernacular
style to ultra-modern design. There are no particular features in the township that
show a development from feudal bond to freehold: no village square, no village pub
to act as a neutral area for local discussion, no visible memorials to the war dead and
none of the outward trappings that conventionally indicate a closely knit community.
Yet, the crofting township *is* a tight social unit, simply because it is the people of the
township who are the dynamic elements; the physical environment is merely a stage
setting.

This is what the visitor will sense and detect, and, armed with even a superficial
knowledge of the history that brought these townships into being, can use this as a
basis for tuning into a form of land use and way of life quite unique in the British
Isles, and thus increase that element of appreciation which makes a visit memorable.

The Impact of North Sea Oil and Gas on Scotland

H. F. WICKHAM

Who would have thought in 1964, when on 26 December that year drilling of the first well was started in the North Sea, that within a few years there would be a new industrial revolution in Scotland? Traditionally the search for oil and natural gas had been in those areas of the world that geologically had indicated the largest reserves, primarily in the Middle East. But given the complex and difficult political situation in that region since the end of the Second World War it was natural that the oil companies should pay more attention to looking for oil in areas closer to their industrial markets in North America and Europe.

The North Sea is a sedimentary basin; an area where geologists would expect to look for oil on the Continental Shelf, that is in depths down to 600 ft. The clue that there might be oil or natural gas in the North Sea followed the find at Groningen in the Netherlands which subsequently proved to be the largest on-shore gas field in the world. This was discovered in 1969 after some 11 years of exploration. It was believed that there were similar geological structures in the southern sector of the North Sea, where indeed, gas was later to be found. So, although it was thought that there might be some gas in the North Sea, very few people were prepared to believe there was any oil there, particularly in the more northerly Scottish waters.

Oil, however, is no newcomer to Scotland. In the mid-19th century Dr James Young founded a prosperous shale-oil industry at Bathgate, midway between Edinburgh and Glasgow. He had begun manufacturing by producing oil artificially from cannel, a sort of coal, which he exhausted in about ten years. He then sought and found a substitute in the oil-bearing shale which was near to the coal seams. In those days he distilled the shale oil to produce paraffin for lamps. Subsequently he also manufactured lubricating oil and paraffin wax for candles, and from this he became known nationally as 'Paraffin' Young. His shale-oil industry was the forerunner of oil refining as we know it today.

It was not until 1964 that the British government ratified the UN Continental Shelf Convention under which the seven countries bordering the North Sea agreed on the allocation of the sea bed between them. The North Sea was divided by a median line: the equidistant point from the various shores. Governments around the North Sea were then able to extend their petroleum legislation to offshore areas and issue petroleum exploration and production licences. The United Kingdom was particularly fortunate as it has the longest North Sea shoreline, from Dover in Kent to Unst, the northernmost island of Shetland. The British government was very quick off the mark, awarding 53 North Sea licences in September 1964. The first gas field was found in 1965, and there were a number of other discoveries shortly afterwards. This encouraged attention to be turned to Scottish waters where proposals were highly speculative because of the lack of geological knowledge.

The first well to be drilled in these waters was in 1967. The first major oilfield to be discovered, the Forties field, was found in 1970 by BP, some 100 miles to the east of

*The Brent Field showing Brent C in the foreground
with Brent's A and B in the background*

(Shell Photo Service)

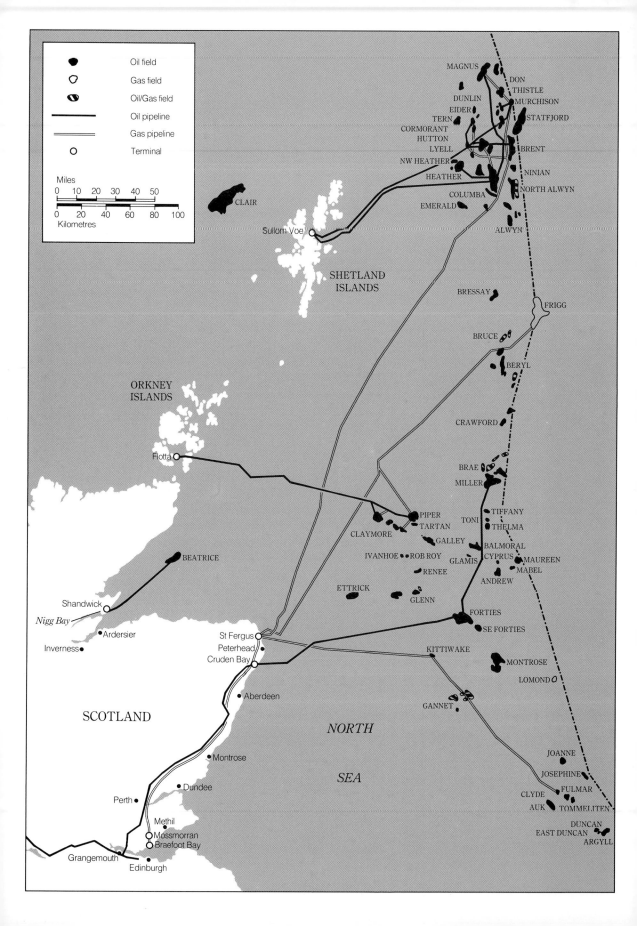

Aberdeen. Early in 1972 Shell/Esso working in partnership found oil in the Auk field, 170 miles off the Scottish coast, due east of Dundee. The oil from the Forties field, which began to flow in 1975, comes ashore at Cruden Bay, south of Peterhead. An on-shore pipeline takes the oil from Cruden Bay to Grangemouth near Edinburgh, Scotland's only refinery, on the southern banks of the Forth estuary. Output from the large fields such as Claymore, Piper and Tartan flows through a second big pipeline to Flotta terminal in the Orkney Islands.

The northern North Sea east of Scotland has proved to be a highly prolific oil-bearing region and development of the fields there has stimulated impressive technical engineering achievements. Enormous production platforms have been designed, built and installed capable of operating in waters at depths of over 600 ft.

By the end of 1985 oil and gas were being produced from 30 offshore oil- and 9 gas fields and brought ashore either through the 2300-mile network of underwater pipelines or by tanker. Altogether more than 1000 exploration wells had been drilled with 200 significant discoveries. All this activity represents a total investment by the oil industry of more than £40 billion and employment for over 100,000 people.

The most significant finds of oil have been those discovered 100 miles north-east of the Shetland Islands in an extensive province containing the fields of Brent, Cormorant, Dunlin, Hutton, Thistle, Murchison and Magnus. The oil flows by pipeline from the Brent system 93 miles to Firths Voe in Shetland, and from there to a marine terminal at Sullom Voe which can berth tankers of up to 300,000 deadweight tons.

Gas has been found in commercial quantities associated with the oil in many of the fields. The longest deep-water offshore pipeline in the world brings the liquids and gas 278 miles from Brent and associated fields to St Fergus on the Scottish coast some 30 miles north of Aberdeen. Here the natural gas is separated from the gas liquids for use in the National grid. The remaining gas liquids are piped south to Mossmorran in Fife where they are separated into ethane, propane, butane and natural gasoline. The ethane is processed in an ethylene plant and used to produce a wide range of chemicals from detergents to plastics.

In 1985 the North Sea supplied just over three-quarters of the United Kingdom's national gas needs, the balance coming from the Norwegian sector. Forty per cent of British gas supplies comes from the British/Norwegian Frigg field. Near by is the large Ninian field, from which oil also flows through a pipeline to Shetland.

In addition to these larger discoveries, a number of small fields have been found from which the laying of pipelines cannot be commercially justified. Oil from these fields is brought ashore to the mainland by tankers which load from single-buoy mooring systems, through which the oil passes from the sea bed. Most of these fields are in Scottish waters. On-shore oil terminals were constructed to separate the gases from the oil, remove impurities, store and ship to the refineries for processing into oil products.

This comprehensive network of pipelines and terminals will provide great benefits in the future as many of the smaller fields discovered, or yet to be found, would not be economic were it not for the facility of feeding the oil into existing pipelines.

Oil and gas development has meant a complete change in the infrastructure of Scottish industry. The first evidence of the oil industry's interest in Scotland was the

North Sea oil fields

Aerial view of the Mossmorran plant, Fife   *(Shell Photo Service)*

setting up of supply bases at Aberdeen and Dundee, and subsequently Montrose and Peterhead. This was soon followed by the search for fabrication sites for the very large oil-production platforms to be erected at the site of the oilfields. The main requirement for these construction sites was deep-water facilities, which were often found in Scotland near places of natural beauty.

The Scottish Office was anxious to maintain the balance between the economic benefits from these developments against possible harm to the environment. After several public enquiries a number of sites were selected and approved. Fortunately much construction work which would otherwise certainly have gone to other countries was retained in Scotland.

The first site was in Moray Firth. Steel production platforms were built at Nigg Bay in Cromarty at Ardersier, near Inverness, and at Methil in Fife. The steel platforms are secured by piles driven into the sea bed and designed to withstand storm waves of 100 ft and gusts of winds up to 150 mph. Some of the latest platforms now tower over 1000 ft.

On the west coast of Scotland fabrication sites were established at Loch Kishorn and at Ardyne Point in Argyll, where the first of the reinforced concrete gravity platforms were built. These structures rely on their weight to keep them in position on the sea bed.

Several new production systems are being pioneered in the North Sea off Scotland for operating in water depths below 1000 ft; one is the tension-leg platform which involves tethering a floating production facility to the sea bed against its own buoyancy by means of a series of steel tubes.

Much of the equipment required by the industry has been produced by the traditional craftsmen of Scotland. Cranes have been manufactured in East Kilbride, compressors and pumps in Glasgow, and generators in Edinburgh. In addition the offshore industry will continue to require maintenance and service work for the next 20 years. Through the Offshore Supplies Office in Scotland, British industry has been given an opportunity to bid competitively for contracts related to North Sea work as well as providing materials and services for the offshore industry. By 1985 about three-quarters of the value of all North Sea orders had been placed with firms based in Britain.

Communications throughout Scotland have been improved and the new roads built benefit both industry and tourists generally. The airports at Aberdeen and Inverness have been extended to receive jet aircraft and to provide an extensive helicopter service between the mainland and drilling and production platforms. Aberdeen is now one of the busiest airports in Great Britain and the busiest heliport in the world.

However, virtually all the larger North Sea oilfields – that is those with estimated recoverable reserves of over 300 million barrels – have already been discovered in the mature areas of the central and northern North Sea. Of all the oil being produced or developed today 96 per cent had been discovered by the end of 1975, the year when production began.

Looking towards the future, it is believed that there could be as many as twice the number of present fields working in the next 20 years although they will be very much smaller. The prospects west of the Shetlands in the greater depths of water beyond the Continental Shelf are promising. A series of seismic surveys have taken place and further wells will be drilled in 1986 and 1987. The speed of development of these prospective fields will depend on the water depths and further development in production platform technology. However, it is likely that underwater developments are more likely to be used than conventional structures and other possibilities, such as floating production systems fed from underwater wells and underwater manifolds, are being examined.

The potential and promise of these future oil developments are great. It is to be hoped that the growing business opportunities for Scotland can be grasped while at the same time maximum concern for local environmental and social considerations is maintained.

The Gaelic Dimension:
the Scots Character

Under the protective cover of the general statement, it might be said that the Scot is like everybody else. But that is not the popular received image. Somewhere along the line there must be evidence of some of the particular, peculiar and at times idiosyncratic elements that go to make up the character of the Scot. A look at Scottish history will go some way to identifying a few of these elements.

At the time when most European ethnic and political factions were putting in a hard day's work trying to conquer their neighbours, the Scots were content to remain within the confines of a country that was slowly emerging as the future Scotland. The Romans tested their patience. Having built Hadrian's Wall, running from near present-day Carlisle to east of Newcastle, they decided to push further north and arrived in central Scotland, to start on the Antonine Wall. They then proceeded to plaster the countryside around Perth with fortresses to maintain it. But the native Scots (if the term may be used, for the sake of simplicity, retrospectively for all the country's inhabitants) retaliated and in AD 115 launched a massive and concerted attack on these outposts. In response, the Romans sent their Ninth Legion to deal with the problem. It vanished without trace and has gone down in history as the 'Lost Legion'. Then, when Rome began to suffer the effects of its domestic problems, the Romans retreated south to hide behind Hadrian's Wall, a move which the Scots took to their advantage and crossed it to reduce Roman Britain to ruins, the only time the Scots went out of their native country to settle old scores. In its own way, the Roman invasion both revealed and shaped a distinct element in the Scots personality: stubbornness, or 'thrawness'. After that experience, as history has demonstrated, the Scots have seldom allowed themselves to be at the beck and call of others. Even when Malcolm Canmore finally united the tribal elements in Scotland, he could only become King of Scots and not 'of Scotland'. He was in his position at the pleasure of the Scots commonalty.

Scottish history is littered with incidents of betrayal, surrender and stony-faced intolerance, bitter fighting over obscure doctrinal issues and bloody splits between factions. Yet it is also chock-full of those moments when the Scots have come together in acts of communal shriving. They have been parochial isolationists, yet have allowed their fellows, failures in a sense in their own land, to infiltrate other countries of the world where they have contributed both deeds and words to the process of creating nations.

The Scots have held down those of their fellows bright with hope, intellectual power, inventiveness and artistic talents. Yet as a nation they have demonstrated, often to the death, the true meaning of tolerance, democracy and humanity and given the world a poet like Robert Burns, whose passion for the equality of men has made him an idol celebrated the world over, even in Russia where the individual is often sacrificed for the sake of the greater societal whole.

Back to one popular image . . . the Highlands and the Lowlands. In reality Scotland comprises a number of districts, each characterized by its own geography,

Highland dancer at the Braemar Games (*Aberdeen Tourist Board*)

Up Helly Aa, Lerwick, Shetland (see p. 49 and 192)   *(Shetland Tourist Board)*

cultural traditions, outlook on life, attitude to life, and linguistic distinctions. Of the last-mentioned, perhaps Gaelic marks out the Highlander from his fellow Scots.

At one time, Gaelic was virtually the only language spoken in Scotland – until Queen Margaret, wife of Malcolm Canmore, decided to import from south of the border Norman-French and English nobles who proceeded to oust Gaelic as the medium through which the work of the Church, the legal system and the court was transacted. From the 13th century, Gaelic has retreated like a receding hairline until its province today lies on the north-west coast of Scotland and the Hebridean islands, and is still under pressure from the dominance of the English-speaking media.

The Gaelic language is a member of a linguistic grouping that also includes Welsh, Irish, Manx, Cornish and Breton, all tongues spoken by the people of the Celtic fringe of Europe. The history of all of these languages has been one of erosion by the sharp edge of the sword, the corrosive ink of the pen, militant legislation, subversive education and religious fervour and fanaticism. Apart from Cornish, which died out but is now revived, they all still exist as living tongues and even, in the case of Welsh and Irish, have received State accolades and recognition. That says something about the tenacity, pride and deeply entrenched attitude of these residual Celts to their only

Opposite: Burning of the Clavie, Burghead (see pp. 49 and 94)   *(Shetland Tourist Board)*

outward mark of difference between themselves and their monoglot neighbours: their language.

All over Scotland many place names betray their Gaelic or Celtic origins, though they have now been anglicized beyond all recognition. They are the only residual evidence that Gaelic was a spoken language throughout much of Scotland, even in Fife, an area not readily associated with the language. Yet, in the 17th century virtually half the population of Scotland still spoke Gaelic. Its repression sprang from the Reformation and was targeted by zealots from the first moment because the main areas where it was spoken, the West Highlands and Islands, were also Catholic. However, Governments also contributed to the repression, as witness the 1609 Statutes of Iona which forbade the inclusion and maintenance in the retinues of clan chiefs the keepers of the Gaelic culture and tradition such as pipers, clarsairs (harpists), bards and sennachies (keepers of the clans' genealogies).

Then other agencies added their militant contribution to the assault on the language. Presbyterian educationalists in Scotland adopted English as the most suitable language for the teaching of the Scriptures, which proved to be a major disaster for Gaelic and became the source of a language problem that dogged Highland education until well into the 19th century. Though the Church of Scotland did lay the foundations for a tradition of Gaelic-medium worship, this was largely through a fear of counter-Reformation in the Highlands. In addition, because of her long-term policy of anglicization, the Church refused to make use of Gaelic in its newly settled schools.

Despite the attitude of the Church, it was in fact lenient in some directions. For instance, it initiated the production of religious works in Gaelic, which enabled the language to emerge from its hitherto deeply entrenched oral tradition to the status of a literary medium, though in fact the Gaelic written word is as old as the 12th century.

Then, from the side wings, came the Society in Scotland for the Propagation of Christian Knowledge (SSPCK), founded in 1707. For all that tolerance was an element in the Christian faith, the SSPCK was determined to exorcize Gaelic from the Highlands. Despite the fact that the Catechism and Metrical Psalms were printed in the language, its schoolmasters were reprimanded for teaching Gaelic-speaking children to read those books. It was an Englishman, Dr Samuel Johnson, no great lover of the Scots, who was instrumental in bringing before the general public the fact that the SSPCK was actively preventing a translation of the Bible into Gaelic from being published. He wrote: '. . . there remains only their language and their poverty. Their language is attacked on every side. Schools are erected in which English is only taught and there were lately some who thought it reasonable to refuse them a version of the Holy Scriptures, that they might have no monument in their mother tongue.'

After the defeat of Bonnie Prince Charlie's Highland army at Culloden in 1746, the process of mass emigration from the Highlands began, to be followed from the early 19th century by more forcible attempts to clear people from their lands. Indeed, the removal of whole swathes of the Highland population, bound together by language, was an act bordering on genocide. In terms of the Gaelic speech community, this could be regarded as the removal of its heartland. Effectively, the clearances were to reorientate the linguistic geography of Scotland, reducing the Gaelic-speaking districts to the fringes of northern and western coastal areas and the Western Isles.

Finally came the teaching out of Gaelic, by means of the 1872 Education Act in Scotland, in the text of which Gaelic and its culture were completely ignored as a matter of educational policy. Nearly 40 years later, Gaelic was given a grudging recognition in the Scottish education system. Even so, there are many native Gaelic speakers living today who remember being beaten for daring to use their own native language in the school playground!

The decline in the Gaelic-speaking population is seen in the statistics. At the turn of the century the number of Gaelic speakers was well over 200,000 of whom 28,000 spoke Gaelic only. Today the figures are: 80,000, with the Gaelic-only population all but gone for ever.

The English language is today sprinkled with Gaelic-derived words: slogan, corrie, glen, loch, dunce, strath; the famous racehorse Arkle is named after Arcuil, a mountain in Sutherland.

If Gaelic has had the unhappy experience of its history, Scotland's second linguistic element (the third and most dominant being English) has suffered from downright neglect: Scots or Lallans. When Robert Burns wrote his poems in his native Ayrshire dialect they were well understood throughout Scotland, though today a glossary has to be provided. The *Scottish National Dictionary* contains over 50,000 words particular to Scots. At the present time, in Scotland, Scots is spoken in various dialects, each peculiar to its district. The Fifer has a means of expression which is different from that of the Aberdonian; he, in turn, is different to the man from Buckie; and he is different from the native of Easter Ross. There is no such thing as a Scots accent: there are hundreds.

Having mentioned trilingual Scotland, there is another linguistic dimension to be found in the northern isles. In the islands of Orkney and Shetland English is indeed spoken, but so heavily leavened with local words that the stranger needs a finely tuned ear to become accustomed to what is being said. At one time the common language was Norn, derived from Old Norse; it has since been diminished but is still strong enough to add a more than interesting facet to what these islands have to offer.

The real face of Scotland is buried deep in its cultural heritage, and only in recent years have the veils been shed to reveal a kaleidoscope of colourful facets derived from the folk traditions of the Scots themselves. Again we must contend with the popular image perpetrated by such comedians as Harry Lauder on the unsuspecting English. The image is both pawky and couthy: tartan, twisted walking sticks, glengarry bonnets, heather-clad hills, the wisp of smoke from the chimney of the wee croft in the Highlands, Granny's Hieland Hame, Hogmanay cantrips, football-mad people, second sight, being canny with the bawbees, Loch Lomond, Brigadoon, and so on – the stage props are vast.

The reality is different, and much better. Perhaps the most accessible aspect of Scotland's cultural heritage is music. It is strange that while other countries, including England, have produced composers whose works are a common feature of the international scene, Scotland's contribution to music, although it has indeed its coterie of able and professional composers, has been at a community level, enriching the leisure life of its people.

For no other reason than that it is the first instrument that springs to the popular mind, the Highland pipes have a popular following which reaches its annual peak in the Cowal Games, where massed pipe bands thrill the spectators, and the Northern Meeting in Inverness, where soloists vie with each other for major piping awards.

Perhaps the most Scottish of all musical instruments is the fiddle. The present-day exponents in this field continue a longstanding and historic association which reflects the life of Scotland. Each year and all over Scotland, folk festivals are held where the audiences are treated to a pungent taste of Scotland's rich and heady musical heritage. In particular, the fiddle music of Shetland has its own brand of appeal, influenced as it is by the long association of those islands with Scandinavia. An insight into the tantalizing repertoire can be had by looking in on the many festivals devoted to folk music and song which run all through the summer months, such as the Keith Festival of Traditional Song and Music.

The Gaelic language, too, has its own stage in October of each year with the National Gaelic Mod. This festival is of a competitive nature with aspirants to the gold and silver medals, the supreme achievements, presenting the best of Gaeldom's rich mine of song and poetry.

The art of the dance is not forgotten, with the popularity of Scottish country dancing fostered by the Royal Scottish Country Dance Society. Dancers are most often seen as competitors in the many Highland Games that pepper the summer season in Scotland. It says something for the country dance that it is still as popular today as it was over two centuries ago.

The point that has to be stressed here is that all this artistic activity is 'folk' or community based, and attracts audiences of all ages, thus proving another aspect of the Scots character: that however much the Scot might contribute to his popular image of being a dour, humourless character, he is in fact a member of a community of lively people who do not give up easily the rich and varied fruits of a culture that has been so long a-growing.

To reinforce this point we might mention the survival of age-old customs in places like Stonehaven (fireball swinging), Burghead (the burning of the clavie), and Lerwick (Up Helly Aa). All these and others tend to emphasize the fact that the Scot takes his history seriously and is more than willing to see the 'old times' echoed in his contemporary society. (*See pp. 44 and 45.*)

There is also the astonishing adulation accorded to Robert Burns. Generally, the Scot has ever been unwilling to afford public recognition in the lifetime of those whose achievements have placed Scotland on the map. Perhaps the phrase 'I kent his faither' might have something to do with this reluctance to honour the prophet in his own country. However, after the prophet has been well and truly buried, then, it seems, is the time for posthumous recognition.

Robert Burns is the Scot who has received the greatest measure of such recognition. The first Burns Club was formed only five years after his death in 1796. Today Burns Clubs are to be found wherever two or three Scots have gathered together in any and every part of the world, even in Moscow. The strange fact is that many of those who find themselves as part of the audiences at Burns Suppers have little or no knowledge of Burns' work. Yet they are attracted to the occasion, to participate in a series of rites devolved round the received notion of what Burns represents: the Scot who articulated for others in love, in homage paid to whisky, in the inherent desire for freedom, in the ideal of the brotherhood of Man. In the latter two concepts we find echoes of the 1320 Declaration of Arbroath, in which was set out the ideals of Scotland as a free nation, and which were to be later incorporated into the American Declaration of Independence, partly drafted by emigrant Scots.

Portrait of Robert Burns by A. Nasmyth   *(National Portrait Gallery, London)*

What does it all add up to, this essential quiddity of the Scot, the product of a nation that consistently throws up so many extravagantly disparate characters?

There really is no summation. Scratch the Scot and you will find pawkiness, arrogance, pride, snobbery, sentiment, tolerance and intolerance, submission and ambition; he is a lover of his own backyard yet has itchy feet; sanctimonious yet he lets his hair down at the tinkle of a glass; parsimonious yet generous to a fault; a nationalist, yet one who seems unable to achieve his own independence; at times unspeakable yet his door is ever open to the stranger.

Perhaps the Scot *is* like everybody else.

Scotland's Wilderness

To use the term 'wilderness' in the context of Scotland's northern Highlands and Islands requires some measure of justification. Certainly the term is not used in accordance with its dictionary definition of an area recognizable as a desert, uncultivated and uninhabited; though it is a fact that much of the Highland area comes close to the Old English concept of wilderness (*wilddēornes*) being an area where wild animals, especially deer, roam. At the present day the area in which red deer are to be found, some 200,000 animals, covers about 7 million acres and represents about 30 per cent of the Highland region. Much of the land occupied by red deer could never be used for anything else apart from recreation of a rather raw nature. Also, to contradict the term further, in certain parts of the country that are eminently qualified to be described as 'wilderness' there are remote pockets of human settlement whose members practise a form of land use, crofting, which provides a means to subsistence living.

Thus 'wilderness' is used as a device to reinforce the popular image of vast expanses of countryside, remote from large centres of population, rich in wild life and offering the opportunity to experience the spiritual, physical and visible aspects of nature in its rawest and most revealing forms; in short, nature in the round.

Northern Scotland is on the same latitude as southern Alaska and southern Sweden, countries that are seldom mentioned without a picture of 'wilderness' springing from the recesses of the mind. Scotland displays an extraordinary range of geographical facets within a small compass: generally poor in natural resources, presenting a rather hostile environment of harsh climate, stony, acid soils and rugged relief. The variety of landscape is kaleidoscopic: steep-sided fjords indenting the north-west coast contrast with the shallow shelving bays of Fife. Plunging mountain torrents compare with the stately meanders of slow-moving rivers across wide, open carselands. The ice-smoothed humps of the Grampian massif contrast with the sharp, jagged and weathered peaks of the Cuillins of Skye. Like largesse scattered with wild abandon, the host of islands of varying size in the north and west emphasize the regular, island-free east coast. Even the climate changes as you move from west to east, from moisture-laden airstreams coming across the Atlantic Ocean, warmed by the Gulf Stream, to the dry and sharply bracing atmosphere on the east coast.

Geology, too, provides another magnificently orchestrated suite of contrasts. North of the line of the Highland Boundary Fault, from Helensburgh to Stonehaven, two-thirds of the total area of Scotland comprises the highest, the most barren and the least populated part of the British Isles. Here the land base is composed largely of crystalline and metamorphosed rocks, rising in parts to over 4000 ft. Barren and unproductive Torridonian or Lewisian formations are juxtaposed with Old Red Sandstone which is easily weathered to form a good soil base, as is evidenced by the great swath of this rock running from Caithness and curving, scimitar-like, along the Moray Firth coast.

The Torridon mountains from Gairloch   *(A. S. Beamish, Natural Selection)*

The sculpting effect of Ice Age glaciers is seen in huge gougings like Strath Conon in Ross-shire, creating U-shaped valleys and straths. Broad expanses of peat-covered moorland, with domes, ridges and hummocks, present the tell-tale signs of an age-old landscape, part of some of the oldest areas of Europe.

To say that all this is merely part of the physical environment is to ignore the impact of Man since his arrival in Scotland many thousands of years ago. As a destroyer, developer and creator, Man has effected significant changes on the landscape, though only in those areas amenable to change with minimal effort. Nature still rules supreme, able to flaunt a flamboyant geography with a mastery which more than impresses the eye and the mind.

The Highland region has been inhabited from the earliest of times, a period of perhaps some 10,000 years. The earliest evidence of the human presence in the British Isles has been found in recent years in caves near Inchnadamph, in Sutherland. The traces he left there, and in other places such as Perth and Oban, bear witness to an era of habitation which goes back far beyond Christian times. Whether or not the occupation of northern Scotland has been continuous is extremely difficult to say; nor can it be said with any certainty that the population was numerically significant. More likely it was small and found in distinct areas amenable to life and living. Of those early inhabitants we know little, except what can be deduced from the civil engineering remains in the form of monoliths, multiliths, burial cairns, earth houses, crannogs or lake dwellings, brochs and the like.

One of the greatest, and continuing, assets of northern Scotland is its forests. In the past, the main element was the Caledonian Forest, an extensive tract of woodland and scrub which, it is believed, when Man first entered Scotland, covered over half of the Scottish mainland area lying below 3000 ft. In time, the woods, seen as a source of

The broch at Glenelg (2/C2)

fuel, building material and, later, charcoal, were depleted; only in the last century or so have attempts been made to replace the original land cover.

That the Caledonian Forest was of significant economic importance in northern Scotland is clear from many documentary references to the uses to which wood was put: from firewood to shipbuilding. Early Man started the process of forest cutting which has lasted to modern times. Then, the extension of land cultivation encroached on more forest, until it was realized by central authorities, such as the old Scots Parliament, that a serious problem was looming which would create a vacuum in the economy, if not in the lifetime of contemporary politicians then at least in that of a future generation. So legislation was introduced by the middle of the 15th century to regulate the destruction of forests, though, in reality, it had little effect. Many woods were burned to the ground to remove the natural cover of wolves, and also of human predators, the criminals and outlaws. Later, iron foundries were established which further depleted the forests.

By the end of the 18th century much of the original land cover as represented by the old Caledonian Forest had disappeared, particularly in the area of the Cairngorms and in the valley of the river Spey. Perhaps the last act of destruction was in the clearance of tree cover to provide sheep runs on a vast scale, and this prevented natural regeneration. Although the pastures were fertile to begin with, they degenerated rapidly as the result of the breaking of the natural cycle of chemical and organic activity associated with forest cover. Subsequent loss by leaching became more pronounced, there being no forest litter to retain a proportion of the rainfall at the surface. Downhill wash initiated peat-forming processes. Bracken, once broken and bruised and kept in check by the hoofs of grazing cattle, ran rife, because sheep and deer are selective grazers and avoid the spreading bracken-infested areas.

From the exploitation of the woodland resources in the 18th century to the exploitation of scenic resources from the mid-19th to the 20th centuries is but a step in the same direction. The latter, in terms of the preservation of fragile areas, is causing as much concern to conservationists as to those worried about the sociological implications for any region subjected to intense developmental and tourist pressures, as the need increases for 'wilderness areas' for those whose normal, everyday environments fail to offer satisfactory opportunities for outdoor relaxation and leisure.

The appearance of tourists in northern Scotland was by courtesy of a process of change in land use in which, paradoxically, the residual human element was gradually pushed out. Land that had over the centuries been nursed to a satisfactory level of crop and livestock production was cleared of people as landlords, many of whom were territorial clan chiefs, realized that cash rentals were more to their advantage than tenants offering their services and kind in return for unsecured tenancies. The landowners' estates were offered on lease to sheep farmers who took advantage of vast areas of grazing. The end result of the sheep invasion was a deterioration of the land and the take-over by coarse vegetation. To improve the situation heavy burning operations were undertaken by the graziers, but in certain types of soil this has an adverse effect: the destruction of basic soil nutrients.

Faced with diminishing returns from the sheep, graziers pulled out to leave the estate owners with only one direction in which to turn: the creation of the deer forest and the introduction of deer stalking as a sport. Thus, the vacuum left by the sheep was filled with deer and, as these animals required a wide foraging area, deer estates increased in size, again requiring the removal of the very element that would have kept the land sweet and productive: people.

During the 20th century, many of the large estates of the previous century were broken up to pay death duties and were made into small sporting estates. After the First World War, the State made its appearance as a landowner with State settlements for crofters and the acquisition of land by the Forestry Commission. Sheep stock continued to decline and the areas thus left vacant were afforested. Deer stocks rose considerably to create a conflict between the requirements of deer and trees. Crofters themselves began to find themselves in need of a second source of income, failing which they moved away from the land with their families. The basic problem today has two facets. One is that the land has been impoverished by the spread of heather and bracken, with much of the soil now peaty podzol of very acid content; the other half of the problem is human. The older people tend to relive the history of their forebears, while the young are being introduced to the community-corrosive influences of the mass media and different standards.

So it is that today when the visitor explores northern Scotland, he or she is exposed to a thick patina of social history laid over the natural pattern of the physical environment. What is enjoyed today, what gives pleasure to both mind and eye, is the product of many factors which, if they are known about and form part of the whole, contribute to a mature understanding of the landscape.

And yet . . . tough though nature is, seemingly unchangeable, untouchable and able to recover from the rigours of the natural elements, it is still susceptible to the impact of the human element. The increasing pressures created by the demand for

Fishing, Loch Fyne   (The Image Bank, David W. Hamilton)

recreation and leisure facilities have placed many areas of primeval and natural beauty in great danger.

An indication of the pressures being created by the heavy tread of many feet in the Grampians was suggested in a survey published in 1970, which showed that the damage people have caused has reduced the covering of vegetation considerably, and in some areas has actually led to soil erosion. Particularly on the high ground on the mountain slopes, chemical weathering is very weak; this, coupled with the fact that there is little available organic matter from decomposing plants able to accumulate in what sparse soil covering exists, produces a serious problem. Mountain soils, in particular, are at a great risk, as are the plant communities. Damage is most apparent on the soils and vegetation near ski lifts. Added to this is the scarring of areas for tourist development, the pollution of lochs and streams, and the unthoughtful scattering of litter of the kind that cannot be broken down by normal weathering processes, and there is created the current concern which, fortunately, is now shared by those very tourists who visit the Cairngorms and learn something about the delicate natural balances that exist there. They have their respect for the countryside enhanced as a result; tourists are often converted to active conservationists.

The emergence of old clan and family lands as sporting estates began towards the end of the 18th century. One of the first, if not the first, to recognize the possibilities for sport, with gun and rod, of the Highland estates was the indomitable Colonel Thomas Thornton, an eccentric sporting Yorkshire squire who pioneered the English sport invasion. In 1804 he wrote a book describing with great gusto and in as great detail his 'bags' of wild animals. His sporting tours in the Highlands were on the scale of the old grand African safaris and conducted in great style. Some idea of the extent of his big tour in 1786 may be had from the fact that he hired a cutter, the *Falcon*, to take his creature comforts from Hull to Fochabers; so extensive were his requirements that it needed 49 carts to take them all from Fochabers to Badenoch in Speyside, while four more horses were employed to transport, on a sledge, two large boats for his own use on the lochs. On one tour he recorded a fantastic gamebag of 561 birds and mammals of 15 species and 1126 fish.

This publicity attracted others who came in droves to conduct their own massive and indiscriminate slaughter of wild life. Anything that moved was shot at or fished with the result that the natural species which had hitherto enjoyed a life of reasonable security were reduced to levels that bordered on extinction. Paradoxically, it is now this scarcity of species which makes the 'wilderness' such an attraction for tourists, who may if lucky catch glimpses of the pine marten or the wild cat, animals which can be seen only in their secluded and restricted native habitats.

Dreadful though this picture might be, there is a silver lining which offers much hope for the future. The case of the osprey, the fish-eating eagle, is one example of recovery.

A rare enough bird last century, its nests were continually made the target of egg collectors and sportsmen who thought nothing of pulling the trigger whenever a specimen came into their sights. By 1916 the osprey had ceased to breed on Speyside. Then, in the 1950s, they began to appear, concentrating their nesting efforts on Loch Garten. However, nest robbers created problems which were immediately tackled by the Royal Society for the Protection of Birds and a programme of security was mounted, the success of which is seen today for the osprey is now a familiar sight in the Loch Garten area.

White-tailed sea eagles being successfully introduced in Rhum   (*Eric and David Hosking*)

Another bird species that seems now to be successfully returning to its old haunts is the white-tailed sea eagle. Until the beginning of this century these birds had a number of long-established cliff eyries on the islands of Canna, Eigg and Rhum in the Inner Hebrides. The last British nesting site of this huge and magnificent bird was in Skye in 1916. Then it disappeared off the list of native British birds. In June 1975 four white-tailed eagles (one male and three females) were reinstated on the island of Rhum, whose environment is controlled by the Nature Conservancy Council. It has taken over a decade for the birds to become accustomed to the island, but success has recently been reported in the mating and breeding of a pair of eagles. Perhaps once again we may have the pleasure of these noble birds adding an extra dimension of interest to West Highland cliffs.

Through the influence of the Nature Conservancy Council, recent legislation has been introduced to identify 'Sites of Special Scientific Interest'. These cover not only areas that have significance for fauna and flora, but also natural habitats, such as flat water, marshland, peat bogs, estuaries, maritime and coastal areas, and even unique rock formations. However, while the identification of these sites has been generally welcomed, their very location has created controversy, particularly where agricultural practices might impinge on those very aspects that make the sites valuable in scientific terms.

The tension created between the need to preserve wild life habitats and the need to continue with certain forms of land use has been highlighted in South Uist, one of the islands in the Outer Hebrides. There, habitats for wildfowl have only recently come into existence, the result of the flooding of land neglected by crofters because they lack the necessary capital to buy the equipment needed to build drainage systems. The Nature Conservancy Council was then accused of putting birds before people.

A similar situation arose in 1985 in Islay when it was proposed to extend the cutting of peat into areas where the greylag geese winter. The peat was needed to add that essential and somewhat mystic ingredient to malt whisky, without which the Islay malts would not have quite the same appeal to the palates of connoisseurs of the golden liquid. Added to the problem was the damage done to farm crops by the grazing geese. The campaign in this instance was led by TV personality and botanist *par excellence*, David Bellamy. The reception accorded Dr Bellamy and his campaigning followers hardly came up to the usual standards of hospitality for which the Highlands are noted.

These are merely two out of many instances creating ripples in the current mainstream of thought and activity which advocates the preservation and maintenance of areas which could be called, in simplistic terms, 'wilderness'. Other parts of the British Isles are under similar pressures: the drainage of land, the clearance of hedgerows and the ploughing of fallow land and meadows.

The very appeal of the 'wilderness' aspect of a certain area will always attract the tourist, with the more accessible areas put under more pressure than those deemed remote. Thus the wild natural places in Sutherland, Torridon, Ardnamurchan, the Trossachs, the Grampians, the Culbin Sands, the Sands of Forvie and the National Forest Parks, all extend a welcome to visitors, coupled with an appeal for the kind of respect for the very elements that make these areas so attractive to those whose everyday environments are overwhelmingly urban and man-made.

At the end of the day, it can only be the informed and educated attitude of 'wilderness' consumers that will help to establish the conditions necessary for compromise between those who wish to develop the leisure and recreation potential of these areas and those for whom 'wilderness' forms part of our heritage as much as does an ancient castle or stately home. The public demand for wholefood products, for cosmetics derived from natural sources and the like, indicates that attitudes are changing as the human species comes to realize that nature in the round is part and parcel of our lifestyle, able to offer an environment to which we can escape to recharge our spiritual batteries.

Scotland's 'wilderness', then, offers a whole horizon of unique experiences: the bodily lightness, akin to feyness, experienced on a mountain top which communicates some degree of elation to the mind; the tranquillity that comes from watching slow-moving water dappled by rising trout; the sensation of fear and awe as your physical being is dominated by the bulk of a massif such as Beinn Eighe; the sense of timelessness experienced when walking in the pinewoods of Rothiemurchus; and the feeling of companionship, the 'at-one-ness', when wild life makes a shy appearance to add that essential living element to what really makes a 'wilderness'.

The West Highland Way

Loch Rannoch

The first long-distance footpath to be established in Scotland was the West Highland Way (*see* Map 6), officially opened in 1980. Following its route, the walker starts on a 95-mile trek from Milngavie, just outside Glasgow, to end, in his own time, at Fort William. The Way can be accessed at points along the route to which motor vehicles can be taken, so that it can be traversed in comfortable sections. Those who wish to indulge in the invigorating experience of trekking its full length will require about eight days; the more athletic, who wish to ignore the excellent opportunities for exploration, will complete the route in much less than that. But it would not do justice to an excellent provision, which opens up so many new vistas, simply to 'do the Way just because it's there'.

Some sections of the Highland Way offer easy walking in good conditions, on old-established footpaths, on forest roads, on historic military roads and along former railway lines. Other sections require a modicum of stamina, but not so much as to deter those in a.reasonable state of physical fitness. Indeed, the ultimate reward, like a marathon, is the personal satisfaction derived from the successful completion of the route.

Milngavie, the start of the West Highland Way, is only 10 miles from Glasgow, but it is the gateway to a countryside of fine hills and moorland, rivers and woods. As the traveller progresses, his eye is continually drawn up 'to the hills', which increase in stature as the southern approaches to the Highlands are reached.

At Drymen, the route takes the walker along the eastern shore of Loch Lomond, the largest body of inland water in Britain, and one of the deepest. Stimulated by the writings of Sir Walter Scott, the area became something of a tourist magnet last century and today the attraction has not diminished, as witness the estimated 40,000 people who visit Loch Lomond on a peak summer day.

Breath-taking scenic panoramas tantalize the eye, as the Luss Hills lend some enchantment to the distant view. Near the north end of the Loch, Inversnaid offers a dramatic view of Ben Arthur, better known as 'The Cobbler'. In this area is Rob Roy's Cave and Rob Roy's Prison, where he is supposed to have hidden hostages and kidnap victims. Whether this is true or not, this is Clan Macgregor country. The clan throughout its history had the unhappy knack of backing the wrong side in a conflict, or else attacked the wrong neighbours, a talent exploited by its enemies to such effect that at the beginning of the reign of Mary, Queen of Scots, the Macgregors took part in an abortive rebellion and 'letters of fire and sword' were issued against them. So ruthlessly were these letters applied that the name of Macgregor was proscribed, the use of the surname being forbidden on pain of death.

The roughest part of the West Highland Way occurs between Inversnaid and Inverarnan (about 6 miles), requiring frequent scrambles over rocks and through trees, best tackled with good strong footwear. But there are rewards. The taste of the real wilderness is ever present, as is the occasional strong whiff of the many wild goats in the area. Nathaniel Hawthorne, an American author, trekked here in 1857 and commented that 'this particular stretch of Loch Lomond, in front of Inversnaid, is the most beautiful lake and mountain view that I have ever seen'.

The Way continues to Crianlarich, the halfway point along the route, and a junction for both road and rail. Though the normal population is less than 200, the village is usually crowded with tourists in the summer months. Because of its accessibility to the big hills around it, Crianlarich is a favourite starting point for those climbers and mountaineers who tackle some of the 'Munros', those mountains of 3000 ft and above. North of Crianlarich the route opens out to Breadalbane (Gaelic: 'the uplands of Scotland') and the bens that form the southern part of the Grampian mountain chain. At Strath Fillan there is the ruined remains of St Fillan's Chapel. He was an 8th-century missionary who is credited with many miraculous deeds, not the least of which was the cure of the mentally ill. In the National Museums of Scotland (formerly the National Museum of Antiquities of Scotland) you can see St Fillan's crozier and his bell, stolen in 1798 by an English tourist but eventually recovered in 1869.

The Way then progresses through part of Rannoch Moor, considered by some to be the most desolate and remote area of country in the British Isles. It is crossed only by the Glasgow–Fort William railway. The railway line was built on large bundles of tree trunks to allow it to 'float' on the boggy ground. Past the dark waters of Loch Ba you reach Kingshouse, Scotland's oldest inn. It is on record that at one time the Government, recognizing the need to maintain a lodging house in this remote area, contributed an annual grant to keep it open, and charged no rent. In 1803, Dorothy Wordsworth stayed here with her brother William. She left with the comment: 'Never did I see such a miserable, such a wretched place.' Things are much better now.

The West Highland Way enters the final phase of its route through Glen Coe, where the infamous massacre of the Macdonalds took place in February 1692, the end result, though happily not final, of a complex interaction between Hanoverians and Jacobites, between Lowlanders and Highlanders, and between rival Highland clans. Kinlochleven is one of the few industrial settlements in the Highlands, built to house the workers of the local aluminium works. The last leg of some 15 miles takes the walker into Lochaber and Fort William, through hills clad in birchwood and forestry plantations. Here the mass of Ben Nevis is never far from the eye. At Fort William little remains to be done, save to offer some self-congratulations on having walked a footpath which, far more than any motorway, offers some of the most magnificent scenery in the whole of the British Isles. 'Footpath' seems such a humble name for the West Highland Way.

Chairlifts stacked for summer, Glenshee

Previous page: Inverpolly (see p. 143)

Gazetteer

Aberdeen, *Grampian* (3/3C) Despite the fact that in recent years Aberdeen has become the offshore oil capital of Europe, the city has retained all the dignified trappings of its long history and traditions. The oil industry is quite out of sight: far to the east, over the horizon and in the turbulent waters of the North Sea. Its presence in Aberdeen is confined to the harbour and is only hinted at in the air of prosperity in the city's busy streets. Aberdeen has also held intact its longstanding association with its rural hinterland acting, as it has always done through the centuries, as the social and commercial sheet anchor that holds this north-eastern corner of Scotland together. Aberdeen's motto is *Bon Accord* (Good Fellowship) and the associated toast is: 'Happy to meet, sorry to part, happy to meet again.'

Although often called 'The Grey City', Aberdeen gives this the lie. It is a city of everything: fish, flowers, parklands, mica-speckled granite, dreaming spires, ships in the bay, golden sands, and 'couthy' people, whose characteristic independence through the centuries has allowed them to absorb anyone from Norman earls to Texas oil barons without losing their grip on their own strong sense of individuality. All this has been achieved over the centuries with not a little sacrifice from its citizens.

The first known settlement, at the mouth of the Denburn on the Green, now overshadowed by Union Street Viaduct, was established by Flemings from the Continent, who kept themselves apart from their Celtic neighbours. Inexorably, however, the community was drawn into Scottish history. When the Scottish kings who came after Malcolm Canmore had extended their rule to the fertile lands along the Moray Firth coast, they considered it necessary to control Aberdeen. The first extant charter goes back to 1179, and was later strengthened by the granting of important trading privileges. From then the city's name began to pepper the pages of Scotland's turbulent story as internal struggles and political and religious factions rose and fell.

In 1336 Aberdeen was totally devastated by England's Edward III. Less than a century later, the city's burgesses saw fit to take part in the Battle of Harlaw in 1411, to prevent a take-over by eager Highlanders. The Reformation in 1560 brought 'fire and spulzie [spoliation]' to the city's churches and the three great monastic foundations: Greyfriars, Dominicans and the Trinitarians. The worst devastation took place in 1644. James Graham, 1st Marquis of Montrose, angered by the shooting of a drummer boy on the Green, unleashed his 'Irishes' to pillage, rape and murder in the city's streets. Though Aberdeen tended to side with the Risings of 1715 and 1745, it escaped much of the punishment meted out to other places that supported the Jacobite cause.

A period of real peace then ensued which allowed the city fathers to concentrate on the development of Aberdeen into the commercial, industrial, shipping, fishing and trading centre it is today. In particular, they saw to it that the city should be built to last – with granite – giving Aberdeen a solid and permanent air of civic pride. Like Edinburgh's Royal Mile, Union Street sums up much of Aberdeen's past. At its eastern end is Castle Street, known to the Aberdonians as Castlegate. It is a square that has been the official centre of the city since the 12th century. Despite today's heavy traffic, the area retains a substantial echo of its long past. Here a crippled child once wandered about in the last decades of the 18th century who was to win a secure place in literature: George Gordon Byron, later Lord Byron. The focus of his attentions was a young girl, Mary Duff, who lived at 17 Castle Street, now the Horseshoe Bar, built around 1760. Many years later, when he had won European renown for his poetry, he wrote: 'Hearing of her marriage years after was like a thunderstroke.'

In the centre of the square is the Market Cross of Aberdeen, erected in 1686, with carved portrait medallions of ten Stuart kings, beginning with James I of Scotland. Off Castle Street runs Shiprow, with Provost Ross's house, the second oldest domestic dwelling in the city, built in 1593; it is now the Aberdeen Maritime Museum. Provost Skene's house, tucked away in the courtyard of the towering glass and concrete of St Nicholas House, the city's administrative headquarters, dates back to 1545 and is now a period domestic museum. On show is a cycle of religious paintings in tempera on the timber vault of the long gallery. These were hidden under plaster for

300 years until revealed during the restoration of the building and are believed to date from 1622.

On the east side of Broad Street is Marischal College with an elaborate neo-Gothic façade. Founded in 1593, it gave Aberdeen its second University for a period of 250 years during which the whole of England could boast only the same number. Down from Marischal College, through Upper Kirkgate, is St Nicholas Church, dedicated to the patron saint of sailors, a fitting choice for this important seaport. The church was first mentioned in a Papal bull of 1157.

Union Street is so named after the Union of Great Britain and Ireland in 1801 and is a noble thoroughfare. Lined on both sides by granite buildings, it was completed in 1805 and the cost nearly bankrupted the city – a fact that may have caused Aberdonians to be rather more cautious about spending money, giving rise to their unjustified reputation for parsimony.

Although Aberdeen came late on the scene as a fishing port, it had a reputation for shipbuilding. In the mid-19th century, clippers for the China tea run and the Australian wool trade were built here: the skippers of the *Thermopylae*, *Black Prince*, *Cairngorm* and many others thought it nothing to cross half the world's seas in 67 days from Melbourne to London. The winds that filled the sails of these elegant ships also brought economic prosperity to the city. Over the years it has been able to weather both economic storms and becalmed periods, and that ability has made Aberdeen perhaps the most exciting, absorbing, and enthralling city in all Scotland, ever looking to its past to guide it through the present to an even more secure future.

Aberdour, *Fife* (5/2B) An air of history overlays Aberdour's rather more superficial present-day popularity as a holiday resort on the Fife coast. Its castle is 14th century, with additions grafted on through the 16th and 17th centuries. In 1688 the building suffered badly through fire and was abandoned to the elements. But the destruction was not final, because the 17th-century painted ceiling was preserved intact and can be seen today. Also, the east range of the castle continued in use as a barracks, schoolroom, Masonic hall, and latterly as a dwelling.

St Fillan's Church is part Norman and part 16th century. Its severely plain interior tends to give a feeling of great security, both physically and spiritually, with no distracting architectural detail. A leper squint in the west wall serves to remind us that this disease was once common in Scotland, and this provision was made so that the lepers could participate in the services, at least at a safe distance.

Building corn stacks, near Aberdeen

Castle Menzies, Weem, near Aberfeldy

Aberfeldy, *Tayside* (5/1B) A prime example of a typical Highland town, relishing its superb setting. Aberfeldy has been a popular tourist centre since it was visited in 1787 by the poet Robert Burns, who extolled the beauty of the surrounding countryside in his song 'The Birks o' Aberfeldy'. These same birchwoods can still be seen and experienced – and perhaps excite the viewer to poetry.

An important feature in the town is the bridge built by General George Wade, the inveterate 18th-century builder of the roads that opened up so much of the Highlands. The bridge, quite the finest designed by the general, was built in 1733. Near by is a large cairn, erected in 1887, surmounted by a kilted figure and commemorating the raising of the Black Watch Regiment in 1739. The Oatmeal Mill in Mill Street is in working condition; a museum explaining the complete milling process from raw grain to oatmeal.

Aberfoyle, *Central* (6/3C) Aberfoyle owes its fame to Sir Walter Scott who immortalized it and the surrounding TROSSACHS in his novels. His vivid descriptions of the unsurpassed scenery caught the imagination of his readers, who had to come to see for themselves that it was not all the product of his fertile imagination. They started to come in coaches and on horseback and so started off the booming tourist industry that Aberfoyle enjoys today. But even without Scott, the village would have achieved fame, for its superb setting beneath crags that signify the boundary between the Highlands and Lowlands of Scotland would eventually have been discovered. There is a virtual kaleidoscope of scenic variations: woodlands, heathery hills, greenings, tumbling burns and the glistening of the sun on loch waters.

Aberlemno, *Tayside* (5/3A) The focal point of interest in this community is the splendid upright cross-slab stone with Pictish symbols in the churchyard, and its three companions beside the road. Rather exposed to the weather, and almost inviting the destructive attention of vandals through the centuries, these stones are in a

Cross-slab stone with Pictish symbols, Aberlemno

remarkable condition considering they are over 1000 years old. What the symbols mean is open to anyone's educated guess, for the Picts left nothing but these sculptures when they so mysteriously disappeared or were absorbed by the ascending Scots. Yet, the striking figures on horseback, or standing with arms, give a tantalizing glimpse into an early society, unique in Europe and one with considerable skills and cultural achievements.

Aberlour, *Grampian* (3/2C; 7/2C) Known officially as Charlestown of Aberlour, after its founder, Charles Grant, this burgh dates from 1812. Its outstanding feature is the width of its main street, lined with trees and well-laid-out houses. In former times, the settlement here was called Skirdustan from the old church dedicated to St Drostan. Delightfully situated on the east bank of the river Spey, the little burgh is surrounded by hills and mixed woodland. Its population has declined in recent years due to a rather unusual circumstance: the closure of the town's famous orphanage, which provided home, care and sympathetic upbringing for some 400 children drawn from many parts of Scotland.

Being in the centre of whisky country, it has its own distillery. Aberlour is also famous for its shortbread, claimed to be the best in the world. A small bakery was set up in 1909 and over the years has won deserved attention for its product and has become a big employer in the area. The shortbread is based on traditional recipes and made by traditional methods. The ingredients are simply flour, sugar, butter and salt, transformed into a magic mixture by decades of expertise.

Aberlour has little in the way of antiquities, apart from the ancient churchyard with an early stone font. However, the surrounding area is dotted with burial cairns, indicating many now forgotten battles. The town is dominated by Ben Rinnes, from which, it is said, you can see the smoke rising from a fair proportion of the 43 whisky distilleries in the district.

Abernethy, *Tayside* (5/2B) Now reduced to the status of a village, Abernethy, just south of the Tay was once an important Pictish capital. Tradition has it that it was here William the Conqueror met Malcolm Canmore, King of Scots, in 1072. The village retains the visible evidence of its past, chiefly in its Round Tower, the lower part of

Opposite: The Round Tower, Abernethy

which dates from the 9th century, one of only two of this kind in Scotland. Abernethy was one of the main centres of the early church in Scotland; the tower acted as a bell tower and a place of refuge for the monks who lived in the nearby monastery. A fragment of Pictish sculptured stone can be seen at the foot of the tower. On nearby Castle Law Hill are the remains of an Iron Age fort, with excellent views of Strathearn, the Grampians and the Firth of Tay.

Aboyne, *Grampian* (5/3A) Aboyne on the river Dee derives its name from the Gaelic: 'Place of Rippling Waters'. The layout of the village is unusual for a Scottish community, with a large green acting as a focal point. Substantial houses and other buildings make Aboyne something more than the term 'village' might imply. It was in fact created a royal burgh in 1676 to act as a centre for the interests of the surrounding communities. Evidence of the area's importance to the people of an earlier age is seen in the extraordinary collection of cairns about 2 miles to the north-west, most of which date from the Bronze Age. A relic from later times is the Formaston Stone in the grounds of Aboyne Castle, a Pictish sculptured cross slab with characteristic symbols and Ogham characters, the latter being an early form of writing (short and long lines cut across a horizontal datum).

A little to the north is Tarland, a quiet country village that was a place of ceremonial importance to the Bronze Age people. What must not be missed, however, lies a few more miles further north: Craigievar Castle which, architecturally, is the most perfect and least altered of 17th-century towerhouses in Scotland. It is open to the public.

It was completed in 1626 and was never added to. Its great tower thus stands alone, decorated with turrets, crow-stepped gables, conical roofs, balustrading and corbelling. The walls, harled in a pale apricot, contrast sharply with the greensward of the slowly rising ground on which it stands. Inside the castle are superb, richly moulded plaster ceilings.

Alford, *Grampian* (3/2C) A small market town near the river Don and the best-known, and best-loved, hill in Aberdeenshire: Bennachie (1733 ft). Alford entered the pages of Scottish history books in 1645 when a battle was fought here with the Covenanters, who lost. Now mainly concerned with serving the local farming communities and welcoming holidaymakers, Alford is a popular base for exploring the surrounding

countryside that is redolent with historic interest. The Grampian Museum of Transport, at Station Yard, off Main Street, has a comprehensive display of transport through the ages, including horse-drawn and steam vehicles, cycles and stationary engines.

Alloa, *Central* (5/1B) Alloa lies on the northern bank of the river Forth and is a busy commercial and industrial centre with spinning, brewing and glassmaking as its main economic activities. The 15th-century Alloa Tower is one of the largest of its kind in Scotland with a number of historic associations, including Mary, Queen of Scots. One of the oldest buildings in Alloa is the Kirkgate, a house dating from 1695 with its original sundial. The massive spire of St Mungo's Parish Church dominates the town; built in 1819, it retains a 17th-century tower.

Alyth, *Tayside* (5/2B) A small market town situated on the Highland Line (the line dividing the Highlands from the Lowlands) and beside the fertile plain of Strathmore. Its pleasant situation at the foot of the Braes of Angus tends to make people stop their cars and walk around. The remains of the 13th-century St Moluag Church stand as witness to a long and peaceful settlement, though the Iron Age hill fort on Barry Hill to the north-east might just hint at trouble in former times. The Alyth Folk Museum just off the Market Square, on Commercial Street, offers a fascinating glimpse into the agrarian history of the area.

Amulree, *Tayside* (5/1B) This tiny village was once an important staging post for Highland cattle drovers on their way south to the cattle trysts at CRIEFF, before they completed the final stage of their journey south on the military road built in the 18th century by General George Wade.

Anstruther, *Fife* (5/3B) Up until the 1940s Anstruther (pronounced 'Anster') was a big herring port; then, mysteriously, the herring shoals disappeared to leave its harbour desolate. In 1881 it reached its peak of fishing activity with no fewer than 221 boats registered, forming the town's own fishing fleet. The catches were salted and sent in whitewood barrels to Russia, Scandinavia and the Baltic countries; smoked haddock and pickled cod found ready markets in

Craigievar Castle

Scottish Fisheries Museum, Anstruther

Liverpool and London. Only an echo of these heady days survives in the few small local boats which fish mainly for crabs, prawns and lobsters.

Anstruther is a fitting home for the Scottish Fisheries Museum, set up in one of the oldest identifiable buildings in Scotland, known as St Ayles Land, with a charter dating from 1318. Part of the 15th-century chapel survives, as does the 16th-century Abbot's Lodging. The museum, situated on the old harbour head, has a large and comprehensive display of all aspects of the Scottish fishing industry, including – a reminder that fish is paid for by men's lives – an area dedicated to the memory of those fishermen who have died in pursuit of their calling.

The Old Kirk in the town itself was founded in the 12th century by Queen Margaret of Scotland. The manse at Anstruther Easter, dating from 1590, is said to be the oldest continuously occupied building of its kind in Scotland. It is to be found to the east of the town.

Applecross, *Highland* (1/3B) This is a rugged peninsula on the north-west coast of Scotland, between Loch Torridon and Loch Carron. It is a sparsely populated area where human settle-ments suddenly appear in view as welcome surprises on the coastal fringe which faces the Inner Sound, looking across to the island of RAASAY. Access is by way of a road through Bealach na Ba ('Pass of the Cattle').

Flanked by soaring cliffs, this narrow glen bites deeply into the ancient sandstone mountains which ascend in bold confident steps up to a barren plateau 2000 ft high, where the bedrock thrusts itself through a threadbare turf and clouds seem to race past your head, and often do so literally, a few feet above. The road through the pass, the highest in Britain, virtually cajoles permission to make its tortuous way through to the main part of the peninsula, and is truly Alpine in character.

The main settlement is Applecross village, the location selected by a 7th-century saint, Maelrubha, for a small monastery. Out from the village, the road turns south to serve four other tiny communities before it comes to an abrupt end at Toscaig pier. These communities are set in a truly marvellous patchwork of vegetation with wild flowers growing by the roadside and tiny fields, yielding crops of potatoes and hay. In summertime the heavy scent of the lush growth mingles with the salt air from the sea with an almost overpowering effect.

Ardclach Bell Tower

Arbroath, *Tayside* (5/3B) Given its status as a royal burgh in 1599, Arbroath is today a fine town combining tourism with fishing. The well-preserved ruins of Arbroath Abbey have for long occupied a deep and significant place in Scotland's history. The abbey was founded in 1178 by King William the Lion and dedicated to the memory of St Thomas à Becket who had been murdered some eight years before at Canterbury: the design is based on the towering Gothic style of the English cathedral. In 1320 the Abbot of Arbroath drew up the most important document in Scottish history: the Declaration of Arbroath. This was in the form of an appeal from the people of Scotland to the Pope in Rome asking him to intervene in the struggle against England's claims to Scotland. One statement has survived for 700 years: 'It is in truth not for glory, nor riches, nor honours that we are fighting, but for freedom – for that alone, which no honest man gives up but with life itself.' All the Scottish nobles gathered at Arbroath to sign the Declaration, thereby asserting Scotland's independence.

Under the influence of the abbey, the town's first harbour was built in 1194, with piers of wood; the fish catches were bought by the monks and distributed to the poor. The abbey was sacked in 1608 and allowed to fall into ruins. But its significance in Scottish history was not forgotten. In 1951 when the Stone of Destiny was taken from Westminster Abbey, it was eventually found on the high altar of Arbroath Abbey, as a reminder of the 1320 Declaration.

Arbroath's long association with the fishing industry continues, with an active fleet of boats bringing in whitefish, prawns, lobsters and crabs. Just south of the harbour is the Signal Tower – now a museum devoted to Arbroath's history – built in the early 19th century to communicate with the lighthouse on Bell Rock, or Inchcape, which stands some 11 miles out in the North Sea.

The town has a place in Scotland's culinary heritage with the Arbroath Smokie: fresh haddock gutted, headed and dry-salted before being hung in the hot smoke of oak chips. The result is a pale copper-coloured delicacy that melts in the mouth.

Ardchattan Priory, *Strathclyde* (4/2A) Standing on the north shore of Loch Etive some miles north-east of OBAN is Ardchattan Priory where King Robert Bruce convened the last all-Gaelic-speaking parliament in 1308. Rather less than half of the buildings remain, though it houses the

descendants of the last lay prior. There are a number of fine carved stones to be seen, with the burial aisles of the Campbells of Ardchattan and Lochnell. The nucleus of the priory is the 15th-century refectory which, after many alterations and extensions, has been in continuous occupation for 750 years. The gardens are worth seeing and open April to September.

Ardclach, *Highland* (3/1C) This little community lies south of NAIRN in lands watered by the river Findhorn and is seen to its best advantage near Ardclach Bell Tower. This curious 17th-century structure was built because the parish church was too well hidden from view for lookouts there to be able to give warning of raiding clans. The tower is on a high ridge overlooking the river, and thus served as a watchtower for the people of the district. The church itself has been rebuilt several times since the original was erected before the 17th century. Scotland's first missionary to India, Donald Mitchell, was born in Ardclach in 1782. He founded many schools and paved the way for continuing missionary work in the Bombay area, all in the space of the year before his early death in 1823. A cairn was erected to his memory in 1961, near the Bell Tower.

Bealach na Ba, on the road to Applecross

Ardersier, *Highland* (3/1B) Just along the coast north-eastward from INVERNESS, is Ardersier, sometimes known as Campbelltown, after its original Campbell inhabitants. It is one of the oldest fishing ports on the Moray Firth, though this role has completely disappeared. It now acts as a dormitory for Inverness and NAIRN. Close by is a gigantic oil-production platform construction yard.

Ardnamurchan, *Highland* (4/2A) This is one of the many peninsulas that make up the deeply indented west coast of Scotland. Its seaward tip is the most westerly point on the British mainland. Its name, derived from the Gaelic, means 'Point of the Great Ocean'. It is quite exposed to the westerly winds but this, far from being a disadvantage, means that large quantities of shell sand are regularly blown inland to sweeten the soil, and allow some significant crofting activity, ensuring some degree of support for the scattered townships.

At Mingary there is the remnant of one of a chain of castles built in the 13th century to guard the western approaches of the Highland west coast. It was roofed and still habitable until the 19th century.

The old parish church of Ardnamurchan, at Kilchoan, was built in 1763 on the site of an earlier 12th-century chapel. It is devastatingly stark inside the building. The chairs are said to have been part of a suite used by Napoleon when he was in exile on St Helena.

Ardoch Roman Camp, *Tayside* (5/1B) This camp is one of a system of earthworks comprising one of the largest Roman stations in Britain. Located at Braco, south of CRIEFF, it has been dated to around the mid-2nd century AD. These stations, including a companion fort at Inchtuthill, were linked with other signal stations and marching camps and were used after the completion of the Antonine Wall to the south. The camp at Braco is on the usual Roman rectangular plan, with substantial remains still to be seen to link the visitor with that period in British history when the Highland tribes faced the might of Rome's legions and held them dead in their tracks.

Ardrishaig, *Strathclyde* (4/2B) On the shore of Loch Gilp, a 3-mile long inlet of Loch Fyne, Ardrishaig stands at the entrance to the CRINAN CANAL. A former fishing port, its past prosperity relied on the excellent quality of the herring that once came into Loch Fyne in great shoals. Now the herring have gone and the town depends on the trade from passing craft as they take the Crinan Canal route to the western coast of Argyll.

Armadale *see* Skye

Arran, *Strathclyde* (4/2C) Sitting snugly at the entrance to the Firth of Clyde, and therefore in a main shipping fairway, the Island of Arran is in an ideal situation. Sheltered from the Atlantic westerlies by the long arm of the MULL OF KINTYRE, and its eastern coast offering easy access to the temptations of Glasgow and its hinterland, this island has attracted the attentions of the human species for some 6000 years. Arran has been justly called 'Scotland in miniature' on account of its widely varied scenery: moors, greenings, sandy beaches, woodlands and hills and mountains, ten of the latter rising to more than 2000 ft, with the brooding mass of Goat Fell (2866 ft) looming over Brodick, the island's main settlement and capital.

Evidence of a long and continuous human occupation is seen in chambered tombs (3500–2200 BC), monolithic structures, stone circles,

hut circles and brochs or duns. For its size, Arran rivals the ORKNEY and SHETLAND ISLANDS in its richness of archaeological remains. In more recent historic times, Arran was part of the ancient kingdom of Dalriada, later called Argyll, a region that once stretched as far south as Lancashire. Later it fell under the domination of the Norsemen who held it until the 12th century, when Somerled, or Sumerled, Lord of the Isles, successfully won it by dint of sharp sword and smart politics.

The King's Caves at Drumadoon offered shelter to King Robert Bruce in 1306, where one of the residents, the legendary spider, gave him the inspiration to venture on the final stage of his long period of fighting to achieve Scotland's independence from England.

The focal point of Arran's history is Brodick Castle whose walls have witnessed more trouble than peace. Built on the site of a Viking fort, the present castle dates in part from the 13th century with additions built in 1652 and 1844. It was occupied for a time by Edward I of England, in an attempt to obtain some kind of advantage over Robert Bruce. And Cromwell's Commonwealth soldiers held it for a short time, before being massacred by the islanders. Once Scotland's destiny began to be formed by politicians' words instead of the sword, the castle settled down to a long period of aggrandisement, with the results seen today: a veritable museum of the gracious life of the Dukes of Hamilton, with priceless collections of furniture, porcelain and paintings. The gardens are equally priceless. There is a walled garden started in 1710 and a woodland garden, begun in 1923, now showing off with no little pride one of the finest collections of rhododendrons in Britain. The castle and its policies are now in the vigilant care of the National Trust for Scotland, which has successfully fended off certain inappropriate proposals for the development of the tourist industry on which the Arran economy largely depends.

Arran's social history in the last century echoed that of many parts of the Highlands, with vast numbers of people being cleared off the land and left with no alternative but to emigrate to Megantic County and Chaleur Bay in Canada, crossing the Atlantic in dreadful conditions. James Hogg, the Border poet, was moved to write: 'Ah! Wae's me, I hear the Duke of Hamilton's crofters are a' gaun away, man and mither's son, frae the Isle o' Arran. Pity on us!' and went on to lament this depopulation. Tourism has not yet dispelled the atmosphere of sadness evoked by those times, particularly in the deserted places off the beaten track on this rather special island.

Brodick, linked by car ferry with Ardrossan on the mainland, hugs the shore of Brodick Bay. Once a huddle of cottages, an inn and a woollen mill, the town is now geared to cater to every whim of the tourist, with substantial buildings exuding a cosy and comforting welcome. Lamlash takes its name from Holy Isle covering the mouth of Lamlash Bay, in a convoluted philological progression from the Gaelic Eileen Molaise, a reference to an early missionary from Ireland. The High School stands on the ground once used by Donald 'Tattie' MacKelvie, who produced the famous seed potatoes that carried the island's name all over the world for their quality: Arran Pilot, Arran Chief and Arran Banner.

The last sea-going paddle steamer in the world, the *Waverley*, plies the waters along the Ayrshire coast and into Brodick. Built in 1945, she has been saved from the breaker's yard and restored to her original glory.

Arrochar, *Strathclyde* (4/3B; 6/2C) Situated at the head of Loch Long, Arrochar is dominated by Ben Arthur (1892 ft), which is better known by its popular name of 'The Cobbler'. Its craggy outline against the sky reminds the viewer of an equally craggy face with a Roman nose and pointed beard. Four other peaks of more than 3000 ft are in the area, which make Arrochar a popular base for mountaineers. In 1263, King Hakon of Norway led a fleet against Scotland and had his longships dragged across land from Arrochar to LOCH LOMOND so that he could make deeper raids into central Scotland. This ploy, however, was to no avail as Hakon was defeated a few months later at the Battle of Largs.

Auchindoun Castle, *Grampian* (3/2C; 7/3C) This castle stands as a stark ruin against the skyline on a high moorland rise above the river Riddich. It is enclosed by prehistoric earthworks and occupies the site of a much older hill fort. Its cornerstones were removed to build part of BALVENIE CASTLE about a mile away in DUFFTOWN. Auchindoun was the work of Robert Cochran, a favourite mason builder of King James III; he was later hanged by the Scottish barons at Lauder Bridge in 1482. The castle has had a stormy history. In the wars during Mary Queen of Scots' period of rule it was held by the picturesque ruffian the Earl of Gordon. From here the Catholic Earls of Huntly and Errol set out to win their victory in the Battle of Glenlivet in 1594, two years after the castle had suffered a burning, the result of a feud with the MacIntoshes of Clan Chattan. The castle has to be viewed from the outside as the interior is unsafe and therefore not open to the public.

Auchmithie, *Tayside* (5/3B) Despite the fact that its cluster of whitewashed cottages are perched on top of an exposed and barren cliff with a tiny harbour 150 ft below, Auchmithie has been a fishing community for hundreds of years. At one time it supplied ARBROATH with the quality haddocks for the famous 'Arbroath Smokie'. The harbour was built in the 1890s. Before that the boats had to be dragged by brute strength up the shingle beach. During the Second World War, a maverick German mine blew a hole in the harbour wall, starting a process of decay that has never since been corrected. The red sandstone cliffs hereabouts are riddled with caves, which made the area popular with smugglers and were used by Sir Walter Scott in his novel *The Antiquary*. A recent locally based scheme of restoration of the houses has been eminently successful.

Auchterarder, *Tayside* (5/2B) An ancient market town with a history going back to the 12th century, Auchterarder has had its sore share of history. In 1715 it was burned down by the Earl of Mar after the Battle of Sheriffmuir, one of the episodes in the Jacobites' struggle for the British Crown. It was here that a religious dispute occurred which had such ramifications that, in 1843, the established Church of Scotland was fragmented by the formation of the Free Church of Scotland. Three miles to the north-west is Tullibardine Chapel, founded in 1446. Once the mausoleum of the Dukes of Atholl, it is now that of the Earls of Perth. The building, for its age, is an unusually complete example of a collegiate chapel.

Auldearn, *Highland* (3/1B) A small village 3 miles to the east of NAIRN where, in 1645, the decisive Battle of Auldearn was fought between the Duke of Montrose and the Scottish Covenanting forces. Three of the defeated Covenanters are remembered by a monument in the north porch of Auldearn Church. An unusual structure, the Boath Dovecot, stands on the motte which is all that remains of the 12th-century royal castle of

Opposite: (above) Tullibardine Chapel, Auchterarder; (below) Boath Dovecot, Auldearn

Eren. It was built in the 16th century as a living larder where pigeons (or 'doos') were kept and fattened for their meat.

Aviemore, *Highland* (3/1C) Lying at the foot of the Cairngorms, Aviemore has been developed in recent years as an all-year holiday resort. Its success is seen in the bustle of activity as tourists take advantage of the wide range of facilities provided. At one time Aviemore was only a small village with a popular inn ('fully furnished, neatly kept, excellent cooking, the most attentive of landlords'), which came into its own with the opening of the Highland Railway between PERTH and FORRES. It had its status further enhanced when it was made a railway junction to provide a direct line to INVERNESS via CARRBRIDGE. Much of the old Aviemore has been swamped with tourist developments, but some houses from the Victorian era echo those quieter times when the surrounding countryside offered a chance to relax and find solace close at hand. Despite modern tourism, the landscape is still able to offer a goodly measure of that quietness, and not too far off the beaten track.

Balfron, *Central* (5/1B) This small village takes its name from the Gaelic: 'Town of Sorrow'. This is said to date from about 300 years ago when all the children in the community were attacked and eaten by wolves. These animals were a common species native to Scotland until the early 18th century – when the last Scottish wolf was reputedly killed in Sutherland, though other places lay claim to the deed.

Ballachulish, *Highland* (4/3A; 6/1A) Once important as a ferry crossing for travellers going south from Inverness-shire into Argyll, this Highland village owed much to the slate industry which began in 1697 and lasted until 1955. The evidence of former times is seen in massive slagheaps, now undergoing a welcome programme of face-lifting. At the southern end of the modern bridge is the cairn of James of the Glens, accused of the murder of Colin Campbell, the Red Fox, and tried by a jury of his Campbell enemies and hanged in 1755 at Ballachulish. The story of the shooting is one of the themes used by Robert Louis Stevenson in his novel *Kidnapped*.

The road going south from Ballachulish runs along the eastern shore of Loch Linnhe and

Previous page: Loch Morlich, with the Cairngorms beyond, Aviemore

passes through the little village of Portnacroish which provides an excellent viewpoint for Castle Stalker. The correct name of the castle is 'Stalcair' from the Gaelic for 'hunter'. It was built in the 13th century as one of a string of strongholds on the western shores of Argyll. The castle sits on a small islet and is perhaps the best sited of all such structures in the area. It has had a rough and vigorous history, one episode in which is commemorated in a granite stone on a crag in the graveyard of the Episcopal Church at Portnacroish: a bloody battle fought in 1468. The castle has been restored recently and can be visited by appointment between March and September.

Ballater, *Grampian* (5/2A) Ballater is largely the creation of the Victorian era, coming into prominence after Prince Albert and Queen Victoria had bought Balmoral Castle. In fact Victoria insisted that the Deeside railway line from ABERDEEN should end at Ballater and go no further west, so that her royal seclusion at BALMORAL could be preserved. As a result, the track, already engineered to take the western end of the line, was converted into a lane. In its time Ballater has seen many royal occasions, all set against the impressive backcloth of forest and mountains, with 'Dark Lochnagar' reaching its highest point in the Forest of Balmoral.

Ballater owes its original existence to an old woman who cured herself of scrofula by obeying a dream and bathing in the water near the foot of Pannanich Hill, about 2 miles east of the town. About 1785 an exiled Jacobite returned home to Deeside and, hearing of the story, built Pannanich Lodge as a health spa and was so successful that his nephew expanded the facilities in 1800, laying out what was to become Ballater and replace the older settlement, Tullich, which had been granted royal burgh status as early as 1295. Tullich is now barely a hamlet while Ballater is a pleasant, tidy and dignified town rather proud of its royal association.

Balmoral, *Grampian* (3/2C) The present Balmoral Castle is the successor of an earlier one built in 1484. Standing on a flat green shelf of meadow on the south bank of the Dee, it has views southward through the Forest of Balmoral to the long ridge of Lochnagar with its eleven summits. Queen Victoria visited here in 1848 and was so taken with the area that Prince Albert bought the estate in 1852. A year later work began on the present building, constructed in the

Scottish baronial style. With its many royal associations, Balmoral has now become a considerable attraction along the route through Royal Deeside. Crathie Church, attended by the Royal family when at Balmoral, dates from 1895 and is the fifth in a succession of churches here, the first being established in the 9th century. The ruin of the medieval church stands in Crathie's old churchyard. Certainly Queen Victoria had a keen eye and sense of place when she chose Balmoral, 'this dear Paradise'.

The castle grounds are open to the public when the Royal family is not in residence.

Balnakeil, *Highland* (2/3A) A tiny community enlarged by a craft village that uses the buildings of a former RAF camp. Close by is DURNESS Old Church, built in 1619, on the site of a much older structure mentioned in Vatican records as having made a contribution to the Third Crusade (1189). In the graveyard is the monument to a fine Gaelic poet, Robb Donn, or Robert MacKay (1714–78). An 18th-century farmhouse to the north-west of the village is built on the original site of the summer residence of the former Bishops of Caithness.

Balnakeil House

Balquihidder, *Central* (5/1B) This little village owes its fame to Rob Roy Macgregor, the Highland folk hero immortalized by Sir Walter Scott. In the churchyard are the tombs of the man himself and his family. This is Macgregor country. The clan was outlawed in the 15th century for atrocities ascribed to them for which they were not wholly to blame. Clan members were forced by law to adopt other surnames, a situation that was not resolved until centuries later. Next to the present church (1855) are the joint ruins of two earlier churches, the first dating from the 13th century and the second, built on the first, from 1631. Inside the church are a number of ancient relics and an 8th-century sculptured stone.

Balvenie Castle, *Grampian* (3/2C; 7/3C) This massive structure stands at the meeting of Glen Rinnes and Glen Fiddich in Banffshire and commands the passes to the towns of HUNTLY, KEITH and CULLEN; it also overlooks the main route to Rothes and ELGIN. In its time it has been a medieval moated stronghold and the seat of a Renaissance nobleman. Though now ruined, there is much of the original 13th-century walls standing, with later 16th-century additions, to impress the imagination and urge the mind back

Crathes Castle, Banchory

through the turbulent pages of history to appreciate the need for such a building. There is a tradition of a Pictish tower having stood on the site of Balvenie, indicating the importance of the strategic position to all kinds of powerful forces. Originally owned by the family of Comyns, it was visited by King Edward I of England in 1304, during his punitive expedition against the Scots. Centuries later it was of interest to the Duke of Cumberland as he made his way westwards to meet the Jacobites on CULLODEN MOOR in 1746, though by then the castle had been abandoned as a residence. Balvenie was evacuated hurriedly by Cumberland's soldiers when they heard of a possible surprise attack by the Jacobite troops.

Banchory, *Grampian* (3/3C) Although of recent origin (1805), Banchory in fact grew from a much older settlement, Arbeadie, with a long history. In the 5th century, St Ternan came over the hills from Fordoun to found a monastery here by the river Dee. This ancient site, still a burial ground, was used for successive places of worship until 1824. The circular watchtower, or morthouse, was built in the 18th century to prevent body snatchers digging up fresh corpses to supply the anatomists in ABERDEEN.

Banchory is now a dormitory of Aberdeen, but also manages to provide a more local base for its economy, for example in the distillery which processes lavender rather than whisky. A tablet in the High Street commemorates the birthplace of James Scott Skinner, one of the best masters of Scots fiddle music, and still unrivalled as the Scots equivalent of that other violin wizard, Paganini. Born in the town in 1843, Skinner became known as the 'Strathspey King', and his influence on Scottish folk music is just as strong today as in his own times when huge numbers flocked to hear him play.

A little over 3 miles east of Banchory is Crathes Castle and Gardens (open Easter to September). The castle is an outstanding example of the Scottish towerhouse and was completed in 1660, though the double square tower is earlier (1553). Inside the castle are rooms with really magnificent painted ceilings. The gardens are equally splendid.

Banff, *Grampian* (3/2B) One of the earliest Scottish burghs, Banff was first granted its status in 1163 which gave it access to the prestigious Hanseatic League of trading towns in the 13th

Opposite: Banff. (Above) The seven-arched bridge; (below) the Market Cross

century. Little of the town from this ancient period remains, except the postern gate from an old fortified castle behind an 18th-century mansion called The Castle. The present Banff Castle was built in 1750 and is now a community centre. The town has a predominantly 18th-century atmosphere which the local Preservation Society has made great efforts to preserve, with the result that many of Banff's fine old properties have been restored; indeed, much of the town is a conservation area.

Banff is built on three river terraces: High Street and Castle Street, Low Street and Deveronside. These are connected by a series of steep narrow lanes which are sometimes stepped, giving this part of the town a unique medieval flavour (the Water Path for instance). Some streets have examples of 17th-century housing; others present whole frontages of buildings from the 18th century.

Banff has always attracted visitors. Dr Samuel Johnson came here in 1773 and Lord Byron's mother had a house on the site of the present Court House. The town was called the 'Bath of Scotland' in the 18th century because of the vast numbers of people who treated it as a spa, taking to the coast here for the bracing sea air.

On the south edge of the town is the former lodge of Duff House, built as a mock Greek Doric temple. Duff House was an extravagance allowed himself by the 1st Earl of Fife and built in 1790 by William Adam. It is modelled on the Villa Borghese in Rome. It cost the earl £70,000 and all but ruined him.

Banff is separated from its neighbour MAC-DUFF by the river Deveron, which is spanned by a fine seven-arched bridge built in 1799.

Barcaldine Castle, *Strathclyde* (4/2A) Sited on the shore of Loch Creran, West Argyll, is Barcaldine Castle, built around 1600 as a tower-house and now restored and occupied, but only occasionally open to the public. The sea provides a theme of interest here in the factory which processes seaweed for inclusion in a wide range of products from medical preparations to ice cream. The Sea Life Centre on the shore of Loch Creran is the largest exhibition of native marine life in Britain, with many species on display.

Barra, *Western Isles* (1/1C) Barra lies at the southern end of the Outer Hebridean chain of islands. In common with its neighbours, there is much evidence of long eras of human occupation: chambered cairns, early Christian cells, standing stones, and the inevitable clan stronghold. Barra is largely covered by great stretches of peat moorland, though some welcome relief is offered by areas of rich pasture and meadows which occur on lower levels of ground. The coastline varies from sheltered inlets and the fine harbours of Castlebay and Northbay, to high cliffs and wide sandy bays guarded by huge sand dunes. Those areas near the shore that have had the benefit of windblown and drifting calcareous sand become flowery carpets of pale yellow primroses in springtime. Indeed, the fragile beauty of this flower belies the steel-cored hardiness of everything that lives on Barra.

Castlebay, the main settlement and the harbour for the car ferry service to OBAN and SOUTH UIST, overlooks Kiessimul Castle, *c.* 1060, with its main tower dating from 1120. It was the stronghold of the MacNeills, who were given Barra by King Robert the Bruce. The clan was notorious for piratical raids in the north of Ireland in medieval times before being persuaded to settle down to a fitful history of occupation until, in 1838, the clan chief sold the island. In 1937 Kiessimul Castle was bought back by a descendant of the MacNeills of Barra who began a programme of restoration now completed.

The island's economy is based on crofting and fishing, the latter enjoying its heyday late last century during the herring boom. In recent years Barra has developed as a tourist attraction, using the Barra Feis or festival in early July as a fulcrum, when traditional aspects of the Gaelic language and culture offer a unique flavour of community life.

Barra is predominantly Catholic, which faith has remained intact, despite persecution in the 17th century, ever since the island formed part of the See of the Isles, with the Isle of Man as the centre. A number of places on the island reflect the early Christian period, in particular at Eoligarry, where a group of three ancient 12th-century chapels stand, with one restored.

Close by Barra is the island of **Vatersay** with its population of just over 100, mostly descendants of the Vatersay Raiders who, in desperate need of crofting land, raided the farm on the island in 1906 and forced its break-up into 58 holdings.

Beauly, *Highland* (2/3C) West of INVERNESS lies Beauly, a name thought to have been derived from the French *Beau-lieu,* and associated with the now ruined priory founded *c.* 1230. Still surviving are three rare and beautiful 13th-century triangular windows, with trefoils in the south-west wall. The chapel was restored in 1909 after it had been used as a burial ground for the MacKenzies of GAIRLOCH since 1470.

Beauly today is a market town and tourist centre, but its grid-planned streets and market square are easy on the eye and present much appreciated aspects of a town of ancient lineage.

Beinn Eighe National Nature Reserve, *Highland* (2/2B) This reserve, marching with the boundaries of the National Trust for Scotland property of TORRIDON, is in the care of the Nature Conservancy. It was the first reserve of its kind to be declared in Britain and was acquired primarily for the preservation and study of the substantial remnants of native Caledonian pinewood. Wildlife abounds here and includes the rare pine marten, fox, wildcat, golden eagle, badger and buzzard, to say nothing of the distinctive flora which takes in many Arctic alpine plants. The Conservancy has established a number of Nature Trails and a Conservation Cabin. Fossils over 600 million years old are seen at Pipe Rock. At Anancaun there is a residential Field Station for naturalists.

Benbecula, *Western Isles* (1/1B) In Gaelic the name of this Hebridean island means 'Mountain of the Fords'. In fact it is a rather flat island, a place of sandy machair, strips of green and fertile natural grassland, with bogland on its eastern side. Its main role in Hebridean history has been as a stepping stone between NORTH UIST and SOUTH UIST, with its fords crossed by foot and by horse-drawn vehicle. These fords have since been replaced by causeways. Remnants of the 14th-century Borve Castle, stronghold of the Clan Ranalds, stand in a field close by the main road. It was last occupied in 1625, when it was burned down and deserted. About 2 miles further north are the remains of the 14th-century Nunton Chapel, destroyed after the Reformation. A number of the island's lochs have traces of ancient duns or forts of the 1st or 2nd century AD.

Ben Lawers, *Tayside* (5/1B) The highest mountain (3984 ft) in the old county of Perthshire, Ben Lawers is noted for its variety of rare alpine flowers and wild birds. The area is a National Nature Reserve with particular ecological importance for the whole of Britain. The mountain is not of volcanic origin but was once a deposit on the floor of a large sea 600 million years ago. As the result of a geological overfold, the oldest rocks are now on the surface.

Ben Nevis, *Highland* (4/3A; 6/1A) Despite its forbidding mass Ben Nevis, at 4406 ft the highest mountain in Britain, is easily accessible by a well-marked path that starts at Achintree Farm in Glen Nevis. The route to the summit is a 4- or 5-hour trek (3 hours down). Walkers are advised to keep to the standard routes and to be well shod and clothed, for the mountain can be a dangerous trap for those who are unfamiliar with this massif. Its micro-climate produces many freak situations, including the possibility of snow falling on any day of any month in the year, the result of the atmospheric condensation that tends to cover the summit even when the rest of the sky is clear.

Bettyhill, *Highland* (2/3A) This village was named after its founder, Elizabeth, Countess of Sutherland, who created it as a settlement for crofters evicted in 1820 during the era of the Highland Clearances. A mile to the east of Bettyhill, in Clachan Churchyard, stands the Farr Stone of about AD 800, an outstanding example of the ancient Celtic art of Scotland. The church (1774) has been converted to the Strathnaver Museum with a thematic exhibition telling the story of the clearances that occurred in Strathnaver around 1812.

South of Bettyhill is the beautiful valley of Strathnaver which, more than most, suffered during the clearances. At Skail is a commemorative cairn erected to the memory of the 93rd Sutherland Highland Regiment who formed the 'thin red line' at Balaclava in the Crimean War.

Black Isle, *Highland* (2/3B) This peninsula on the eastern seaboard of the Highlands faces the Moray Firth and rather belies its name, which is derived from St Duthac whose missionary work, around AD 1000, earned him a place in Highland memory here and elsewhere. The Black Isle enjoys a temperate climate and a high degree of fertility, which is exploited by agriculture and forestry. The area, with other parts of Easter Ross, leads Scotland in the production of virus-free seed potatoes. Its communities lie along the coast and include FORTROSE and CROMARTY. Avoch is a thriving fishing village whose people are said to have descended from survivors of a wreck from the Spanish Armada – both the surnames and local dialect are quite distinctive.

Rosemarkie, to the east of Fortrose, was once an important salmon fishery; indeed so plentiful were the fish that it was the staple food of the farm servants in the area. But enough was enough and they petitioned their employers, saying that they would refuse to eat it more than twice a week. Salmon are still caught at Rosemarkie, which is now a little holiday resort. Munlochy stands at the head of a very attractive small bay. Kessock was once the northern landing stage for the INVERNESS ferry, now displaced by the new bridge that links Inverness with the Black Isle.

Blair Atholl, *Tayside* (5/1A) A small feudal village that has grown under the protection and patronage of successive owners of Blair Castle, the ancestral seat of the Dukes of Atholl. The castle has had its inevitable share of Scottish history. A fortalice, or small fort, is known to have been built here in 1290, part of which is thought to be incorporated in the north-eastern tower of the present mansion. In 1653 the castle was blown up by Cromwell's Roundheads, but restored in 1689, in which year it was occupied just before the battle of KILLIECRANKIE. After the battle, the castle was dismantled to prevent it falling into Jacobite hands. In its time it gave lodging to Prince Charlie on his march south into England in 1745 – and again when he dragged himself northwards a year later, having made the fateful decision to do a U-turn at Derby. In 1746

Shrine and well, near Munlochy, Black Isle – leaving articles of clothing here is thought to bring luck

the castle was besieged (the last siege laid on British soil) and was bombarded with red-hot shot. The castle, open from Easter to mid-October, was restored by successive dukes as a white, turreted baronial-style mansion. The Duke of Atholl is the only British subject allowed to maintain a private army, the Atholl Highlanders. Inside the castle are visible reminders of past social and military splendour, with fine collections of Highland arms, furniture, lace, portraits and Jacobite relics.

Much of the extensive woodland plantations now covering Scotland owe their origin to one of the Dukes of Atholl, known as the 'Planting Duke'. He began with a variety of species, but found the larch to be the best tree for planting in the Highland environment. From about 1764 the Atholl Forests were developed and by the time the 4th Duke died in 1830 it was estimated that over 14 million trees had been planted.

Blairgowrie, *Tayside* (5/2B) At one time this substantial town thrived on its flax and jute industries. These have now gone and Blairgowrie depends on the soft fruit grown in the district. In 1898 a local man was so impressed with the quality of wild raspberries in the area that he started to grow the fruit commercially. Since then, climate, soil and altitude have all combined

to make the area one of the major fruit-growing districts in the British Isles. Blairgowrie's substantial red sandstone houses are witnesses to the town's former and continuing prosperity.

Three castles are within easy reach of the town: Glascune (not open to the public), Newton (not open to the public) and Ardblair (open to the public by arrangement: contact Blairgowrie Tourist Information Centre). The last-named is a 16th-century towerhouse, incorporating parts of an earlier 12th-century castle. Reputed to be haunted by a Green Lady, it contains relics of Bonnie Prince Charlie.

Boat of Garten, *Highland* (3/1C) The name of this Speyside village derives from the fact that there was once a chain-operated ferry here to take passengers across the river Spey. It was replaced by a bridge in 1899. The village grew up with the advent of the Highland Railway in 1863 and is now a popular holiday centre. Although Boat is a comparative youngster in the Spey valley, there is close by the site of early fortifications known as Tompitlac; the tell-tale 'pit' element in the name indicates a Pictish origin.

The Strathspey Railway, Boat of Garten

Boat forms the northern terminus of the Strathspey Railway, which runs steam trains from a special platform in AVIEMORE station. The engines and rolling stock have been rescued and restored to working order by the Railway Company and now offer a unique opportunity to taste and smell the old days of railway steam in the short run of about four miles between Boat and Aviemore.

Near here is Loch Garten, now the home of the fish-eating osprey. For nearly half a century this bird of prey was not seen in Scotland, until the 1950s when a pair returned to their ancestors' family domain and chose to nest in the ancient Caledonian Forest of ABERNETHY. Since then, the osprey has reached 27 breeding pairs, flying each year from their winter quarters in North Africa to nest here.

Bonar Bridge, *Highland* (2/3B) This little village, known as the 'Gateway to Sutherland', lies on the north side of the Dornoch Firth, spanned by an iron bridge originally built in 1812 (rebuilt in

1892 after a flood) by Thomas Telford, whose works are still to be seen all over the country as monuments to a brilliant 19th-century civil engineer. Though Bonar Bridge relies heavily on tourism, a busy salmon fishing industry provides something of an economic sheet anchor.

Bonawe, *Strathclyde* (4/3A) On the southern shore of Loch Etive in Argyllshire lies Bonawe, its neighbour Taynuilt and the remains of the Lorne Furnace. In 1730 an Irish company went to Argyll to set up an iron-smelting industry based on imported iron ore and wood from the surrounding forests. All went well until the two partners quarrelled during a drinking bout one night at the inn at Dalmally, and a fight started that ended with one man being fatally stabbed by the other. That might have put an end to the venture had not a consortium of local interests taken the factory over, backed by a 110-year lease of all the woodlands in the surrounding area as a guarantee of a plentiful supply of fuel. The ore was imported from Ulverston in Cumberland and unloaded at a jetty in Loch Etive, still known as Kelly's pier. The operations continued until 1883 when the works were closed down. One of the products was cannon balls, which were used to good effect at Trafalgar.

Today the site, furnaces and buildings have been restored as a monument to a past Highland industry, and are surrounded by a crofting community whose activities are perhaps more in keeping with the environment.

Braemar, *Grampian* (3/1C) Although now a more-than-popular holiday resort with royal overtones, the district of Braemar can lay claim to a long historical significance. The village is strategically located at the convergence of the old military road from the south over the Cairnwell Pass with the mountain tracks from Atholl in Perthshire and Speyside, by way of Glen Feshie. Braemar itself did not come into being until 1870 when two small settlements, Auchendryne and Castleton, the former Catholic and the latter Presbyterian, were combined in an example of Christian tolerance to be noted in our own times.

The original Braemar Castle, the 14th-century fortress of Kindrochit visible from the bridge over the river Clunie, was already in ruins by 1618. The present Braemar Castle was built in 1628, to be burned down 60 years later and then rebuilt by surrounding the original traditional

Waterfalls, Glen Orchy, Bonawe

Scottish towerhouse with battlements, crenellations and a star-shaped wall all round, pierced for shooting muskets. The overall effect is a rather incongruous whole, but still catches the eye with its position on a slight rise of ground.

Braemar was the location of the raising of the Jacobite standard in favour of the Old Pretender in 1715, an attempt to gain the British Crown which fizzled out with the Battle of Sheriffmuir in the same year, after which the Jacobites had to wait for the Forty-five to get their swords out from their thatched roofs.

Today Braemar's fame rests on its Highland Gathering. This annual event started in 1817 as a simple walk to raise funds for charity and was eventually established as a Highland Games in 1832. It received a royal accolade from Queen Victoria in 1848 and since then has had the honour of the presence of royalty. The Games themselves have an international flavour, with competitors from overseas joining with locals and others to participate in a memorable day (the first Saturday in September) of tartan, massed pipe bands, Highland dancers, 'heavy events' and track athletics. Tradition has it that King Malcolm Canmore used to summon Highland clansmen to the Braes of Mar for martial contests that enabled him to select the best men as soldiers more than 900 years ago.

Brechin, *Tayside* (5/3A) Brechin's focal point is the cathedral, a rather squarish building founded in 1150 and still used as the parish church. At the time of the Reformation, the choir was ruined but re-roofed in 1807 with subsequent restoration carried out over the years. Next to the cathedral is the Round Tower, one of the only pair of their kind in Scotland (the other tower is at ABERNETHY). It was built *c.* 1012 by Irish clergy who carried over to Scotland some of their country's architectural ideas. Both the Round Tower and Brechin Cathedral are a delight to the eye. In Maisondieu Lane can be seen parts of the walls of the 13th-century chapel of the hospice.

Present-day Brechin devotes its time to making linen and paper, and also serves as a market town for the hinterland.

Bridge of Allan, *Central* (5/1B) In Victorian times, visitors flocked to this spa for the saline waters of the Aithrey mineral springs. Now a rather quiet residential town for STIRLING, Bridge of Allan still attracts visitors in plenty, who lodge in the many solid and imposing mansions built for the Victorian tourist boom which even enticed royalty to stay awhile. Just south of the town are the modern buildings of Stirling University, situated in the fine parklands of the Aithrey estates.

Broadford *see* Skye

Brodie Castle, *Grampian* (3/1B) This castle lies west of FORRES and was until recently owned by one of the oldest untitled landed families in Britain. It dates from the 15th century but what is seen today are 18th- and 19th-century reconstructions. Now placed under the care of the National Trust for Scotland, Brodie Castle contains fine French furniture, English, Continental and Chinese porcelain, and a major collection of paintings. The castle is open from May to September, and the grounds all year.

Brora, *Highland* (3/1B) Brora is full of surprises. Though now defunct, its coalmine dates from 1529, and so important did the fuel become that in 1601 King James VI of Scotland granted the village a charter as a 'free burgh of Barony'. A saltworks was also established in the 17th century but eventually it failed. The Brora brickworks was started in 1818, when the Duke of Sutherland decided he needed bricks to supply his building programme. But it closed down after only a decade of activity. In 1901 a mill for spinning wool was established by a local entrepreneur which, happily, still survives. Also thriving is the Clynelish Distillery, producing a fine, full and mellow single malt whisky with a fruity tang.

Yet the scars and visual horrors associated with industrial towns that might be expected are hardly apparent here, for these staple economic activities provide a low-profile background to Brora's attraction as a small holiday resort with a picturesque harbour that lies within the bar of the river Brora, and pleasant sandy beaches near by.

Broughty Ferry, *Tayside* (5/3B) Though today Broughty Ferry is an eastern suburb of the much larger DUNDEE, it once had an independent existence – and some importance. Evidence of the latter is Broughty Castle, built in 1498 on the Craig which thrusts itself into the Firth of Tay. The castle experienced occupation by the English (after the Battle of Pinkie in 1547) and three years later by French mercenaries employed by the Scots. Today Broughty Castle is a museum devoted, though not exclusively, to the whaling industry of the last century.

The little harbour here was built in 1872, at the height of Broughty Ferry's prosperity when the fishing industry was booming. Ten years later came the advent of the steam trawler, when it was found that the harbour was too small to accommodate these larger boats. The fishing declined as a result. But all was not lost, for many of Dundee's wealthier citizens had decided the town was good for their health and their substantial houses can be seen today, strongly contrasting with the cluster of old fishermen's houses along the sea front.

To the north-west of the town is Claypotts Castle, an outstanding example of 16th-century Scottish architecture. Built in 1588 as a towerhouse, it is in a near-perfect state of preservation. The castle is open to the public.

Buchlyvie, *Central* (5/1B; 6/3C) A small village with international connections, for in a large house, used as a training college, missionaries of the St Patrick's Missions are prepared for their vocations before going to Africa or South America.

Buckie, *Grampian* (3/2B) This fishing and boat-building port on the Moray coast started as three separate hamlets which have existed at least since 1645. Today the town stretches some three miles along the coast. By the early 18th century Buckie had become a place of importance for the fishing industry, in particular the curing of herring in brine, an activity that began soon after the Napoleonic Wars.

Its first harbour was built with timber in 1843 and lasted until it was swept away to be replaced by another inadequate provision. The present solid and substantial installation, called Cluny Harbour, was completed in 1880. It consists of a harbour wall running parallel to the coast, with the harbour itself divided into five basins. This facility pushed Buckie well into the forefront as a centre for fishing and by 1900 nearly 500 boats were registered at the port. In its heyday Buckie was second only to ABERDEEN as the fastest-growing town in Scotland.

In keeping with its importance, offering a base for many fishermen following a wide range of religious beliefs, Buckie has for its size an over-provision of churches. The most striking is the Roman Catholic Church with its twin spires, consecrated in 1857.

Opposite: Brodie Castle. (Above) The exterior; (below) the kitchen

Many of Buckie's industries are based on the sea: ships' chandlers, three boatyards, marine engineering, iceworks, a fishmarket and the biggest 'scampi'-processing factory in Scotland. The town's long association with the sea is excellently displayed in Buckie Maritime Museum in Cluny Place, which has a section devoted to a well-respected historian of the sea, the late Peter Anson, artist and writer.

The town is rather well laid out and exudes an air of prosperity, even though the hustle and bustle of the heyday of the herring fishing are now gone. A number of the earlier buildings are to be seen in the Yardie and Seatown areas of the town. In past years all Buckie folk were better known by their nicknames, a necessity that arose because so many of them had the same surnames; the tradition continues.

A mile or so inland from Buckie is the tiny village of Rathven which, as early as 1260, had a bedehouse (a kind of almshouse) for lepers, now only a few stones.

Bullers of Buchan, *Grampian* (3/3C) These cliffs, taking the full brunt of the North Sea, are an awe-inspiring work of natural art, created by wind and waves. The 200 ft deep chasm was once an immense cave whose roof has collapsed. In rough weather the sea pounds in through the natural archway, adding its roaring to the noise of thousands of seabirds darkening the sky. Dr Samuel Johnson visited these cliffs and asserted that if he ever had to witness the true reality of a storm, this was the place to do it from.

Burghead, *Grampian* (3/1B) This Moray Firth fishing town has a long history. Its name refers to the *borg* or fortress of a Norse jarl, Sigurd of Orkney, which was established here in 889. But even before this it was a place of great significance for the Picts. Before that still the Iron Age vitrified fort on a strategic headland near the town (on the site of the old coastguard station) points to millennia of continuous habitation of the area. A number of incised Pictish stones bearing the carved symbol of a bull have been found in the locality.

The town was developed as a fishing port during the early 19th century, an activity still carried on though at a much reduced level. The harbour is surrounded by fine stone-built granaries from which the grain from the fertile lands of Moray was once loaded on to ships to be transported along the coast to larger centres, when sea transport was much quicker and safer than the roads of the 18th and 19th centuries.

Burghead maintains an age-old tradition, the 'Burning of the Clavie'. This ceremony takes place on 11 January, the 'old' New Year, when a tar barrel is carried round the streets to end up in a bonfire on a nearby hill (*see p. 44*).

Of particular interest is the Burghead Well, a marvellous rock-cut structure situated under a hill slope on the shoreside of the town. A staircase carved out of the rock leads to a chamber containing a well cut into the floor. It is believed to be a very early Christian baptistery. A key is available from the key keeper in a nearby house.

Burntisland, *Fife* (5/2B) Secular and spiritual interests lie cheek by jowl in Burntisland, the former in the shipbuilding industry and the latter in one of the most remarkable post-Reformation churches in the whole of Scotland. It started life as a concept in 1120 when King David I granted land for a church. But it took a century before the building was complete and the original concept manifested in stone and mortar. The present building, erected on the first, dates from 1592 and has a canopied central pew (1606) and a Trades' Loft which shows off the craftsmanship of the 17th-century woodcarvers. It was here in 1601 that James VI (James I of England) suggested the need for a new translation of the Bible: another concept which, in this case, took only a decade to complete and find life as the Authorized Version.

The harbour was supposed to have been used by Agricola in AD 83, and his troops built a fort on nearby Dunearn Hill. One of the few women who breached the male-dominated society of her times was Mary Somerville, an astronomer, who lived in Burntisland in the 1780s.

Bute, *Strathclyde* (4/3B) Bute is a small island, about 15 miles long and 3 wide, yet it has an infinite variety of scenery, from the wilder northern end to the gentler landscape of the south. It is tucked into the southern end of the COWAL peninsula from which it is separated by the Kyles of Bute. The chief town is the popular tourist resort of Rothesay, much featured in Glasgow's litany of folk song and the pleasures of going 'doon the watter'; the car ferry sails from here to Wemyss Bay on the mainland.

The massive red sandstone remains of Rothesay Castle (13th century) indicate a former

Scots pine on the lower slopes of the Cairngorms (see p. 96)

strategic importance. It stands on an immaculately tended greensward and has square and circular towers. It was used many times by the Scottish kings, among whom was Robert III, who made his eldest son Duke of Rothesay, a title held today by Prince Charles.

St Mary's Chapel, dating from the 16th century, stands as a ruin beside the High Kirk (1796), and contains two canopied tombs dating from 14th century.

Cairngorms National Nature Reserve, *Highland* and *Grampian* (3/1C) The Cairngorms are the highest mountain mass in Britain and form a ridge running from the southern reaches of the river Spey to Deeside in Aberdeenshire. Six peaks are over 4000 ft. The bedrock is mostly granite, a material so resistant to climatic erosion that the peaks are almost as nature formed them millions of years ago.

The Cairngorms high plateau forms a wide undulating range dominated by broad summits, the highest of which is Ben MacDui (4296 ft). The edges of the plateau often end abruptly in the vertical cliffs of large cauldron-like corries scoured out by glacial action. Lairig Ghru pass cuts right through the mountain block, from east

Above: Ski centre in the Cairngorms
Opposite: Ptarmigan in summer plumage in the Cairngorm mountains

(J. F. Young, Natural Selection)

to west. The mountains form an impressive backcloth to the broad sweep of the Spey valley.

The Nature Reserve was established between 1954 and 1966 and is the largest of its kind in Britain. Covering some 100 square miles, it offers a wide range of habitats for both flora and fauna. Many of the plants are alpines.

Public use of these high places has always been in contention, as the thin vegetation cover is often eroded by large numbers of visitors. The Cairngorms offer one of Britain's prime skiing areas, an attraction that contributes to the all-year tourist influx.

Caledonian Canal, *Highland* (2/3C) About the middle of the 17th century, some 150 years before the Caledonian Canal was built, Coinneach Odhar, the semi-mythical Brahan Seer, prophesied: 'Strange as it may seem to you this day, the time will come, and it is not far off, when fullrigged ships will be seen sailing eastward and westward by the back of Tomnahurich, near Inverness.' It is recorded that the person who

took down the seer's words thought this prophecy so ridiculous that he threw his notes in the fire. Today, the Caledonian Canal is a fact, and while the gift of prophecy might be questioned, it is quite possible that a man of great natural shrewdness would see that the Great Glen's long chain of inland lochs could one day be joined to form an inland waterway. It is to this fault, this natural gash of the Great Glen across Scotland, between Loch Linnhe and the Moray Firth, that one of the world's best-known canals owes its creation.

The idea for such a canal link between the north and south highlands was put forward in 1726, to be followed over the years by other proposals until, in 1801, Thomas Telford was asked to survey the route. His commission resulted from fears that if such a canal were not available, British shipping would be exposed to attacks from French privateers. Work began in 1804 against a background of financial and labour problems. Workmen deserted their posts to attend to their seasonal fishing or potato harvesting. Drinking on the job was rife.

James Hogg, the Scottish Border poet, visited the southern end of the canal in 1804 and commented forlornly on the lack of urgency displayed by the workmen, 'how apt they were to look around them at everything which was to be seen, while others were winding slowly out with each a little gravel in a wheelbarrow', and continued, 'I could not help viewing it as a hopeless job: my head grew somewhat dizzy, and I felt the same sort of quandary as I used to do formerly when thinking of eternity.'

By 1812 less than half the canal had been finished with Telford forecasting that, with luck, the whole might be completed by 1817. In the event the official opening did not take place until October 1822. Then followed a long catalogue of trouble, including the collapse of the canal's banks, problems with locks, and flooding, all of which purged the national purse of vast sums.

The Caledonian Canal, however, was well used, though more by passenger traffic than commercial shipping. Passage through the canal in the 1850s took three to four days, with no complaints at all about detention by unfavourable winds. It is still a popular short cut, saving ships the long journey from the Moray Firth through the Pentland Firth and down the precarious west coast of Scotland to the Clyde.

The total length of the Caledonian Canal is 60 miles, which includes 20 miles of artificial canal and 40 of natural loch. The canal summit occurs at Loch Oich (106 ft above sea level). There are 29 locks and 10 swing bridges. Day trips are popular; the passage through Loch Ness offers an extra dimension of interest – the far-famed Loch Ness monster might make a hoped-for appearance.

Callander, *Central* (5/1B; 6/3B) To be located in magnificent scenery is a commonplace for many of the villages and towns in and around the TROSSACHS. Callander is certainly no exception. Overlooked by Ben Ledi (2882 ft) and other crags like beetling eyebrows, Callander's setting provides everything for the eye's delight. Its substantial houses, many in their own wooded grounds, give the clue to its prosperity: a magnet for tourists who are catered for in many small details. Callander attracted the Romans, too, as witness the mound that was once Bochastle Fort, at the west end of the town and built by Agricola in the 1st century AD. The inevitable Sir Walter Scott was a frequent visitor, as was James Hogg, the Border poet and novelist. Another literary association connects J. M. Barrie, creator of *Peter Pan*.

Four handsome churches are among the buildings of architectural interest, which also include the 17th-century Roman Camp Hotel (originally built as a hunting lodge for the Duke of Perth) and Leny House, now a guesthouse. It saw much activity during the Forty-five Rising, when arms and ammunition were stored there by its owner, Francis Buchanan. He was eventually arrested and hanged at Carlisle, not only for his Jacobite support but for a murder committed in the house, which he denied. One of Rob Roy Macgregor's sons, James, used Leny House as a base, acting as a double agent, carrying false information to the Hanoverian forces.

The little village of Kilmahog, to the north of Callander, was once the proud possessor of three mills operated from one lake, producing meal, wood and woollens. James Hogg, a shepherd by trade, said he disliked the village's name, with its dark implications for the pig species.

Campbeltown, *Strathclyde* (4/2C) This large burgh lies at the head of Campbeltown Loch, at the southern tip of the MULL OF KINTYRE. Once famous for its role in the Loch Fyne herring industry, it now relies on a number of important industries which have given the town an air of well-being. Activities here include fishing for prawns and whitefish (replacing the now decimated herring), shipbuilding and whisky distilling. Although its location on the map might at first sight seem to make it remote, it is in fact just 40 minutes by air from Glasgow.

At the head of the loch is Davaar Island, once inhabited but now used only for grazing. On its southern side are a number of caves, in one of which is a wall painting of the crucified Christ. It was executed in 1887, in secret, by the artist Alexander MacKinnon when aged 33. Its subsequent discovery caused something of a sensation and the cave became a place much visited by curious sightseers. In 1934, when he was 80, MacKinnon returned to restore the painting. Today it is still kept in good condition by a local artist.

Canna, *Highland* (1/2C) The most westerly island of the Small Isles parish of the Inner Hebrides, Canna has held a special place in Highland clan and religious history over many centuries. It has a base of basaltic rock and this forms a soil that grows good, lush grass on which high-quality sheep and cattle are raised. Since 1938 Canna has been under a form of land ownership that is somewhat rare in the Highlands: committed, progressive, sympathetic, and caring for both land and population. Its resident owner is one of the foremost of Gaelic scholars, Dr John Lorne Campbell who, in addition to his valuable contributions to the corpus of Highland history and the Gaelic language and its culture, has been in his lifetime what the Scots call 'a bonny fechter'. In the 1930s he, with the famous author Sir Compton MacKenzie, started up the Sea League while they both lived on Barra, to promote the interests of island fishermen against interloping English-based trawlers. During Dr Campbell's 43 years on Canna he has been an advocate against the sometimes offhand attitudes of local government to communities who choose to live on small islands. In 1981 Canna was handed over to the care of the National Trust for Scotland, along with Dr Campbell's large and extensive library of Gaelic literature and Gaelic song collections, many of the latter recorded by himself and his wife in the Outer Hebrides.

Canna contains many relics of bygone occupations, from the well-preserved Viking ship burial to the remnants of an early 7th-century church and a medieval prison tower.

Cape Wrath, *Highland* (2/2A) The most northwesterly point on the Scottish mainland. There is no access for cars, but a ferry is met by a minibus which takes visitors to Cape Wrath lighthouse. The name is derived from the Old Norse *hvarf*,

'turning place', named no doubt by raider Vikings who, with some relief after sailing westwards through the turbulent Pentland Firth, turned south down past the Hebrides for rich pickings. The cliffs teem with seabirds, occasionally disturbed by naval ships using the rocks for target practice. Clo Mor cliffs are the highest on mainland Britain, rising to 900 ft from sea level.

Carnoustie, *Tayside* (5/3B) Now a holiday centre offering a championship golf course as a main attraction, Carnoustie is a 20th-century town, though its site featured in a battle in 1010 between the Scots and the Danes.

Carrbridge, *Highland* (3/1C) This Speyside village lies on the banks of the brawling river Dulnain, whose waters from the Monadhliath Mountains make no small contribution to the flood and flow of the Spey. Now a popular holiday resort, in past decades it was a thriving health centre, which boosted its trade when the Carrbridge section of the Highland Line was opened in 1892. Carrbridge was at one time an important staging post for the INVERNESS mailcoaches. The site of the old inn is now occupied by an hotel. The old, high-arched bridge spanning the Dulnain was built in 1717 so that funerals could pass safely to the old churchyard at Duthill, after an incident in which two men were lost trying to cross the river in flood.

The first-ever visitor centre in Europe is at Carrbridge. Set in 30 acres of ancient pine forest, it offers a variety of attractions, including an audio-visual display of the history of Man in the Highlands. It is just beside the main road and is amply signposted.

Catterline, *Grampian* (5/3A) There has been a village here since it was first recorded in the 12th century as 'Katerlin', a name derived from the ruined old church dedicated to St Catherine. Though it was never an important fishing station, its population was mostly fishermen who supplemented their income by smuggling, if a mention in the *New Statistical Account for Scotland* (1845) is to be believed. The pier is still used for landing salmon.

Cawdor Castle, *Highland* (3/1C) This castle stands about 5 miles from NAIRN, and is probably one of the best-known in Scotland, being mentioned in Shakespeare's *Macbeth*. No part of the

Overleaf: Cawdor Castle

structure dates from the Thane of Cawdor's period, however. The oldest part of the castle dates from 1372, a fortified tower now surrounded by 16th-century building remodelled during the following century. The family of Cawdor has the enviable record of having an unbroken tenure of the land hereabouts for over six centuries.

The castle, which is open to the public, is a very pleasant building with attractive battlements, turrets and gables and, in the bedroom of Lady Cawdor, tapestries imported from Arras in 1682, covering the original unplastered stone walls. The village church (1619) strives to match Cawdor's splendour with a castellated belfry.

Ceres, *Fife* (5/2B) A tiny village near CUPAR which houses the Fife Folk Museum, situated in the 17th-century Weigh House and devoted to the domestic and agricultural past of Fife. Ceres Church dates from 1806 and has an attractive horseshoe gallery and double row of communion tables. Adjoining the church is the Crawford mausoleum.

Ceres claims a place in aviation history. It was to here, in 1785, that Vincenzo Lunardi flew in a balloon from the then Heriot's Hospital in Edinburgh. He landed in a field near the village, much to the surprise and delight of the locals. The minister, however, was not impressed. When Lunardi remarked that he had been at the gates of heaven, the minister replied: 'It's a great pity you did not go in, for you'll never be so near it again.'

Charlestown of Aberlour *see* Aberlour

Clackmannan, *Central* (5/1B) Sitting astride the river Black Devon, Clackmannan has been a burgh since 1551, but its roots go back further into history. Clackmannan Tower, overlooking the river Forth on a hill top known as King's Seat Hill, was a royal residence in the time of Malcolm IV in the 14th century, and is what is left of a much larger structure. In the town square stands the Mercat Cross and Tolbooth, both of 17th-century origin. The *clach* (or stone) of Mannan, an ancient pagan god, was placed on its present perch, beside the Mercat Cross and Belfry, in 1833; its origin is now lost in the mists of antiquity but was of sufficient significance to have the town named after it.

Clava Cairns, *Highland* (2/3C) This remarkable and important Bronze Age site lies near to the CULLODEN MOOR battlefield just off the B851. Three large burial cairns are surrounded by standing stones, with a small stone circle on its own. Two of the cairns are of the passage grave type. The central cairn is a ring type, with no entrance, and is unique in having mysterious stone pavement strips radiating from it. Many of the standing stones bear ritual cup indentations and other markings. The whole area has an atmosphere that borders on the menacing, enough to leave some visitors with the impression that they are intruding on an ancient, jealous privacy.

Clickhimin Broch *see* Shetland Islands

Coll, *Strathclyde* (4/1C) This island lies opposite the eastern side of MULL. It is composed of Archaean gneiss, an extremely old rock formation which does not of itself break down easily into good soil. Characteristically it forms low rocky hills with numerous lochs, and this is the general nature of the island: low-lying with poor soil. Machair land exists, however, formed by the everlasting pounding of minute calcareous shell forms that create a rich sandy soil when mixed with peat. At the turn of the century, Coll cheese was renowned and reached connoisseur degrees of perfection. *Aficionados* would claim they could detect the very farm that had produced the cheese. This product, sadly, is now no longer available as a challenge to the taste buds.

The island was given to Angus Og of the Isles by King Robert Bruce in the 13th century, and was then held by the MacLeans, who built the 15th-century Breacachadh Castle, now a ruin. Beside it is the castle's 18th-century successor. It was in this house that Dr Samuel Johnson was entertained by 'Young Coll' during the former's tour of the Hebrides in 1773. In 1840 the island supported a population of about 1400 people, most of whom were cleared off Coll. Today only about 150 live on the island, which can be reached by car ferry from OBAN.

Collieston, *Grampian* (3/3C) A charming fishing village whose prosperity once depended on smuggling. Its neat houses stand in a refreshingly unplanned pattern overlooking the small harbour. In the middle of the last century, over 250 people were fully employed in herring fishing until the 1880s when the larger fishing boats could no longer use the harbour. Lawrence of Arabia stayed here in 1929 under the name of Aircraftman Shaw, with two companions.

Just south of Collieston are the Sands of Forvie National Nature Reserve, one of the largest, and untouched, sand dune systems in Britain. The sands are thought to have been left by the river Ythan during the Ice Age when it had a much greater flow of water. The largest pearl in the ancient Scottish Crown was found in the Ythan. The area was not always so desolate as it is today. The remains of a 12th-century Forvie Kirk are all that can be seen of the old village buried by a nine-day sandstorm in the 16th century. Excavations of a Bronze Age village have indicated a long continuous human habitation. The Reserve is of considerable botanical interest, apart from its importance as a wintering area for wildfowl and several kinds of tern.

Colonsay, *Strathclyde* (4/1B) One of the islands of the Inner Hebrides, Colonsay lies in the Firth of Lorn, south of MULL, about 8 miles long and some 3 miles at its widest part. The Colonsay vegetation pattern is of heather and grass moorland, but of a sweeter kind than is found on more acid soils. Small areas of natural scrub add interest to the scenic aspect which is quite broken, with sharp escarpments above the shore in the north-west part of the island. A number of raised beaches offer good arable soil conditions which, coupled with a mild maritime climate, provide excellent growing conditions for the semitropical gardens at Kiloran, beside Colonsay House. The gardens were created by Lord Strathcona from 1929 and rival those at Inverewe in Wester Ross.

Colonsay's evidence of a long human occupation is seen in standing stones and the remains of Iron Age *duns*, the most important of which is Dun Eibhinn, overlooking Scalasaig, the island's village capital from where the car ferry to OBAN sails.

However, the most important evidence of Colonsay's significance, to ecclesiastics at least, is on the sister island of **Oronsay**, which can be reached on foot at low tide. Here are the ruins of Oronsay Priory, a magnificent structure built about 1380 and said to be among the finest of its kind in the Highlands, and second only to IONA in importance. The cloisters are quite beautiful though many of the arches are broken. The medieval high altar is still intact, which is rare. One of the best of Scotland's stone crosses stands here as an excellent example of the art of the early church in the Highlands.

The Prior's House, re-roofed in 1927, contains many fine 16th-century tomb slabs depicting Highland warriors of the period.

Comrie, *Tayside* (5/1B) If you wish to experience an occasional earth tremor, then the Perthshire village of Comrie is the place to visit. It stands immediately over the geological fault that separates the Highlands from the Lowlands. (It is as well to mention that the tremors are scarcely sufficient to rattle more than a few teacups.) However, in 1831 and 1841 fissures did appear in the earth and a few house walls cracked. Fortunately the 1805 parish church with its castellated steeple remained unharmed and can be appreciated today.

Comrie is the home of the Museum of Scottish Tartans, the only place anywhere devoted entirely to the subject of tartan and the Highland dress. The collection includes a small piece of his own clan tartan which Neil Armstrong took with him to the moon. Truly the Scots get everywhere! Tartan weaving is demonstrated, and of particular interest is the plant garden where natural dyes are obtained.

Corrieyairack Pass, *Highland* (2/3C) There are many passes in Scotland, those syncopations in a geological theme that play so many important roles in the history of human settlements. Some are famous: GLENCOE and KILLIECRANKIE conjure up a vivid pageantry with little effort. Some others are, however, equally well deserving of fame, but tend to remain obscure and out of the public eye by their very inaccessibility.

The Corrieyairack Pass carries a road of sorts built by General Wade in 1732, running from Cullachy, just south of FORT AUGUSTUS on Loch Ness, to DALWHINNIE at the head of another pass, Drumochter. Much of the route of this road follows the young river Spey as it flows towards NEWTONMORE. The road was built primarily to allow easy movement of Government troops between the barracks then being constructed in the Highlands. The period that followed the 1715 Jacobite Rising was one of considerable unrest in the Highlands. The Disarming Act of 1719, forbidding, among other things, Highlanders to wear the kilt, only served to increase the feeling of bitterness among the Highland clans.

In 1731 General Wade began building the road; it was no easy task. Some 500 men were employed on the project. The road runs for 22 miles and was completed in about six months, a feat that would be impressive even today with sophisticated earth-moving machinery. In a later century it was used extensively by drovers, herding large numbers of cattle to the trysts or markets at Falkirk and CRIEFF.

You can still traverse Wade's old road, though it has deteriorated considerably in parts. Parts of the road make for difficult walking, but it can be done in about five hours. The Corrieyairack Pass is undoubtedly a route of scenic importance, with an exciting history almost every step of the way.

Cowal, *Strathclyde* (4/3B; 6/1C) This is a long peninsula between Lochs Fyne and Long; part of its coastline lies in the Firth of Clyde. It has a wide variety of scenery, so much so that it might be called 'Scotland in Miniature'. There are vast forests, moorland, wooded lochs, mountains of respectable heights and, if all this were not enough for one area, there is the sea which drives deep sea lochs into the land.

The land area contains the Argyll Forest Park, not all wooded, and to the north of DUNOON at the southern tip of Loch Eck the Younger Botanic Garden, with some of the original plantings going back to the 1820s. It is an outstation of the Royal Botanic Garden in Edinburgh. An extensive collection of rhododendrons are magnificent in their flowering season and the conifers enjoy the clean air and high humidity.

In August each year DUNOON, Cowal's chief town, sees the spectacle of the Cowal Highland Gathering, at which hundreds of aspiring Highland dancers, pipers, and pipe bands compete for world-status honours. Even for the visitor who is not quite won over to the pipes, the Gathering is an event which, once experienced, is never quite forgotten.

The fjord-like Loch Goil is an inlet of Loch Long and is fed by the waters of a river flowing through Hell's Glen, a desolate steep-sided moorland depression. Overlooking Loch Goil is Carrick Castle which dates mainly from the 15th century. Once an Argyll stronghold, it was burned down in 1685 after being fortified 30 years earlier in expectation of a siege by Cromwell's Commonwealth forces. The castle walls are virtually entire, though the structure is now roofless.

Cowdenbeath, *Fife* (5/2B) Underneath the greening of Fife lies the black wealth of coal, won at an often terrible price to the people who toiled in the mines. Cowdenbeath is only one of a number of coalmining communities that grew up in the 19th century around the pitheads. Its growth was spectacular, with a gain in population of some 20,000 in three decades. All along the line of the measures other communities dependent on coal came into being: Lochgelly, Kelty, Lochroe, Lumphinnans. Lying as they did among huge slagheaps, and dominated by the gaunt winding towers, they were hardly places of beauty. Rather, their character lay in the people who lived their lives in the seemingly endless rows of miners' cottages, in communities that were all closely knit by the common need to survive in the harsh conditions of their industry.

Although that industry is now a shadow of its former self, there are many reminders of the past to present an interesting lesson in social and industrial history. Many of the scars have been landscaped and derelict areas revitalized: the new parkland of Lochore Meadows is one fine example.

Cowie, *Central* (5/1B) Impossible though it might now seem, Cowie was a royal burgh in the Middle Ages and had its own castle to protect its interests, built in the 11th century by Malcolm Canmore. Only vestiges of the castle now remain. Last century Cowie was an important fishing station, until 1864 when survivors from a Swedish wreck came ashore with the dreaded cholera. The disease spread quickly among the locals; many died and Cowie never quite recovered from the experience. It is still an attractive village, however, with quaint street names such as Helen Row, Boaty Row and Amy Row.

Craigellachie, *Grampian* (3/2C; 7/3C) This little village has a Victorian character and is built in terraces above the confluence of the rivers Spey and Fiddich. Its main feature is Craigellachie Bridge, built by Thomas Telford in 1814, which consists of a single cast-iron span supported at each end by a pair of castellated granite towers. The metalwork was cast at Plas Kynaston in North Wales. Craigellachie boasts the inevitable distillery.

Crail, *Fife* (5/3B) According to the records, Crail was exporting salt fish to the Continent as long ago as the 9th century: thus far back goes the association with the fishing industry of this town on the East Neuk ('corner') of Fife. Its early charter of 1310, which gave it royal burgh status, confirmed its importance to the medieval Scottish trade. Indeed the charter always allowed the people of Crail the unusual privilege of trading on the Sabbath. This fact did not escape the attention of the Scots religious reformer, John Knox, who preached one of his most violent sermons in the parish kirk above the harbour.

Although this most easterly Fife town never achieved the renown of some of its East Neuk

Craigellachie Bridge, built by Thomas Telford, 1814

neighbours during the boom years of the herring industry in the 19th century, it did hold its own as an important fishing station. In particular, the expertise of the Crail folk in smoking and curing fish gave it a particular advantage. The local delicacy is the 'Crail Capon': smoked haddock, which puts the taste buds into a fast-forward reaction.

Many of the buildings in the town have been carefully restored. Dating from the 17th and 18th centuries, they proudly show off their architectural virtues. The partly cobbled and tree-lined streets catch the eye at every turn. Add to that the salt-sea air and its unspoiled hinterland, and Crail becomes the epitome of what the East Neuk is all about.

Crail's 16th-century church of St Mary, incorporating parts of an earlier 12th-century building, has an 8th-century Pictish cross slab at its entrance. Another stone near the door has an indentation which is said to have been made by bowmen sharpening their arrow tips. The Town Hall's attractive tower houses the oldest bell in Fife which is inscribed in Dutch and carries the date 1520. It is still rung at 10 o'clock each evening to advise the citizens of Crail to withdraw to their sober beds.

Crarae, *Strathclyde* (4/3B) This little village on the western shores of Loch Fyne has been the site of extensive quarrying since 1852. The stone is tough and long-lasting, and was much sought after for street improvements in many of Britain's cities. Because of its hardness massive amounts of explosive were needed, so much so that the 'big bangs' became a tourist attraction. In June 1883 a 'Monster Blast' was advertised which drew hundreds of spectators. Three years later another blast was advertised. This time nearly 1000 watchers arrived on the ferry *Lord of the Isles*. Just after one o'clock, the explosion took place and some thousands of tons of rock heaved, bulged and fell on to the quarry floor. Half an hour later people were seen to collapse unconscious, the result of an unexpected concentration of gases which proved to be toxic. Some 40 people were affected, of whom 6 died. Only chance prevented the gases from blowing on to the loch and across to the *Lord of the Isles*.

Crarae is better known for the Forest and Lodge Gardens all contained within the setting of a typical Highland glen. Minard Castle, a couple of miles south, dates from the 16th century and contains fine collections of the Franco-Scottish royal house.

The gardens are open to the public all the year round and Minard Castle from May to October.

Crianlarich, *Central* (4/3A; 6/2B) It was here that the 59th Roman outpost was established nearly 2000 years ago. Later, St Fillan arrived from IONA in the 7th century to set up his chapel, re-established in 1314 by a thankful Robert Bruce after his victory against the English at Bannockburn. It is now ruined. Surrounded by mountains, Crianlarich is today a popular base for hill walkers and climbers.

Crieff, *Tayside* (5/1B) This town was once an important tryst or centre for the great cattle-trading activities of the Highlands. Along the old drove roads great herds of livestock were brought through countless Highland passes to the south. The town acted as a gathering point for the cattle from no fewer than 25 points of origin, ranging from Caithness and Aberdeenshire to the Outer Hebrides. Until the mid-18th century Crieff, which had acquired statutory market rights in 1672, was the main tryst; but then, owing to an increase in the number of English buyers, it was displaced by Falkirk, which then developed to become the greatest Scottish cattle mart of all time (though its role ended in 1901 with the advent of the railway).

In the earlier years of this century Crieff was regarded as a health resort and built up a reputation which it holds today in the minds of tourists. It still retains its original charm, with narrow streets that have changed little over the years. In the High Street are some grim reminders of the town's past: ancient stocks in use until 1816. Also in the High Street is a 10th-century sculptured stone cross.

Just north of Crieff is the tiny village of Fowlis Wester with the church of St Bean (*c.* 13th century and restored in 1927) standing on the site of a much older religious building. When the astronaut Alan Bean went to the moon he took with him some McBean tartan, a piece of which he donated to the church, where it can be seen with some moon pictures.

Crinan Canal, *Strathclyde* (4/2B) The Crinan Canal stemmed from an idea thought up by the magistrates of Glasgow who, with a keen eye to its commercial potential, wanted an 'easy and short communication' between the Clyde and the west coast of Scotland to save a long and hazardous journey round the MULL OF KINTYRE. In 1793 an Act was passed authorizing the cutting of a canal from ARDRISHAIG on Loch Gilp to Loch Crinan,

The birthplace of Hugh Miller, Cromarty (see p. 108)

which opens on to the Sound of JURA. Work started in 1794 with a scheduled completion date in 1796. However, the company set up to promote the work experienced a history of difficulties, not the least of which were financial, and it was not until 1801 that the canal was opened in an unfinished state. In August 1809 the Crinan Canal was pronounced officially complete. Five years later, that ubiquitous engineer Thomas Telford had to be called in to survey the canal. He called for significant improvements which were carried out, and by 1817 Telford declared himself satisfied. In the event, he need not have bothered, for the canal has never really fulfilled its original commercial purpose because of its restricted capacity for large vessels.

The main traffic now consists of yachts making for the sailing experiences to be had off the west coast of Scotland, and Crinan itself is a yachting centre in its own right.

The canal extends from just to the north of Ardrishaig, through LOCHGILPHEAD to Crinan, a distance of about 9 miles. There are 15 locks, with 8 reservoirs feeding the canal. The passage through the canal varies from 3 to 5 hours.

Croick, *Highland* (2/3B) This little church, built in 1827 by Thomas Telford, stands at the head of Strath Carron as a mute witness to the forcible eviction of Highland families from the lands of Sutherland. It was once the centre for worship attended by a weekly congregation of 200 drawn from many of the small communities in the area. In 1845 these people all disappeared within months. Before they emigrated to Canada, Australia and New Zealand, they gathered for the last time in Croick Church and scratched their names and comments on the east windows as a poignant reminder for future generations of their tragic circumstances, over which they had no control.

Cromarty, *Highland* (3/1B) This attractive little town stands at the tip of the BLACK ISLE which pushes its snout into the Moray Firth. As the millionaire Andrew Carnegie reported in 1902: 'Cromarty is a most picturesque resort and, approached from the sea, unsurpassed. It only requires to be better known to become very popular.' It is certainly better known nowadays and retains the same character that so attracted Carnegie. Its historical lineage goes back to the 6th century when a church, now covered by the sea, was founded by St Moluag, one of the Columban missionaries sent out from IONA to

Christianize the Highlands. In the 8th century Cromarty was the assembly point for a large Pictish fleet of 150 ships preparing for a battle over a dispute to the Pictish throne. This armada was wrecked on Troup Head on the Banffshire coast. The town became a royal burgh in 1685.

Cromarty is divided into two parts; Fishertown retains its old character and layout, so much so that it has been described as a gem of Scottish vernacular architecture. During the 19th century the town had a flourishing fishing industry which has now all but become an echo in the memory of the older townsfolk.

The town was the birthplace of Hugh Miller (1802–56), a self-educated stonemason who rose to become a noted geologist, writer and theologian. His home, a 17th-century thatched cottage, is now a museum devoted to his life, work and times. It is situated at the corner of 'The Paye' and Church Street. The Old Gaelic Chapel, now roofless, was built to accommodate the religious needs of Gaelic-speaking Highlanders who went to Cromarty to work in the hemp factory in the 18th century. It is now roofless and to be found to the left of 'The Paye' as you go down to the shore.

In the 16th-century parish church there is a memorial to Sir Thomas Urquhart (1611–60), an eccentric but brilliant Scottish scholar who translated Rabelais. He died as an exile on the Continent: in a fit of laughing, it is said, on hearing the news of the Restoration of Charles II to the throne.

Cruden Bay, *Grampian* (3/3C) A small, popular holiday town offering as its main attraction a large expanse of pink sandy beaches backed by high dunes. Close by are the ruins of Slains Castle visited by Bram Stoker, creator of *Dracula*, whose imagination seems to have been triggered off by its stark appearance, inspiring him to write what was to become a literary – and film – classic. The castle was blown up in 1594, but still commands attention, standing as it does on the high cliff tops.

Cruden Bay is the landfall of the oil pipeline from the Forties Field over 100 miles away.

Culbin Sands, *Grampian* (3/1B) This area lies to the west of Findhorn Bay on the Moray Firth coast. The ancient village of the Kinnaird estate once flourished here until, in 1694, it was overwhelmed by a great storm which caused its complete obliteration by sand. For years it lay a desert until the first stages of reclamation began in 1870, a process that has been continued by the Forestry Commission by planting trees. The Commission used up to 40 tons of brushwood per acre to thatch the naked sand and prevent it from moving, and to provide in course of time humus to feed the young trees. It is one of the few sand deserts in Britain.

Cullen, *Grampian* (3/2B) Cullen is one of a string of royal burghs along the northern coast of the Moray Firth and officially dates from the 12th century, when its charter was issued. However, it first entered the annals of Scottish history as the presumed site of the Battle of the Bauds, in AD 961, in which an early king of Scots was killed by Vikings. It justly deserves its name as the 'Pearl of the Banffshire Coast', with its mile-long stretch of golden sand. It is a divided town, however, not so much because its people fell out with each other, but because in 1822 part of the old town was moved as the houses were too close to the Earl of Seafield's mansion. Near the shoreside are the freshly painted and well-maintained houses of the fishermen, though many are now holiday cottages, and the twisting lanes of old Seatown. The upper town boasts a spacious square and broad streets.

The most outstanding visual feature of the town is Cullen House, which stands on a rocky promontory above a winding stream. The main part of the building dates back to *c.* 1543. Its architectural rival is the series of railway viaducts built in 1886 because the Countess of Seafield refused permission to let the railway cross any part of the Cullen House policies (grounds). The three viaducts offer some of the best views of the coast.

Although Cullen's fishing activities are now only a shadow of past times, the industry has a history of some 500 years. Seatown, with its huddle of houses, dates in part from the 17th century and still suggests to the imaginative mind former scenes of colourful activity. The town once specialized in the export of smoked haddock, from which the local delicacy 'Cullen Skink' is derived: a fish soup based on the smoked haddock and now firmly implanted in the repertoire of true Scottish foods.

In Cullen Square is the 17th-century market cross, moved from Old Cullen, which has a carved stone plaque of the Virgin and Child, dating from an earlier period. The Auld Kirk dates from the 14th century and incorporates earlier work. The 'interior parts' of King Robert the Bruce's second wife were buried here in 1327. Most of the building dates from the period 1536 to 1543 and contains a number of rather interesting features, including the Believers' Loft and the Fishermen's Loft. The building was a collegiate church before the Reformation, indicating its ecclesiastical importance. Near by is the Castle Hill of Cullen, on which stand the vitrified remains of an ancient stronghold of the Iron Age. Bin Hill, once an old landmark for mariners, is associated with the revels of witches' covens, and rates a mention in the Aberdeen Witchcraft Trials of 1592.

Culloden Moor, *Highland* (2/3C) This is the site of the last battle fought on British soil and was the decisive conflict which ended the hopes of the Jacobites for a refurbished Catholic ascendancy. It lies about five miles east of INVERNESS. The battle resulted in the loss of 1200 men from the Highland army of Prince Charles Edward, against 310 lost from the Duke of Cumberland's forces. Scattered in the field are simple headstones, marking the communal graves of clansmen, identified by their clan tartans. Old Leanack farmhouse, used by the Jacobites as a headquarters, is now a museum, and stands close by an interpretive centre run by the National Trust for Scotland. A memorial cairn, erected in 1881, is the scene each April of a commemorative ceremony arranged by the Gaelic Society of Inverness. Much of the area is covered by Forestry Commission trees, which are now in the process of removal, as is the road that once ran through the gravestone area.

It was after this battle, on 16 April 1746, that the Highlands suffered the unnecessary atrocities perpetrated by Cumberland's troops who, unlike the Jacobites, killed even wounded men, and then rampaged through the Highlands creating a desert which they called peace.

See also Clava Cairns.

Culross, *Fife* (5/2B) It has taken the National Trust for Scotland some 40 years to restore the many 16th- to 18th-century houses in this Fife town. Discarding the trappings of the present, the imagination can be allowed to run freely in the narrow cobbled streets with such names as Stinking Wynd and Wee Causeway. All aspects of the old Scottish vernacular architecture are here to see: crow-stepped gables, outside stairs and decorative stone lintels. Of particular interest are the Palace (1597), the Study (1600) and Snuff Cottage (1673). The Palace and the Study can be visited; Snuff Cottage viewed from the outside.

Culross Palace

Culross was the birthplace of Glasgow's patron saint, the 6th-century St Mungo or Kentigern; the spot where his mother is said to have given birth is marked by St Mungo's Chapel, built in 1513. In the 16th century Culross thrived on the proceeds of the local industries of coal and salt panning, the exporting of which made Culross an important seaport. The coal was mined by monks from the 13th-century Culross Abbey who cut tunnels into the hillsides to reach the upper seams.

There are few towns in Scotland so genuinely able to stretch a hand from medieval times to the present day and pull the visitor back into such an intriguing past.

Cupar, *Fife* (5/2B) Although Cupar claims a long history, stretching back to 1276 when King Alexander III held an assembly there, much of the evidence has now gone. Standing as a witness to the past is the parish church (1785) with a 15th-century tower and 17th-century spire. Supporting evidence is in the form of the Cross at the head of the Crossgate, dating from 1683, which symbolizes the ancient right, reaffirmed in 1327, of Cupar to hold a market for the surrounding area. Cupar has the air of an old town, with its narrow wynds or alleys and 18th-century houses lending some slight relief to the noise of traffic in the streets.

South of Cupar is Scotstarvit Tower, an L-shaped, five-storey building erected *c.* 1579. Hill of Tarvit House is a 1906 copy of a 1696 building. It is now a convalescent home housing a fine collection of paintings, furniture, tapestry and porcelain, and can be visited. For anyone seeking the unusual, a walk around Dalgairn House Garden, on the outskirts of Cupar, will reveal a magnificent display of 'weeds' and old-fashioned plants. These are in fact a living catalogue of the medicine chest used by country folk in former times for the cure of ailments – and contrast with the modern reliance on drugs.

Dalwhinnie, *Highland* (5/1A) This rather remote village at the northern end of the equally remote Pass of Drumochter started life as a gathering place for the huge herds of cattle driven in from all parts of the West Highlands before making the slow journey to the markets or trysts at Falkirk and CRIEFF. It was here, in 1745, that the famous General John Cope (remembered in the song 'Hey, Johnny Cope') declined to meet the

Culross market cross with the Study beyond (see p. 109)

Jacobites in their own familiar terrain. Cope retired to INVERNESS leaving the way open for the Highlanders to make their easy and unopposed way to Edinburgh and, subsequently, for his own defeat at Prestonpans, near Edinburgh.

At 1188 ft, Dalwhinnie is the highest village in the Highlands. The inn, built in 1729 and now a hotel, did not impress Queen Victoria who, arriving there by pony and carriage after a 13-hour journey from BALMORAL in 1861, had to dine on 'two miserable starved Highland chickens'. The fare is much better now. A distillery offers some employment locally and is open to the public.

Daviot, *Highland* (2/3C) This little village lies a few miles south of INVERNESS and first appeared in records about 1210 as 'Daveth'; thought to be similar in derivation to the Welsh county name Dyfed, it refers to the tribe Demetae, from the Pictish word for 'sure' or 'strong'. The old castle of Daviot was by all accounts an impressive structure. Little remains now except one part of the angle towers overlooking the river Nairn. Until 1757 it stood almost intact but then within a few years had been demolished to provide building material for the nearby farmhouse. The old kirkyard of Dunlichity – connected to Daviot – is one of those secluded places full of atmosphere. The church, reconstructed in 1758, is built on the site of the old chapel of St Finan (AD 575). It has interesting heraldic tombstones. Daviot's own attractive church, dating from the early 19th century, is a striking piece of architecture.

Dingwall, *Highland* (2/3B) The Old Norse *thing* element in Dingwall's name indicates its origin as an old Viking council or meeting place for debate and the dispensation of their customary law. The town received a royal charter in 1226. The stones of its original obligatory castle were incorporated in the 18th-century tolbooth tower in the High Street and all that remains of it is a flanking tower at the foot of Castle Street. Dingwall is mainly a market town, serving the farming communities in the area, and an administration centre.

Overlooking the town, on a hill, is the grand monument to Sir Hector MacDonald (1853–1903) who rose through the ranks to become a general, the hero of the Battle of Omdurman and latterly Governor of Ceylon. Known popularly by his men as 'Fighting Mac' he was made the victim of scurrilous attacks which led to his suicide in Paris in 1903. He is buried in Edinburgh; the funeral was closely guarded to prevent the thousands of public mourners from giving vent to their emotions which, had they spilled over, would have created a disturbance close to riot.

Dingwall is the reputed birthplace of King Macbeth, who died in 1057; he was given by Shakespeare a reputation that was not wholly deserved, for he reigned for a long time as a good, humane, and just sovereign.

Dollar, *Central* (5/2B) Dollar lies below the Ochil Hills and takes some pride in its association with Castle Campbell, on a steep mound with extensive views to the plains of the Forth. Built towards the end of the 15th century by the first Earl of Argyll, it was known as Castle Gloom, more from its derivation from the place name Glume than from its prospect. It was burned by Cromwell's troops in the 1650s, but still stands foursquare as an impressive example of a late medieval defended house.

Dornoch, *Highland* (3/1B) This is a popular holiday seaside resort. Once the seat of the Bishops of Caithness, Dornoch still retains something of the character of a cathedral town. The cathedral itself is more functional than a mason's hymn to the glory of God. Even so, it has a simple

Dornoch Cathedral

and dignified charm. First erected in 1224, it was destroyed by fire in 1570 during a clan feud between the Murrays of Dornoch and the Mac-Kays of Strathnaver. It was then restored over a long period of time until 1835 when the final stages were completed. In 1924, to commemorate the 700 years of its existence, the whole of the lath and plaster work, with the exception of the fine vaulted ceiling, was removed, to reveal the building's 13th-century natural masonry which, apart from the nave, is original.

Local excavations have revealed a history of continuous habitation of the area going back some 3000 years. It was in Dornoch that the burning of Janet Horne, 'the last witch in Scotland', took place in 1722. In a garden near the golf course stands a simple slab of rough whinstone marking the spot where the unfortunate woman breathed her smoky last.

Golfing as a recreation in Dornoch dates from 1616, and the links are the third earliest mentioned in the history of the game. The Royal Dornoch Golf Club sponsors an Open Amateur Tournament held annually in mid-August.

Doune, *Central* (5/1B; 6/3C) What Doune lacks in size it makes up in its history. With two rivers, the Teith and Ardoch, flowing through it, Doune

was once an important venue for fairs and markets of Highland cattle and sheep. In the 17th century it was noted for its pistolmakers, who made guns for the droving trade. These weapons now fetch enormous sums at auction, as much for their antique aspects as for their fine workmanship.

The bridge over the Teith was built in 1535 by a former tailor to King James IV who, in a rage at a ferryman who had refused him passage, erected the structure which put the latter out of business. Doune Castle is one of the largest and best-preserved examples of 14th-century military–domestic architecture in Scotland. It is difficult to conceive that the castle was a roofless ruin by the end of the 18th century, remaining so until 1883 when the restoration began. At times the castle served as a royal palace and the rooms and halls echo this long historical association.

At Doune Motor Museum (on the same site as the castle) is a unique collection of historic cars. Two miles south is Scotland's Safari Park at Blair Drummond, where wild animals enjoy Scotland's rather uncertain weather.

Both Doune Castle and the Motor Museum are open to the public.

Doune Castle

Dounreay, *Highland* (3/1A) This is the site of the Experimental Reactor establishment opened in 1958. It has had a marked effect on the economic and social life of Caithness, and particularly on the neighbouring burgh of THURSO. Whatever controversy might be raised about the use of nuclear power, there is no doubt that the shining steel sphere of Dounreay is a sign of the future in the present. To help explain the nature of atomic power, there is an interpretative visitor centre.

Drumnadrochit, *Highland* (2/3C) This Loch-ness-side village is a collection of farm townships living in communal rural harmony. It houses the permanent Loch Ness Monster Exhibition, devoted to the history of the sighting of this creature over the past half century. A mile or so on the road south of the village is Urquhart Castle, now ruined but still impressive enough to fire the imagination. A 13th-century fortification built on the site of an Iron Age fort, it was occupied by English forces in 1296 and finally captured by the Scots in 1308. The castle was then in use until 1689 when it was blown up and left in ruins after the Jacobite Rising. The 16th-century tower is in good condition and the whole environs are a pleasant and interesting walk back into the past.

Drymen, *Central* (5/1B) Small though it is Drymen, to the east of LOCH LOMOND, has plenty to boast about. The Clachan Inn is one of the oldest in Scotland and was once owned by the sister of Rob Roy Macgregor. West of the village is Buchanan Castle, now in ruins, a 19th-century seat of the Duke of Montrose.

Other attractions include the Buchanan Smithy where a swordsmith produces traditional weapons. There is also a 'craft trail' centred on Drymen and ruined Ross Priory lies on the shore of nearby Loch Lomond, and so does the Loch Lomond National Nature Reserve.

Dufftown, *Grampian* (3/2C; 7/3C) A once-popular jingle went: 'Rome was built on seven hills, Dufftown stands on seven stills.' Depending on which way the wind blows, you can often catch a tantalizing whiff of roasting malt in the air from the many whisky distilleries in and around Dufftown. The village was founded in 1817 by James Duff, Earl of Fife, to give much-needed employment to locals after the Napoleonic Wars. Its four main streets converge on the battlemented Town House tower, built in 1836, once a jail and now an information centre and the Dufftown

Opposite: Doune Castle
Below: Duffus Castle

Museum. The Clock Tower, completed in 1839, boasts the famous 'clock that hung MacPherson'. The latter was a freebooter from KINGUSSIE condemned to death for robbery in Banff. Knowing that a reprieve was on its way, the executioners put the clock forward one hour to make sure MacPherson was well and truly dead before the pardon arrived.

A link between Dufftown and Canada exists in Lord Mountstephen, who was educated here. He and his friend Donald Smith, later Lord Strathcona, were the chief promotors of the Canadian Pacific Railway.

Of particular interest is Mortlach Church, one of the oldest places of Christian worship in Scotland. It was founded by St Moluag in the 6th century but the structure dates from the 12th century. Last renovated in 1930, it boasts the famous 'Elephant Stone', dating from about AD 500, which bears the incision of an animal that looks uncommonly like an elephant.

Near Dufftown are two important castles: BALVENIE (open from April to September) and AUCHINDOUN (not open to the public).

Duffus, *Grampian* (3/1B) About 4 miles northwest of ELGIN stands the massive ruins of Duffus Castle, a fine motte-and-bailey structure surrounded by a moat still entire and water-filled.

The original seat of the de Moravia family, it dates from about 1300. In 1452 the castle was plundered and wrecked, but was later partially restored. A considerable part of the heavy stone keep, built on the forced soil of the Norman motte, has broken off and slipped bodily down the slope; large portions of the curtain wall round the bailey have also tilted forward or slid down.

A little distance away is the old ruined parish church of Duffus, in existence as early as 1226. The base of the 14th-century western tower remains, as does a fine vaulted 16th-century porch. Outside stands a tall and rather elegant 14th-century parish cross.

Dull, *Tayside* (5/1B) A small village west of ABERFELDY. From about the end of the 7th century there was a Christian college here, later transferred to ST ANDREWS in Fife to form the basis of the university. The founder of Dull was Mansuteus who, it is suggested, took the disgraced Pontius Pilate back to FORTINGALL, close by, the latter to end his days in some kind of uneasy peace.

Dumbarton, *Strathclyde* (4/3B; 6/2C) Although now very much an industrial town, Dumbarton has a longer recorded history than any other stronghold in Britain. In the 6th century it was the capital of the kingdom of Strathclyde, which then stretched from LOCH LOMOND south to Lancashire. The focal point was the castle, built on Dumbarton Rock, which rises steeply from the Clyde waters. Only 17th-century fortifications survive, but the castle foundations go back much earlier, to the 13th century. It has seen such figures from Scottish history as William Wallace, the 13th-century Scots patriot, and Mary, Queen of Scots.

Dumbarton's industrial history is no less interesting. Here was built the famous tea clipper *Cutty Sark*, now in retirement on the Thames. Launched in 1869, her name is a reference to one of the witches in the Robert Burns poem 'Tam o' Shanter'. She was to win a reputation on the high seas for her beauty and speed, to say nothing of the valuable cargoes from the Far East which earned for her owners the pick of the London market and, in consequence, the highest prices.

Though now largely redeveloped, Dumbarton has had the sense to retain some of the fine buildings that reflect prosperity in former days. Glencairn (Greit House) dates from 1623, while other buildings such as the North Church, the Burgh Hall, Sheriff Court and the Old Parish Church all date from the 19th century. Old Dumbarton Bridge (1765) replaced the wooden rafts on which coaches formerly crossed the river Leven.

Dunadd, *Strathclyde* (4/2B) A tiny village just above Bridgend, north of Lochgilphead in Strathclyde, which at first glance has little of interest. In fact, this area has been rightly called the 'Cradle of Scotland'. There are old churches, castles, carved stones, Celtic crosses, sun circles, standing stones, vitrified forts, chambered cairns, all of which bear witness to a continuous human occupation going back some 4000 years. Dunadd was once the capital of Dalriada, one of the early Scottish kingdoms. The main point of interest in the Dunadd area is the fort, built on a natural hill. From all cardinal points, Dunadd was to the west of Scotland what Rome was to its empire: a focal point of great military and political importance. All approaches to Dunadd are safeguarded, by no fewer than 70 forts within a 10-mile radius. On top of Dunadd Hill is a stone slab with a human footprint, cup holes and the outline of a boar. This is a crowning stone, used in the ceremony of the coronation of a new king who, placing his foot in the imprint, pledged himself to uphold, not so much his own ideas of kingship, but the ancient laws of his forefathers.

Dunadd was besieged in the 8th century AD by both the early Britons and the Picts, but remained the seat of Scottish power until the reign of Kenneth MacAlpine. When he conquered the Picts in 843 he removed his capital to Forteviot and SCONE in Perthshire. Dalriada, which had been a separate kingdom for three and a half centuries, became a 'remote' region and even had its name changed to Argyll.

Dunbeath, *Highland* (3/1A) A small fishing village on the north-east coast with a small harbour. Dunbeath Castle, *c.* 1430, is a magnificent edifice, made more prominent by its position on a high cliff overlooking the small river and beach. At one time it was a stronghold of the Sutherlands. They lost favour with King James IV, who gave it to the Innes family. It then descended through the female line to a branch of the Sinclair Earls of Caithness. It is not open to the public.

Dunblane, *Central* (5/1B) The main feature of Dunblane is its cathedral, standing beside houses dating from the 17th to 19th centuries, which complement its grandeur. It was founded in about 1150 on the site of an earlier church dedicated to the 6th-century Saint Blane. The present structure is mainly 13th century but it has a 12th-century Norman tower incorporated. The cathedral suffered at the hands of reforming zealots and remained neglected until the collapse of the nave in the late 16th century, though the choir continued in use for 300 years as the parish church. Late last century the nave was restored. The west front, with its central doorway and lancet windows, was considered by John Ruskin as a masterpiece of Scottish architecture, praise which is still remembered today in 'Ruskin's Window'.

The Allan Water winds its way through the town, lending an extra dimension of interest to the quaint narrow streets. The Old Bridge was built in 1409; above it sits resplendent an Old Coaching Inn, well known in former times, particularly to Robert Burns who was inspired to write some of his poems here in 1787.

In the centre of Dunblane is The Ramoyle, once a small hamlet of weavers, which has retained its medieval character over these past 300 years. Film buffs will be interested to know that the jail (now a collection of modernized flats within the original walls) was the scene for Kenneth More (alias Richard Hannay) making his escape from a top window made of the usual barley sugar in the 1959 version of John Buchan's *The Thirty-Nine Steps*.

Some three miles south of Dunblane is **Sheriffmuir**, where in 1715 an indecisive battle was fought between the Jacobite forces of James, the Old Pretender, and the Duke of Argyll. The right wing of each army was victorious, but the left on each side was routed. In the end it was the Jacobites who retreated and Argyll claimed the day.

Close to Sheriffmuir Inn, near Dunblane, is a stone known locally as the Wallace Stone, a reminder that it was in this vicinity that the Scots patriot, William Wallace, fought a successful guerrilla action against the army of King Edward I of England, just before the Battle of Falkirk in 1298.

Duncansby Head, *Highland* (3/2A) This headland is Scotland's north-easternmost promontory and faces the entrance to the turbulent Pentland Firth. Just south of the Head are the three Stacks of Duncansby, standing like obelisks rooted to the seabed.

Dundee, *Tayside* (5/2B) Dundee is Scotland's fourth largest city and one of the oldest of the royal burghs. Though its origins can be traced to prehistoric times (as witness the finds uncovered at Stannergate at the turn of the century), its real

The Unicorn *and HMS* Discovery, *Dundee Harbour*

growth from an embryo settlement began in historic times as a small fishing community, clustered near the sheltered bay between Craig Pier and the Castlehill promontory. The prevalence of Pictish stones and Celtic cross slabs found in the area are further evidence of a considerable degree of status and importance. Recorded evidence begins in the late 12th century, when Dundee was granted a royal charter by King William the Lion, whose brother had lands in the vicinity – suggesting a personal influence in the welfare of the new burgh.

The city's temporal importance was confirmed in the 13th century by religious building; later, the main church was replaced in the 15th century by a structure of which only the tower (St Mary's Tower) remains. Later St Paul's Cathedral (1853) was erected on the site occupied by Dundee Castle, destroyed in the 14th century.

Historically, Dundee was much involved in the turbulent events that often wrenched Scotland apart into warring factions. In 1547 the forces of King Henry VIII of England held the town for a week, during which the citizens felt the heavy hand of the occupying troops, and emerged from the experience to see their homes ablaze. About a century later it was stormed by the Duke of Montrose and was treated with no less severity. Hardly had the city recovered from that assault than General Monck arrived in 1651 to mete out some harsh treatment once again. Dundee was occupied by the Jacobites in 1745. They held the city for a year, during which time the citizens were relieved to be treated with courtesy.

By the 13th century Dundee had established a reputation as a trading port, with considerable sea links with the Continent, particularly the Low Countries, France and, later, the Baltic ports. Three hundred years on, Dundee was the second city in Scotland in terms of both wealth and importance, with a Merchants' Guild set up to complement the Incorporated Trades Guilds. Textiles became a significant element in Dundee's economy, with large exports of 'hemp clayth', 'narrow blew clayth' and 'lyning and plaiding' adding to the prosperity. The Treaty of Union between the Scots and English Parliaments in 1707 ruined Dundee's woollen industry. All was not lost, however, and the expertise was transferred to the development of a linen or flax industry, helped in no small measure by the foundation of the Dundee Bank in 1763. The linen cloth produced went as far afield as the American colonies; by the late 18th century the manufacture of coarse linens was a staple occupation. At one time all the Royal Navy's sails were made in Dundee.

In its turn, the flax industry suffered when cotton cloth was imported from America, but this time Dundee enterprise looked to jute products for its continuing prosperity. Indeed, so vast was the wealth created that the city invested in the development of cattle ranching and railways in America and in jute manufacture in India. Some of the wealth was turned to the development of the city itself, resulting in the many fine buildings seen today, though little of Dundee's historic past remains, having paid the price of rapid industrial and commercial progress.

While all this activity was going on ashore, the sea was not forgotten. More than one successful shipyard carried on operations. Fishing, too, became important for a time, but the money was to be made elsewhere: in whaling. From the early 18th century Dundee's participation in the international whaling industry was an important element in the city's economy. By the mid-19th century Dundee-built whalers were scouring the North Atlantic for these valuable leviathans. The last whaler launched in Dundee was the *Terra Nova* (1884), later used by Sir Ernest Shackleton in his polar research expedition. The *Unicorn*, a frigate launched in 1829, the oldest extant British-built warship, is permanently anchored in Dundee's docks as a reminder of the city's connections with the sea. She is now a Royal Navy museum. In 1986 Captain Scott's *Discovery*, also Dundee built, was given a permanent berth here as part of a large waterfront redevelopment scheme.

Dundee's old reputation as the centre of 'jute, jam and journalism' has been replaced by a multifaceted economy based on modern industries, reflected in the city's new buildings that blend tastefully with Victorian styles of architecture, all reflecting prosperity in one form or another.

Among Dundee's famous names are Mary Wollstonecraft Shelley, creator of *Frankenstein* (1818); Sir Robert Watson Watt, inventor of radar; William McGonagall, the world's best-known worst poet whose verses are still in print; and Mary Slessor, the missionary to Africa.

Dunfermline, *Fife* (5/2B) The 'Auld Grey Toun' of Dunfermline has a firm place in Scottish history, being the seat of kings and the capital of Scotland for 200 years. The only visible remnant of its royal role is a mound and ruin in Pittencrieff Glen. What is rather more impressive is Dunfermline Abbey, begun in 1128 and added to in

1250, only to be wrecked by Reformation zealots in 1560, and finally swept away in 1818 to make way for the new church. In the choir beneath the pulpit is the grave of King Robert Bruce, marked by a magnificent memorial brass. During the excavations in 1818 the king's body was discovered wrapped in a shroud interwoven with threads of gold and encased in lead covering. It was placed in a new coffin and re-interred. Of the old abbey, the refectory remains as does the kitchen.

Dunfermline is today an industrial town, with its foundations in the 18th-century linen industry which established the town's reputation for fine cloth. At the corner of Moodie Street and Priory Lane one of the handloom weavers' cottages remains today as a museum. But it is more than that, for it was the birthplace of Dunfermline's most celebrated son: Andrew Carnegie who emigrated to America to become one of the greatest industrialists of the emerging steel and railway age. He never forgot Dunfermline and in 1902 he set up the Carnegie Dunfermline Trust which, among other gifts, enabled the townsfolk to enjoy the glen and estate of Pittencrieff. Pittencrieff House in the grounds of Pittencrieff Park is a 16th-century building now a museum of costume and local history.

Dunkeld, *Tayside* (5/2B) A few places situated along the Highland Boundary Fault line claim to be the 'gateway to the Highlands'. Dunkeld and

its twin, Birnam, seem to have the best claim to the name. Here the river Tay breaks through a gap in the wooded hills to create a natural gate.

Dunkeld's main feature is the cathedral. Though now roofless, there is to be experienced within its walls a quiet dignity. Some parts of the building date from the 12th century, but most are 14th and 15th century. The north-west tower was completed in 1501, just 60 years before the cathedral became the focus of attention of Scottish religious reformers who were responsible for its destruction.

Much of Scotland's turbulent history has been enacted in or around Dunkeld. Its name, derived from 'Fort of the Celts', goes back to the time when an older abbey was founded in 729 as a refuge for monks who had been driven from IONA. In 1689 the town was the setting for a savage battle in the aftermath of KILLIECRANKIE. The town had been held by the Cameronians, a Border regiment of extremist Covenanters, against a Highland army. The latter managed to penetrate the defences but were frustrated by the Covenanter commander who set fire to the town. The Highlanders withdrew and so the Jacobite cause was lost, leaving William and Mary sitting comfortably on the British throne.

Dunkeld takes its history seriously, as witness the recent renovation of the Little Houses on Cathedral Street, 18th-century buildings which are now a delight to the eye.

Across the Tay is Birnam, made famous by Shakespeare because it was the trees of Birnam Wood that moved themselves to Dunsinane some

Birnam Wood, near Dunkeld

eleven miles away and heralded the end of King Macbeth. Birnam is linked to Dunkeld across the Tay by a fine multi-arched bridge built by Thomas Telford in 1809.

Dunnet Bay, *Highland* (3/1A) A promontory of sandstone rising to over 400 ft and the most northerly tip of the British mainland. The view seawards to Orkney and along the coast is breathtaking. The lighthouse is sometimes open to visitors. Dunnet Head is the Cape Oreas of the Greek historian Diodorus Siculus and thus the first-ever place in Scotland to be mentioned by any writer.

Dunoon, *Strathclyde* (4/3B; 6/1C) Dunoon is the chief town of south Argyll and a focal settlement on the COWAL peninsula. Its main role today is as a holiday capital of Glasgow. For many centuries Dunoon was an unimportant village until 1779 when the first recorded account appeared of a Glasgow family's 'safari' there. The trip proved so dangerous that they spread the news that here, within sailing distance of Glasgow's Broomielaw, was a place that was out of this world. When they arrived they found that the only person who could speak English was the minister, the rest of the inhabitants being Gaelic speakers. Now that language has disappeared. When Henry Bell's steamer made its maiden voyage down the Clyde in 1812, Dunoon was a stop-off and the locals, realizing that tourism was on their doorstep, began to develop their properties for visitors. They have not stopped since and today everything in the town is geared to ensuring that the holidaymaker goes back home with the memory of a good time and two weeks of glorious refreshment – even if the sun does not shine all the time. During the summer months, Dunoon trebles its population.

Despite its pervading Victorian aspect, Dunoon in fact has an ancient lineage; it goes back to the 13th-century castle, built on the site of an earlier fort, of which now little remains, for it was destroyed in 1685. The rent for the castle was a red rose, should it be demanded. When Her Majesty the Queen visited Dunoon in 1958, she was duly presented with a red rose, as the castle was officially a royal possession.

Dunrobin Castle, *Highland* (3/1B) Built on a terrace left by an ancient inland sea, Dunrobin Castle stands as an example of ducal splendour. Open to the public from May to September, its outer walls and high-spired turrets hide a massive

inner keep which dates back to *c.* 1275. This is the seat of the Dukes of Sutherland, whose family fortunes were continually kept in credit by marriage to wealthy heiresses. The interior decoration and the Louis XV furniture exude an atmosphere of wealth and stylish comfort. The gardens are modelled on those of Versailles. On the other side of the coin, it was this family in the 19th century who implemented policies of clearing crofters from the wide fertile straths of Sutherland. Some 15,000 people were moved from their homes to find a new life in Canada. The resultant 500,000 acres of cleared land were then populated by sheep.

Early morning at Edzell Castle

This process of removal continued for half a century, and on such a scale that even Napoleon and Karl Marx were moved to commit their thoughts on the subject to paper. One eyewitness described his experience counting on one night in 1819 the flames of 250 crofts, including his own.

Durness, *Highland* (2/3A) A pleasant, clean village overlooking the waters of the Pentland Firth. Close by is Smoo Cave, of cathedral dimensions and comprising two chambers, one 200 ft long and 120 ft high and open to the public. A small chamber runs some 80 ft into the brooding sandstone cliff. This is not open.

A few miles to the west is Loch Eriboll, the deepest natural anchorage in Britain. In 1945 German U-boats came here to surrender, thus fulfilling the prophecy of the Highland Brahan Seer, who foretold that a war would one day end at Eriboll.

Dysart *see* Kirkcaldy

Edzell, *Tayside* (5/3A) The old village was moved in the 19th century from the environs of Edzell Castle to its present site, straddling the road that

*Above: Ivory eagle carved from over 2,000 separate
pieces of ivory, Fasque*
*Opposite: The largest cantilever staircase in the world,
Fasque, near Edzell*

exits south through a magnificent red sandstone
arch erected in 1887. A quiet, almost deserted
settlement, Edzell in the 18th century was
renowned for its pistolmakers.

Edzell Castle was built by Sir David Lindsay in
1604 as a towerhouse. Reflecting the elegant taste
of an educated and much-travelled Scottish
aristocrat, he took his ideas to the limit and
created a formal walled garden or 'pleasance'.
Even the red sandstone walls are divided into
compartments, displaying the Lindsay armorials
and sculptured portraits of all aspects of the arts
and muses. The overall effect is quite outstanding, particularly when the rosebeds are in flower.
The Lindsays were a gifted family, renowned for
gallantry and artistic taste, and rather sophisticated for their times, despite the streak of tragedy
that ran through their line. Extravagance of living
led to their lands being sold in 1715.

The Castle is open to the public.

North of Edzell is the village of Fettercairn,
close by which is Fasque, built in 1809 and home
to the Gladstones, one of whom was the Victorian
Prime Minister, W.E. Gladstone. It contains
much of interest: impressive 'public' rooms and a
quite extraordinarily complete 'downstairs'
quarters. Gladstone's memorabilia have been
assembled in his former bedroom. Fasque means
'shelter' in Gaelic, though it was no cover for the
builder, for he ruined himself in the process and
eventually had to sell the house to Gladstone's
father.

Egilsay *see* Orkney Islands

Eigg, *Highland* (1/3C) The island of Eigg (Gaelic:
'a hollow') lies close to the Scottish mainland,
almost opposite MALLAIG. Once a fertile island,
its productivity has been allowed to fall into
decline and much of the land is now derelict.
Generally low-lying, it makes up for its overall
lack of height in An Sgurr, a craggy sugarloaf
peak rising to 1289 ft. Standing sheer from the
1000 ft contour, it is a residual block of pitchstone
lava. Eigg's main settlement is Cleadale, a rather

packed crofting township. The island's chief land-use feature is the extensive home farm, established by the Runciman brothers: James was a writer and Walter was a shipowner. They created an estate, now lush woodland, and a semitropical garden. When they took over Eigg, they ploughed back all profits in an effort to develop the island, more for the sake of the resident population than for their own pockets. The island is owned today by a wealthy but energetic and committed landlord, Keith Schellenberg, who has tried to secure its future by introducing innovations in land use. Even so, Eigg hangs by a thread which a harsh economic climate could easily snap.

A cave on Eigg, Uamh Fhraing (near the southernmost tip of the Eigg coast), was the scene in 1577 of a massacre of MacDonalds by Macleods of SKYE who, after the former had used the cave for shelter, piled brushwood at the cave's entrance and set fire to it. Two hundred MacDonalds died in this avenging of a supposed wrong.

In the Bay of Laig, on the west side of the island, are the Singing Sands which emit sounds under the walker's feet, resembling the strains of an Aeolian harp. This sound occurs at times of changes in temperature, such as at sunset.

Elgin, *Grampian* (3/1B; 7/2A) Elgin, the chief town of Morayshire, can lay claim to be a city, though its cathedral is now in ruins. It has been for centuries the focal point of much of the history of the surrounding district, which has on occasion tumbled on to the pages of Scotland's own national story. Elgin's townspeople are justifiably proud as they crowd the High Street. It is in this street that over a dozen historic houses of great charm can be seen – No. 7, Braco's House, is a three-storey house with typical Scots crowstepped gables and dates from 1694. The small streets off the High Street are worth investigating, for they all reveal something of Elgin's past and are typical architectural examples of a Scottish 17th-century town boasting commercial wealth and civic pride.

Created a royal burgh in the 13th century, by which time it was already a thriving settlement, its focal point was Elgin Cathedral, founded in 1224. In 1390 it was burned along with nearly the whole of Elgin by the Wolf of Badenoch, an outlawed son of King Robert II. Lost in the burning were valuable books and charters. In 1567 the lead was stripped from its roof, to pay

Opposite: Elgin Cathedral.
Below: Old Mills, Elgin (see p. 126)

Elie harbour   *(Scottish Tourist Board)*

the wages of the soldiers of Scotland's Regent Moray, an indignity that was added to on New Year's Day, 1640, when the precious rood screen, with its 'starris of bricht golde' was torn down. Perhaps as sign of divine disapproval, on Easter Sunday in 1711 the great central tower fell down, after which the ruins were left to assume the dignity of a 'noble pile'. But even that was to be denied the cathedral when it was then used as a quarry for building stone. In 1825, the nation assumed responsibility for the preservation of the structure, which is today undergoing restoration.

The street plan of the medieval town is still fairly well preserved, and some of the buildings retain the arched façades typical of much of 18th-century Elgin. The Little Cross, in the High Street, was erected in 1733, replacing an earlier 15th-century stone. At one time this was a place of punishment for Elgin's wrongdoers, who were forced to suffer the 'stocks and the jougs'. The Elgin Museum, just off the junction of High Street and College Street, is an unusual Italian-style building, housing material of local interest. The existence of a watermill at Old Mills is

recorded in documents dating from 1203. It has now been restored to full working order and demonstrates the process of producing flour from grain. It is situated on Oldmills Road.

Elie, *Fife* (5/3B) At one time in the 16th century Elie harbour was the most important on the Fife coast, thriving on an extensive trade with cities across the North Sea. The harbour now only accommodates pleasure craft. To the east of the village is the ruined Lady's Tower, named after a local beauty who used to bathe from it – after she had sent a bellringer round the village to warn the inhabitants to keep away while she took her ablutions. Fife's answer to Coventry's Lady Godiva?

Ellon, *Grampian* (3/3C) Ellon has a present-day role as a commuter dormitory for the growing population of ABERDEEN, but is heir to a proud history that goes back to the times of the Picts in Scotland, well over 2000 years. Occupying a strategic site where the river Ythan can be forded, it was the main settlement of the Pictish province of Buchan *c.* 400 BC. In medieval times its importance was increased with the construction of a motte fortification, on Moot Hill, where the later Celtic Mormaers or princes held court and dispensed the justice encoded in the Brehon Laws. The Norman Earls of Buchan (the Comyns) also operated from Ellon until, in 1308, the castle and Ellon were burned in the 'Harrying of Buchan' following the defeat of the Earls by King Robert Bruce. The site is now marked by a monument in Market Street.

Thereafter Ellon declined and today offers service as a market town for the surrounding communities. The latter had their work cut out to turn the land around Ellon, once poor and infertile, into the rich productive agricultural area it is today. For a time last century the town was a popular fresh-air lung for holidaymakers, if an 1858 comment is anything to go by: 'Ellon has many attractions, and therefore many visitors in the summer season. Some resort to it for a mere change of scene; others again for its pleasing situation and pleasant accommodations, its salubrious air, and, though last but not least, its admirable fishing.' That prospect, despite changes, still holds good today.

Ellon Castle, an 18th-century ruined tower to the east of the town, was built by the 3rd Earl of Aberdeen to accommodate a brown-eyed mistress from Sussex, who was displaced, after the Earl's death, when his son found he could not afford the upkeep of his father's amusement.

Eriskay, *Western Isles* (1/1C) A small island in the Outer Hebrides, lying south of SOUTH UIST, Eriskay has a number of claims to fame. Under the disguised name of Todday it featured in the film *Whisky Galore*, based on the wreck of a ship loaded, among other freight, with cases of whisky many of which were recovered by the resourceful islanders when she ran aground during the Second World War.

The island was the first British landing place for Prince Charles Edward Stuart when, in 1745, he made his eventful bid to recover the British Crown for his father.

Although crofting is the main activity of the islanders, by necessity, they have also had to become first-class fishermen. Their spirit of independence is evidenced by the recently formed community cooperative which caters for the island's needs and handles the production of hand-knitted jumpers with patterns peculiar to Eriskay.

The island is famous for the Eriskay pony, a small and docile, but hardy, beast. The breed,

An Eriskay pony

which has been an island native for many years, went into decline some years ago but has now recovered, thanks to the attention of an association of interested owners. As a class the Eriskay pony is of great antiquity, the nearest in type to the native race that roamed Scotland before the arrival of recorded man.

Evanton, *Highland* (2/3B) A pleasant and well-laid out village with an open aspect. To the west is the Black Rock of Novar: a gorge some $1\frac{1}{2}$ miles long and over 100 ft deep through which the river Glass makes its strangulated way; yet it is so narrow in places that a man could leap from one side to the other. A footbridge spans it at a vantage point.

To the west of Evanton a remarkable representation of the Gates of Negapatam can be seen, an Indian town captured by Sir Hector Munro of Foulis (1726–1805) in 1781. Sir Hector saw military service in India, rose through the ranks to become a general and in doing so acquired a considerable fortune, some of which he used to create local employment. The 'folly' was one such project.

Fair Isle (3/3B) This island lies midway between ORKNEY and SHETLAND. The population of around 80 sustain themselves by crofting and some fishing, with a small additional income derived from tourists who come here to see the seabirds. Since 1954, Fair Isle has been administered by the National Trust for Scotland. The island is one of the most important ornithological habitats in the world, with well over 300 species of migratory birds using it as a staging post on their flight to, and return from, southern climes. A Bird Observatory hostel caters for birdwatchers.

The island is far-famed for its knitted garments, based on the intricate Fair Isle patterns, said to have been derived from Spaniards from the Armada who were wrecked here in 1588. Some 20 miles of spectacular cliff scenery round the island is continuously and relentlessly worked on by the waters of the Atlantic.

Falkland, *Fife* (5/2B) This town offers something of a 'time-warping' experience with Falkland Palace dominating the main street where the cobblestones and stone-fronted houses of the 17th to 19th centuries thrive in an attractive setting at the foot of the Lomond Hills. The palace, open to the public April to September, was begun before 1500 as a royal residence by

James II, and the town became a favourite country retreat for the Scots court. James V completed the building with a flourish of embellishments. It saw the return of James V from his defeat at Solway Moss in 1542, and here he died, just after hearing the news that he had become the father of a newborn daughter: Mary, Queen of Scots. With that clear sense of the future which seems to come with death, he said: 'God's will be done. It cam wi' a lass and it'll gang wi' a lass.' That prophecy came true when the Stuarts eventually lost their claim to the throne of Britain; they had originally achieved royal status by marriage to the daughter of King Robert Bruce.

Some excellent restoration work has been carried out over the years, including the garden, which was faithfully replanted according to an old print design. The royal tennis court, still playable, dates from 1539 and is the oldest in Britain.

Fetlar *see* Shetland Islands

Findhorn, *Grampian* (3/1B) The present village of Findhorn is the third of that name to have been built in this district, and dates from 1701. Its predecessor was swamped by the sea, and the first hamlet lies buried under the CULBIN SANDS at the estuary of the river Findhorn.

The original Findhorn was an important port trading with the Continent in wines, silks, tapestries and other luxuries, imported in exchange for local produce such as salmon, hides, beef, grain and malt. No commercial fishing is done from the harbour today, which mainly serves pleasure craft and yachts associated with the local Yacht Club which has Royal status.

The village is the centre for the Findhorn Foundation, an international spiritual community, founded in 1962.

Findochty, *Grampian* (3/2B) This fishing village (pronounced 'Finnechtie') dates from 1717, though it was known as a fishing port before that. In a report of 1797 a comment reads: '. . . the fisherfolk of Findochtie were distinguished for their decency and decorum and for curing their fish, great and small, superlatively well'. The neat, brightly painted cottages that cluster round the tidal harbour are more reminiscent of the Mediterranean than the traditional Scottish dourness usually bestowed on vernacular architecture. To the west of the village stands the sorry ruin of an old castle of *c.* 1560.

In 1855 more than 140 fishing boats worked out of Findochty, after which the port declined as nearby BUCKIE with its superior harbour facilities took over. The present harbour is more used by pleasure craft, and is overlooked by a striking whitewashed church, standing on a low rise to emphasize its importance to the community.

Findon, *Grampian* (3/3C) A little fishing village that had its prosperity cut from under it by an Act of Parliament in the 1870s. This forbade the smoking of fish over open cottage fires. The local product was far famed as the 'finnan haddie'; these smoked haddock were 'known and esteemed in most parts of Scotland'. As the smokehouses of nearby ABERDEEN took over, Findon assumed its present role as a dormitory for that city.

Fochabers, *Grampian* (3/2B; 7/3A) Most of the buildings in this Morayshire town date from the reconstruction of the former village in 1776 by the Duke of Gordon, who thought the houses of his tenants too near his residence, Gordon Castle. The original village was created a burgh of barony in 1598. The town boasts a magnificent square, with Bellie Kirk (1798) and its neighbouring house lending a classic Georgian elegance to the spacious aspect. Most of the buildings are very much as they were when first erected two centuries ago.

North of the town stands Gordon Castle (not open to the public), which was in its heyday the finest Georgian house in Scotland. It has an imposing battlemented façade, almost 600 ft long, with 365 windows. This was the home of the famous Duchess of Maxwell, who helped to raise the Gordon Highlanders regiment by rewarding new recruits with a kiss and a King's shilling.

Surrounded by farmland, forest and market gardens, Fochabers is the home of a well-known food firm, producing from good home recipes, and a well-established nursery garden.

Fochabers Folk Museum has the largest collection of horse-drawn vehicles in the north of Scotland. It is located in Pringle Church, High Street, and is open daily.

Fordyce, *Grampian* (3/2B) This little village lies a few miles inland from PORTSOY. Built round a small compact 16th-century castle, which is open to the public, its winding lanes flanked by charming houses make the whole area a visual delight. The castle itself was built in 1592 as an L-plan

towerhouse with all the Scottish vernacular architectural trimmings, including crow-step gables, angle turrets and a stair turret. Near by are the remains of the old church of Fordyce, first mentioned in 1272, and now restored. Until 1964 Fordyce Academy, dating from early in the 18th century, was well known in the world of education for its high standards which laid the foundations of the careers of many famous people, one of whom became personal doctor to Queen Victoria.

In 1840, buried in the ring cairn of a recumbent stone circle called Gaulcross, to the south-west of Fordyce, an important hoard of Pictish silver was discovered, the surviving items of which are now in the National Museums of Scotland (Queen Street), Edinburgh.

Fire hydrant, Fordyce

Forfar, *Tayside* (5/3A) A busy town lying at the eastern end of Forfar Loch; it witnessed one of the last battles fought between the Picts and the Scots before the two kingdoms combined to become the embryo Scotland in AD 845. The town was granted a charter for commercial activities in the 13th century, which was renewed in 1665. In 1056 King Malcolm Canmore held his first Parliament in Forfar, a reminder of the town's significance in the past. Today some of that atmosphere of history still exists, such as in the Little Causeway, a picturesque square behind West High Street. The Town Hall dates from 1788. A well-deserved place in the Scottish culinary repertoire is occupied by the 'Forfar Bridie', a half-moon-shaped pastry filled with baked meat and onions, to which anyone could readily become addicted.

Forres, *Grampian* (3/1B) It is thought by some that the place marked 'Varris' on maps drawn by the Romans almost 2000 years ago is the present town of Forres, a few miles inland from the Moray Firth coast. If that claim to antiquity cannot quite be established the fact that there was a royal residence at Forres by the end of the 9th century gives the town a healthy and ancient lineage. Of the medieval castle that stood here nothing remains to be seen. Forres rates a mention in Shakespeare's *Macbeth*, where it is the locale of the opening scenes of that play. The famous 'blasted heath' is supposed either to be Macbeth's Hill, 5 miles to the west of the town, or the Knock of Alves, 8 miles to the east.

Much of the present layout of Forres reflects its medieval importance, with the main street widening to accommodate the marketplace, and linked to parallel streets by a series of narrow lanes. Many of the houses survive from the 17th and 18th centuries with the typical Scots architectural feature of crow-stepped gables.

The Market Cross is reminiscent of the Walter Scott monument on Princes Street in Edinburgh. On Cluny Hill, overlooking the town, stands the Nelson Monument, erected in 1806 after the Battle of Trafalgar. It was the first national monument in Britain raised to commemorate Nelson's victory.

Present-day Forres is mainly a residential town, with a pleasant welcoming character enhanced by extensive open spaces and parks. It is a consistent winner of the annual 'Britain in Bloom' competition. Situated on the A96(T) road east out of the town is the mysterious Sueno's

Fordyce Castle (see p. 129)

Stone, a superb sculptured monument supposed to commemorate a victory over Norse invaders and standing 23 ft high. Sueno was the father of England's King Canute and is better known as Sweyn Forkbeard of Denmark. The stone, however, predates the Danish monarch and is thought to have been carved and erected in the 9th century. As an example of Pictish art – all they ever left as records of their society – it is one of the most remarkable witnesses of their sophisticated culture.

Some 3 miles north-east of Forres lies the remains of Kinloss Abbey, founded in 1150 by King David I. After the Reformation the buildings gradually fell into disrepair and were extensively quarried by Cromwell's troops for the building of the Citadel in INVERNESS.

Fort Augustus, *Highland* (2/3C) This town at the southern end of Loch Ness takes its name from William Augustus, the Duke of Cumberland who made the fort his quarters after his success at CULLODEN in 1746. Besides its more recent history this village, originally called Kilchumein, after a follower of St Colomba, has an ancient lineage.

Much of the site of the old fort is now occupied by a Benedictine Abbey and a highly regarded school. The Abbey School was erected in 1876, a fine building with many architectural features that catch the eye.

In the old cemetery of the parish church lies the grave of John Anderson, a carpenter friend of Robert Burns made famous in the latter's poem 'John Anderson My Jo'.

Fort George, *Highland* (3/1B) About 6 miles west of NAIRN, on B9006, this is one of the most outstanding examples of Hanoverian military architecture, begun in 1748 and the last in a chain of three built in the Highlands (along with Fort Augustus and Fort William). Overlooking the Moray Firth, it formed part of the government's scheme to prevent armed Highland threats to Hanoverian law and order. By the time the fort was completed in 1769, the Highlands were more or less peaceful, but it was kept in use as a military barracks. From 1881 until 1961 it was the depot of the Seaforth Highlanders. The plan is arranged as an irregular polygon with six bastions and can accommodate 2500 men. Within the fort are barracks, a chapel, workshops and the regimental museum of the Queen's Own Highlanders (Seaforth and Camerons). The fort, newly restored, is open to the public all the year round.

Fortingall, *Tayside* (5/1B) A picturesque estate village off B846 a few miles west of ABERFELDY. It has a claimed history stretching back to the days of the embryo Christian faith. Fortingall is reputed to be the birthplace of Pontius Pilate, born at a Roman camp established in the village during the Roman occupation of Britain. The hill fort behind the village was once occupied by a local kinglet. This tradition relating to Pilate has puzzled many, yet some of the evidence contains at least an element of feasibility. It is suggested that Pilate was sent to Rome as a boy slave, and taken into the Roman family of the Pontii, later to be given a *pilateus*, the felt cap worn by a freed slave. His marriage to Claudia Procula, the illegitimate granddaughter of Emperor Tiberius, gave him access to rank and promotion and ultimately to the governorship of Judea in AD 26. After his fall from grace 10 years later he vanished from Roman records, but it has been suggested that he returned to Fortingall to die there; and a stone burial slab was discovered at the turn of this century bearing the initials 'PP'!

The Fortingall yew tree in the churchyard is reckoned to be 3000 years old; it now shows its age but still clings longingly to life. Inside the church is a 7th-century font and a monk's bell of equal antiquity.

Fortrose, *Highland* (2/3B) This ancient BLACK ISLE town was once the cathedral town of Ross-shire and a noted seat of learning in medieval times. The cathedral was completed in the late 15th century and built of red sandstone, which lends a degree of charm and beauty to the now ruined strucure. Close by Fortrose is Chanonry Point and its lighthouse, where a stone marks the spot where Coinneach Odhar, the Brahan seer, was executed. He was a rather misty character in Highland history, given credit for many proph-ecies that have since come true, such as the building of the CALEDONIAN CANAL. He proph-esied the downfall of a number of great Highland chiefs in circumstances that were fulfilled down to small details. He died because his noble lady employer asked him to tell her what her husband was doing in France. What the seer saw was not to her liking and she had him burned in a tar barrel.

Fort William, *Highland* (4/3A; 6/1A) As in the American West, the prefix 'fort' indicates a gar-rison town, which Fort William once was. The original fort was built in 1645 by General George

Monck, acting for Oliver Cromwell. About 40 years later the structure was strengthened and named Fort William after King WIlliam III, replacing the settlement's brief name of Maryburgh, after his Queen. It then formed part of a chain of Highland fortifications, with FORT AUGUSTUS on Lochness-side and FORT GEORGE, near INVERNESS, as visible deterrents to the clans who supported the Jacobite cause. The fort was demolished to make way for the West Highland Railway, which appeared in 1884, to connect the town to Glasgow. Only the archway and parts of the old walls now remain. A little to the north of the town, off the A82, are the remnants of the 13th-century Inverlochy Castle which saw much action from the Wars of Scottish Independence of that period to the Covenanting Wars in the 17th century. The present Inverlochy Castle, a granite 19th-century edifice, is a hotel.

Today Fort William is both a holiday centre and an industrial town, although the latter aspect has a low enough profile. The main industries are aluminium and whisky distilling. The metal-refining plant was completed in 1934 with the help of Canadian troops and has since been a stable source of employment for the town. The distillery was founded and built in 1825 by a John MacDonald who was later to become known as 'Long John'.

Fort William is squeezed between the shores of Loch Linnhe and the steep slopes of Cow Hill, so that at first sight it seems that it has only one long street. In fact the burgh sprawls where it can, which adds an element of character and interest. Dominated by the loch on one side, and the brow-beetling mass of BEN NEVIS, it exudes a character that is truly West Highland, but with a touch of industrial prosperity.

Foula *see* Shetland Islands

Foyers, *Highland* (2/3C) The little village of Foyers, on the B852 beside Loch Ness, was once famous for the Falls of Foyers which were impressive enough to move Robert Burns to write: 'Among the heathy hills and rugged woods, the foaming Foyers pours his mossy floods'. The construction in the 1890s of the first-ever aluminium-reduction works in Britain, which required a massive hydroelectric scheme to operate economically, reduced the falls to the present trickle, although they are still worth a visit. The factory closed in 1967 and the waters of the area are now used to feed an underground power station.

Previous page: Cottages, Fortingall

Fort William with Ben Nevis beyond

Fraserburgh, *Grampian* (3/3B) This Aberdeen-shire town was founded in 1546 as a fishing port, and still serves the local fleet based on the rich North Sea fishing grounds. It is also a base for onshore operations connected with the North Sea oil industry. On Kinnaird Head north of the town are the remains of the squat 16th-century tower built to guard the embryo settlement and converted into a lighthouse in 1786. Close by is the Wine Tower, a three-storey 15th-century building whose purpose remains a mystery, despite its name. There are no stairs between its three floors! The Broadsea area of Fraserburgh presents an attractive old-world atmosphere, with houses catching the eye with their bold red-tiled roofs. It was here that the Marchese Guglielmo Marconi, the radio pioneer, had a research station from which signals were sent to receiving stations in England.

Furnace, *Strathclyde* (4/3B) This little village on the A83 on the western shore of Loch Fyne has a place in Scotland's industrial history. Its name is derived from the furnace connected with the iron smelting that was established in 1754. It was such an important event in the district that the community's former name of Inverleacainn was changed to Furnace. By 1813 the iron smelting had ceased, to be replaced in 1841 when a licence was issued to 'erect mills and other engines for making gunpowder'.

The fact that a powder store was within 100 yd of the post office and the school caused some concern, but nothing more, until the fatal day of reckoning. This occurred in September 1883 when 23 tons of gunpowder exploded in an accidental fire. A chance of fate had decreed that the wind that day should be from the north-east. Had it been in the normal prevailing direction, the whole of Furnace would be rubble today. In the event only the factory was destroyed, after which the locals presented an iron-bound case for its closure. Only the cottages remain and Furnace is now a quiet backwater resting on its well-earned laurels.

Fyvie, *Grampian* (3/3C) This little Aberdeenshire village lies beside the A947 and the banks of the river Ythan, with its 'pride of place' atmosphere making no small contribution to its scenic setting. There was a settlement in this place before work was begun on nearby Fyvie Castle, just north of the village, around 1296. The castle is one of Scotland's finest and perhaps the most grandiose. Its five towers are named after the families that built them, reflecting its various owners. The building, in its present form, was begun by Sir Henry Preston who used the proceeds from a ransom received for one of the great English Percy family captured at Otterburn in 1390. Ownership then passed to the Meldrum lairds who added a tower of their own. The Setons took over and used their influence with James VI to improve the building. Alexander Seton had for a time the care of James VI's young son (later Charles I) who spent some of his youth at Fyvie. The Gordons of Haddo took possession from 1733 to 1847, when the castle was left neglected until bought by Alexander Forbes-Leith, a steel magnate who made his fortune in the United States. He restored the castle and grafted an inevitable Leith Tower on to the Gordon Tower. The castle is now in the care of the National Trust for Scotland and open to the public.

To the east of the village is Fyvie Church, reached by an imposing avenue of beech trees. First mentioned in records of 1179, the church was rebuilt in 1808. In 1902 the chancel was added, with a memorial window designed by the New York glass designer Louis Tiffany. A short distance from the church is a tall cross marking the site of St Mary's Priory, established in 1285 and abandoned at the time of the Reformation in Scotland.

Gairloch, *Highland* (2/1B) This is a busy West Highland coastal village situated at the head of the loch of the same name and on the A832, and serves as the focal point for a number of small communities in the area. It is popular with visitors who enjoy the pleasures of the sea coast and sandy beaches, and the hinterland which constitutes one of the largest parishes in Scotland and contains no fewer than 23 mountain peaks of 2000 ft and over. Flowerdale House, an 18th-century mansion with rather fine gardens, looks over the loch to distant views of SKYE. The intense interest in local history in recent years has culminated in the establishment of the Gairloch Heritage Museum, in a converted farmstead, which has on display a comprehensive overview of life in the area from prehistoric times to the present. The village itself is a port for whitefish landings.

Gardenstown, *Grampian* (3/3B) Better known as 'Gamrie', which is also the name of the bay it overlooks, this Moray Firth coastal fishing village was founded in 1720. Over the years the houses have had to be built up the sides of the steep hill above the harbour in serried ranks and narrow terraces. Why this village was ever placed here is something of a mystery, for it has a tidal harbour that is all but inaccessible. Perhaps it was the determination of the founders to establish a close-knit community bound together, as they still are today, by staunch religious beliefs and intent on preserving their identity.

Some of the houses are so built that each of their three floors has a doorway opening out on to the steeply sloping street. Indeed, parts of the old village can only be reached on foot. Above is the

ruin of St John's Chapel with its origins going back to the routing of an 11th-century Viking raid. It survived as a parish church until 1830. It was built by the Thane of Buchan in 1004 in fulfilment of a vow to erect a church dedicated to St John the Evangelist if that saint would help him defeat the invading Danes. The skulls of the three Danish chiefs who were killed in the ensuing battle were inserted in the wall of the church and remained there 'grinning and hollow' for the 800 years the church was in use. Within the ruins is a 1547 monument to Patrick Barclay, one of whose descendants (Mikhail Barclay de Tolly) rose to be a Russian general at the time of the Napoleonic Wars and was subsequently made a prince and field marshal.

Garelochhead, *Strathclyde* (4/3B) Despite being close to the Royal Naval Base at Faslane, this village at the head of the Gare Loch seems to have managed to maintain its own identity. White, slate-roofed houses nestle among trees that have failed, as yet, to reach the high slopes behind the village. The peaceful setting belies the ever-present submarines and defence installations. Glen Fruin, about 2 miles away, was the scene in 1603 of a bloody conflict between the Macgregors and the Colquhouns, the end product of a cattle-lifting raid by the former. The Colquhouns' dependants took a load of bloodied shirts off to King James VI at STIRLING and pled – to use the Scots term – so effectively that he outlawed the Macgregors and proscribed their very name.

Garmouth, *Grampian* (3/2B; 7/3A) This Morayshire village was founded in 1587 as a port from which to export timber from the forests of Strathspey, the trees being floated down the Spey in great rafts. Its role as a coastal port lasted until the late 18th century when the great Spey floods of 1829 altered the course of the river estuary to a few miles away, leaving the town stranded. Garmouth was the port of landing of King Charles II in 1650, where he reluctantly signed the Solemn League and Covenant, a document whose purpose was to impose a Scots-style Presbyterianism on Episcopal England. A plaque on Brae House in Spey Street marks the site of the house where the Covenant was signed.

There are many buildings of both architectural and historic interest and the village has altered little from a description given in an early guide book: 'The streets are nearly as sinuous as the houses, which, as regards size and position, are nearly as irregular as it is possible to make them.'

The 'Maggie Fair', held annually on the last Saturday in June, is one of the few ancient Scottish fairs still surviving. It commemorates the creation of Garmouth as a burgh of barony.

Gigha, *Strathclyde* (4/2C) This Inner Hebridean island lies off the western shores of the MULL OF KINTYRE, with which it is connected by ferries. Six miles long and three across, its name is said to mean 'God's Island', which suggests that the early Christian missionaries found it a pleasant place on which to establish their lonely cells. A backbone of rock runs down its centre, flanked by rich fertile fields benefiting from this sheltered island's moderate rainfall and virtually frost-free climate. Its main attraction is found at Achamore House, in the extensive gardens created by Sir James Horlick. These include some 50 acres of glades, shrub and woodlands, which offer a home for many semitropical plants. (The gardens only are open to the public all year round.)

The island was occupied in the 15th century by MacNeills, until they were dispossessed by Macleans in 1530. In 1554 Gigha was sold to the Macdonalds but was bought back by a MacNeill, whose family held it until 1865. The main feature of antiquarian interest is the ruined 13th-century church of Kilchattan.

Glamis, *Tayside* (5/2B) This pleasant little village, situated where the A94 and A928 cross, has won fame through its association with Glamis Castle, the childhood home of the Queen Mother. But it has its own attractions, such as the charming row of one-storey 17th-century cottages which now form the Angus Folk Museum. In the garden of the nearby manse stands a beautifully sculptured 9th-century Pictish stone with intricate decorations and symbols, the meaning of which is lost to present-day scholars.

The attraction *par excellence* is Glamis Castle, standing on the site of an 11th-century royal hunting lodge. The present building dates from *c.* 1687 and later, as successive Earls of Strathmore left their permanent marks. Its size and the magnificence of the massive pinkish structure are a testimony to the repute and standing of the Lyon family, from the first Sir John Lyon who, in 1376, married the daughter of King Robert II, to the present-day owners. Legend is mixed with history at Glamis, with not a little leavening of fancy provided by William Shakespeare in his play *Macbeth*. But even so, there is sufficient evidence of wealth, ambition and sheer extravagance to merit a full day of sightseeing both inside the castle and in the attractive grounds.

Glencoe, *Highland* (4/3A; 6/1A) Glencoe has earned an unenviable place in the history of Scotland for the massacre committed in February 1692 when, on the order of the Government, soldiers who had for days enjoyed the hospitality

Glencoe

of the Macdonalds of Glencoe attacked their hosts and killed 40 members of the MacIan clan, including the chief and his wife. The Government had decided that an example should be made of those clans who were still inclined to rebel against the reigning king and who had previously supported the Stuarts. Through no fault of his own, MacIan was delayed in getting to INVERARAY to sign the oath of allegiance to King William III. Once his signature was dry it was sent to Edinburgh, only to be rejected as being six days late. But skulduggery was also afoot. It was discovered that the signature had disappeared, being clumsily erased by another hand. Orders were then given for the whole of the MacIan clan to be destroyed, root and branch. Even babes in arms and old men over 80 years of age were not spared. The massacre still remains a dark stain on Highland history.

As if to reinforce a 300-year-old memory, Glencoe itself has a gloomy and even forbidding atmosphere, given an extra dimension by the variety of mountain forms, gullies, walls, ridges, corries, buttresses and peaks. While the traveller on the A82(T) road through the glen can sample some of the scenic beauty, the real pleasures are available only to the muscular and well shod.

The Glencoe and North Lorn Folk Museum in the village includes Jacobite relics among its collections.

Gleneagles, *Tayside* (5/1B) The mere mention of this name conjures up high-class living and the excellent golf course. The name comes from the nearby scenic wooded and moorland glen in the Ochil Hills, the setting for Gleneagles House, built in 1624 with material from a former castle.

Glenfinnan, *Highland* (4/2A) Glenfinnan marks a significant point in Highland history. Above the headwaters of Loch Shiel is the monument erected in 1815 commemorating the Forty-five Jacobite Rising. It was at this spot on 19 August 1745 that the standard of Prince Charles Edward was raised to rally the Highland clans in his attempt to win back the British Crown for the Stuarts. The figure on top of the high column is not Prince Charles, as popularly believed. The monument in fact remembers 'Those who fought and bled in that arduous enterprise' – those Highland clansmen who paid so dearly for the Prince's hopes.

The Visitor Centre is run by the National Trust for Scotland and is mainly devoted to telling the story of the Rising.

Glenrothes, *Fife* (5/2B) One of Scotland's new towns established to provide a fresh focal point for modern industrial development. Now the centre for light industry, its planners have had to create a living and working environment of astonishing variety. In starting virtually from scratch Glenrothes has also had to work out its own contemporary architecture. St Columba's Church (1960) has a high detached steel and glass tower and contains a mural by Scots artist Alberto Morrocco; St Paul's Roman Catholic Church boasts a fine altarpiece by the late sculptor Benno Schotz; the High School fronts a remarkable patterned façade of glass; open spaces in the town have been filled with many examples of contemporary art.

Grantown-on-Spey, *Highland* (3/1C) A planned town of the 18th century founded in 1776 in an effort to provide a new economic focal point for the fertile area where it stands. Within a few years it had become the main market town for a large part of the Spey valley. As well as linen goods, woollen clothes were produced, some of which gained an export market as far afield as West Africa. By the time the linen industry failed, in the face of the competing cheap cotton from the Americas, Grantown had become sufficiently well established to benefit from the impetus of its own fast growth and went on to become one of the finest planned towns in the north of Scotland. In 1863 the railway arrived to set the seal on future prosperity.

The Square, a former marketplace, has been presented as a gift to the townsfolk to mark the bicentenary of the founding of Grantown. Some of the oldest buildings line this square, along with trees a century old – but showing little signs of their age, so much do they benefit from the sharp, clean air of the area. Grantown now caters mainly for the holidaymaker who seeks something more than the brashness of AVIEMORE.

Just north of the town is Castle Grant, part of it 15th century, the seat of the Earls of Seafield. It has 18th-century additions by John Adam and contains some fine period furniture. When Queen Victoria visited the castle, she described it in her *Journal of My Life in the Highlands* as 'a very plain-looking house, like a factory'. In 1618 it was visited by John Taylor, the 'Penniless Poet' who anticipated modern sensation-mongering by making a tour of the British Isles with empty pockets and writing up his observations for the gossip-reading fraternity of his time. Robert Burns was a guest there, and in the days of the

Forty-five Rising, the Jacobites enjoyed some of the welcome liquid stores found in the cellars.

Castle Grant is open to the public April to September.

Handa Island, *Highland* (2/2A) This island is near to SCOURIE on the north-west coast of Sutherland. It stands proudly with 400 ft high sandstone cliffs and was once populated by an island 'queen' and seven families, living in glorious isolation. After the potato famine in 1845 the island was deserted and it is now a bird sanctuary. Separated from the parent island by only a few yards is the Stack of Handa, standing on three pillars, a remarkable piece of sea sculpture. Access to Handa Island is by boat hire from Scourie.

Harris, *Western Isles* (1/2B) Despite the fact that Harris is often called an island, it is connected to its larger neighbour, LEWIS, by a 6-mile neck of mountain and moorland. Harris is a land of contrasts. On the western coastline are high cliffs, often dropping sheer to the sea. The hinterland is a wilderness of bare rock and small lochs. The eastern coastline, however, is a magnificent suite of flat expanses of sandy beaches fringed by lush green pasture. This is where much of the original Harris population lived over a century ago, until they were cleared to the eastern shores where the visitor can see with his own eyes the product of a century of untold toil in the conversion of thinly slippered rock into small patches of fertile earth for growing produce. Now, thus far on in time, the string of coastal crofting townships on the east coast still eke a living from meagre resources. They are linked by a twisting road between Tarbert, the urban centre of Harris, connected by ferry with SKYE and NORTH UIST, and Rodel in the south.

Despite its inhospitable appearance, Harris has always provided a homeland for a continuing population, from prehistory, through the Norse hegemony, the clan period and to the present time. Many traces of an ancient occupation exist, such as duns or forts and standing stones.

The most outstanding example of ecclesiastical architecture in the Hebrides is St Clement's Church at Rodel. Dating from before 1549, when it was first recorded, the church is built as a cruciform, with choir, nave, transepts and a tower with exterior sculptured panels. Its main feature is the marvellous carved tomb of Alastair Crotach (1528), a Macleod chief from Dunvegan in Skye.

Helensburgh, *Strathclyde* (4/3B) A seaside town situated at the entrance of the Firth of Clyde, Helensburgh has long been a dormitory resort for the people of Glasgow. Its substantial buildings indicate that in former times it was more than favoured by the wealthy merchant class of that city. Today it is more cosmopolitan. Its symmetry owes much to the 18th-century plans of Sir Alexander Colquhoun, after whose wife the town was named.

Two famous men are associated with the town. Henry Bell was the designer of the *Comet* (1812), Europe's first commercially successful steamship, whose original flywheel stands in Hermitage Park. An obelisk on the sea front commemorates this citizen who was Helensburgh's provost in 1807. John Logie Baird (1888–1946) was born here and grew up to become a pioneer of television. A visit to Hill House (1902–3), in Upper Colquhoun Street, is essential for anyone interested in Charles Rennie Mackintosh (1868–1928), the influential Scots designer and architect. He designed the building, which contains many valuable examples of the functional yet austerely beautiful furniture produced by this leader of the Glasgow School. The house is open to the public all the year round.

Helmsdale, *Highland* (3/1B) Although the herring fishing, which once gave this village on the north-east coast its now-vanished air of prosperity, has largely disappeared, Helmsdale still holds jealously to the echoes of its past glory. The old harbour today enjoys some degree of muted prosperity from fishing boats loaded with whitefish and lobsters. As far back as 1841 salmon were packed in ice and sent south to London to satisfy that city's gourmets. Helmsdale was chosen to be a showplace by the Duke of Sutherland, who settled a few of the families his agents had evicted from the hinterland. His stamp of authority is still evident in the streets running east to west which bear the names of his Scottish estates; those running north to south commemorate his English possessions.

The ancient ruins of a medieval castle overlooking the village was, in 1567, the setting of a tragedy said to have inspired the poisoning scene in *Hamlet*. A cup of poisoned wine intended for the Earl of Sutherland was inadvertently drunk by the Countess's son, much to the chagrin of his mother.

The action of the sea over many centuries has exposed the inner secrets of rock formations, to reveal many kinds of semiprecious stones such as amethyst, rose quartz, jasper and chalcedony, to say nothing of interesting fossils and even coral.

Fronting the waters of the Moray Firth, and on the A9(T) coast road and served by rail, Helmsdale exudes a comforting atmosphere of stability and reassurance.

Hopeman, *Grampian* (3/1B) Once a thriving fishing community on the shore of the Moray Firth, Hopeman is now an attractive township, although rather spare in appearance. Its streets slope down to the sea and run at right angles to each other, reflecting the fact that it was laid out as a planned village in 1805; it owed its foundation to the need to ship out sandstone from nearby quarries.

Hoy *see* Orkney Islands

Huntly, *Grampian* (3/2C) This town, set in a sheltered position in the heart of the scenically beautiful area of Strathbogie, has always enjoyed its strategic location. Commanding the routes from Strathdon and ABERDEEN to Moray, it has over the centuries received the welcome, and at times unwelcome, attention of both friend and foe. Two standing stones in the Square suggest a significant importance before the Norman earls came north to set up as kinglets in the 13th century. The conical, flat-topped motte, just west of the present ruins of Huntly Castle, marks the 12th-century peel or palisaded enclosure of Strathbogie. It was here that King Robert Bruce fell ill during his campaign against the Comyns of Buchan. By the early 15th century the wooden structure on the motte had been replaced by the first stone buildings, which were added to as the power of the Gordon family increased. The main fabric of the present castle ruin dates from around 1550, though in 1594 it suffered much damage after the Gordons fell from grace as the result of a slight contretemps with King James VI. This temporary setback was laid aside when, three years later, the 5th Earl made his peace with the king and was enhanced in status as the 1st Marquess of Huntly. The castle was restored, with many architectural innovations introduced. The 2nd Marquess lost his head for supporting Charles I after suffering the indignity of being imprisoned in his own castle. The castle then slowly succumbed to the ravages of time and neglect. Even so, despite the alterations – and complications – of its 'Auld Werk' and 'New Werk', the ruins remain an impressive sight.

Huntly Castle

Huntly today is a busy and prosperous town, benefiting from its situation on the main road and rail route between Aberdeen and INVERNESS. Located as it is in the middle of cattle and sheep country, it also enjoys its role as an important market town.

Just south of Huntly is Leith Hall, a graceful country house added to by succeeding generations of the same family for over 300 years. The mementoes of that long history adorn the rooms – such as the personal jewellery of the last King of Oudh, trophies from the Indian Mutiny. Built *c.* 1650 and now in the care of the National Trust for Scotland, Leith Hall exudes an atmosphere of comfort, well-being and stability, despite the family's lust for globetrotting. Leith Hall has something of a reputation for being haunted – no particular ghost but simply the occasional feeling of a presence.

Innerpeffray, *Tayside* (5/1B) This rather unassuming little place was in fact of great importance in Roman times. Today it is the location of the oldest public library in Scotland, with a borrowers' ledger dating from 1747. It was founded in 1691 and contains some extremely rare books, with a large collection of early Bibles, including the copy carried by the warring Marquis of Montrose. Next to the library building, dating from 1750, is Innerpeffray Chapel, founded in 1508 as a collegiate house and built on the site of an older chapel.

Inveraray, *Strathclyde* (4/3B; 6/1B) This small burgh near the head of Loch Fyne was established on its present site in a grand scheme of rebuilding and town planning that took place in the second half of the 18th century: it included the razing of an older castle and the erection of the present attractive Inveraray Castle. From about 1457, when Colin, the second Lord Campbell, was created the first Earl of Argyll, the old castle had been the Campbell seat. But by 1743 it was beginning to show its age. In 1744 the third Duke of Argyll began rebuilding, taking advantage of the skills of architect Roger Morris to establish Inveraray anew and, indeed, allowing him his head. This freedom was extended to the employment of William Adam, builder of Hopetown House, and the father of the better-known Robert Adam, who actually followed his father on the Inveraray project.

The result is seen today: a little town designed not by town planners, but by architects and artists in their own right. If Inveraray is approached from the Glasgow road, the framework of six tall arches heralds some eyecatching delights. In fact the Historic Buildings Council has declared that Inveraray is 'an entirety designed to delight the eye from every angle of approach, both by land and water'.

Inside Inveraray Castle, the visitor cannot fail to be impressed by the sumptuous decoration, paintings, furniture and the armoury hall, displaying weapons dating from the 15th to the 18th centuries.

In the castle grounds is a museum of the Second World War, the Combined Operations Museum, the only one of its kind in Britain, opened in 1984. Inverary was the first Combined Operations Training Base where the techniques of seaborne landing assaults were evolved, and to which nearly every such raid during the last war owed something.

Inverbervie, *Grampian* (5/3A) There is little sign of the past in Inverbervie in spite of its being an ancient royal burgh with a charter going back to 1342. This east coast town on the A92 is now mainly an industrial community basing its economy on textiles. The first machine for spinning linen in Scotland was set up here in 1788. The designer of the wool and tea clipper the *Cutty Sark*, Hercules Linton, was born here. For a time during the late 18th century Inverbervie was a herring port, but when that fish disappeared from the coast, the town went back to concentrating on its more stable activity of textile production.

Inverewe Gardens *see* Poolewe

Invergordon, *Highland* (2/3B) Invergordon, on the shores of Cromarty Firth, first came into its own in the 18th century as a sheltered port with a safe anchorage to which easy access was gained at all times. Its use by the Royal Navy as a base in two world wars has tended to define its one and only function. However, in an account written in 1797 it was said: '. . . very few situations indeed in the north of Scotland seem better adapted for a manufacturing village than the Ness of Invergordon'. This was somewhat prophetic, for Invergordon has since become an industrial town with a distillery, which is the largest single unit of its kind in Europe, and an aluminium reduction plant, now sadly closed down with the loss of hundreds of badly needed jobs. For all its industrialization, the town has a number of pleasing features: its broad High Street, an esplanade on the sea front, and a purposeful atmosphere.

On the very last day of 1915, the armoured cruiser *Natal* exploded, the result of an accident with ammunition. She sank in minutes with the loss of half the ship's company, nearly 400 men. The sound of the explosion was heard miles away in the hinterland. In 1931 the famous Invergordon Mutiny by naval personnel took place, on grounds of bad conditions in the Senior Service. Across the water from Invergordon is Nigg, now the scene of high-technology engineering for the oil industry, with production platforms as high as cathedrals scoring the skyline with their precise geometry.

Inverkeithing, *Fife* (5/2B) One of the ancient royal burghs of Fife, standing on the shores of the Forth estuary. An industrial town, part of its economy is based on the local shipbreaking yard, which has seen some of the world's most famous liners and naval ships reduced to mere heaps of scrap iron. The 14th-century Greyfriar's Hospice is now restored as a community centre along with the museum devoted to local history. It is on the outskirts of town on the road to the Forth Bridge.

The Town Hall dates from 1755, and the church (1826) incorporates a medieval tower containing a rare 14th-century font. The market cross at the east end of the town dates from 1399 and is topped by a unicorn made in 1688.

Inverness, *Highland* (2/3C) If Edinburgh has been given the title 'Athens of the North' Inverness, the capital of the Highlands, is worthy of the title 'Paris of the North'. Its situation on the banks of the river Ness, complete with midstream islands, has provided it with a scenic asset that has not always been used to best advantage. Like Paris, modern planners have juxtaposed multi-storey jungles with the buildings of an older generation, and physical changes made in an effort to pull the town out of its planning backwater have not altogether been easy on the eye. Having said that about Inverness, it must also be declared that some areas of the town still exude a pleasing atmosphere, echoing the days when the streets were crowded with the more leisurely horse-drawn dray, cart and coach. The riverside fringes have been largely left intact, though in some places they have been encroached upon to serve the needs of the growing commercial centre that Inverness has become in recent years.

The origins of Inverness are obscure, but there is sufficient evidence to indicate that it has been a place of significance as a human settlement for some 2000 years. One of the first documentary references dates from the 6th century, in the

Inverness

biography of that much-travelled cleric, St Columba. He visited the town in AD 565 to confront the Pictish King Brude. The exact site of Brude's fortress is uncertain, but some place it west of Inverness at Craig Phadraig, some miles away. Later, in the 12th century, the old castle of Inverness was built on a ridge to the east of the present Castlehill. This castle saw the bloody murder of King Duncan of Scotland, so dramatically portrayed in Shakespeare's *Macbeth*. The history of the castle itself was subsequently to prove destructively eventful.

In 1150 Inverness was made a royal burgh on the strength of its importance as a trading port; it exported furs, hides, skins, and wool as far afield as the Mediterranean. The Inverness hinterland at that time was a densely wooded area; the trees were used for building a ship, the *Comte de St Paul et Blois*, which accompanied Louis VII of France on his Crusade to the Holy Land. In the Scottish Wars of Independence in the 13th century, Inverness was a target for both English and Scots. It was occupied by English forces three times and when King Robert Bruce recaptured it in 1307 he destroyed the castle. In 1427 James I convened a Scottish Parliament in Inverness to which he invited all the important Highland chiefs. Some 40 attended and were promptly arrested and imprisoned; two were executed *pour encourager les autres*. But the incident had little effect on the chiefs, one of whom, Alexander Macdonald, Lord of the Isles, took revenge for the treatment he received in prison and pillaged and burned the town:

The present Inverness Castle is a Johnny-come-lately. Built in 1834 it now accommodates the Court House. Other older buildings include the Parish Church, rebuilt in 1772, with its 14th-century vaulted tower remaining intact. In the adjoining churchyard some prisoners taken at the Battle of Culloden were executed in 1746, and the execution stone still shows the bullet marks. Cromwell's Clock Tower is all that remains of the large Citadel or Sconce, built around 1657 by his Commonwealth army. When the garrison troops left in 1662, the people of Inverness demolished the building but left the clocktower as a useful landmark.

In Church Street can be seen Abertarff House, built *c.* 1592 with an old turnpike stairway. Almost opposite is Dunbar's Hospital, erected in 1688 as an almshouse for the town's poor. In Friar's Street is all that remains of the large Dominican Priory built in 1233: a graveyard. St Andrew's Cathedral dates from 1869. It is richly decorated with illuminated windows and carved pillars. The baptismal font is a copy of the one in Copenhagen Cathedral.

Now very much a commercial and administrative centre for the Highlands, Inverness is also a popular tourist base. As the northern terminus of the CALEDONIAN CANAL, its shipping tends to be varied, lending another aspect to a town that is full of vitality, interest and retains a measure of charm.

Inverpolly National Nature Reserve (2/2B) This reserve is some 12 miles north of ULLAPOOL in Highland and has as its centrepiece the sandstone peaks of Cul Mor (2787 ft), Cul Beag (2523 ft), and the unusual Stac Pollaidh (2009 ft), with its startling serrated ridge.

The area is an expanse of moorland, bog, burns, lochs and mountain peaks, and the natural home of some rare animals and birds. This is a desolate part of the north-west Highlands with the character of a primeval wilderness (*see pp. 64–5*). Because of this it is best to consult the Nature Conservancy Warden at the visitor centre before venturing into the hills.

Animals to be seen include: red deer, goat, wild cat, fox, and pine marten (Britain's rarest mammal); birds include: merlin, snow bunting, golden eagle, peregrine falcon, raven and ptarmigan.

Inverurie, *Grampian* (3/3C) This town developed from medieval times at a junction of three main roads (to HUNTLY, BANFF and FRASERBURGH). It is situated in an area full of historical associations, from Pictish stones to stone circles, from motte and bailey mounds to the usual castles. The Bass of Inverurie is a conical 60 ft grass mound, once the site of a wooden peel tower built in the 12th century and the first of its kind in north-east Scotland. Keith Hall is a Z-plan castle of the late 16th century with gardens laid out by the incomparable Capability Brown (Gardens open all the year round: dogs on lead.)

Within a five-mile radius are two important reminders of prehistory: the Loanhead Stone Circle (near DAVIOT, off the B9001, 5 miles north-west of Inverurie) and the East Aquhorthies stone circle (3 miles west of Inverurie). Two miles west can be seen the monument erected in 1911 to commemorate the Battle of Harlow (1411) where the advance of Donald, Lord of the Isles, was checked by forces that included the worried citizens of ABERDEEN who hardly relished the presence of wild Highlanders in their city. 'Red

Harlow' ensured that Gaeldom would never be a dominant political and military force in Scotland.

Today Inverurie is a thriving town serving a fertile, intensively farmed hinterland.

Iona, *Strathclyde* (4/1A-1B) After Whithorn, in the south-west of Scotland, Iona is the cradle of Christianity in Scotland and, indeed, so far as the Highlands of Scotland are concerned, the status of Iona in the Scottish Christian mind was a combination of Paradise and Valhalla. It lies just off the southern tip of MULL and was the place chosen by St Columba in AD 563 to establish a centre from which radiated missionary journeys on behalf of the new faith both in his own time and in later centuries. Though it was a place of peace, it did not escape the attentions of the Vikings who paid frequent raiding visits and on one occasion, in 806, killed 68 monks at 'Martyrs Bay' near the present jetty. Of the first monastery built by Columba and his followers nothing much remains. By 1074 Iona had assumed a special dimension in Christian Scotland and the monastery was rebuilt by Queen Margaret. In 1203 it was again rebuilt by Reginald of Islay, Lord of the Isles. In 1500 Iona achieved cathedral status. During the Reformation all the buildings were dismantled and some 350 of the island's crosses were destroyed.

In 1899 the ruins of the old abbey were gifted to the Church of Scotland and had been restored by 1910. Since 1938 the monastic buildings have been undergoing a continuous programme of restoration supervised by the Iona Community, founded by Lord George MacLeod of Fiunary. More recently the island has come under the administration of the National Trust for Scotland.

Because of its religious association, Iona was the required burial place for many of Scotland's early kings and queens, and for a number of Norwegian and Irish monarchs. Reilig Odhrain graveyard was their last resting place, though the tombs have long since vanished. The massive influx of visitors each year tends to militate against the atmosphere that might be expected in such a place, drenched as it is with over 1500 years of spiritual brightness, devotion and inspiration. Even so, in quieter periods, there are occasions when that very special atmosphere can be sensed by receptive hearts and minds.

The island is reached by passenger ferry (no cars) from Fionnphort on Mull or by sea excursion from OBAN.

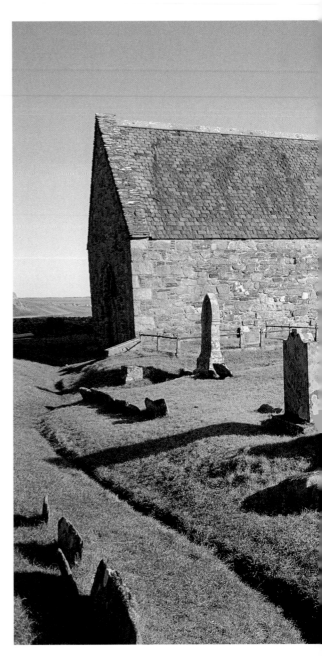

St Oran's Chapel and the old abbey, Iona

Islay, *Strathclyde* (4/1B) This is the largest island of the Inner Hebrides, with ferry connections to TARBERT. Because its geology is a mosaic of various rock types, its aspect ranges from good, green arable land to peat bog, the latter a most essential ingredient in Islay's economic sheet anchor, the whisky industry. The three main population centres are Bowmore, Port Ellen and Port Charlotte.

Throughout its history, Islay has featured prominently in both ecclesiastical and secular roles, the latter often as witness to clan feuds between Macdonalds, Campbells and MacLeans. The Cross of Kildalton, the finest of its kind in Scotland, dates from *c.* AD 800 and is a memorial of an intense early Christian activity on the island. Islay was once the council place of the Lords of the Isles, a Gaelic autonomous principality in the 14th century which was power-ful enough to have made treaties with the Kings of England against the Scottish interest. The ceremony of proclaiming new chiefs was carried out on an island in Loch Finlaggan, where many carved stones remain.

The Round Church at Bowmore, built in 1769, took a circular shape so as to deprive the Devil of corners to hide in and thus prevent him from tempting the congregation.

Both Port Ellen and Port-Charlotte are planned villages of the 18th century. At the latter is the Museum of Islay Life, with displays showing

Islay through the centuries. Farming, fishing and distilling are the main Islay activities; the last-named claims the greatest attention. The island's seven distilleries have been known to malt whisky connoisseurs since the early years of the 19th century. The product tends to be strong in flavour, reflecting the influence of the maritime climate on the peat, all combining to impart a unique experience to the taste buds.

On a hill overlooking Bridgend village is a memorial to John Francis Campbell (1822–85), who spent a lifetime collecting and preserving much of the all-but-lost traditions and folk tales of the Gaelic West Highlands: his pioneering work in this field rivalled that of the Brothers Grimm.

Jarlshof *see* Shetland Islands

John o'Groats, *Highland* (3/2A) John o'Groats is not quite the most northerly point on the British mainland as is often claimed. That distinction belongs to Dunnet Head, further to the east. Even so, it is the place twinned in the popular mind with Land's End in Cornwall and is certainly the last village on the main A9 route from the south. Its unusual name is derived from Jan de Groot, one of several Dutch brothers who settled in Caithness in the 16th century. They became successful businessmen, but their very prosperity generated a quarrel among their descendants as to who had precedence at family gatherings. It was Jan who solved the problem by designing a house with eight walls, windows and doors and an eight-sided table so that each claimant could imagine his own importance. The original house has since disappeared.

This village has been spoiled by its fame, with little to offer the discerning tourist. The beach hereabouts is well known for the 'Groatie buckie', a small cowrie shell that is now the basis of an unusual form of jewellery which has, in fact, an origin in the prehistoric ornaments found in the area. The shells are rather difficult to find. The small harbour is mainly used by lobster boats.

Jura, *Strathclyde* (4/2B) Jura is one of the largest islands of the Inner Hebrides. Lying north-west of the MULL OF KINTYRE and north-east of ISLAY, it is 28 miles long and about 8 across at its widest. Its aspect is wilder and hillier than most of its neighbours, so much so that the entire western part is trackless and holds no human habitation. The three main peaks of the Paps of Jura, in the

southern half of the island, rise to 2576, 2477 and 2407 ft and their lower slopes run down to the sea clothed in blanket bog.

The name of Jura is derived from the Gaelic and means 'Deer Island', which reflects its long history as a hunting ground. The present deer population is in the region of 5000. The island is served by one main road. The main settlement is Craighouse, which has a modern distillery built on the site of an early works established in 1810 and in full production until 1912.

To the north of Jura is Scarba Island, separated by the Strait of Corriebhreacan (or Corry-vreckan). This is the most formidable tide race in the British Isles and has been officially deemed unnavigable by the Royal Navy; its speed is about 8 knots. It is at its worst when the flood tide is opposed by a westerly wind, when its roar can be heard many miles away.

Keith, *Grampian* (3/2C) The burgh of Keith has a history that goes back to AD 700, when the much-travelled St Maelrubha, of APPLECROSS in Wester Ross, converted the inhabitants to Christianity. The settlement seems to have had some early significance, as evidenced by an important circle of monoliths and a holy well nearby, and its location, straddling essential routes to all cardinal points. The name Keith appears in a religious charter dated 1195. The connection with religion was strengthened by the birth here in 1580 of John Ogilvie, a Jesuit missionary. After studying in Paris and Germany he returned to Scotland, where he was arrested and hanged in Glasgow in 1615 for his refusal to take the anti-Catholic oath. He was beatified in 1929 and canonized in 1970, thus becoming Scotland's first post-Reformation saint.

Keith was revamped in 1750, in one of the many planning exercises popular with lairds of the period. It then established its position as a main marketing centre. At one time its industries were linen manufacture and tobacco processing. The main activities now include woollen goods and the making of whisky; the local distillery, founded in 1786, is the oldest in Scotland. The oldest building in Keith is Milton Tower, once part of a larger castle, built in 1480.

Kenmore, *Tayside* (5/1B) A delightful little estate village at the eastern end of Loch Tay, with its whitewashed houses standing in a fine luxurious green setting. Both the parish church and the inn date from about 1760; in the latter Robert Burns wrote some lines that gave his favourite

'Soldier's Leap', Killicrankie

impressions of the district. The bridge over the outfall of the loch flowing into the river Tay dates from 1774.

Killiecrankie, *Tayside* (5/1A) This wooded pass in Perthshire carries the hasty river Garry on its way to join the Tummel. A far-famed beauty spot, it was the scene of the battle in 1689 at which the Jacobites defeated the army of King William III. A Visitor Centre run by the National Trust for Scotland explains the battle in considerable detail using an audio-visual display. The actual pass is a narrow gorge threaded by both road and railway. Tracks lead down through oak trees to view the 'Soldier's Leap', a gap of some 18 ft across which an English soldier managed to jump in escaping from pursuing Highlanders after the battle.

Killin, *Central* (5/1B; 6/3B) At the western end of Loch Tay, Killin was once the headquarters of the Clan MacNab, whose burial ground is on a small island in the river Dochart. Killin Church, in use from the 9th century, was rebuilt in 1774.

The font is at least 1000 years old and is the only seven-sided example of its kind in Scotland. A little to the north is the now-ruined Finlarig Castle, a 17th-century towerhouse on the site of an earlier stronghold, with what is claimed to be a beheading pit, where wrongdoers paid the price for their misdeeds.

In a small field close to Breadalbane Park lies a stone said to mark the burial place of Fingal, a Celtic hero of the 3rd century AD and Gaelic warrior king.

Kilravock Castle, *Highland* (3/1C) Situated about 7 miles south-west of NAIRN, this ancient home of the Roses of Kilravock has been lived in continuously for 700 years. The earliest part of the building dates from 1460, with additions in the subsequent centuries. The lands around the castle have had a long association with Christianity, and many churches were built in the valley. This tradition is continued to the present day, for the castle is now a Christian guesthouse. It is not open to the public.

It was here, just before the decisive battle of Culloden in April 1746, that Bonnie Prince Charlie dined as a guest of the owner, who was not a Jacobite – while in Nairn his opponent, the Duke of Cumberland, slept in his own town house after celebrating his birthday.

Kincardine, *Fife* (5/1B) A small port on the river Forth before it widens out into the Firth, Kincardine has as its most conspicuous feature a bridge built in 1936 with a central swing span of 300 ft. Picnickers will be forever grateful to John Dewar (1842–1922), a native of the town, who invented the thermos flask. Across the bridge, at Airth, is 'The Pineapple', a rather strange structure built in 1761 and standing in a double-walled garden. To the north of Kincardine is a roofless 17th-century church, behind which is Tulliallan Castle, dating from the 14th century, now a police college.

Kincraig, *Highland* (5/1A) A small village on the main INVERNESS–PERTH road, with Loch Insh as a scenic feature. Insh Church, on a moraine knoll above the loch, is built on a site said to have been sacred to the druids, and then used continuously for Christian worship from the 6th century. An ancient Celtic bell is worth seeing, as is the hollow stone said to have been used as a font by St Adamnan, the biographer of St Columba. The low-lying and often flooded Insh marshes are a reserve for waterfowl. Observation hides are operated by the RSPB.

At Kincraig the Highland Wildlife Park specializes in animals that were once common in Scotland. A few of the now all but extinct breed of Przevalski, or Asiatic, wild horses are also on proud display.

Kingston, *Grampian* (3/2B; 7/3A) This Morayshire village derives its name from the two men from Kingston upon Hull, in Yorkshire, who were its founders in 1785. They had originally come north to buy timber from the Speyside forests, then decided to stay and establish a shipbuilding industry. This activity continued until the Spey changed its course, leaving a vast area of stones and pebbles to mark where large ships were once launched. One family engaged in the shipbuilding industry were the Kinlocks, who eventually moved into shipping by founding the Chief Line, plying around the Cape and the East and West India trade routes. One ship built at Kingston was the *Chieftain*, which went in search of Sir John Franklin's 1845-7 expedition to the Arctic.

The oldest building in Kingston predates the shipyards by several centuries: Dunfermline House, *c.* 1654, originally built by the monks of nearby Urquhart Priory, a daughter house of Dunfermline Abbey.

Kingussie, *Highland* (5/1A) Kingussie is the capital of the Badenoch area of Speyside. A guidebook of some 50 years ago insists that, because of the great pine woods in the vicinity, 'the air of the place is highly beneficial to sufferers of chest complaints'. Certainly, standing at 750 ft above sea level, between the Monadhliath Mountains and the Cairngorms, Kingussie exudes a feeling of exhilaration. Before the advent of the railway, the town was the centre of a busy spinning and weaving industry which lasted for a few decades. But when the railway opened in 1880, the town became the centre for the Highland shooting season and saw the building of large Victorian houses, many of which survive today.

Ancient history abounds in the area, with the Old Church of Kingussie, chapels and a monastery, and, older still, stone circles and cairns. (For more information *The Visitors Map to Strathspey*, published by the Landmark Centre, CARRBRIDGE, is most useful.)

Dominating the eastern skyline are the old Barracks of Ruthven built in 1716 to keep the Highlanders in check. After the defeat of the Jacobites in 1746 at Culloden, the remnants of Prince Charlie's forces gathered here hoping he might take the field again; but when they realized the cause was hopeless, they blew up the buildings. What remains is more than impressive.

In Kingussie is the Highland Folk Museum, founded in 1935 in a pioneering attempt to preserve much of the fast-disappearing artifacts associated with Highland outdoor and domestic life. In the grounds of Pitmain Lodge, the main museum facility, there are realistic replicas of an old Highland 'black house', a clack mill run by water and a turf house.

Kinlochbervie, *Highland* (2/2A) The size of this fishing village belies its economic significance for the Scottish west coast fishing industry, with two harbours accessible from its two sea lochs, Bervie and Clash. The catch is worth £2 million per annum. A popular tourist base, Kinlochbervie gives access to the mountains of Sutherland's north-west wilderness areas, and a coastline of high cliffs and magnificent stretches of white sandy beaches.

Kinlochleven, *Highland* (4/3A; 6/1A) This village lies at the head of Loch Leven and was once

Trawlers, Kinlochbervie

nearly called 'Aluminiumville' on account of its importance as a centre for the reduction of aluminium from bauxite, an industry that is still a sheet anchor for the resident population. The factory was completed in 1907. The energy needed for the aluminium processing comes from a hydroelectric plant which in turn relies on the Blackwater Reservoir, with its capacity of almost 4000 million cu ft. With an annual rainfall in the area of more than 80 in, there is no shortage of water, which is one reason why this industrial development was started eight decades ago.

Overshadowed by its dominant mountains, Kinlochleven tends to be a sunless place even in summer, which seems hardly to deter the large number of tourists who make it a holiday base.

Kinross, *Tayside* (5/2B) Lying on the western shore of Loch Leven, Kinross boasts a 17th-century tolbooth in the High Street. Historically it tends to be overshadowed by Loch Leven which contains several islands, on one of which is Loch Leven Castle, a compact, square 14th-century tower standing in a court and surrounded by a curtain wall. It was here in 1567 that Mary Queen of Scots was imprisoned for nearly a year,

until her escape was engineered by some of her faithfuls. Less than a fortnight later, she fled to England and her eventual execution. Loch Leven is now a nature reserve and the most important expanse of freshwater in Britain for migratory wildfowl.

Kintore, *Grampian* (3/3C) A small town proud of its status since it was created a royal burgh in 1506 – though its history as a settlement goes back to the 9th century when its people were granted a charter from Kenneth II after they had valiantly assisted him in a battle against the Picts. The Town House in the square dates from 1737 and has external curving stairs which adds a dimension of quaintness. It can be opened on request. The church has a rare 16th-century sacrament house with an early Pictish sculptured stone in the churchyard which combines both Christian and pagan symbols.

Kirkcaldy, *Fife* (5/2B) One of Scotland's industrial towns, Kirkcaldy on the Firth of Forth has that solid long-lasting look about it which reflects the down-to-earth character of its buildings and the townsfolk. Not that everything is functional here. Spiritual welfare and leisure are well catered for, the latter in the many parks and open spaces acting as welcome lungs for the citizens of 'The Lang Toun', a name derived from the fact that Kirkcaldy was once little more than one long street.

Kirkcaldy's prosperity was founded on the linoleum industry, the first factory being built in 1847. Now in decline, its place has been taken over by other industries to give the town a firm base of what is called in present-day jargon 'economic pluralism'.

The town has sprawled over into next-door **Dysart**, an old seaport that has gone out of its way to preserve many of its old buildings and to help out its larger neighbour with some borrowed history. The Pan Ha' in Dysart, for example, is a small row of restored houses showing off their fine 17th-century architecture. The ruined Church of St Serf is much older than the date 1570 which appears on one of its windows. The Tolbooth (1576) might still have survived intact had it not been blown up by accident by Cromwell's troops in 1656 when someone entered the powder room, rather the worse for drink, with a lighted torch.

The Stuart McDouall Museum bounds the War Memorial Gardens and is devoted to the life and times of this Dysart native who traversed the great Australian desert in 1862, the first man to do so from north to south.

Kirkcaldy's Museum and Art Gallery in Rectory Lane has a good representation of material of local interest, including examples of the much-sought-after Wemyss Ware pottery and a comprehensive and important selection of work by Scottish artists. Adam Smith, the author of the influential *Wealth of Nations* (1776), was born here and has not been forgotten by Kirkcaldy.

Kirkwall *see* Orkney Islands

Kirriemuir, *Tayside* (5/2A) The warmth of the welcome offered by this friendly old Tayside town is complemented by the red sandstone used in many of its buildings. Here the creator of Peter Pan (J. M. Barrie) was born in 1860 and the house (at 9 Brechin Road) is now a museum devoted to his life and work.

Though Kirriemuir is still a jute manufacturing town, it was at one time a place full of weavers, whose idiosyncratic activities are reflected in the narrow wynds that separate the houses, and in the steep streets. It is said that to preserve their privacy, no house front door faced that of any other, which helps to explain the apparently haphazard nature of the layout.

Lairg, *Highland* (2/3B) This small Sutherland village, with a refreshing open aspect, is the venue for one of the biggest one-day sheep sales in the whole of Britain. Apart from its tourist attractions (it is at the southern tip of Loch Shin, 16 miles long), Lairg acts as a junction of five roads and has a railway station. Evidence of a long history of continuous habitation is seen at Auchinduich, south of Lairg, where one of the largest chambered cairns found in Scotland was once excavated. Some miles to the east, through Strath Fleet, is Rogart, a scattered crofting community that boasts the memorial to Sir John Alexander Macdonald (1815–91), the first Prime Minister of Canada, whose family originated in the area.

Lake of Menteith, *Central* (6/3C) Of all the thousands of lochs in Scotland, the Lake of Menteith is among the very few so called. Not only that, but it boasts the Port of Menteith, from which a ferry carries visitors to one of the islands on which is built the Augustinian Priory of Inchmahome. Founded in 1238, it was a favourite resort of Scots royalty. In 1979 the lake was completely frozen over and offered some 3000 curlers a bonspiel (tournament), one of the biggest in the world with competitors enjoying the chance to indulge in a Scottish sport now too often held on ice rinks indoors.

Largo, *Fife* (5/3B) Although little or no commercial fishing is now pursued from the harbour of Largo on the Firth of Forth, it once had a significant part to play when the herring industry was enjoying its boom years last century. In reality the present town is in two parts. Upper Largo is the old Kirkton, with a parish church first consecrated in 1243. Only the chancel remains as an echo of its pre-Reformation days. However, a Pictish cross slab suggests a much longer occupation.

Lower Largo is better known these days as the birthplace of Robinson Crusoe – in reality Alexander Selkirk, who left home to become a sailor and, at the age of 28, was marooned for four years on the island of Juan Fernandez, 400 miles off the Pacific coast of Chile. His story inspired the prolific Daniel Defoe to write his novel in 1719. It was an immediate success and has remained so ever since. Towards the eastern end of the main street can be seen the house with its statue of Selkirk gazing out to sea, dressed in goatskins.

Alexander Selkirk, the 'real' Robinson Crusoe

WM. BURNETT A.R.S.A.
1885

Latheron, *Highland* (3/1A) This is one of the most attractive places in Caithness, as witness the derivation of the name: 'Haven of Seals'. Its harbour was created by building a wall round a natural cove; this area is known as Latheron-wheel or Janetstown. In its heyday it had a significant share in the boom days of the herring fishing industry. Today, the harbour tends to silt up and only a few lobster boats and pleasure craft use it. The old parish church is now a museum devoted to the Clan Gunn (Gunn is a common surname in these parts, going back to Viking days). Latheron is a favourite haunt of painters, drawn by the splendid seascapes and the magnificent coastline it offers.

Lerwick *see* Shetland Islands

Lewis, *Western Isles* (1/2A) Lewis is the largest island in the Outer Hebrides and as such has maintained a significant influence on the history of its neighbours, so that today it is the seat of the Comhairle nan Eilean, the Western Isles Council. The main town, Stornoway, has the largest population – about 26,000 – in the north-west of Scotland, including the mainland. This has been a decisive factor in the attention given by successive governments to these islands.

Lewis consists largely of rolling moors, generously sprinkled with lochs and, to the south-west, high mountains. A feature of its landscape is the many crofting townships, most of which lie on the fertile coastal areas of the island. Often these are contiguous, so much so that you drive through what is effectively one long village. Apart from crofting, which yields little more than a subsistence, the island activities are fishing and the weaving of the world-famous Harris tweed. This latter occupation, partly industrialized in Stornoway, has been something of an economic sheet anchor for the island. It is a unique industry for, although the spinning, washing, dyeing and finishing processes are carried out in the Stornoway mills, all the weaving is done by crofters in their own homes on foot-operated looms.

The history of Lewis goes back to 2000 BC, with the Standing Stones at Callanish an astonishing witness to the presence of a significant population and culture. Evidence of an early conversion to Christianity is seen in the many remains of chapels and temples, with a large church, dating from the 14th century, at Aignish near Stornoway, now roofless but containing carved commemorative stone slabs.

The history of the island's fishing industry has been one of a tragic denuding of the rich waters of the Minch, that stormy channel of water which separates Lewis from the Scottish mainland. Since the coming of steam trawlers at the turn of the century, and of devastatingly efficient methods of catching fish, the local fleet has never recovered, never experienced again the boom days of 100 years ago when king herring ruled for six busy days every week in season. The main harbour facilities in the town are often deserted, though construction works for the oil industry at the mouth of the harbour point to a future potential.

In recent years the Lewis community has gathered itself together to work out its own salvation in the form of community cooperatives: a new spirit of self-help has been a trigger for enterprise and success. These cooperatives have extended the economic base of the local people to include crafts, knitting, marketing of livestock and fish farming, and have provided much-needed work for an island whose unemployment rate has for many years hovered around the 20 per cent mark. A unique cooperative is the seaweed-processing factory at Keose, taken over by the workers themselves when its closure was threatened.

The well-preserved Iron Age broch at Carloway is a notable sight standing about 30 ft on one side. Evidence of a long Norse occupation is contained in numbers of Lewis place names and in the origin of many of the island surnames (with the Gaelic Mac- replacing the Scandinavian -son in many cases): Macleod, MacIver, MacAulay. Stornoway itself has contributed significantly to world history. Sir Alexander MacKenzie (1755?–1820) discovered the MacKenzie River in Canada. Colin MacKenzie became Surveyor-General of all India in 1819. MacIvers from the parish of Uig were co-founders of the Cunard line. In this century Robert MacIver became Lieber Professor of political philosophy at Columbia University and adviser to the United States Government.

Stornoway Ever since the Vikings pushed their way into the almost landlocked natural harbour of the town 1000 years ago, there has been a settlement here that has acted as a focal point not only for the island of Lewis but for the whole of the Western Isles. From its original collection of 'rude huts', Stornoway has grown up round the castle of the major Lewis clan: the

The Standing Stones at Callanish, Lewis (Richard Muir)

Macleods. The structure, now lost under the magnificent pier and harbour installations, saw much activity in the 15th and 16th centuries, mainly repelling incomers intent on exploiting both the island and its people.

Today Stornoway, connected by a car ferry with ULLAPOOL on the mainland, is a rather splendid-looking town, though many of its older buildings have been cleared away and it has lost its former characteristic originality. Even so there are still a number of fine houses and churches with aspects of Scottish vernacular architectural interest.

Its present castle was built in 1850 by Sir James Matheson, a native of Sutherland who made his fortune in the Far East. He was once called 'Mr Drug' by Disraeli in the House of Commons, on account of part of that fortune being made from opium. Matheson purchased Lewis in 1844 and his regime lasted until Lewis was bought in 1918 by Lord Leverhulme, of Sunlight Soap fame. The latter's scheme for the development of Lewis ended in frustration, but not sourness. Before he left, he gave the castle and its wooded policies (park) to the people of Stornoway as public property. The managing agency, the Stornoway Trust, is the only body of its kind, with its land held in common trust, in Britain. The castle is now part of the only technical college in the Western Isles.

Lismore, *Strathclyde* (4/2A) This 10-mile-long island lies in the mouth, as it were, of Loch Linnhe. Its name is derived from the Gaelic and means 'Great Garden'. The first element, *lios*, also means a residence or fortified place with an enclosure, which might refer to a garden at the ancient monastic site at Kilmoluaig. Evidence of a long occupation is seen in three castles and several *duns* or forts. Achadun, or Achaduin, Castle, built in the 13th century, was at one time a bishop's palace. The island is built up on a bedrock of limestone, which gives a fertile soil and maintains lush green grazing.

Kilmoluaig dates from the 13th century and is still in use, but no longer enjoys its former elevated status as a cathedral. The dedicatee, St Moluaig, also founded sees at Mortlach in Banffshire and Rosemarkie in Ross-shire. The old cathedral was burned to the ground during the Reformation. The present building is the residual old choir, given a roof in 1749. It tends to look like a rather ordinary parish church.

Lismore is linked by passenger ferry to Port Appin and by car ferry to OBAN.

Lochaline, *Highland* (4/2A) A small village with a sheltered anchorage on the southern shoreline of the Norvern peninsula opposite the island of MULL. Its importance lies in the fact that in the area there is a bed of white cretaceous sandstone which, during the Second World War, was Britain's only source of sand for optical glass, a material that had hitherto come from the Continent. The sand is exceptionally pure and free from iron. The rock is still being mined, and the operations present a rather ugly scene.

Nearby is the turreted structure of Lochaline House (*see p. 153*).

Lochcarron, *Highland* (2/2C) Loch Carron, a long inlet of the sea, feeds an area that combines the old and the new. The village of Lochcarron, which straggles along the north shore of the loch, was once an important fishing community. (*See pp. 156–7*). A 19th-century comment sets the scene in former times: 'In a calm evening, when hundreds of boats are seen shooting their nets, and scores of vessels lying at anchor, Loch Carron exhibits a scene of rural felicity and of rural beauty that seldom is to be witnessed.' The 'rural felicity' remains and the village now mainly relies on tourism as its *raison d'être*.

On the shore of the loch south-west of Lochcarron is Strome, boasting the ruins of Strome Castle, blown up after a clan feud in 1602. Strome has two places in Highland history. In 1881 the SS *Ferret*, a ferry owned by the Highland Railway, was 'hired' by a James Henderson, alias Smith, who exceeded the conditions of his contract and made off with the ship, a coaster of 346 tons. She sailed to South America, Africa and finally Australia where, though under a different name, she and her pirate crew were arrested and eventually sentenced.

In June 1873 two steamers arrived at Strome with cargoes of fish, which were unloaded. At any other time of the week this activity would have passed without comment. But the time was one o'clock on a Sunday morning. About 50 locals appeared on the scene, took possession of the pier, stopped the unloading and blockaded the ships. The following day a party of six policemen arrived but were unable to cope with the situation. The affair blew up to such proportions that 160 policemen were drafted in from as far away as Lanark and ELGIN, to cope with the mass rally of 2000 people on the following Sunday. The situation was resolved by local ministers who, by their intervention, prevented what might have become a sore and bloody affair.

Plockton, Lochcarron

Close by Lochcarron is Kishorn, presenting the 'new' face of the Highlands: a massive yard for the construction of giant concrete oil-production platforms.

On the southern shore of Loch Carron is the delightful village of Plockton in an idyllic setting, helped in no small way by the warmth of the Gulf Stream and its sheltered location. It is a haven for west coast yachtsmen.

Lochearnhead, *Central* (5/1B; 6/3B) Situated at the western end of Loch Earn, this small village has exploited its only advantage: the loch's large expanse of water, the focal point for a sailing school and facilities for a range of water sports. To landward there are the contrasts of Glen Ogle and Ben Vorlich, with scenic gems such as the Falls of Edinample, in Glenample, where the remains of ancient St Blane's Chapel can be seen.

Lochgilphead, *Strathclyde* (4/2B) This popular Argyll holiday centre nestles comfortably in the crook of Loch Gilp, itself an offspring of the greater Loch Fyne. Its substantial stone-built houses give a feeling of well-being and hug the shore in a long line with an outward view to the hills of ARRAN, whose notched crests hang high on the south horizon. The administrative centre for mid-Argyll, Lochgilphead's streets are always full of traffic, giving an impression of purposeful haste.

Lochindorb, *Grampian* (3/1C) This ruined 13th-century castle stands on an island in lonely Lochindorb about 10 miles north-west of GRAN-TOWN-ON-SPEY. It was occupied in person in 1303 by Edward I of England, the 'Hammer of the Scots', when on a punitive mission in Scotland to try to bring its people to heel. Its fame came with its occupation by Alexander Stewart, the vicious Earl of Buchan, known as the 'Wolf of Badenoch', who was the outlawed son of Robert II. He was responsible for the sacking of FORRES and the burning and destruction of ELGIN Cathedral, the heart of the bishopric of Moray. The terrified burghers of Elgin fled with their families into the surrounding countryside. Tradition has it that some of them, like Lot's wife,

Overleaf: Lochcarron

looked back at the burning cathedral, with its Gothic windows a tracery of stone against the flames, and were frozen in their tracks with horror. Lochindorb was dismantled in 1456.

Lochinver, *Highland* (2/2B) A small but busy fishing village on the west coast of Sutherland lying under the shadow of Suilven (2399 ft), an intriguing sugarloaf mountain. The magnificent coastal scenery in the area makes Lochinver a popular base for tourists, and sea and freshwater anglers who have a choice of some 300 lochs within easy reach.

On the shores of Loch Assynt lie the ruins of Ardvreck Castle, built *c.* 1590, the seat of the Macleods of Assynt.

Loch Lomond, *Central* and *Strathclyde* (4/3B; 6/2C) This is the largest stretch of inland freshwater in Britain, some 24 miles long and 5 miles at its widest. With its wooded shores overlooked by Ben Lomond, and its waters studded with 30 islands, the loch has won deserved praise in both song and poetry. One song in particular, 'The Bonnie Banks o' Loch Lomond', was written over 200 years ago by a Jacobite supporter imprisoned in a cell in Carlisle. Facing death, he was truly to take the 'high road' back to the scenes he knew and loved.

The loch attracted the attention of many. In 1263 King Hakon IV of Norway dragged his longships overland so that he could use it to gain access to central Scotland for raids. Early Christian missionaries from IONA and Whithorn, in the south-west of Scotland, set up bases for their evangelizing work. Along its shores have marched armies, marauding bands of clansmen, and drovers from the north with their herds of cattle.

Many pleasure boats offer a chance to sail round the loch and visit the islands, including Inchmurrin, with its ruins of Lennox Castle, and Inchcailleoch, the burial place of Clan Macgregor. Boats can be hired from a number of places including Balloch, Inversnaid, LUSS, Rowandennan and Tarbet.

The whole area has been identified as being of special natural interest, with Forest Reserves and the Queen Elizabeth Forest Park offering many attractions, including a wide variety of wildlife. Loch Lomond boasts a natural rarity, the powan. This is thought to be descended from the salt-

Opposite: Near Lochinver. (Above) Loch Assynt; (below) Ardvreck Castle

water herring which may have been trapped there after the last Ice Age when the loch was cut off from the sea.

Loch Maree, *Highland* (2/2B) Loch Maree in Wester Ross is perhaps rivalled only by LOCH LOMOND and England's Lake Windermere in its beauty (*see overleaf*). It impressed the 7th-century St Maelrubha enough for him to establish a cell on Isle Maree, one of several islands in the loch. In 1877 Queen Victoria came to marvel and a stone with a Gaelic inscription commemorates her visit. On this island are the graves of a Danish princess and her lover still marked by ancient crosses. Loch Maree was the site of iron-smelting activities about three centuries ago. Much of the ore came from neighbouring bogs, though eventually it was imported from other parts of Britain. There are still traces of these old furnaces in the area. Some of the employees were English and near by there is a spot known as Cladh nan Sassunach, the burial ground of the English. The metal produced in the locality was used for swords and armour, for which, with the many clan feuds in progress at the time, there was a big demand.

The BEINN EIGHE National Nature Reserve lies near the south-eastern end of this 12-mile-long loch.

Loch Morar, *Highland* (1/3C) This Inverness-shire loch lies about a quarter of a mile inland from silver-sand-fringed Morar Bay. It is one of Scotland's geological freaks. The deepest loch in Britain, its depth is 987 ft and, though it lies close to the shallow seas to the west of Scotland, there is no other equivalent depth until the Continental Shelf dips into the Atlantic 170 miles north-west between St Kilda and Rockall. Loch Morar is said to be the home of 'Morag', a sister to the Loch Ness monster. Many sightings of a strange beast have been reported over the years. As with 'Nessie', no conclusive evidence has yet been presented to verify its existence.

Lossiemouth, *Grampian* (3/2B) This Moray coast town is really a collection of small, formerly separate villages. The old seatown of Lossiemouth, around the original harbour, was the main port for ELGIN and was founded in 1698. The New Harbour was cut out of solid rock in 1830, to avoid the silting to which the old harbour was subject at the mouth of the river Lossie. During the heyday of the Scottish herring industry in the 19th century, Lossiemouth was

Loch Maree (see p. 159)

one of the big ports in Scotland. From here, in 1879, a new type of sail-driven fishing boat was launched, the *Nonesuch*, the first of her kind. The type was called a Zulu after the colonial South African war which was successfully concluded in the same year. The design of the craft was ideally suited for fishing and became so popular that within four years, there were 3665 Zulus registered in Scotland, ranging from 20 to 80 ft in length. The main feature was a tall mast, made from Norwegian pinewood and trimmed down from a baulk of timber 60 ft long and 2 ft square. In keeping with Lossiemouth's tradition for fishing innovation, the first modern seine-net fishing boat was designed here by a local boatbuilder. The town still relies on fishing for its economic base.

1 Gregory Place, Seatown was the birthplace of James Ramsay MacDonald, Britain's first Labour Prime Minister. He died in 1937 and is buried in Spynie churchyard a few miles inland close by Loch Spynie.

About 1 mile north of Elgin at Spynie is Spynie Palace, the home of the Bishops of Moray. The prominent square tower dates from 1461. It was once one of the largest keeps in Scotland, and illustrates how the bishops were as feudal and as military in character and life style as the temporal lords.

Luss, *Strathclyde* (4/3B) Lying on the western shore of LOCH LOMOND, Luss has earned for itself the title of the prettiest village in Scotland. Its cottages are overgrown with roses which give the place a distinct charm and entice the visitor to leave the car and enjoy a walk around. Luss Church has an impressive interior, with magnificent oak beams setting off a 14th-century effigy of St Kessog, who Christianized the area in the 6th century. When William Wordsworth and his sister toured here last century they were particularly taken with the whole setting provided by the waters and islands of Loch Lomond, with its eastern shores dominated by the beetling heights on the skyline.

Lybster, *Highland* (3/2A) This fishing village has one of the largest harbours on Scotland's north-east coast south of WICK. It began as a wooden pier built in 1810 by a local landowner to help his crofter tenants to earn a little extra from fishing. Some 20 years later the pier was replaced by a large stone-built structure and Lybster went into the fishing charts as the third largest fishing station in Scotland. Prosperity lasted until the herring fishing declined towards the end of the 19th century. Today only a few boats operate commercially from here.

Just north of Lybster is the Hill o' Many Stanes, a fascinating Bronze Age monument consisting of 22 rows of 8 small stones. The monument is thought to date from *c.* 1850 BC and is unique in the far north of Scotland. The low stones are set out in fan-shaped rows running roughly north to south.

A little further to the west are the Camster Cairns, huge burial tombs of the New Stone Age peoples who were the first settler-farmers to arrive in Britain. The larger of two cairns is about 200 ft long and contains an estimated 3000 tons of stone.

Macduff, *Grampian* (3/3B) This Moray Firth fishing port twins with BANFF, just across the river Deveron. It was established in 1783 and given the name MacDuff in place of Doune, the original name of the earlier hamlet here. When the harbours of Banff began to silt up, MacDuff took the initiative and its facilities were developed to such an extent that the town is still an important fishing port. In the middle of the 19th century much of the fish caught was exported direct to the Baltic countries. The economy today is largely based on fishing; a boatbuilding yard operated by successive generations of the same family offers significant employment.

The open-air swimming pools at Tarlair are close to the old Well of Tarlair, a spring of mineral water discovered in 1770 which had an effective purgative property. In its heyday it enjoyed an immense popularity and would still be an attraction had not a wartime mine, washed in on the tide, exploded and destroyed everything. Doune Hill is crowned with an Italian-looking church of 1805.

Despite its being of more recent origin than its rival Banff, MacDuff has succeeded in preserving no fewer than 123 listed buildings of architectural or historic interest, mainly among the fisher cottages in High Shore and Low Shore.

Maes Howe *see* Orkney Islands

Mallaig, *Highland* (1/3C) In 1900 this west of Scotland port was little more than a huddle of houses. Since then it has, by the determined effort of its people, jumped into prominence as one of the main fishing ports on the west coast, and one with a European significance. (*See overleaf*). It is the ferry terminal for the island of SKYE and the Small Isles of the Inner Hebrides, a railway terminus, and is also at the end of the A830(T) from Fort William.

Meigle, *Tayside* (5/2B) This tiny village boasts the Meigle Museum which contains 25 sculptured stones from the 7th to the 10th century, all originally located in the old churchyard. They are magnificent examples of an early Christian art form that incorporated Pictish symbols. The stones indicate a highly cultured people who used a variety of symbols as a kind of code. This is the largest and most notable collection of Dark Age sculpture in western Europe. Further information on sites is available at the museum.

Mey Castle, *Highland* (3/2A) This structure on Scotland's north coast dates from *c.* 1572. It was originally called Barrogill Castle and was used as a seat of the Earls of Caithness. Over the years it fell into disuse until, in 1952, it was bought by the Queen Mother who has carefully restored it to something of its former glory. The castle is of course a private home, but during the year the gardens are open to the public. The area around Mey has always been regarded as the garden land of Caithness and inspired many 18th-century travellers to verse, if not quite to poetry.

Monifieth, *Tayside* (5/3B) A straggling village on the northern shore of the Firth of Tay, Monifieth is in an area that has yielded much evidence of a long occupation. Several Pictish stones have been found (now in the National Museums of Scotland, Queen Street, Edinburgh) and there are a number of sites of archaeological interest.

Montrose, *Tayside* (5/3A) Situated at the mouth of the South Esk river, Montrose has been in existence as a coastal settlement for at least 1000 years. It was important enough in 980 to attract the attention of the marauding Danes, and for King William the Lion (1143–1214) to build a royal castle which was occupied by Edward I of England in 1296 and destroyed by William Wallace, the Scots patriot, the year after. It was in Montrose that Baliol, the Scots king, submitted to Edward I personally after he formally abdicated at BRECHIN, a town inland from Montrose. In 1330 Sir James Douglas, one of King Robert Bruce's most trusted companions throughout the Scottish Wars of Independence, set sail from

Montrose bearing the casket with Bruce's heart to the Holy Land. He reached his destination two years later and was killed in a battle against the Saracens. The casket was found, however, and returned to Scotland, to be buried at Melrose Abbey in the Borders.

In 1534 the first school in Scotland for teaching Greek was built in Montrose, which paved the way for Protestantism in Scotland. The first harbour was built in the Middle Ages, around which were erected shipyards, granaries and warehouses to promote trade across the North Sea with Scandinavia. Fishing came into its own from the 17th century and a century later herring were being exported in large quantities to the Baltic ports, Germany, Holland and France. Today fishing is much less in evidence, though the harbour gives this east coast town a busy cosmopolitan air. The present involvement with North Sea oil gives the visitor the impression that there is no spare time for leisure, there is so much bustle in the town.

There is, however, plenty to see and do in Montrose. The Basin, a tidal lagoon through which the South Esk flows, is now a nature reserve and adds a rather special dimension to the town's aspect. There are few really old buildings, but the Old Town Hall (1763) and the Old Church (1834) in the High Street and Montrose Academy, close to the museum, are worth a look. Sunnyside Royal Hospital (1781) behind the links was the first mental hospital in Scotland.

Mousa *see* Shetland Islands

Muchalls, *Grampian* (3/3C) A 'model' village built in 1865 to replace the ancient hamlet of Stranathra. Many of the cottages have been restored. One of the smaller castles in Scotland, Muchalls was built in about 1620 and rebuilt after a fire in 1746. Its elaborately moulded ceilings are a particularly delightful feature. It is open to the public from May to September.

Muck, *Highland* (1/3C) One of the Hebridean Small Isles, Muck extends to about 1600 acres, with one hill which rises sharply to 451 ft. The island is rather low-lying, on basalt and quite fertile. It has around 24 inhabitants who rely on farming for their survival. If Muck is ever deserted by its residual population it will be the result of a reduction in sea communications (foot ferries sail here from MALLAIG and Arisaig) rather

Nets, Mallaig harbour (see p. 161)

than a hostile environment, for the island is eminently viable and an excellent environment for any community. So far this has held together only through the tenacity and benevolence of private ownership.

Muckle Flugga *see* Shetland Islands

Mull, *Strathclyde* (4/1A) This island of the Inner Hebrides lies off OBAN at the seaward end of the Firth of Lorn. It can be reached by car ferry from Oban or LOCHALINE. Mull is large and peninsulated, so much so that its coastline is over 300 miles in length. Its ground rock is largely basalt, though at Carsaig, on the Ross of Mull, there is a chalk layer beneath which is an expanse of lias constantly washed by lime-laden water. It is one of only two places in the West Highlands where watercress grows in a stream as it does in the chalk streams of southern England. Mull boasts one respectable mountain, Ben Mor (3171 ft), with a number of companions whose heights rising above the rolling moorland and hilly areas add an extra dimension of visual interest.

The first inhabitants have left many stones, cairns and circles scattered all over the island. Crannogs (lake dwellings built on wooden stilts) can be seen in a number of lochs (Ba, Assapol, Frisa and Sguabain). In later centuries forts and duns were built and still survive to tell the tale, though now in a ruinous state. Early Christian and medieval chapels tell the story of the missionaries from IONA, off the Ross of Mull, after St Columba established that island as his base of light and peace. Duart, 12th century (open to the public May to September), and Aros Castle, 14th century (open to the public but only a fragment), remind us of the period of the Lords of the Isles. The former, with the exception of a short period, has always been the home of the chiefs of the Clan MacLean, and has seen much bloody history as the result.

Tobermory is the chief town on Mull. It fronts onto a small bay, on the seabed of which lies the wreck of the *Florida*, a Spanish Armada galleon, still the target of treasure hunters. Founded as a fishing port in 1788, it struggled to perform this role until the railhead came to Oban, when stagnation set in. It is now mainly a tourist attraction, though some fishing boats still use the harbour (*see pp. 66–7*).

At Ardmeanach, for those who can endure the difficulties of a long hard walk over mud, rock and bog, there is a geological wonder: implanted in the cliff face is a high fossil tree, engulfed by a

lava flow some 50 million years ago. It is one of the most spectacular of Scotland's geological phenomena.

At Grulin is the mausoleum of General Lachlan MacQuarrie, the 'Father of Australia'. He was born on the offshore island of Ulva from where the ancestors of Scots missionary David Livingstone also came.

Mull of Kintyre, *Strathclyde* (4/2C) Now made famous by pop singer Paul MacCartney, who has a house on the Mull, this long finger of land has much of the remoteness associated with a Hebridean island. It is, however, less of a crofting area; rather it is a district of small and medium-sized farms concentrating on the production of grass, potatoes and turnips, and with livestock husbandry. At Machrihanish there are deposits of coal, worked until 1967, which, with BRORA in Sutherland, were the only commercial coal operations in the Scottish Highlands. Historical records show the coal was worked in the Machrihanish district from the 15th century.

There are a number of places on Mull of archaeological and historical interest. At Saddell are the scanty relics of the Abbey founded before 1207. Although little remains there are several sculptured tombstones to be seen, carved in Argyll between 1300 and 1560. They portray warriors in pointed helmets and armour against a background of weapons, foliage, deer and war galleys.

Near Southend, a little holiday resort with sandy beaches, is a ruined chapel; it stands at Keil Point, supposed to be the place where St Columba first set foot on Scottish soil. The caves below the Point contain a slab with the prints of two right feet incised into the rock, known as 'St Columba's Footsteps', but they may in fact be as much as 3000 years old.

Muthill, *Tayside* (5/1B) A small village which has altered little since the early 19th century and is now identified as an area of outstanding interest worthy of conservation. Its history goes back to the early Iron Age settlement near by. Much later, in the 12th century, came church buildings to which an Abbey School was attached with a significant reputation for the teaching of music and the skills required by persuasive preachers. Muthill Church, now ruined, dates mainly from the 15th century but incorporates part of an earlier 12th-century square tower. The church

was in use until 1818. In the graveyard are many interesting stones bearing the carved traditional symbols of the trades once carried out in the area. At one time Muthill was heavily involved in the growing and weaving of flax. A reminder of this activity is the Dog's Head Well, where the cloth was washed and bleached.

Near by is Drummond Castle, incorporating part of a 15th-century structure which was attacked by Cromwell's troops in 1650. It also suffered the attentions of the Jacobites in the 1745 Rebellion. The gardens have, however, been well preserved and developed. Two features are a multiple sundial dated 1630 and a very attractive formal Italian garden. (The gardens only are open to the public.)

Nairn, *Highland* (3/1B) This royal burgh is a popular holiday resort, enjoying in north-east Scotland a climate that is one of the sunniest and driest in Britain, rivalling that on the Cornish Riviera. It has a remarkable stretch of coast with sand and shingle beaches and offers a championship golf course among its tourist attractions.

Established as an important commercial settlement in the 12th century, Nairn was the seat of the Thane of Cawdor, whose great castle has long disappeared. However, a latter-day witness to the town's significance can be seen about three miles south in the ruins of the early 14th-century Rait Castle, on a site that commands views over the Moray Firth. The substantial ruins reveal a unique ecclesiastical architecture discerned in the unusual windows, which once lit the first-floor banqueting hall.

Nairn was the centre of a flourishing fishing industry in the 19th century. The old Fishertown has a very different atmosphere and appearance, with tiny houses huddling together for comfort in a rather haphazard fashion. The more prosperous fishermen moved into substantial villas at the east end of Nairn at the beginning of this century. The Fishertown Museum on King Street has an exhibition devoted to this former activity.

Shortly after he ascended to the throne of Britain in 1603, King James VI of Scotland and I of England boasted that he had a town in his northern kingdom 'sae lang that the inhabitants at one end didna understand the language spoken at the other'. This was Nairn where, it is claimed, the Highland Line intersects the High Street: Gaelic was spoken by the people on one side and English on the other. Gaelic is rarely heard today.

Opposite: Millstone on Mull

Overleaf: Tobermory harbour, Mull (see p. 163)

The harbour was built in 1820 by Thomas Telford, but it is now mainly used by pleasure craft.

Colonel James Grant was born here in 1827. In 1860–3 he accompanied the explorer John Speke in his search for the source of the river Nile.

Newtonmore, *Highland* (5/1A) The origins of Newtonmore on the river Spey are obscure but it is supposed that its first permanent settlers were connected with cattle droving. The low arable ground in the vicinity of the present golf course is where the cattle, after being brought over the CORRIEYAIRACK PASS from FORT AUGUSTUS and the west of Scotland, were herded together before being taken south to the markets at Falkirk and CRIEFF.

A rather quiet village with a clean and refreshing aspect, it houses the Clan MacPherson Museum, devoted to the relics and history of that clan and proudly showing off the Bratach Uaine, the Green Banner, under which the MacPhersons never knew defeat in their battles. Among the exhibits is a massive silver epergne depicting an incident in the life of Cluny MacPherson during the Forty-five Jacobite Rising, and the broken fiddle of James MacPherson, the freebooter hanged in BANFF in 1701.

North Queensferry, *Fife* (5/2C) This little village lies under the towering girders of the Forth Railway Bridge (1890) which heralded the end of some 800 years of acting as a royally approved and regular ferry service between Lothian and Fife. The real end came when the Forth Road Bridge was opened in 1964. Down but not out, the people of North Queensferry have revamped their village into a thriving marina for small boats.

North Ronaldsay *see* Orkney Islands

North Uist, *Western Isles* (1/1B) This island displays many of the topographical features of its Outer Hebridean neighbours, with the eastern coast riven by long sea lochs while the western side is flat and fertile. There is much evidence on show to indicate human occupation stretching back some 4000 years: many standing stones, stone circles and chambered cairns, and at Eilean an Tighe in Loch nan Geireann the remains of a Neolithic pottery workshop, the oldest recorded example of its kind in Europe. The pottery found

Tossing the caber, Newtonmore (Scottish Tourist Board)

at this site is of a very high quality, and in such quantity that nothing less than a pottery factory must have existed here to supply the needs of the island and its neighbours.

Of particular importance is Trinity Temple at Carinish, founded *c.* 1200, in its time something of a Celtic university where Highland chiefs sent their sons to study Latin and the law. A programme of excavation near Sollas township has revealed many layers of human occupation, with interesting and unique finds from Viking times. The main settlement is Lochmaddy which acts as the port of call for the car ferry from HARRIS and SKYE. In the 17th century it saw some activity as a fishing station, part of the fishery schemes of Charles I. This died the death until the middle of the 19th century, when the herring industry created boom conditions for some decades.

See also Benbecula; South Uist

Oban, *Strathclyde* (4/2A) The chief town of Argyll, Oban nestles snugly in the bay from which it takes its name (Oban is Gaelic for 'little bay'), and is sheltered by the island of Kerrera. Its harbour, one of the best on the West Highland coast, serves not only the local fishing fleet, but is the ferry link for the islands of both the Inner and Outer Hebrides. Oban's setting is more than just functional: it is almost an environment, and as such has proved to be a strong attraction to both the tourist and those who wish to spend their retirement days in an invigorating climate. The Oban hinterland is criss-crossed by the roads that serve the communities in the district of Lorn.

The plan of Oban suggests a far-from-formal approach. Few of its streets run according to that monotonous grid system which unimaginative town planners have too often accepted as the easiest way of providing a town with footpaths and roads. Oban displays an almost offhand preference for the ever-changing vista. Roads curve, dive round bends, run back on each other, short-circuit fine sweeps and present the traveller on foot with a continuous and ever-changing feast for the eye. As it is, Oban can be described as a well-preserved, clean and proud Victorian town.

It is more than this, however, for the burgh stands on a site that has had a period of continuous occupation estimated at some 8000 years. Towards the latter part of the 19th century, when the town was expanding, workmen uncovered seven caves in a stretch of low cliff where the present George Street runs north to south. There were found the remains of Azilian Man (6000 BC), a Stone Age people who had migrated from the Continent to Britain after Britain had become an island.

From a small settlement in medieval times, Oban's real period of growth began in the early years of the 19th century as shipbuilding took root and as farming developed in the hinterland. It was created a burgh in 1801, after which piers were built to cater for steamboats from the Clyde coast. Its status was further enhanced with the arrival of the railway from Glasgow in 1880. Economic activities today include tweed-cloth weaving, fishing, glassware and tourism.

McCaig's Folly, inspired by the Colosseum in Rome and the desire to provide work for unemployed masons, dates from the 1890s and dominates the town.

Dunollie Castle ruins, to the west of Oban's marvellous esplanade, are of considerable historical interest. The castle was the ancient stronghold of the MacDougalls, the Lords of Lorn, who were barons so powerful that they once laid claim to a third of Scotland's territory. In the days before Scotland became a single kingdom, they were hereditary enemies of King Robert Bruce.

About four miles north of Oban is Dunstaffnage Castle, originally the property of the MacDougalls but given the status of a royal castle by King Robert Bruce. It was to this place that the incoming Scots, in their wandering from Ireland, brought the famous Stone of Destiny, which now lies under the Coronation Chair in Westminster Abbey in London. The castle dates from the 13th century, with a contrasting 17th-century towerhouse above its entrance. The adjacent ruined chapel is the burial place of the Campbells of Dunstaffnage.

To the north of Oban is the 18-mile-long arm of Loch Etive offering a wide variety of scenery. The loch, though connected to the sea, is almost tideless, the effect of the cataract at the Falls of Lora at Connel where the waters are crossed by a large cantilever bridge. Connel Church is a much reduced copy of Iona Cathedral. The loch and its glen are associated in Scotland's prehistory with Deirdre of the Sorrows.

She was the loveliest woman in Gaeldom and as such attracted the unwanted attentions of the King of Ireland. She, on the other hand, had no love for anyone but Naoise with whom she escaped to Scotland and Glen Etive. The King sent for them, saying that all was forgiven. Deirdre, however, suspected treachery, foretelling a bloody tragedy if they returned. But return they did, and the manner of their deaths became in time enshrined in the great stories of Celtic mythology.

Old Man of Stoer, *Highland* (2/2A) This is one of Scotland's family of old men: pinnacles of rock standing sheer out of the sea. The Old Man of Stoer is off Stoer Point, on the north-west coast of Sutherland, and rises 200 ft. For many decades it was declared unclimbable until 1966 when Dr Tom Patey and Brian Robertson scaled the mass to breach the Old Man's privacy.

Oldmeldrum, *Grampian* (3/3C) Created a burgh of barony in 1672, this town was the main settlement in the district until it was superseded by INVERURIE. Though much development has taken place, the town still has the irregular plan of a medieval market town, with narrow streets and the houses displaying typical Scottish vernacular architectural details. The market square, with its fine Town Hall (1877), is now a conservation area.

A little to the east is Pitmedden Garden (*overleaf*), a 17th-century 'great garden' laid out in 1675 and re-created by the National Trust for Scotland. It is the centrepiece of some 100 acres of woodland and farmland.

About 5 miles or so north from Oldmeldrum lies Haddo House in undulating wooded grounds that might be mistaken for Sussex. Built in 1731 by William Adam as a Palladian mansion for the 2nd Earl of Aberdeen, the building is in the care of the National Trust for Scotland. Its internal splendour makes it a perfect setting for its role as an important musicmaking centre in the northeast. Many eminent musicians present recitals, operas and concerts organized by the Haddo Choral Society.

On the road going east towards ELLON is Tolquhon Castle, a late 16th-century conversion of a square mansion – albeit fortified – built by a laird of culture and taste. Though now ruined, there is still much to see that reflects life in bygone times including kitchens, a brewhouse and a cellar with hooks for hanging prisoners (or meat!). In the church at nearby Tarves can be seen the elaborate tomb of the laird, designed and built by Thomas Leiper, the master mason responsible for much of the castle structure.

Ord of Caithness, *Highland* (3/1B) This is a bold solid granite promontory overlooking the Moray

Opposite: Haddo House, near Oldmeldrum. (Above) The Pheasantry; (below) view of the house from the garden

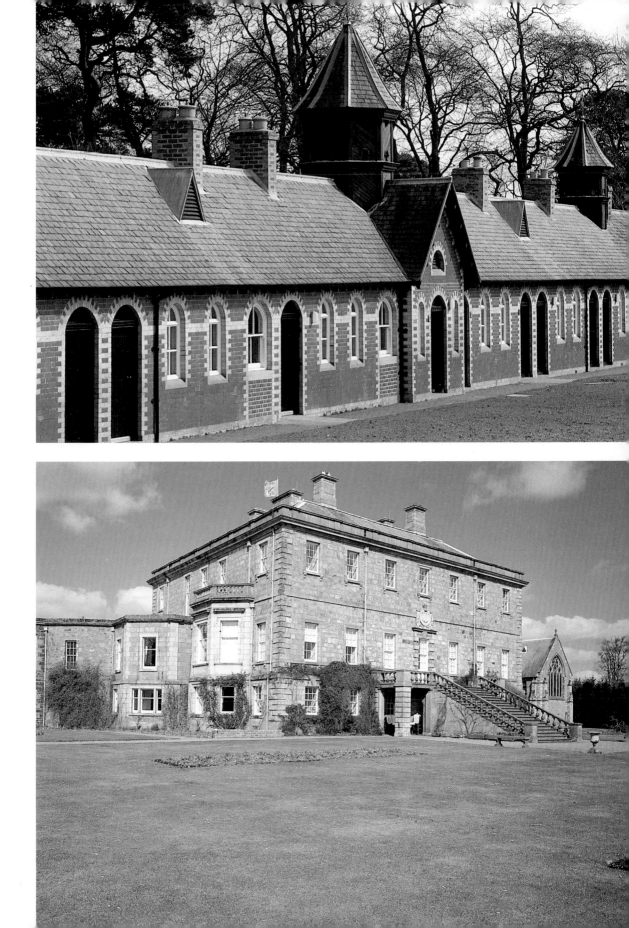

Firth; across its eastern end the A9(T), the main road from the south, snakes its way into Caithness. A comment of an early 18th-century traveller reads: '. . . the Ord of Caithness had been represented to me by many in so frightful a Shape, that I longed much to see it, and when I came to it, my imagination had far outshot Reality; for I rode up every inch of it, a thing rarely done by any Persons, and all along looked down ye dreadful precipice to the Sea, on the Right Hand, of some Hundred Fathoms from the edge of the Road down to the Sea, and frequently perpendicular . . .' Happily the new road looks down on the old road overhanging the sea and gripping the cliff edge for its very survival. It was always considered unlucky for a Caithness Sinclair to cross the Ord on a Monday, ever since a large party of armed men went south to fight at the Battle of Flodden (1513), from which none of them returned.

Orkney Islands (3/2B) The Orkney group of islands, separated from the Scottish mainland by the turbulent waters of the Pentland Firth, total some 70, of which about one-third are still occupied, though many more were inhabited over the centuries as the ruins of deserted dwellings indicate. In general, the land is fertile and has thus offered the islanders a two-pronged economic advantage, with the sea providing an excellent source of income and employment. In sharp contrast with, say, the SHETLAND ISLANDS and the Outer Hebrides, those who work on the land tend more to be farmers than crofters. Indeed, Orkney's many green, lush fields often stretch to the very edge of precipitous cliffs or encroach on to sandy beaches. That these islands have attracted people for thousands of years is evidenced by the fact that there are said to be three sites of historical interest to every square mile. Neolithic relics and ruins are more numerous and better preserved here than anywhere in the British Isles.

The prevailing historical ambience of the Orkney islands is Norse, reflecting the colonization from the 8th century onwards by Vikings and farmers from Scandinavia. The islands came under Scottish rule only in 1468, when they were pledged to the Scottish Crown in a marriage settlement. Not that this made any difference to the cultural heritage and integrity of the islanders. The rhythm and syncopations of island life and living owe more to Scandinavia than to

Scotland, which has given the islanders a healthy outward-looking attitude towards the many problems now associated with living on any of the Scottish island groups.

One aspect of Orkney independence is shown by the fact that, whereas elsewhere in Britain the seashore belongs to the Crown, in Orkney the coastal land is owned by the islanders as far as the low-tide mark, a relic of the old Norse udal mode of land tenure that dates from before the feudal system. Freshwater fishing is also free, thanks to the udal tradition and residual Norse law that still obtains in these islands.

Orkney culture extends into the everyday language, which is English heavily larded with words and phrases – often of Norse origin – that require the visitor to have the ears well tuned, which can take a day or two. But this is no real disadvantage to anyone who desires to visit a part of the British Isles which is 'different' in so many ways. The concern of the Orkney people to maintain their community as a cohesive whole is seen in one aspect: the comprehensive network of sea lanes and air routes, which ensures that no island community is remote from the hub of things in Kirkwall, the capital (*see below*). Call this aggressive independence, if you like, but it is at the very foundation of a concern for a community to keep itself intact and maintain its distinctive identity in a world that tends increasingly to require conformity to norms.

Egilsay is a small island that has both historical and ecclesiastical significance. It was here in 1116 that Jarl Magnus was murdered – or, in the context of his subsequent elevation to sainthood, martyred. A cenotaph marks the site of this event. St Magnus Church, *c*. 12th century, is today roofless but otherwise in a fine state of preservation. Its high round tower is unique in Scotland. The church was in regular use until last century.

Jarl (Earl) Magnus was a grandson of Thorfinn the Mighty, a Norse king whose dominion included the Hebrides, a large part of Scotland and a realm in Ireland. In the early 12th century, Magnus was one of two jointly ruling earls, respected for his humane approach to his fellows. But this was not a factor considered by his co-earl, Haakon, who suggested a meeting on Egilsay to discuss matters of common interest. Magnus was killed and greatly missed by the people of Orkney. His nephew, Rognvald, reflected Magnus' lifestyle in being both cultured and humane. He founded St Magnus Cathedral in Kirkwall (*see overleaf*) in memory of his uncle.

Pitmeddem Garden, near Oldmeldrum (see p. 170)

Hoy (3/2B) This island is famed for its isolated red sandstone rock stack, The Old May of Hoy, which stands as high as St Paul's Cathedral in London: 450 ft. Hoy itself is heather-covered and hilly and is quite unlike the rest of Orkney. On the Atlantic side of the island are the highest perpendicular cliffs in Britain, rising to 1140 ft from the sea, at St John's Head. Behind this headland lies the ruined hamlet of Rackwick, once a thriving crofting community and now a mere visual memory striking a responsive chord from the past. The Dwarfie Stane on the island of Hoy is a Stone Age rock tomb, with a corridor and two chambers carved out of the solid stone; it is the only example of its kind in Britain. Hoy has two Martello towers, at Crockness and Hackness. Unlike those built in the south of England, to warn against the approach of Napoleon's ships, these were built as a defence against American privateers.

Kirkwall (3/2B) This is the capital of Orkney. It was founded by the Norsemen and remains one of the best-preserved medieval towns in Scotland. It is dominated by the red sandstone of St Magnus Cathedral, founded in 1137 by Rognvald, the nephew of Earl Magnus. Both men, saint and founder, are buried in the cathedral: the axe wound in the skull of Magnus corresponds exactly with the account of his death in the *Orkneyinga Saga*. The building is not owned by any religious assembly but belongs, by a 1486 Royal charter, to the citizens of Kirkwall.

Two other buildings in Kirkwall are of particular interest. The Bishop's Palace was built in the 16th century on top of an earlier 12th-century structure and is open all the year round. It was here that King Haakon IV of Norway died after his disastrous defeat by the Scots at the Battle of Largs in 1263. Just across the road is the Earl's Palace, built by the infamous Earl Patrick Stewart by forced labour c. 1607. The magnificent great hall is in keeping with the luxurious lifestyle which the earl enjoyed before he was, for his oppressive rule of the islanders, placed on trial and executed in Edinburgh. It is said of Earl Patrick that he was so ignorant that he 'could scarce rehearse the Lord's Prayer' and thus had his execution stayed for a week until he could 'better inform himelf'. It is open to the public.

Kirkwall has always been the main town of the Orkneys, though for a time its importance was taken over by Stromness (*see below*). The present harbour was built in the 1850s. During the 18th and 19th centuries huge quantities of grain were exported to the West Highlands, Ireland, Nor-way, the Netherlands, and even as far as Spain. Facing the harbour is a 17th-century granary in which taxes, called 'skatts', were collected and paid in grain.

A number of Kirkwall's old houses still survive to echo former times, along with narrow, twisting streets snaking up to the cathedral, all of which adds an extra dimension of interest to an intriguing scene. The town's main thoroughfare is known simply as 'The Street'. Tankerness House is a restored 17th-century merchant's dwelling, now a museum with some four millennia of Orkney life and living on display.

Kirkwall today is a base for a large fishing fleet, landing whitefish and lobsters, and a port for passenger ferries to ABERDEEN and the Shetland Islands.

Maes Howe (3/2B) This huge Stone Age chambered cairn lies near the A965 on Mainland. It is massive by any standard being 24 ft high and over 300 ft in circumference. A low narrow passage leads into a large chamber, off which are open burial cells, each floored and roofed by single stones. Some of the stones here weigh well over two tons each. Around AD 1150 the Norseman left evidence of their presence in the form of runic inscriptions. Some were carved by Crusaders thought to have been members of Earl Rognvald's Christian expedition to the Holy Land which stopped off at Orkney on their way south. One intriguing inscription indicates that some of the tomb's treasure was removed and hidden to the north-west of Maes Howe. There are 14 personal names and some animal figures among the incised inscriptions, the largest collection of runic characters to be found in any one place in the world. The sun shines into the passageway only during the winter solstice.

North Ronaldsay (3/3A) This is the most northerly island of Orkney. The fertile central area is surrounded by a stone wall, outside which the small native sheep live almost entirely on the local seaweed. The sheep are among the dwindling number of rare breeds of animals in the British Isles. Because of their peculiar and rather distinctive diet, and fears that the animals might become victims of oil pollution from the sea, a number are now kept in England to ensure that, should such a disaster occur, some of the breed's genes might survive for posterity.

Sanday (3/2A) On this island is the Quoyness chambered tomb, dating from c. 2900 BC, with an elongated central chamber and more cells than Maes Howe (*see above*). The island is a favourite resting place for terns and rare migrant birds.

Scapa Flow (3/2B) is a large protected sea area that has earned its name in British history as an important naval base in both world wars. It contains Flotta, now an oil tanker terminal and landfall for undersea pipelines from the oilfields of the North Sea to the east. Scapa saw some 74 warships, the greater part of the German fleet, brought here and either beached by their crews or scuttled in June 1919 on the orders of Rear-Admiral Ludwig von Reuter. Many of the ships have since been salvaged. Others remain as an attractive underwater prey for divers on the hunt for souvenirs or just to satisfy curiosity. In the Second World War, huge convoys of ships gathered here before being escorted across the seas to Russia and to America.

In an attempt to close off the eastern approaches to Scapa Flow, the massive Churchill Barriers were erected in the 1940s, mainly by Italian prisoners of war. A reminder of their stay in Orkney is seen on the little island of Lamb Holm where, inside two Nissen huts, the Italians constructed a beautiful chapel, using scrap materials with a high degree of ingenuity. The chapel was rededicated in 1960 when the designer, Domenico Chiocchetti, a gifted artist, returned to restore some of his paintings.

Skara Brae (3/2B) A celebrated archaeological site on Mainland, near the B9056. It is a 4000-year-old Neolithic village completely buried under sand for nearly two millennia until a violent storm uncovered its existence in 1850. It is a remarkable settlement with much of its original 'furnishings' remaining intact: stone bed frames, shellfish tanks, hearths and primitive furniture all fashioned from stone. Some 10 houses and a workshop comprise this prehistoric village which is easily the best-preserved of its kind in Europe. Close by Skara Brae are the Standing Stones of Stenness and the Ring of Brogar, known as the 'Circle of the Sun'. The former are a henge monument of which only four stones now remain upright. The latter is a great ring of stones, of which 27 out of a possible original 60 stand as a witness to the intense lifestyle of the folk who lived here in the ancient past.

Stromness (3/2B) Situated in the west of Mainland, this is the second largest town of Orkney after Kirkwall (*see above*). It began its existence in a small way, offering shelter for French and Spanish ships sailing to the New World. In 1670 there were only 13 houses, but during the following century Stromness expanded and prospered as the result of increased trade. When the Hudson's Bay Company began its operations in

Canada, the town became its British base for the stocking and preparation of ships before their voyage across the Atlantic. Around 1760 Stromness had also became a supply base for whaling ships bound for the Davis Straits and northern Atlantic and Arctic waters. The piers once provided the Stromness inshore fishermen with space to make and mend their nets, bait lines and shelter their boats from the winter storms. The town is the ferry terminal for the passage across the Pentland Firth from SCRABSTER in Caithness. The fishing industry provides a steady income for Stromness, with many sites in the town echoing the past relations with the sea.

Much of the charm of Stromness lies in the many stone-built piers, stairs and slipways which support the houses on one side of the mile-long narrow main street. In the early part of the 18th century the infamous pirate John Gow lived in Stromness. He left his native town as a young man and returned several years later in a ship under his command. But the pride of the townspeople was dashed when they discovered that Gow and his crew had mutinied and murdered their officers, which made them pirates. The truth being out, Gow and his companions made off but were shipwrecked on the Calf of Eday.

Stronsay (3/2B) A flat and fertile island. Evidence of past inhabitants is seen in the Lamb Head broch close by, a formation running into the sea that some used to think was an old Norse pier. Towards the end of last century Stronsay made the headlines with the 'Stronsay Beast'. Though history has since shown that the remains found on the island's shore were those of a large basking shark, at the time it created a heated debate among scholars in London and Edinburgh, who, as might be expected, agreed to disagree on the origins of the beast. As early as 1319, Stronsay was a fishing community, which industry the islanders still practise.

Westray (3/2A) The main feature of this island is Noltland Castle, reconstructed by Gilbert Balfour, who was Master to the Household of Mary, Queen of Scots. It was burned by the Covenanters in 1650. The castle, one of the earliest of the Z-plan type, is notable for its over-provision for artillery defence. The ruins of two ancient churches, Holy Cross (12th century) and St Mary's (13th century) are part of the numerous religious settlements erected in the Orkneys soon after the Norsemen adopted Christianity, for political rather than religious reasons at first. To the north-west of the island is the Gentlemen's

Elcho Castle, near Perth

Cave, where a number of fugitive Jacobites hid after the disastrous battle of Culloden in 1746. A large cemetery of Viking graves was discovered in the sand dunes during the 19th century near the village of Pierowall, which was once the Vikings' second harbour in Orkney after Kirkwall (*see p. 174*).

Oronsay *see* Colonsay

Out Skerries *see* Shetland Islands

Papa Stour *see* Shetland Islands

Pennan, *Grampian* (3/3B) Though perhaps the smallest village in this book, Pennan merits a mention because it is one of the most picturesque fishing villages on Scotland's north-east coast. The cliffs here are of red sandstone and the village is at the end of a steep zigzag road (B9031) its cottages backed on to a sheer wall of rock 100 ft high. Like Crovie, just round Troup Head to the west, Pennan is an example of the kind of grim determination demonstrated by the human species in finding a most unlikely place to settle and making things work.

Perth, *Tayside* (5/2B) The 'Fair City' was once the capital of Scotland, though little of this ancient association now remains. Much was destroyed in the 16th century during the turbulent times of religious division in Scotland, promoted by the fiery preaching of the reformer John Knox in St John's Kirk in 1559. Even so, recent archaeological digs have revealed at least 1500 years of continuous occupation. Some parts of the city have rather a hang-dog look, the result of civic neglect; but, strangely, this aspect has its own kind of fascination, an atmosphere that conjures up something of the past.

St John's Kirk stands at the heart of the history of Perth. The record of its early foundations begins in 1126 when David I granted it with its tithes and parsonage to the Abbey of DUN-FERMLINE, the burial place of his parents, Malcolm Canmore and Queen Margaret. The complete fabric was consecrated in 1242. In the intervening years, the building saw much damage, but was completely restored in 1928, and a carillon was placed in the Gothic tower ten years later.

Perth today contains good measures of all the elements that go to make up a well-balanced economic settlement: industry, theatre, and recreational facilities, with the agriculture of the hinterland using Perth as a focal point. In particular the annual pedigree cattle sales are world-famous, with buyers coming from South America to replenish their stocks. Other industrial activities include whisky distilling, and Perth's impressive dyework mill is a reminder of the forward-looking Sir John Pullar who exploited the commercial possibilities of the first aniline dyestuff, known as 'Perkin's Mauve', in the last century.

Straddling as it does both banks of the river Tay, Perth is in an outstanding scenic situation, and in the past the city fathers exploited every natural advantage in their efforts to make Perth a city to be proud of. For example, the Salutation Hotel, dating from 1699, is the oldest-established building of its kind in Scotland; and the Fair Maid's House is an attractive medieval structure made famous in the novel of the same name by Sir Walter Scott. The Round House was the first Perth city waterworks built in 1832 and was restored in 1974 to act as a tourist information centre.

Standing to the north of the Perth to CRIEFF road is one of Scotland's most historic castles: Huntingtower. Its two main towers, dating from the 15th century, are joined by a late 17th-century building. The castle was the scene of an attempt, in 1582, by some Scottish earls to take over the Scottish throne from King James VI, then only a youth of 16 years. The earls' ascendancy lasted only some months and they paid the price for their ambitions by being beheaded.

About 3 miles south-east of Perth stands Elcho Castle (c. 1530) on the site of an older building which was once used by William Wallace as a hiding place.

Peterculter, *Grampian* (3/3C) This village derives its name from an old chapel dedicated to St Peter, on the north side of the river Dee, though some claim that the 'culter' element (pronounced 'cooter') comes from the Gaelic *cuilter*, meaning 'back land'. The area on the other side of the river is known as Maryculter, from the chapel (now ruined) founded by the Knights Templar in 1187 on lands granted to them by King William the Lion of Scotland. Before that, this district was known to the Romans who had a camp here. To the east is Blairs College, a Roman Catholic foundation of 1827 for the training of priests. There are many treasures here, including a Papal Bull issued by Pope Alexander III to the monastery of Ratisbon, once staffed by Scots monks. Present-day Ratisbon is Regensburg in Bavaria and is, appropriately, ABERDEEN's 'twin' city.

Peterhead, *Grampian* (3/3C) After ABERDEEN, Peterhead is the largest town in Scotland's north-east region. Yet Peterhead's origins date back only to 1593, when the small village of Peter Ugie was founded on the island promontory of Keith Inch, on lands ceded at the time of the Reformation by the Abbey of Deer. Small it might have been, but the political influence of its founder, George Keith, the great 5th Earl Marischal of Scotland, who also founded Marischal College in Aberdeen, brought it burgh status at once. From then Peterhead has never looked back except, with some justifiable pride, to its past.

Peterhead's first harbour was built in 1593 and took advantage of the shelter provided by the long rocky islet of Keith Inch, now joined to the mainland by a fine new area of reclaimed land, which provides a breakwater and creates a natural and safe anchorage. It was a popular place for Dutch fishing boats during the 17th century; they even tried to buy Keith Inch as a depot. By the late 18th century the harbour had fallen into disrepair and work was begun in 1775 to re-create the facility, finished by Thomas Telford in 1822. Improvements since then have made Peterhead one of the most important ports on Scotland's east coast. In the 19th century whaling brought much prosperity. When that industry faded, the port assumed significance for the Scottish herring fishing fleet. And when that activity failed, white-fish landings made Peterhead what it is today: the foremost fishing port in the whole of Europe. Add to that its proximity to the North Sea oil industry and you need only walk round the harbour to sense the atmosphere of 'boomtown' bustle, which fortunately has not destroyed much of Peterhead's firm grasp of its history.

Many of its red granite houses reflect the period in the 18th century when Peterhead was far-famed as a health spa. The Town House (1788) overlooks the statue of James Keith (1696–1758), who became a Field Marshal of Prussia; it is a replica of the similar memorial in Potsdam and was presented to the town in 1868 by Wilhelm I of Prussia. At the foot of Broad Street is the square parish church of 1804 with an

Overleaf: Inverewe Gardens, Poolewe

attractive slender steeple. The Arbuthnot Museum, St Peter's Street, is devoted to the whaling period of Peterhead's history, among other displays. To the south of the town stands the ruins of the pre-Reformation Kirk which stands on the site of an earlier religious building attached to the Monastery of Deer. The chancel arch is of architectural note.

Pitlochry, *Tayside* (5/1A) Boasting a claim to be the geographical centre of Scotland, Pitlochry has exploited its setting in a quite dramatic and varied scenery to become a great attraction for the holidaymakers who swell the population in the summer months. Its tourist face is clean, well-appointed and attractive. Even the nearby Tummel–Garry hydroelectric scheme is given a tourist function. Thus the reservoir, Loch Faskally, created from the river Tummel in 1950, offers watersports (*see p. 11*) and the Fish Pass is a popular venue for those who wish to see salmon making their way to their spawning grounds.

The now well-established Pitlochry Festival Theatre, founded in 1951, began life literally in a tent and now offers a wide range of drama all the year round in a more permanent building. It is one of the prime examples of an arts enterprise that started as a sheer act of faith and achieved a dramatic reality.

Pittenweem, *Fife* (5/3B) Unlike many of its neighbours on the southern Fife coast, Pittenweem has maintained its importance as a fishing centre and is today the busy home port for the East Neuk fleet. Created a royal burgh in 1542 to foster trading links with the Low Countries and the free ports of the Baltic, Pittenweem has always depended on the sea for its prosperity. At the eastern end of the harbour, built in 1830, is a group of restored 16th-century houses called The Gyles. They and other buildings in the town, with Flemish gables and designs, reflect the style of the merchant class and their penchant for the up-market living of their time.

The parish church has a tower dated 1588 which was once a prison. More spectacular is St Fillan's Cave in Cove Wynd, where it is believed the 7th-century saint lived. The large cave, with a tiny well and dramatic stone staircase, was rededicated in 1935 and is still occasionally used for worship.

Pluscarden Abbey, *Grampian* (3/1B) In the year 1230 Alexander II of Scots sent to France for monks from Val des Choux in Burgundy and granted them land for a priory at Pluscarden, 3 miles south-west of ELGIN. The Order, the Valliscaulins, prospered until 1454, when the abbey became Benedictine. After the Reformation, the abbey escaped the destructive attention of zealots and was simply allowed to fall into disuse, though the monks continued to live there. In 1943 the abbey and its land was given to the Benedictine community at Prinknash, in Devon, who then continued the restoration work begun by the donor, Lord Calum Crichton-Stuart. In 1974 Pluscarden achieved abbey status again.

The abbey lies in a sheltered valley, a fitting place for both solitude and the hard work of restoration carried out by the monks. As well as the original frescoes the building has some magnificent modern stained glass.

Poolewe, *Highland* (2/2B) This attractive little Highland village at the head of Loch Ewe, where the river enters it after flowing across the neck of land from LOCH MAREE, owes its fame to the nearby **Inverewe Gardens** (*see pp. 178–9*). In the 1860s Osgood Mackenzie came into possession of a small estate which included Am Ploc Ard ('the High Lump'), a piece of bleak desolate peat-covered land, its only vegetation heather, crowberry and two dwarf willow trees. Mackenzie had a love of nature and, aware that the district had a mild winter climate due to the influence of the Gulf Stream which sends warm water round the shores of the West Highlands, he decided to establish a garden. This vision presented a number of practical problems, but he persevered by planting shelter trees and bushes. He commented: 'For four or five years my poor peninsula looked miserable, but at last we could see some bright specks appearing above the heather.' These were the pine trees, which required another 20 years of growing before they were able to offer the necessary shelter for the exotic plants that Mackenzie wanted in his garden.

The end result can be seen today, a tribute to a man who disregarded failure and realized the impossible: a garden chock-full with trees, plants and shrubs which give pleasure to the more than 100,000 visitors annually who journey to Inverewe. Now in the care of the National Trust for Scotland, it is essentially a spring garden, best visited in late May or early June when the magnificent rhododendrons are at their peak. But other splendid sights can be seen at other times during the year.

Inverewe Gardens were no rich man's folly. The work for local people employed by Mac-

Portsoy

kenzie helped them to stave off bad times. In fact there were no clearances of people off the land in the GAIRLOCH area. On the contrary, the Mackenzie family subsidized the fishing industry by buying wood for local boats and guaranteeing sale money for catches.

Portessie, *Grampian* (3/2B) This fishing village on the Moray Firth coast was founded by a local landowner in 1727 and given the name Port Easy, which was corrupted into Portessie. The choice as a fishing station is rather surprising because there was never a harbour here and boats had to be dragged up the beach at a spot where there is a natural small bay. Essentially, Portessie is a suburb of its larger neighbour, BUCKIE, but still retains a strong sense of identity and individuality. The houses are generally at right angles to the sea as protection from the winter gales.

Portknockie, *Grampian* (3/2B) A fishing village on the Moray Firth coast founded in 1677 by emigrant fishermen from nearby CULLEN who took advantage of its natural harbour sheltered by Greencastle Hill to the north. This same hill has yielded evidence of an Iron Age fortification which occupied the promontory in prehistoric times.

Portknockie is made up of parallel rows of neat stone cottages, most of them Victorian and substantial, reflecting the former times of prosperity when the herring industry was booming in many other places on the east and north-east coasts of Scotland. The development of the village can be seen, from the cottages, built gable-end to the sea, to the houses on the later straight streets occupied by skippers and boat owners who had acquired a degree of social status. A common feature in the houses of the village is the immense pride taken in their appearance, with attractive decoration, cleanliness and neatness. Along the clifftop, overlooking the harbour, there are some magnificent views across the Moray Firth to the hills of Sutherland and Caithness.

To the east of Portknockie is an example of Nature's sculpting work: the Bow Fiddle Rock.

Portree *see* Skye

Portsoy, *Grampian* (3/2B) Set alongside a wide sheltered bay on the Moray Firth coast, Portsoy was created a burgh of barony in 1550 and grew around the old commercial harbour, built in 1693. It once had a claim to fame in the 18th century when the Portsoy marble industry was at its zenith. Fireplaces of this colourful soft green serpentine, popularly called marble, were installed in the palace of Versailles and in many of the great houses of the period in Britain and on the Continent. It is an old-world town, with wynds and closes, and crow-stepped gables. Reflecting Portsoy's importance for both shipping and international trade, many of the warehouses and grain stores still stand, proud reminders of the town's former activity. One warehouse near the harbour is now a craft shop working in Portsoy marble.

The marble industry was organized by Lord Boyne who succeeded in having the import of foreign marble to Britain banned, thereby giving his interests a monopoly.

The oldest house in the town is Soy House in Church Street, c. 1690. It has a circular staircase and a William and Mary window with some of the original imperfect panes. The Star Inn in North High Street, built in 1727, was a gathering place for smugglers in Napoleonic times and was the scene of a sea captain's murder.

East of Portsoy at Boyndie is Boyne Castle, now ruined, built c. 1575 by Alexander Ogilvie of Boyne and his wife, Mary Beaton, one of Mary Queen of Scots' 'Four Marys'. Boyne Water protected this courtyard castle on three sides.

Raasay, *Highland* (1/3B) This island of the Inner Hebrides runs some 13 miles along the eastern coast of SKYE. The ferry to Raasay sails from Sconser on Skye. It has a diverse character which presents much of interest to the botanist, geologist and archaeologist. Bedded ironstone occurs at the south-eastern end of the island in sufficient quantities to have been exploited during the First World War. The mines were worked by prisoners of war who, it is said, sabotaged the production by shovelling dirt out along with the ore. The mines were abandoned in 1920. The rich vegetation that covers the basic rock distinguishes Raasay from other Hebridean islands and gives it a fine green look. A Forestry Commission plantation also offers some relief to the eye.

The population is around 160, a third of what it was a century ago the result, as in so many other parts of the Highlands, of a programme of clearances. The main activity is crofting which, although prosecuted with some intensity, is not sufficient to offer other than subsistence living. Young people are not easily persuaded to stay on the island. Raasay House at Clachan, the traditional home of the Macleods of Raasay, was visited by Dr Samuel Johnson. Years of neglect have turned this handsome building into a sorry nondescript ruin.

Rhum, *Highland* (1/2C) The island forms part of a group of islands south of SKYE, and differs from its neighbours in that it is particularly mountainous, with some peaks over 2000 ft. A peculiar geological feature is the vein of bloodstone at the north-west corner of the island. Rhum's coastline is generally steep, with the main access on the eastern side at Loch Scresort. For many years Rhum has been known as the 'forbidden island': it is the property of the Nature Conservancy Council who took it over in 1957 because of its intrinsic value as an outdoor nature reserve for the study of the island's stock of red deer. Visitors are welcome, in fact, but on a restricted basis, and then only because they offer the introduction of an essential ecological element which, were it lacking, would create a false environment for research.

Rhum was bought in 1888 by Sir John Bullough, who made his fortune designing milling machinery. He used some of his wealth to build Kinloch Castle, an extravagant monument to contemporary Edwardian opulence. At one time turtles and alligators were kept in heated tanks.

The island can be reached from Arisaig on the mainland, on the A830(T) south of MALLAIG.

Rosehearty, *Grampian* (3/3B) Small though this Moray Firth town may be, it is one of the oldest seaports in Scotland. Its origins go back to the time of the Viking raids. In the 14th century it came into its own as a major settlement and was granted burgh status in 1681. In the 1850s Rosehearty almost rivalled FRASERBURGH as the chief herring port of north-east Scotland with 88 boats working out of its harbour. With the advent of the larger steam-driven herring drifters, Rosehearty lost its advantage and today offers refuge to small sailing craft and a few salmon cobles, the characteristic rowing boats of this coast. Just south of the town is Pitsligo Castle, now ruined, dating mainly from 1663 but with some earlier elements.

The 4th and last Baron Forbes of Pitsligo was an unusual man for his times who came under the influence of the French mystic, François Fénelon, whose philosophy was called by Sir Walter Scott 'a species of transcendental devotion' – what we today would call meditation. In 1700 Pitsligo set up a community at Rosehearty centred round a school of mystical science, rather similar to the present-day Findhorn Foundation in Morayshire. Many of the contemporary eminents went to the school, including Andrew Ramsay, the man who reorganized Scottish Freemasonry in 1737.

St Andrews, *Fife* (5/3B) The Kingdom of Fife wears a thick patina of history and St Andrews makes no small contribution to the whole pageant of a lively and event-laden story, all firmly fixed in the nationhood of Scotland. Here you are conscious of rubbing shoulders with the Middle Ages as you walk the streets of this old town. The houses have long gardens, called 'riggs', which are still intact after 500 years. The grace and dignity of the design of many of the town's notable buildings compete with and complement the Scottish vernacular as expressed in the architecture of more modest dwellings. Here there is both character and atmosphere, enhanced by the influence of the sea-girt, rocky shoreland.

St Andrews Castle is now a ruin with a history as turbulent as the North Sea it overlooks. Erected early in the 13th century and isolated from the land by a moat on the south side, its walls have seen the ebb and flow of fortune during the Wars of Scottish Independence in the 14th century. It was captured and recaptured, dismantled and rebuilt by both Scots and English, and it was besieged during the 16th-century religious strife. In the same century it was splendid enough to extract a comment from the English ambassador: 'I understand there hath not been such a house kept in Scotland many days before, as of the late archbishop hath kept, and yet keepeth; insomuch as at the being with him of these lords, both horses and men, he gave livery each night to twenty-one score horses.' After that period of glory, the Town Council in 1654 ordered part of the fabric to be used for the repair of the harbour walls, to leave the rest of the building to succumb to the ravages of time.

St Andrews University, founded in 1411, is the oldest seat of learning in Scotland and still a living entity. Of the Cathedral, on the other hand, only the 12th-century east end wall remains to indicate its former splendour. It was once the largest church in Scotland. The priory ruins (1144) lie close by. The unique St Rule next to the Cathedral was built in the 12th century and was the first church of the Augustinian canons in Scotland. Its square tower offers the visitor a climb of 158 steps to gain the reward of a panoramic view of St Andrews town.

Schiehallion and the river Tummel (see p. 184)

(see p. 184)

If Falkland Palace has the oldest tennis court in Britain, St Andrews offers another sporting claim, this time in golf. The Royal and Ancient Golf Club was founded in 1754 and is the world's premier club. In keeping with the non-exclusive character of the Scots, you can play St Andrews without the need to become a member, nor is an introduction required. Payment of a green fee will take you on to the greens where so many of the world's famous players have teed off.

St Monance, *Fife* (5/3B) This Fife fishing village has as its motto: 'We live by the sea.' And so it has been for centuries, as witness the many graves of fishermen buried in the cemetery by the church founded in 1362 by King David II, Robert Bruce's son, in gratitude for a miraculous recovery from a wound. The church is built on the site of an earlier building dedicated to St Monance and associated with a spring which, until modern times, was used for washing nets – not so much for luck, but because the iron in the water made the nets more durable. Close to the harbour is one of the oldest surviving boat-builders in Scotland. Established in 1714, the yard still builds fishing boats with the consumate skill and expertise acquired over two centuries.

St Ninian's Isle *see* Shetland Islands

St Vigeans, *Tayside* (5/3B) In a small cottage in this village (now called St Vigeans Museum) lie some of the finest examples of the sculptured work left by the mysterious Picts, with early Christian stones that are among the most important of their kind in Scotland. The Drosten Stone bears three proper names and has an inscription in the Pictish language.

Although it is much restored, St Vigeans is one of the oldest churches in Scotland. Built on top of a steep conical hump it is surrounded by antique gravestones, many of which commemorate fisherfolk of the district.

Sanday *see* Orkney Islands

Scalloway *see* Shetland Islands

Scapa Flow *see* Orkney Islands

Schiehallion, *Tayside* (5/1A) This is one of the most perfectly contoured mountains in Britain. Rising to 3554 ft, it is an isolated and rather graceful conical peak of white quartzite (*see p. 183*). It was used in 1774 in early experiments carried out to determine the weight of the earth. Although these were not an unqualified success, one of the members of the expedition, the mathematician Charles Hutton, invented contour lines now familiar on present-day maps. In early times it was used as a place of ceremony by the Picts. Its name means 'The Fairy Mountain of the Caledonians'.

Scone, *Tayside* (5/2B) The district around Scone is of great historic interest: it is the site of a Pictish capital and the location of the Stone of Destiny brought from DUNADD in Argyll in the 9th century. At Scone, it was used as the Coronation Stone for the Kings of Scots until it was looted by Edward I of England and became part of the Coronation Chair in Westminster Abbey. Beside the present Scone Palace is Moot Hill where the coronation ceremonies were enacted. The old prophecy, 'the Scots in place must reign where they this stone shall find', was fulfilled when James VI of Scotland ascended the English throne as James I in 1603. In the grounds of Scone Palace are the few stone remains of the ancient abbey that once played a central part in the temporal and spiritual government of Scotland. It was destroyed by the zealous followers of John Knox at the Reformation.

The present Scone Palace, castellated, enlarged and embellished in 1803, incorporates the 16th-century and earlier palaces. Still used as a home of the Earls of Mansfield, its contents include fabulous porcelain, fine furniture, superb paintings and ivories. The palace is open to the public Easter to October and at other times by arrangement. (*See pp. 186–7 and 188*).

New Scone is a village established in 1805 when the then earl decided to remove the original settlement out of the palace grounds for the sake of his privacy.

Scourie, *Highland* (2/2A) A mainly crofting community in the far north-west of Scotland with a concentration of tourist facilities offering easy access to good fishing, sea and freshwater, and sheltered sandy bays.

The presence of a few palm trees is evidence of the mild climate, despite the fact that Scourie is in almost the same latitude as the southern tip of Greenland. Scourie tends to be rather overcrowded in summer with visitors who give it a rather cosmopolitan air.

Opposite: Replica of the Stone of Scone
Overleaf: Scone Palace

Scrabster, *Highland* (3/1A) A small but important harbour on Scotland's north coast facing the
Pentland Firth, a treacherous stretch of water
notorious for its fast-flowing tides (6–10 knots).
Pentland means 'Pictland', the Picts (the 'painted
people') being a race in Scotland whose only
remains are the many carved stones and some
elements of their language in place names – for
example Pitmedden in Aberdeenshire.

Scrabster harbour is the terminal for the ferry
to Stromness in ORKNEY and, in the summer
months, a once-weekly car ferry to the Faroe
Islands and Iceland. It is one of Britain's larger
sea-angling centres, with claims to records for
both the largest catches of fish and world-record
sized giant halibut (the current record stands at
232 lb). It was from Scrabster that Lord Kitch-
ener sailed in the ill-fated HMS *Hampshire* in
June 1916. The estate of Scrabster once belonged
to the Crown, and the reigning sovereign is called
locally the Laird of Scrabster. To the east of the
village is Holborn Head, where that rather rare
flower the Scottish primrose (*Primula scotica*)
grows in some small profusion.

Sheriffmuir *see* Dunblane

Shetland Islands (3/3A) The islands that comprise the Shetland archipelago are Britain's most
northerly community, whose lives pulse more to
a Scandinavian rhythm. This is not so surprising
for Shetland is only some 200 miles from Norway
and nearly 1000 miles distant from London.
Evidence of continuous inhabitation goes back
some 4000 years and many of the remains from
those early times are still to be seen scattered like
largesse among the islands.

Though essentially an island community,
Shetland is well integrated through comprehensive travel facilities which include regular ferry
and air services. The largest island is Mainland
where the administrative capital, Lerwick (*see
below*), is located. In recent years, the impact of
North Sea oil has been significant if somewhat
controversial, with Sullom Voe acting as an
onshore pipeline terminal for the oilfields to the
north-west of Shetland. Sullom Voe handles the
equivalent of well over one million barrels of oil
each day.

Despite the presence of high technology based
on oil, the Shetlanders have determined to keep
intact their links with the past, by fostering
traditional craft industries, such as Shetland knit-

Some of the fine furniture, Scone Palace (see p. 184)

ting, and by the development of a tourist industry
which aims to ensure that their way of life
remains as it ever was: vibrant, lively, colourful,
and outgoing, yet still reflecting those age-old
values inherent in true community living.

During the 6th century the Christian faith
came to these islands and established many early
churches, some of which still survive. That on St
Ninian's Isle (*see below*) yielded a rich hoard of
Celtic ecclesiastical silver, now on display in the
National Museums of Scotland in Queen Street,
Edinburgh. From the 8th century the arrival of
the Norsemen imposed a new culture on the
islands to the extent that the old Norn language
still contains thousands of Norse words. The
islands were taken under the protection of the
Scottish Crown in the late 15th century, which
heralded a rather grim era in Shetland's history,
with the islanders being ruled with an oppressive
rod of iron by two members of the Scottish
aristocracy; these were later executed in
Edinburgh. Then came a steady stream of Scottish court favourites who carved up the islands
into personal estates. With that history behind
them, it is little wonder that the islanders regard
strangers who come with an intent to settle with a
modicum of uneasiness. Island memory tends to
be strong and unforgiving.

Clickhimin Broch (3/3A) This structure lies
about a mile from Lerwick at the end of a causeway in the Loch of Clickhimin. Excavations of
the site have revealed a succession of buildings
dating from the 7th century BC to the 6th century
AD. First used as a Bronze Age farmstead, it was
later developed into a ring fort, a broch and then a
wheelhouse settlement. On a nearby causeway
there is a large slab stone with two footprints
carved out of the rock. It was at one time the
custom at the inauguration ceremony for a new
king to place his feet in the footprints to sym-
bolize his agreement to continue the just rule of
his predecessors.

Fetlar (3/3A) This green and fertile island well
deserves its name, which means 'Fat Isle'. Until
1967 Fetlar was the only British breeding site of
the snowy owl. The resident male bird died
there in 1975. Now only non-breeding females
are still to be seen. One peculiar structure on the
island is the Tower at Brough Lodge, built in
the 1820s as a folly. The Giant's Grave has eight
stones arranged in a boat-shaped oval mound,
marking the spot where a Viking died after being
rescued from the sea. Both broch and standing
stones witness to a long continuous human habitation of the island.

Foula (3/2A) This is the most westerly island in the Shetland group, lying 27 miles out in the Atlantic, and is the remotest inhabited island in the British Isles. It has a population of about 40. At one time the population was around 300, all employed in fishing. The natives had a far-famed skill in rock climbing, to gather birds' eggs which formed a staple food. Until 1800 the old Norn language of Shetland was spoken on the island, and even today the islanders still celebrate Christmas in January – they stuck to the old Julian calendar after 1753 when the new calendar was introduced.

The island's name is derived from the Old Norse: *Fugl-ey*, 'Bird Island'. One of the most prolific species here is the great skua, locally called the 'bonxie', which nearly became extinct but has now recovered in numbers. About 3000 pairs breed on the island. Visitors to Foula are advised to bring their own provisions because spells of severe weather have been known to isolate the island for up to six weeks at a time.

Jarlshof (3/3B) This remarkable archaeological site is right in the south of Mainland near Sumburgh Airport: the old and the new. The name is suspect, however, for it was invented by Sir Walter Scott for his novel *The Pirate*. Even so, it conjures up the romance of a past that dates back to 2000 BC. It was discovered by an accident of nature, when a violent storm eroded the south face of the great mound beside a medieval farmhouse of the 14th century. Excavations indicate at least eight distinctive phases of human occupation, from the New Stone Age onwards and including Viking and medieval remains.

Lerwick (3/3A) The main port and capital of Shetland, and linked by car ferry with ABERDEEN, Lerwick has developed from its 17th-century role as a safe anchorage sheltered by the bulk of Bressay Island to the east across the sound. Its potential was realized by the British Government as far back as 1653, when no fewer than 94 ships were anchored there to prevent its use by the Dutch. In the 18th century, trade developed between Lerwick and Scandinavia and North Germany; private merchants each had his own jetty and storehouse, often used for the concealment of contraband. Indeed, smuggling tobacco, brandy and gin introduced a period of prosperity which was manifested in some of the substantial buildings in the town. Smuggling was so well developed during the 19th century that contraband from abroad was even carried to

Previous page: Skye from Bealach na Ba

London. Ships leaving Lerwick, bound for England, would obtain customs clearance for a coastal journey only. They would then leave British waters, load up with taxable foreign goods, and complete their voyage as if they had been merely held up by bad weather.

The older parts of Lerwick are particularly attractive with buildings fashioned from local sandstone and each displaying the idiosyncracies of their owners. Commercial Street is a stone-paved thoroughfare that narrows at its southern end where the sea laps at the walls of the buildings. Fort Charlotte was begun in 1665 and burned by the Dutch a few years later when Lerwick was sacked. It was subsequently repaired in 1781.

Each January, Lerwick becomes a city of fire, with the Up Helly Aa Festival, a Viking-inspired shindig which celebrates the return of light after the long winter darkness. Hundreds of torch-bearers, dressed as Vikings, march through the streets, all eager for the final touch: the setting alight of a Norse longship.

Annual sales of the famous Shetland ponies are held in Lerwick in early November.

Mousa (3/3B) This tiny island off the southeast coast of Mainland has one of the best-preserved brochs in Scotland, standing some 43 ft tall and dating from the Iron Age. The broch merited a mention in the *Egils Saga* when, in AD 900, a shipwrecked couple took refuge within its walls. It was also mentioned in the *Orkneyinga Saga* when the broch was besieged in 1153. With its galleries and staircases constructed within its thick stone walls, it is a fine example of the craft of ancient builders and belies the popular idea that these Iron Age people were mere primitives.

Muckle Flugga (3/3A) These rocks lie to the north of Unst (*see below*) with a lighthouse on the isolated Out Stack, fully exposed to the storms, swell and heaving waters of the Atlantic. Wind strengths here can be unbelievably high. On Unst, in 1962, the highest British wind speed was recorded just before the anemometer was blown away: 177 mph.

Out Skerries (3/3A) These comprise a group of islands to the east of Mainland. Only two, Bruray and Housay, are inhabited, by a population of about 100. With the land providing only subsistence economy, the islanders have ever looked to the sea for their living and have prosecuted their fishing industry with a vigour and enterprise that eventually led to the building of a highly mechanized fish-processing factory in 1970.

Until the Out Skerries lighthouse was built in

1852, these island rocks were a graveyard for shipping, the main casualties being Dutch East Indiamen laden with treasure. Divers still recover coins and other valuables from the wrecks.

Papa Stour (3/3A) An island just off the west coast of Shetland's Mainland. Formed from lava and ashes and then sculpted by the sea, Papa Stour has some of the finest sea caves in the British Isles. The largest is Kirstan's Hole which extends some 240 ft underneath the island to end in a tiny beach accessible only in calm weather. The island of Brei Holm, off Papa Stour, was used as a leper colony in the 18th century. The fertile soil bears a profusion of wild flowers and their heavy pungent scent was used by fishermen as a guide when the sea was covered with haar (mist).

St Ninian's Isle (3/3B) This small island is linked to the south-west coast of Mainland by a sandy isthmus. Until 1958 the 12th-century church was only one of many similar buildings scattered throughout the Shetland Islands. However, in that year excavations under a stone slab in the chapel revealed a magnificent hoard of 8th-century Celtic silver, including bowls and brooches decorated with Pictish symbols, now known as the St Ninian's Treasure. When the treasure was taken south to the National Museums of Scotland in Queen Street, Edinburgh there was a great outcry that a part of Shetland's heritage was being wrenched out of its provenance. Today the originals are still in Edinburgh, but there are perfect replicas housed in the Shetland Museum in Lerwick. It is thought that the treasure was buried under the cross-inscribed slab by monks who were faced with the threat of Viking raiders.

Scalloway (3/3A) Scalloway on Mainland was once the chief town in Shetland until its position was taken over by Lerwick. It has a busy harbour overlooked by the ruins of Scalloway Castle, a four-storey towerhouse built by Earl Patrick Stewart in about 1600. Both he and his equally tyrannous son, imports from the Scottish mainland, ruled with exceptional cruelty, imposing a regime of terror which ended in 1615 with their joint execution in Edinburgh.

During the Second World War, Scalloway was the base for the 'Shetland Bus', an operation designed for landing saboteurs by sea in German-occupied Norway and for bringing out Norwegian freedom fighters.

Scalloway's main economic base is the fishing industry, a carry-over from the earlier part of this century when the herring fishing provided the town with important trade links with Germany,

to where it exported lightly cured *Matjes* herring and kippers.

Unst (3/3A) Unst is the most northerly point of the British Isles, reached by a small roll-on/roll-off car and passenger ferry. The population of just over 1000 live by crofting, with some quarrying for serpentine and talc. The principal employer is the Royal Air Force which has an important early warning station on the island. Baltasound on the east coast of Unst was once the largest herring port in Britain, a status later lost to Lerwick (*see above*), which was better able to offer the berthing facilities required by fishing boats when steam replaced sail.

Despite the island's relative remoteness, the presence of Muness Castle, a towerhouse almost structurally complete and built in the late 16th century, indicates that Unst then had some significance for those who ruled over Shetland.

Remains of brochs, cairns, and old churches and secular buildings, scattered throughout the island, also demonstrate a former importance.

Whalsay (3/3A) An island off the east coast of Mainland, which still carries on its centuries-old trade with the sea. A witness to its former importance is the 17th-century Bremen Böd, the Hanseatic booth used for the storage of brandy, tobacco, linen, salt, fruit and other exotic goods which were bartered for the main Shetland products of salted and dried fish, wool and butter. This is the only complete building of its kind to have survived in Scotland. The trade lasted from the 14th to the early 17th century. Whalsay is one of the most densely populated islands in the Shetland group: about 1000 people live here and fishing – inshore and from trawlers – is important.

Yell (3/3A) This island is almost entirely peat moor, studded with archaeological sites, including those of no fewer than 15 chapels. The oldest surviving building is Old Haa of Burravoe, which dates from 1637. Recently acquired by the local community it is now being restored to form a local museum and exhibition centre for the island's crafts.

Scenic interest here lies mainly round the coasts – notably the wild cliffs of the north-west.

Skara Brae *see* Orkney Islands

Skye, *Highland* (1/2B) The island of Skye, which can be reached by ferries from MALLAIG and the Kyle of Lochalsh, is a large mass dominating the west coast of Scotland and cut deeply by long sea lochs, so much so that no place on the island is

more than 5 miles from the sea. This feature has led to the creation of peninsular communities, each of which tends to have a distinct history within the Skye whole. Much of the land is poor, supporting crofts that offer only subsistence living. The result is that many crofters tend to rely on other sources for their income. Even so, there are pockets of fertile soil which yield good returns from cattle and sheep. In the southern tip of the island, at Sleat, there is a marked contrast to much of the rest of the Skye landscape: green hills, woodland, scrub and comparatively prosperous crofts and farms.

The Skye scenery is often spectacular, with straths (wide valleys) dominated by magnificent mountains, including the Cuillin Hills in the west which rise to over 3000 ft, gashing the skyline with sharp peaks and dramatic rock formations. During the 19th century, when it was thought that only the Swiss Alps offered any real challenge to the embryo sport of mountaineering, the Cuillins were discovered, and the area soon became a nursery for many famous climbers, and still is today. In fact, in the 19th century, the Cuillins were more popular with painters than climbers. J. M. W. Turner, Horatio MacCulloch and other eminent British artists found inspiration in these mountains, which suggests they were no mean climbers themselves.

Much of the history of Skye from about AD 800 is taken up with the hegemony of the Vikings. They founded such clan families as the MacDonalds, Macleods and MacKinnons, who were later to become involved in protracted internecine warfare which too often prevented the ordinary folk from getting on with the more serious business of living.

Skye was for a number of centuries of little interest to Britain, save for the accounts of such intrepid travellers as Dr Samuel Johnson on his Highland jaunt in 1773. But it caught the national attention in the 1880s when crofters, after a long period of enforced emigration and starvation, rebelled against their harsh conditions and were in the forefront of the battle to win legal rights. These came with the passing in 1886 of the Crofters Act, which gave them security of tenure and a rather limited scope for developing better forms of land use. In the period 1881–5, after a succession of bad harvests and poor fishing, Skye had been the scene of serious crofter riots which made headlines in the national press. The situa-

tion was often serious enough for the Government to send armed troops and policemen to quell the rebels.

There are only two major settlements in Skye, Broadford and Portree (*see below*). The island community is largely made up of crofting townships which, though scattered throughout Skye, have sufficient interrelated interests to allow communal effort for the general good.

Apart from crofting, fishing, fish farming and tourism form the economic base for the islanders. Skye boasts a distillery at Carbost and a small electronics industry which specializes in making transducers for medical use – proving, perhaps, that high technology can be introduced in areas remote from the marketplace to offer small but significant pockets of employment.

The northern gateway to Skye is by way of Kyle of Lochalsh, where a short car ferry journey lands the traveller at Kyleakin. On the road to Kyle you pass one of the most-photographed castles in Scotland: Eilean Donan standing on the site of a 13th-century fort. In 1719 it was garrisoned by Spanish troops who had landed to support the Old Pretender, father of Bonnie Prince Charlie, and for its sins was battered by an English gunboat. Early this century it was faithfully restored on the basis of original plans.

Armadale (1/3C) This is the terminal in Skye for the ferry from MALLAIG on the west coast of Scotland. Apart from the magnificent views offered across the Sound of Sleat of the mountains of Knoydart and around Glenelg the village holds little of interest to the traveller. However, a couple of miles or so north lie the remains of the once-imposing Armadale Castle, the seat of the MacDonalds of Sleat. The castle was partly razed a few years ago and its environs have now been developed into a highly innovative and successful tourist attraction: the Clan MacDonald Centre, devoted to telling the story of the clan. Set in lush woodlands, this area exudes the atmosphere of former times when comfortable and elegant living was pursued by those who could afford it.

Broadford (1/3C) This Skye township on the bay of the same name consists largely of a long main street, dominated by the red granite mass of Beinn na Caillich (2403 ft). It is Skye's biggest crofting township. Beyond the town are the ruins of Coirechatachan, home of the chief of the Clan MacKinnon, in which Dr Samuel Johnson and his companion James Boswell were entertained in 1773. Off Broadford, Pabay (the 'Priest's Isle') has the ruins of a chapel. It was once the haunt of pirates and 'broken men'.

Opposite: (above) Portree; (below) The ferry at Kyle of Lochalsh

Elgol, Skye

Dunvegan (1/2B) This attractive township owes much to Dunvegan Castle, the home of the chiefs of the Clan Macleod, reckoned to be the oldest continuously inhabited castle in Britain. The earliest part was built in the 9th century and stands on a rock crag facing the sea. The present structure dates from the 14th century, but additions and alterations continued into the middle of the 19th century. The woods to the east of the castle were planted in 1780. Among the treasures displayed in the building is the Fairy Flag, supposedly given to an early chief by a fairy lover. A condition attached to the gift was that if the flag was waved when the Macleods were in desperate straits in battle, they would win. It has been displayed twice to give the clan victory. The third time has yet to come. The castle is open to the public Easter to mid-October.

Portree (1/3B) This small town is the 'capital' of Skye, with a population of about 1000. It is a straggling settlement, with only its magnificent square offering a saving grace. It got its name (Port Righ – 'King's Harbour') in 1540 when King James V of Scots landed here in a personal attempt to end a longstanding and bitter feud between the two main clans on the island, the Macleods and the MacDonalds. Portree was also the scene of another royal occasion, when Prince Charles Edward Stuart arrived after being harried by Government ships and troops following his defeat at the Battle of Culloden in 1746. The room where the Prince and Flora MacDonald parted after she had smuggled him across the Minch from SOUTH UIST is now part of the Royal Hotel. Apart from fishing – the boats berth at Portree's attractive harbour – the only considerable productive industry is a small woollen mill.

South Uist, *Western Isles* (1/1C) This is the second largest island in the Outer Hebrides, about 22 miles long, connected by car ferry to OBAN. It offers sharp physical contrasts. All along the western seaboard are flat sand-based strips of machair grassland, supporting a string of crofting townships. The eastern side of the island, virtually unpopulated, is wild, with boggy moorland that rises west to east to meet a long spine of high hills running the length of the island. As with other Hebridean islands, South Uist has some wealth of evidence of its ancient past. In particular there are the 2nd-century wheel houses at Kilphedar and Drimore: circular structures built radially to accommodate a number of families.

Ormaclett Castle, now ruined, was the home of the MacDonalds of Clanranald. At Milton can be seen the remains of the home of Flora Mac-Donald, who earned a place in Highland history by her successful attempt to whisk Bonnie Prince Charlie out of the clutches of the English soldiers after Culloden in 1746. At Stilligarry are the remains of the home of the MacVurichs, an ancient bardic family which lasted from the 14th to the 18th centuries and whose members have contributed much to the corpus of Gaelic literature and tradition.

At the north end of the island is a military rocket-testing station whose presence has caused controversy in the past, and occasionally does today. The Loch Druidibeg National Nature Reserve is one of the most important breeding grounds in Britain of the native greylag goose. The variety of habitats offered by the Reserve has made the area a centre of attraction for ornithologists.

See also Benbecula; North Uist

Spean Bridge, *Highland* (4/3A) A small village lying at the junction of the north–south A82(T) road through the Great Glen and the A86 going eastwards through Glen Spean. Near the village is the Commando Memorial, a tribute to the strenuous training undergone by these men during the Second World War. Close by, Glen Roy shows off its 'parallel roads', of Nature's making. The origin of these parallel terraces goes back to the end of the last Ice Age, when a huge glacier, flowing northwards off the BEN NEVIS massif, dammed up the outlets from the glens. Mountain waters, flowing in from behind, formed deep lochs from which the 'parallel roads' formed the beaches. As the ice retreated, or was more likely breached, the water level fell and new beaches were formed at successively lower levels. The 'roads' stand out because of their different colouring: they have coarse grass or bent which is in contrast to the surrounding heather and bracken.

Speyside Way, *Grampian* (7) The Speyside Way is only the second long-distance footpath to have been officially designated by the Countryside Commission for Scotland. It has a total length of 60 miles and is eventually scheduled to run from Glenmore Lodge, near AVIEMORE, to Spey Bay on the Moray Firth. Still under development, at present only the northern section (the 30 miles from Ballindalloch to Spey Bay) has been routed and signposted. It was opened in July 1981.

Following as it does the northern run to the North Sea of the fast-flowing river Spey, the Speyside Way offers the walker an infinite variety of vistas: from low-lying straths, as wide valleys in the Highlands are called, through woodlands and low hills to the rising massifs of the Grampian Mountains.

The northern end is at Tugnet on Spey Bay. This village has for centuries based its economy on salmon fishing. The Spey is among the very best salmon rivers in Scotland. Running in from the north Atlantic waters, the mature salmon make for home with an uncanny instinct: to the tributaries of the Spey where they were spawned. Entering the Spey with a flowing tide, the fish swim against the river's strong currents to reach their spawning grounds, often in streams near the Monadhliath Mountains nearly 100 miles away.

At the height of the fishing season at Tugnet, some 30 men are employed by the River Spey Commercial Fishery, operated by the Crown Estates since 1937, in netting the salmon and then preparing the fish for export to southern markets packed in ice. At the appropriately named Tugnet there can be seen an ice house, with a permanent display devoted to the history of salmon fishing in the area, both commercial and as a sport.

Starting at Tugnet, the Speyside Way takes a leisurely route south through FOCHABERS to Boat of Brig, a village whose name is derived from an old collapsed bridge which was later replaced by a ferry boat before the present structure was built. The route then continues through Forestry Commission plantations to CRAIGELLACHIE, where the bridge built by Thomas Telford in 1814 spans the Spey in a combination of visual grace and solid engineering. The cast-iron girders were made in North Wales. The traveller now enters whisky-distilling country, an industry once sustained by smuggling the product to southern markets until it was legalized in the 1820s. The Speyside Way passes three distilleries, one of which, at Tamdhu, has converted the former railway station into an attractive visitors' centre devoted to the telling of the story of the alchemic conversion of barley and pure Highland water into liquid gold. The Speyside Way ends (temporarily, until it is fully developed) at Ballindalloch.

A Countryside Service operates on the Speyside Way, with a ranger providing help, advice and information, and there is a first aid service for those who use the route. The Way itself takes the walker through a kaleidoscope of scenic variations: woodland, forest, vistas of the

View of the Spey

Spey, lush river valleys, challenging, though not daunting, hill climbs, and rolling moorland. The history of Speyside, too, is never far away; nor is the wildlife, with roe deer, kestrels, a varied flora and butterflies. The impact both of Nature and of Man on the countryside and environment, sometimes acting in concert and at others creating a visual dissonance, adds an extra dimension of interest to a thoroughly enjoyable journey which requires only the enthusiastic participation of those who prefer their legs to a motor vehicle to extract the maximum pleasure from the Speyside Way.

Staffa, *Strathclyde* (4/1A) This tiny, uninhabited island lies 7 miles to the west of MULL and remained virtually unknown to the outer world until it was visited by the naturalist Joseph Banks

Binn, 'the Melodious Cave', so named on account of the strange music which the sea makes among the pillars of this natural cathedral. The cave itself is well over 200 ft long and 60 ft high at its entrance.

Boats from Croig on Mull and from OBAN will land visitors on the island – if the weather is suitable; and cruises around Staffa, with views of Fingal's Cave, and the other famous caves, are organized from various departure points.

Stirling, *Central* (5/1B) The importance of this historic town is based on its strategic situation on the Forth; it is the most southerly crossing point on that river. Once the capital of Scotland and thus an important settlement by AD 1000, as suggested by an early charter granted by Alexander II in 1260 which gave an already long-established community of merchants and craftsmen certain valuable trading rights and privileges. Stirling Castle, open all year round, is built on a volcanic plug and commands an unrivalled view of the surrounding plains and hills, and the famous battle sites of Bannockburn and Stirling Bridge. History points to the occupation of this site by the Romans and the early Britons. Legend has it that King Arthur fought a battle here with the Saxons. The present castle site has been a focal point for much of Scotland's history. In 1296 it was occupied by the English and retaken by William Wallace the following year, an act that so enraged Edward I of England that he had the lead roofs of churches as far away as PERTH stripped to weight down his catapults to bombard the castle. In 1314 the Scots laid siege to the castle, which Edward II tried to raise but suffered defeat at Bannockburn. From then it attracted the attention of many through the centuries, including General Monck in 1651 and Bonnie Prince Charlie who unsuccessfully besieged it in 1746. Although there has been a stronghold on this site since the 11th century, the present structure dates from the 15th century (notably the splendid Renaissance great hall) and later.

Much of Stirling town still reflects its historic past. The church of the Holy Rood saw the coronation of James VI in 1567 when one year old. Argyll Ludging, at Castle Wynd, is one of the finest surviving examples of 17th-century Scottish domestic architecture, and has been in its day a military hospital and is now a youth hostel. Cowane's Hospital (or Guildhall) in St John Street, was built in 1639 and is an attractive building though its interior was much altered in 1852. The neighbouring bowling green is, at 250

in 1772. He marvelled at its caves and extraordinary basaltic formations, the result of intense volcanic activity which produced the famous columns, similar to those on the Giant's Causeway in Northern Ireland.

After Banks came many famous visitors to view, in particular, Fingal's Cave, which inspired Felix Mendelssohn to write his Hebrides Overture. The name of the cave is an English rendering of a misunderstanding of the Gaelic An Uamh

years, the second oldest in Britain – after Sir Francis Drake's famous green at Plymouth.

Stirling Auld Brig was built in the later 15th century to replace a series of earlier wooden structures. The prominent Wallace Monument was erected in 1869 in honour of Sir William Wallace, whose part in the Wars of Independence in the 13th century has earned him a place in Scottish history as a national hero. Bannockburn, 2 miles south of Stirling, is now a site under the care of the National Trust for Scotland. The Bruce Memorial is at the Borestone site, traditionally Bruce's command post during the battle. An interpretive information centre is devoted to telling the story of the event, which was a turning point in Scotland's history. A mile to the east of Stirling is Cambuskenneth Abbey, founded in 1140, and used from time to time as accommodation for the old Scots Parliament. In 1604 the abbey was given to the Earl of Mar who promptly reduced it to ruins to build his palace, Mar's Wark, in Stirling. This structure is now itself reduced to a fragment at the head of Broad Street.

Stonehaven, *Grampian* (3/3C) This east coast port is really two towns, with the older element clustered round the harbour. The new town was established in the early 19th century and was very much a residential quarter for merchants and professional people. Though little remains of Old Stonehaven, except the Tolbooth (late 16th century on the Old Pier in the harbour), there is still the feel of medieval times. The town was developed largely as a fishing port, but this industry had a fitful history, and only came into its own during the herring boom in the 1880s. After the herring disappeared, the town went into decline, a situation not helped by the rising prominence of ABERDEEN not far to the north. Today fishing is still carried on, but at a lower level, and much of the economy is based on tourism.

Stonehaven's history includes a painful encounter with General Monck's Cromwellian troops who sacked the town in 1645. History repeated itself in 1746; this time the iron hand was that of the Duke of Cumberland.

Robert William Thomson (1822–73), the man who invented the pneumatic tyre in 1845, was born here; every year a Thomson Rally takes place in late June to commemorate the man who also turned his brilliant mind to the road steamer, the portable steam crane, the hydraulic floating dock and the ribbon saw – to say nothing of the

Mar's Wark, Stirling

glass fountain pen with its novel exhaust piston which caught the Victorian imagination at the Great Exhibition in London in 1851. He was not so successful as a businessman, with the result that 35 years later, Lewis Waterman filched the idea and made a fortune.

At the New Year, the people of Stonehaven celebrate Hogmanay by the ancient ceremony of fireball swinging. Wire netting bags are filled with combustible materials, set on fire and swung round the head in a parade down the High Street of the Old Town.

Just south of Stonehaven is Dunottar Castle (*overleaf*), a unique structure perched on sheer cliffs facing the North Sea. This promontory site was once occupied by a Pictish fort and later an early Christian chapel. The collection of buildings date from the early 13th century on and have seen not a few important episodes in Scottish history. In particular, it was from here that in 1651 the Honours of Scotland were taken, to prevent the Scottish Crown, Sword and Sceptre from falling into the hands of Cromwell's besieging troops. Smuggled out of the castle under the garments of the local minister's wife, they were taken to Kinneff Church, five miles to the south, and hidden under a flagstone for safe keeping. The castle was dismantled in 1720, but partly restored in 1925 in a scheme to provide work for the unemployed.

Stornoway *see* Lewis

Strath of Kildonan, *Highland* (3/1A) In 1868 a native of the Strath returned from gold prospecting in Australia. Lured on by stories of sheep with golden teeth, he began panning the waters of the Helmsdale river and its tributaries, the Kildonan and Suisgill burns. Rather unwisely he advertised his gold strike and within a year extensive digging in the area by hundreds of hopefuls brought the Kildonan Gold Rush to the Highlands. No one ever made a fortune; the largest nugget ever found was valued at £9. Eventually the Highland Klondyke petered out and the camp site was deserted. However, flecks of gold are still found today by those who pan for the precious metal, under licence from the Suisgill Estate Office.

Strathpeffer, *Highland* (2/3B) In the 18th century it was discovered that the several mineral springs in the valley here had curative properties and in no time at all a resort was created for hordes of visitors who travelled from far and wide

Dunottar Castle, near Stonehaven (see p. 201)

to take the waters. A pump room was built and by the end of the 19th century Strathpeffer had become the 'Harrogate of the North', with a pavilion, a rheumatic hospital and five mineral wells of different strengths. The waters of the spa, both sulphur and chalybeate, are still available from a small Pump Room re-opened in 1960. So popular was the town that it had its own branch railway line from DINGWALL, with its own Strathpeffer Express which included through coaches from London.

Much of the former spa stands complete and the town retains its original Victorian charm, which makes it a popular tourist attraction. Dominating the valley is the mass of Ben Wyvis (3433 ft), where a proposed mountain railway and ski development threatens to bring in more tourists. Overlooking Strathpeffer is the ridge of Knockfarrel where a vitrified fort can be seen. Close by the Ben Wyvis Hotel is the Eagle Stone, a carved Pictish monument with an ornamented arch and an eagle – possibly a marriage stone.

Strathyre, *Central* (5/1B; 6/3B) Long famed in Scots folk songs, Strathyre has a romantic ring to it as it rolls round the mouth. Sir Walter Scott was so taken with the atmospheric scenery that he used the hills as locales for two of his works: *The Lady of the Lake* and *A Legend of Montrose*. Today Strathyre is a popular tourist watering place and houses a Clan Gregor Heritage and a Forest Information Centre on the A84 at the south end of the town.

Stromness *see* Orkney Islands

Stronsay *see* Orkney Islands

Strontian, *Highland* (4/2A) This small Highland village on the A861 at the head of Loch Sunart has given its name to the element strontium. In 1787 this was discovered in the local lead mines and it was isolated by Humphrey Davy in 1808. It is hard, yet ductile and is used in the manufacture of fireworks, since it burns with a brilliant crimson flame. Lead was mined here from the 17th century until about 1904. The old workings are still to be seen and are a memorial to an industrial aspect not often associated with the Highlands. Strontium 90 is an unwelcome derivative in these nuclear times.

Tain, *Highland* (3/1B) Tain was once an important port on the south shore of the Dornoch Firth, but progressive silting prevented development and the town had to rely on other means to maintain its existence. Its name apparently derives from the Old Norse *thing*, meaning 'council' or 'meeting place'. Its significance for the Norsemen continued to the 12th century, when the St Duthus Chapel, dedicated to the celebrated Celtic saint associated with this town, was built; it is now an ivy-covered ruin. Its sister building, St Duthus Church, built *c.* 1360, was an important place of pilgrimage in medieval times. James IV of Scots came here annually over a period of 20 years in atonement for his part in the death of his father. The church contains some stained-glass windows portraying a number of scenes from Scottish history. In the centre of the town is a 16th-century tolbooth, with a conical spire and small angle turrets. Among the town's industries are a cheesery, making Highland cheeses based on old recipes, and a distillery producing an excellent and widely favoured single malt whisky of some distinction.

Tarbert, *Strathclyde* (4/2B) This little town on the western shore of Loch Fyne was once an important herring fishing centre. Only echoes remain of the hustle and bustle of the days when the harbour was filled with the great brown sails of fishing luggers and the quaysides thronged with fish curers and gutting women. The Loch Fyne herring, known as 'Glasgow Magistrates', are still excellent in their season. They are big, plump, full of oil and have a delicious melting taste when eaten fresh cooked; when kippered in the slow smoke of oak chips they are a sheer delight.

Just north of Tarbert is Stonefield Castle, now a hotel on the grand scale. Built and designed by William Playfair in 1838, it boasts 50 acres of shrubs and woodlands on a dramatic site overlooking Loch Fyne. Some of the Himalayan rhododendrons are a century old, raised from seed collected by Sir Joseph Hooker around 1850 on his expeditions to Sikkim.

In the late 11th century the narrow isthmus between Loch Fyne and West Loch Tarbert was the scene of a 'sailing' across land. A treaty had been signed under which King Magnus Barefoot of Norway was assigned all the lands he could circumnavigate. So, to gain a little extra, he had his men drag a longship across the isthmus and thus lay legitimate claim to Kintyre.

Thurso, *Highland* (3/1A) While most coastal settlements have had their economic history based on the fishing industry, Thurso in the far north-east was from medieval times more of a commercial port. As far back as the 14th century Caithness was an important grain producer, exported and the cereal through Thurso to Scandinavia. Indeed, so significant was this trade that King David II decreed that a common weight should be used throughout Scotland: the *pondus Cathaniae*, or 'weight of Caithness'. The trade between Thurso and the other countries of northern Europe helped the town to establish a firm economic base and in the 17th century the export of meal, beef, hides and fish all contributed to the prosperity of this royal burgh. Indeed, the town's Rotterdam Street is an apt reminder of the thriving sea traffic of former times.

When the Caithness flagstone industry developed, again Thurso was ready to act as a commercial seaport and enjoyed renewed prosperity until the advent of concrete paving blocks. Thereafter the town went into decline, witnessing a significant fall in its population until the arrival of the atomic energy establishment at DOUNREAY, some few miles to the west along the coast.

Thurso has a long continuous history of settlement, going back to Viking times (Old Norse *Thorsá*: 'Thor's River'), and a number of its existing buildings reflect this. The ruined Old St Peter's Kirk, close by the harbour, is one of the finest religious buildings of the Middle Ages to have survived in Scotland. It dates from the 13th century, was reconstructed in the 17th century and last used in 1862. Much of the town's layout was due to Sir John Sinclair, 'Agricultural Sir John', so called from his interest in improved farming methods. His broad, evenly spaced streets and pleasant squares built in the early 19th century are a witness to his vision, and its integrity has been largely maintained by subsequent developers.

Thurso and its immediate environs have produced some notable men. Robert Dick (1811–66), a baker, botanist and geologist, was a self-taught genius who was influential in his chosen fields. Almost every day he rose at 3 o'clock in the morning to attend to his daily baking chores before he finished the remainder of a crowded day with his studies and research. Sir William Smith was born in Pennyland House, on the outskirts of Thurso; he founded the Boys Brigade in 1883. Thurso Folk Museum, in the High Street, in addition to presenting a kaleidoscopic display reflecting local life in past centuries, houses the enigmatic Ulbster Stone, carved with ancient Pictish and Christian symbols.

The old part of Thurso, close by the west side of the river, was called the Fisherbiggins, where the fishermen lived. The area was rebuilt in the early 1950s with the houses renovated to traditional standards but provided with modern amenities.

Tillicoultry, *Central* (5/1B) In the 19th century the existence of this town owed much to the manufacture of textiles, and its economy is still based on knitwear, tartans and tweeds. Today, however, it is rather more a residential area and its buildings give it some significant character. Ben Cleuch (2364 ft) rises to the north of the town to add a touch of interest to the setting.

Tiree, *Strathclyde* (4/1C) Tiree is a low-lying island to the west of MULL and is seen from a distance seaward as a thick line on the approaching horizon. Its popular name in Gaelic is Tir fo Thuinn, the 'Land below the Waves', though the island does sport four hills of just over 100 ft. A large island of about 34 square miles in extent, its flatness causes the Atlantic winds to race unhindered across its terrain. Even so, Tiree's long-standing reputation as a fertile place has given it another nickname: the Granary of the Islands. Though some moss does occur in the interior parts, most of the soil is based on calcareous sand, both free-draining and readily ploughed, with the result that crops grow easily and cattle have excellent pastures. Thus, Tiree's economy is very much based on the land. Its very fertility created social problems last century when many people were cleared from the island so that large tenanted farms could be established. Those who remained in the summer of 1885 agitated for the break-up of one of these farms, an action that resulted in HMS *Ajax* arriving on the scene with a force of 30 soldiers. But the matter was settled after the ringleaders were arrested and imprisoned. The troops stayed on to help with the harvest. After the passing of the Crofters Act in 1886, which gave crofters security of tenure, the big farms were broken up to provide an admirable pattern of land use, finalised in 1921.

Being 'remote', Tiree's community is very close-bound and its members are very interdependent. However, social problems tend to come first among the fears for the future: young people prefer to leave the island, thus creating a distorted population age distribution.

Evidence of a long human occupation goes back to at least 800 BC, and continues through the early Christian period to the Vikings and beyond into the more accessible past, with the various Highland clans of MacDonalds and MacLeans laying disputed claims to the island.

The extensive sandy beaches around the island's shores have created a welcome boost to the tourist element in Tiree's economy, though it does take over four hours by ferry from OBAN via Tobermory to Gott Bay, the island's port of call. An air service flies daily to Glasgow.

Tobermory *see* Mull

Tomintoul, *Grampian* (3/1C) Tomintoul lays claim to being the highest village in the Highlands. It stands 1150 ft above sea level, a fact that gives it a bracing atmosphere. Set between the river Avon and Conglass Water, it came into existence in 1776 through the efforts of the 4th Duke of Gordon. For long the settlement remained 'primitive'. Indeed, it earned for itself some cruel observations from both Queen Victoria and James Hogg, the Border poet. The latter described it thus: 'We came to large and ugly-looking village called Tomintoul, inhabited by a set of the most outlandish ragamuffins that I ever saw in my life; the men were so ragged and rough in their appearance, that they looked rather like savages than creatures of a Christian country; and the women had no shame or sense of modesty about them, and of this the Highland soldiers seemed quite sensible and treated them accordingly.'

The village has come a long way since that time and is now established as a centre of economic activity based on tourism, whisky distilling, farming, forestry and limestone quarrying. Its layout betrays the original 'planned' conception, with a long main street, a central square and gridiron pattern. These lend an open aspect to the village, where space is the first and most essential of the viewer's impressions. The whisky distilleries in the district form part of the now famous and intoxicating 'Whisky Trail', which is rather more educational and informative than the name suggests. The hills and glens around Tomintoul offer many outdoor pleasures, including skiing at the Lecht, where developments include ski tows.

North of Tomintoul are the two glens, Livet and Avon, both maintaining their association with the malt whisky industry. In the 18th century no fewer than 200 illicit stills were producing the nectar. In particular, the Glenlivet brand, though illegal, was reputed to be a favourite of King George IV, though he could hardly admit it in public.

A corrugated-iron church, Elfin Assynt, Torridon

Tongue, *Highland* (2/3A) A beautiful gem of a Sutherland village, on the eastern shore of the Kyle of Tongue, giving some welcome relief from the desolation of moors to the south. Its ancient lineage is evidenced by the ruins of Castle Varrich, thought to have been a Norse stronghold. Tongue House nearby dates from the 17th century and was the seat of the Clan Mackay chiefs. The attractive parish church has a Laird's Loft worth seeing.

The area around Tongue has many archaeological sites indicating its attraction for human habitation for at least 2000 years.

Torridon, *Highland* (2/2C) The west and north-west coasts of Scotland have some of the finest mountain scenery in Europe, and the peaks of the Torridon area in Wester Ross make a substantial contribution to this splendour. In 1967 the Torridon estate fell to the care of the National Trust for Scotland, in part payment of estate duty ensuing from the death of the 4th Earl of Lovelace. Its north-western boundary runs along the summit of Beinn Eighe (3309 ft). To the south is the domineering mass of Liathach (3456 ft) which has seven tops linked by narrow ridges nearly 5 miles long. To the west is the jewelled mountain, Beinn Alligin (3232 ft). This area shows Nature's sculpting of the landscape to the best advantage, with Liathach, the 'Grey One', providing an impressive sight. Viewed from Glen Torridon this massif of red sandstone calls to mind some ancient Stone Age knife-edge used by mythological giants. Beinn Eighe is another multi-peaked mass, with seven peaks running along its 7-mile ridge.

For the person with adequate footwear and clothing who observes the rules for hill walking and climbing, these mountains are accessible for viewing at close hand some of the natural scenic riches not seen from the roadside. The two principal peaks of the group, Liathach and Beinn Eighe, are outstanding for their corries, crags, pinnacles and soaring ridges.

Trossachs, The, *Central* (5/1B; 6/3B) Not until Sir Walter Scott wrote his novel *Rob Roy* (1817) about the Highland folk hero did the area known as the Trossachs leap into the public eye. It was, however, wild country known only to the Macgregors (Rob Roy's clan) as they went on their cattle-lifting forays. Now it is more accessible. The main attraction is Loch Katrine, on whose waters plies the steamer *Sir Walter Scott*. Built in 1900 in Dumbarton, then dismantled and re-assembled on Loch Katrine, it is vintage Victoriana. The loch has been Glasgow's main water supply since 1859.

Overleaf: The Five Sisters of Kintail, Tomintoul

Loch Lubnaig, The Trossachs

The variety of scenery in the area is quite astonishing and represents in miniature all of Scotland's topography.

Turriff, *Grampian* (3/3C) The long-standing reputation of Turriff as a market town for its hinterland farming communities is reflected in its substantial red sandstone dwellings. Over a thousand years ago it was the ancient capital of Lathom, a Pictish prince. Later, in the 11th century, the Old Church was built at the end of Castle Street, with associations with St Congan, a Pictish missionary, and Malcolm Canmore, King of Scots. It has an unusual double belfry added in 1636. Though now roofless, it stands as a mellowing witness to the passing centuries.

Although Turriff experienced some action during 1639 when the Covenanting Wars were beginning to wrench Scotland apart, the town has had a fairly peaceful existence. In 1913, however, shots in a different kind of battle were fired. When Lloyd George introduced the National Health Insurance Act in 1911, which required employers to pay a compulsory stamp for their employees, a local farmer refused to participate in the scheme. To extract payment, the authorities eventually sent the Sheriff to impound a cow in default of payment. The beast, the now famous white 'Turra Coo' and a legend in local folk song, was auctioned in Turriff Market but received no bids. After various adventures, including a trip by train to Aberdeen, the cow was privately bought back and returned to Lendrum Farm near the town with full honours.

The 19th century saw years of prosperity in Turriff with the great 'Feeing' markets, where farm employees were re-engaged for a new term, or changed their employers. Today the markets, including the famous Turriff Show (early August), echo the lively bustle of former days.

Tyndrum, *Central* (4/3A) Tyndrum is an important railway junction where the line splits to go north to FORT WILLIAM and west to OBAN. Thanks to the Friends of the West Highland Line the traveller can once again enjoy the old-time pleasure and smell of steam trains. The village has always served as a stopping place on the routes to and from the north, both for cattle drovers on their way to CRIEFF and Falkirk, and for soldiers on the military roads. The Ben Lui National Nature Reserve is reached from Tyndrum, with Ben Lui (3708 ft) displaying a sequence of contrasting rock types.

Tyndrum is the most recent area in Scotland to be explored for gold. In the 19th century a gold mine was actually in operation just north of the village, from which its owner took a fair quantity of the precious metal. Alluvial gold was once found in the streams. The local people collected it by placing sheepskins on the river beds. The precious grains, being heavier, would sink to the bottom and gather in the wool. After a time a truly golden fleece would be recovered.

To the north-west of Tyndrum lies Glen Orchy through which the river Orchy flows, or rather rushes, from its source on the Black Mount at the edge of Rannoch Moor. In season salmon can be seen challenging the river's tremendous currents. The waterfalls present an awe-inspiring sight, particularly after a heavy rainfall when the waters run dark brown and foam-flecked.

Ullapool, *Highland* (2/2B) Over 400 years ago, Loch Broom, one of the sea lochs of the north-west stretching into the mainland of Scotland, was famous for its herring. But the fishing fleet was not local. Rather it was the Dutch who reaped the benefit of the 'silver darlings'. Their success did not escape the attention of the Scottish Parliament in Edinburgh, whose members, in 1587, passed an Act which penalized the Dutch when fishing there. Early in the 18th century, the Government called for a report on the commercial exploitation of the herring, and from this the British Fishery Society was formed. The Society lost no time in creating a fishing station at what is now Ullapool. Since 1788, when the pier, an inn and storehouses were erected, Ullapool has enjoyed a fluctuating prosperity which has been enhanced in recent years with the appearance of 'Klondyker' ships. These are factory ships mainly from eastern Europe, but also from as far away as Egypt and Taiwan, which buy huge quantities of mackerel from local and north-east fishing boats for freezing and processing. The economic spin-off from these ships, coupled with its role as a popular tourist base, and as the ferry terminal for the Minch crossing to Stornoway on LEWIS, has provided this West Highland town with a well-to-do atmosphere. Pride of place is seen in the many small but substantial dwelling houses, whitewashed and prim, many of which date from the early 19th century.

Custom House Street, Ullapool

The quality of the fish caught in the waters at the mouth of Loch Broom has made Ullapool attractive to anglers and some international sea angling festivals have been held here.

Unst *see* Shetland Islands

Vatersay *see* Barra

Westray *see* Orkney Islands

Whaligoe, *Highland* (3/2A) This is a small fishing station on the Caithness coast about 6 miles south of WICK, and was once used to take the overspill when the latter harbour was full. The only access has always been by steps down the cliff – some 365 of them. To get the fish to market, women carried loaded baskets on their backs up the steps, and on occasion along the road into Wick. Whaligoe can still be reached by the same steps, a number of which are worn and rather dangerous in wet weather.

Whalsay *see* Shetland Islands

Wick, *Highland* (3/2A) The origins of Wick (from Old Norse *vík*, 'bay') go back to Viking times when a small settlement was established here in the far north-east of Scotland. It matured over the centuries until, in 1589, it was accorded royal burgh status. Even then, its claim to 'fame' was rather muted until, in 1767, its foundations as a herring port were laid by three local men. In 1808 the British Fishery Society obtained land on the south side of the town's harbour and a model fishing village, Pulteneytown, was built under the direction of Thomas Telford, who named many of its streets after his friends. From then on Wick became one of the most important ports while the herring swarmed in huge shoals round the northern coasts of Scotland. In its heyday 1100 fishing boats used the port and you could walk from Wick to Pulteneytown across the harbour stepping from one boat to another. Old photographs of the period show Wick harbour looking like a massive defoliated forest, so many are the masts to be seen.

The herring fishing industry began to fail by the turn of the century and Wick had to turn to other economic bases to survive. Happily, the whitefish industry has offered a partial salvation, though the heady days of last century have quite disappeared. Echoes of those days are much in evidence with fine wide streets and attractive wooded squares. The houses show the sombre colour of the local stone used in their construction: Caithness flagstone. This material was once so popular that an industry was founded on cutting and polishing the stone, which was then exported south to London, to the Continent, and even as far as Melbourne in Australia. The former use of the flagstones, as dykes around farms, is still seen in the Caithness hinterland.

In keeping with the enterprise that the Wickers have always displayed, there is a variety of industrial operations in the town, ranging from high technology underwater television systems, for use in North Sea oil rig and pipe maintenance, to the continuation of the age-old craft of glass-making. Some of the world's finest glass paperweights are made here, while the engraved-glass products are superb examples of this art form; the works at Harrow Hill have in fact become a great tourist attraction. The local distillery produces 'Old Pulteney', of which the Highland novelist Neil Gunn, himself a native of Caithness, once said 'It has to be come upon as one comes upon a friend, and treated with proper respect.'

Echoes of the past fishing history of Wick are displayed in the Wick Heritage Centre on Bank Row, housed in buildings which were once part of Telford's plans. Wick's past is also seen in the most complete collection of Victorian photographs of any Scottish town: over 100,000 glass negatives, many prints from which are on display to offer a unique experience and link with the heady days of yesteryear.

Yell *see* Shetland Islands

Further Information

The Nation's Estate Over 330 historic buildings and monuments from prehistoric remains to the industrial archaeology of the 20th century. All these national possessions are in the care of the Secretary of State for Scotland and, on his behalf, administered by the Historic Buildings and Monuments Directorate of the Scottish Development Department. The 'Friends of the Scottish Monuments', through Membership, gives free access to all these properties including privileges south of the Border. Details and special publications from PO Box No. 157, Edinburgh EH3 7QD .

The National Trust for Scotland Details of access to nearly 100 Properties, of the Membership that supports these Properties, and of the opportunities for volunteer work parties at the Trust's Thistle Camps, from 5 Charlotte Square, Edinburgh EH2 4DU, or from Properties and Trust Shops.

Royal Commission on the Ancient and Historical Monuments of Scotland The Commission, which was established in 1908, is responsible for compiling a national record of archaeological sites and historic buildings of all types and periods. The Commission makes this record available both through its publications – details of which can be obtained from 54 Melville Street, Edinburgh EH3 7HF (031–225 5994) – and through the maintenance of a central archive of information, known as the National Monuments Record of Scotland. This contains an extensive collection of pictorial and documentary material relating to Scotland's ancient monuments and historic buildings and is open daily for public reference at 6–7 Coates Place, Edinburgh EH3 7AA.

Publications include Anna Ritchie *Orkney and Shetland*, and Graham Ritchie and Mary Harman *Argyll and the Western Isles.*

Scotland's Gardens Scheme Nearly 250 gardens open from February to October, many regularly, some daily, to support a wide variety of charities. Most of the gardens are open by kind permission of private owners. Handbook available from 31 Castle Terrace, Edinburgh EH1 2EL.

Scottish Wildlife Trust Details of the Trust's more than 70 Reserves and its Visitor Centres, of Membership and Branches across Scotland, of publications and opportunities for voluntary conservation and education work: all from HQ at 25 Johnstone Terrace, Edinburgh EH1 2NH.

Royal Society for the Protection of Birds Details of Society's Reserves open to the public available from the Society's Scottish Office at 17 Regent Terrace, Edinburgh EH7 5BN.

Scottish Conservation Projects Trust Opportunities for volunteers to work on practical outdoor conservation projects, attend skilled training courses and help local conservation groups throughout Scotland. Membership details, programmes and reports from HQ at Balallan House, 24 Allan Park, Stirling FK8 2QG.

The Nature Conservancy Council Details of all National Nature Reserves (NNRs) and Sites of Special Scientific Interest (SSSIs) from Scottish HQ, 12 Hope Terrace, Edinburgh EN9 2AS.

Bibliography

The number of books that have been written about Northern Scotland and the Highlands and Islands is vast and covers virtually everything from socio-economics to cultural aspects. Research carried out in the last two decades or so has revealed much that was unavailable to earlier writers, and the selected titles in the following list reflect some of these recent studies. They offer a deeper insight into aspects only touched on in this book and are recommended to the reader who wishes to gain a greater understanding of, and empathy with, the region covered here.

Aitken, R. *The West Highland Way*. Edinburgh 1986

Campbell, J. L. *Canna*. Oxford 1984

Cooper, D. *Skye*. London 1983

– *Century Companion to Whiskies*, 2nd edn. London 1984

Cowan, E. J. (ed.) *The People's Past*. Edinburgh 1980

Edwards, B. *Scottish Seaside Towns*. London 1986

Eyers, M. *Scottish Place Names*. London 1983

Fawcett, R. *Scottish Medieval Churches*. Edinburgh 1985

Graham, C. *Portrait of the Moray Firth*. London 1977

– *Aberdeen and Deeside*. London 1980

Graham-Campbell, D. *Portrait of Argyll and the Southern Hebrides*. London 1978.

– *Portrait of Perth, Angus and Fife*. London 1979

Grimble, I. *Clans and Chiefs*. London 1980

– *Scottish Islands*. London 1985

Hanley, C. *The Scots*. Newton Abbot 1980

Hunter, J. *The Making of the Crofting Community*. Edinburgh 1976

Maclean, C. *The Fringe of Gold*. Edinburgh 1985 (Fishing villages, Fife to Shetland)

Macnab, P. A. *The Isle of Mull*. Newton Abbot 1970

Magnusson, M. (ed.) *Echoes in Stone*. Edinburgh 1983

Mercer, J. *Hebridean Islands*. Glasgow 1974 (Colonsay, Gigha, Jura)

Muir, R. *The Shell Guide to Reading the Celtic Landscape*. London 1985

Nethersole-Thompson, D., and Watson, A. *The Cairngorms: Their Natural History and Scenery*. London 1974

Nicolson, J. R. *Shetland*. Newton Abbot 1983

Peck, E. H. *North-east Scotland*. Edinburgh 1981

Prebble, J. *The Highland Clearances*. London 1963

Schei, L., and Moberg, G. *The Orkney Story*. London 1985

Scottish Tourist Board *1001 Things to See*. Edinburgh 1983

– *Walks and Trails in Scotland*. Edinburgh 1986

Thompson, F. *Harris and Lewis*. Newton Abbot 1973

– *The Uists and Barra*. Newton Abbot 1974

– *Crofting Years*. Barr, Ayrshire, 1984

Withers, C. W. J. *Gaelic in Scotland*. Edinburgh 1984

For use of maps see Editorial Note on p. 7.

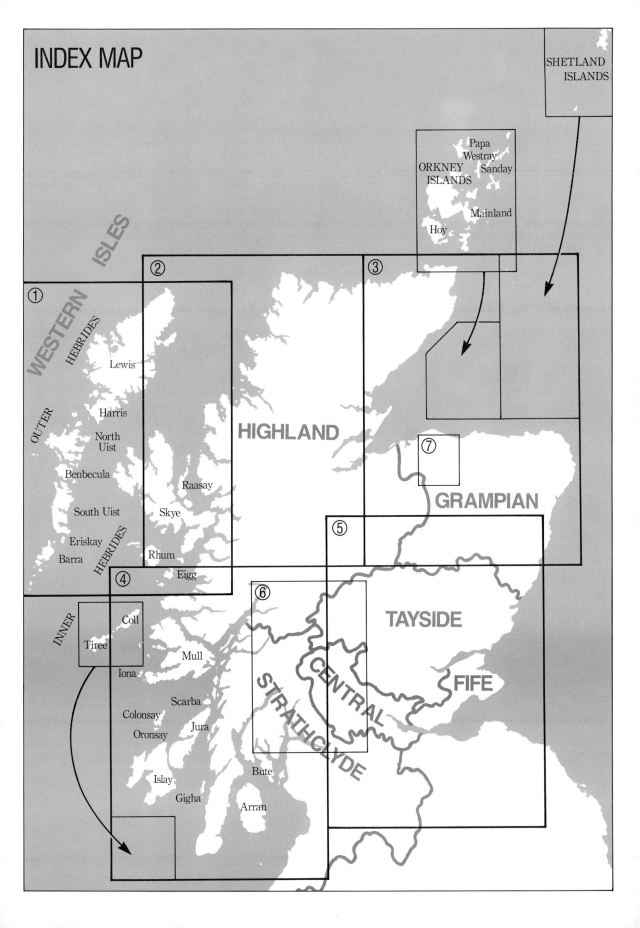

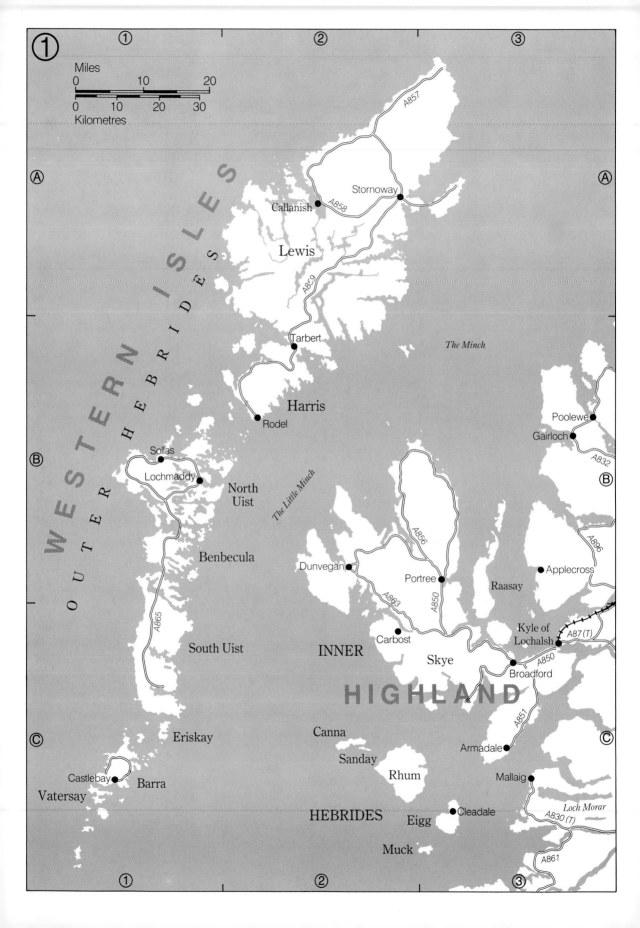

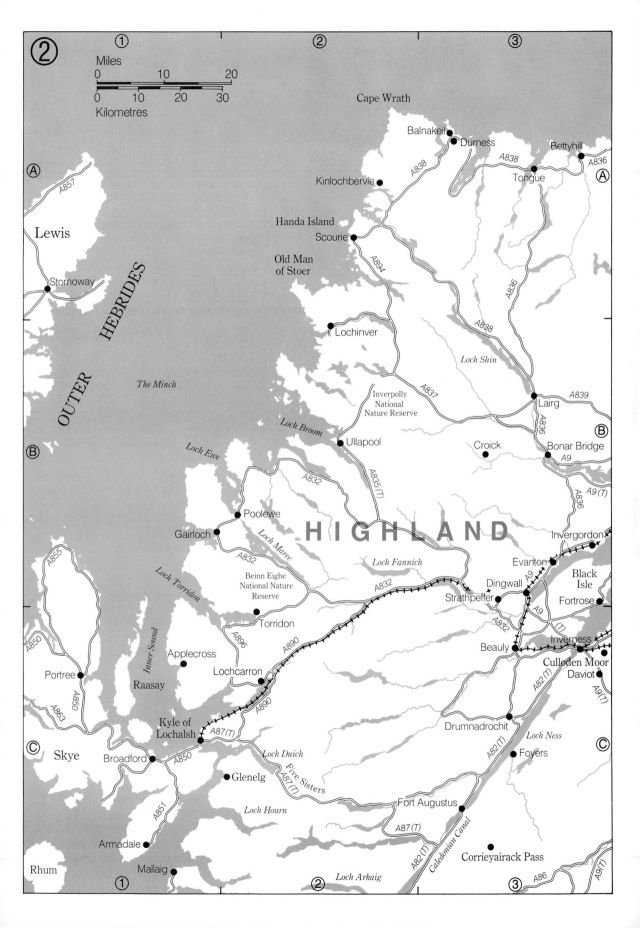

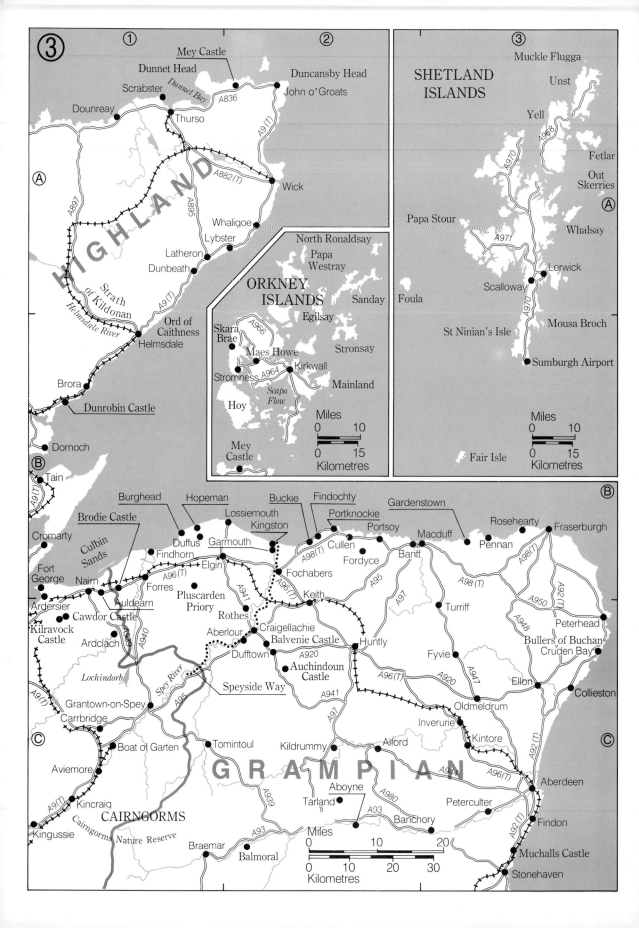

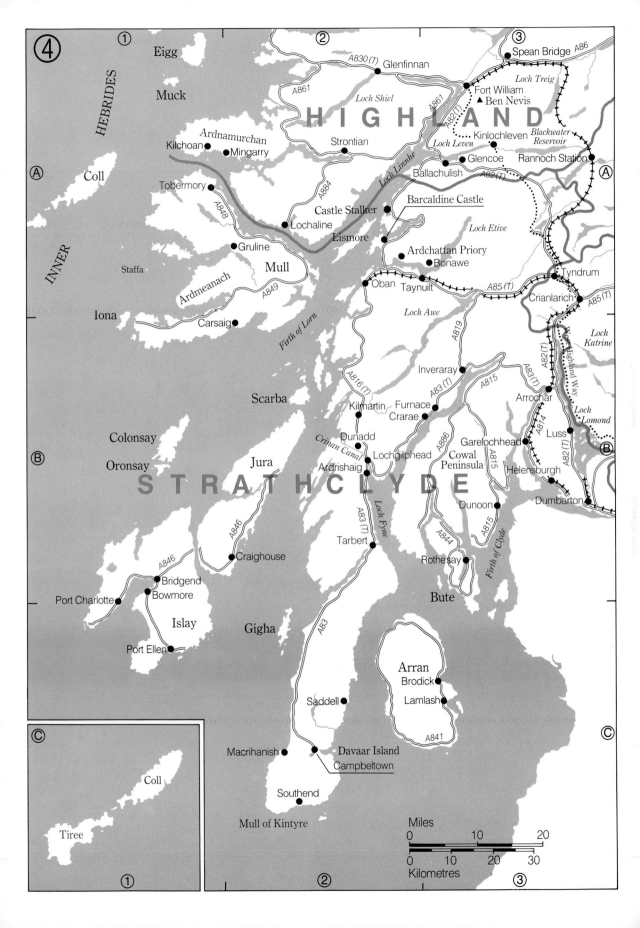

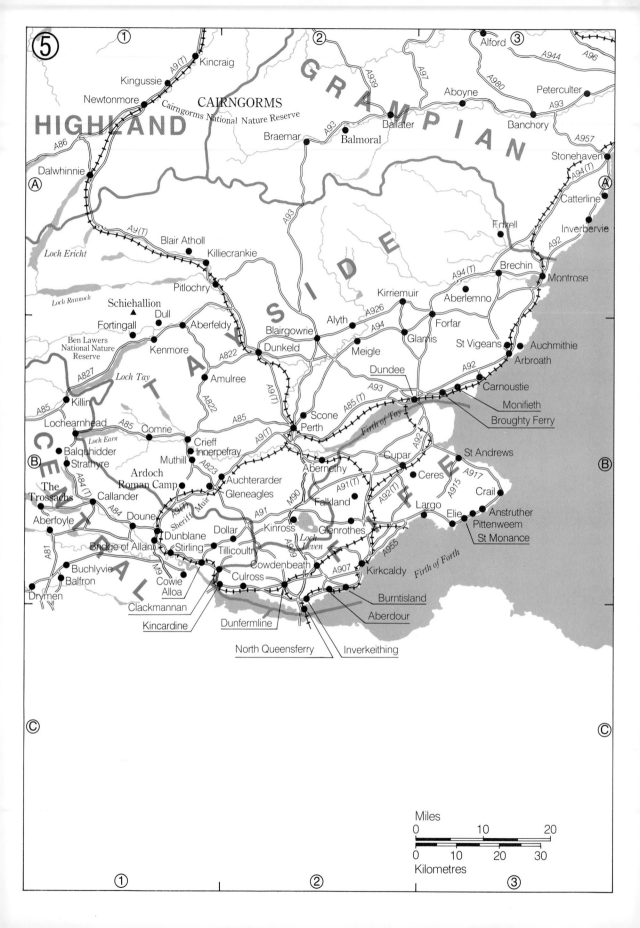

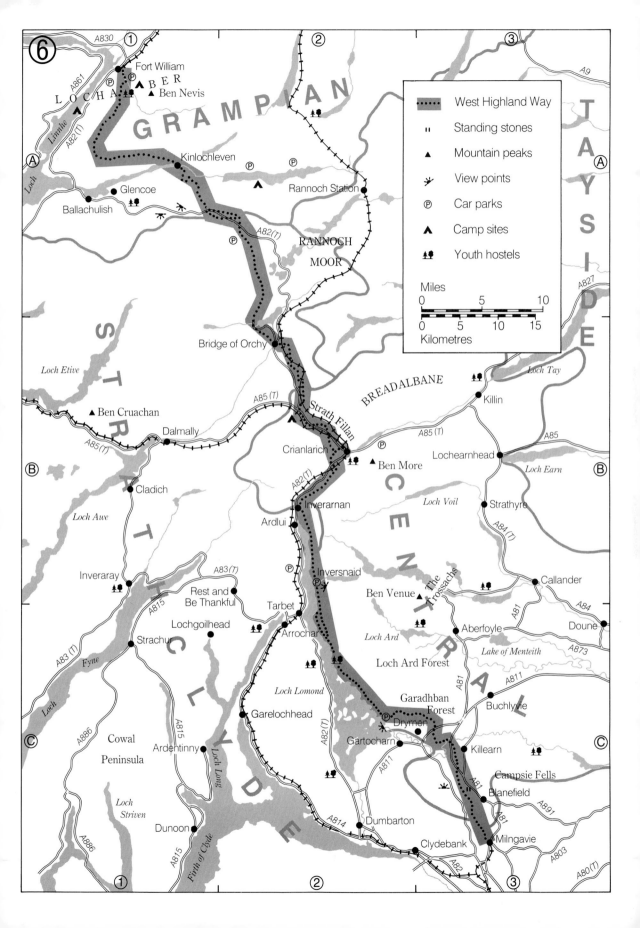

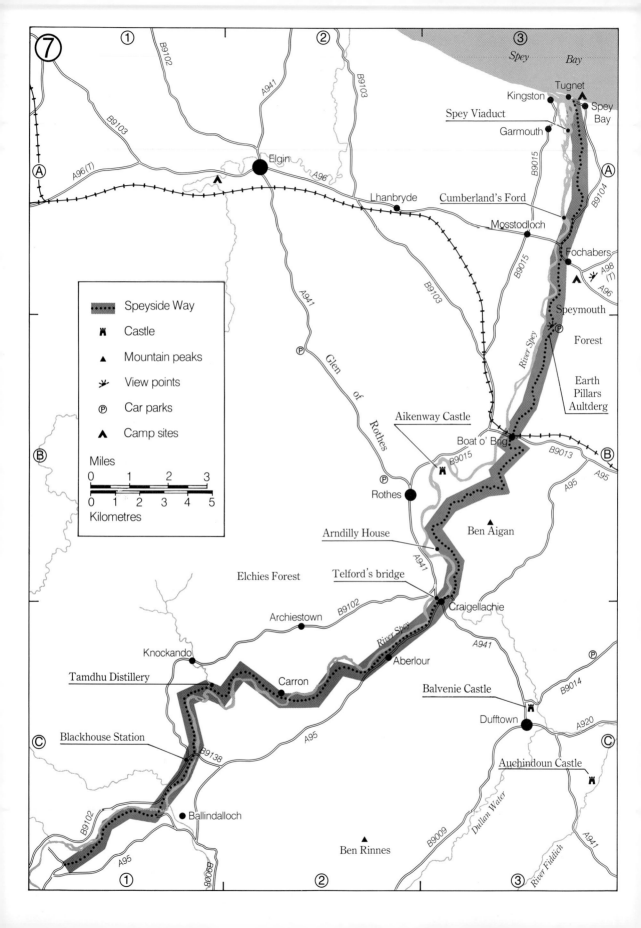

Index

Numbers in *italics* refer to illustrations

Aberdeen 67–8, 84, 126, 129, 143; airport 41; Marischal College 68, 177; Maritime Museum 67; oil industry 39, 41, 67; Provost Skene's house 67–8; Union Street 67, 68
Aberfeldy 69, 134
Aberdour 68; St Fillan's Church 68
Aberfoyle 69
Aberlemno 69–70; Pictish stones 59–70, 70
Aberlour 70
Abernethy 70–2, 89; Round Tower 70, 71, 72, 91
Aboyne 72
Aboyne Castle, Formaston Stone 71
Achadun Castle, Lismore 154
Adam, William 86, 141, 170
Agnew of Lochnow, Sir Crispin 22
Alford 72; Grampian Museum of Transport 72
Allan Water 117
Alloa 72
Alloa Tower 72
Alyth 72; Folk musuem 72
Amulree 72
Anancaun 87
Angus 11, 12
Angus Folk Museum, Glamis 137
An Sgurr (Eigg) 123
Anstruther 72, 74; Scottish Fisheries Museum 74, 74
Anstruther Easter manse 74
Antonine Wall 43, 77
Applecross peninsula 74, 75
Applecross village 74, 146
Arbroath 75; Abbey 75; Declaration of (1320) 49, 75; Signal Tower 75
Arbroath Smokie 75, 78
Ardblair Castle 89
Ardchattan Priory 75–6
Ardclash 76
Ardclash Bell Tower 76, 76
Ardersier (Campbelltown) 40, 76
Ardmeanach, Mull 163, 165
Ardnamurchan 60, 76–7
Ardoch Roman Camp, Braco 77
Ardrishaig 77, 107
Ardvreck Castle 158, 159
Arydyne Point, Argyll 41
Argyll Forest Park 104
Armadale, Skye 195
Armadale Castle 16, 195; Clan Donald Centre 13, 195
Aros Castle, Mull 163
Arran, island of 77–8; Brodick 77, 78; Brodick Castle 9, 19, 77; Goat Fell 9, 77
Arrochar 78
Atholl Highlanders 88
Auchindoun Castle 78, 115
Auchinduich 150
Auchmithie 78
Auchterarder 78, 79
Auldearn 78; Battle of (1645) 78; Boath Dovecot 78, 79, 82

Aviemore 19, 80–1, 82, 89, 138, 197
Avoch 87
Azilian Man 169–70

Badenoch 58, 148
Baird, John Logie 139
Balfron 82
Ballachulish 12, 82
Ballater 82
Ballindalloch 197
Balmoral Castle 82–3
Balnakeil 83
Balnakeil House 83
Balquihidder 83
Baltasound, Unst 193
Balvenie Castle 78, 83–4, 115
Banchory 84; Crathes Castle and Gardens 84, 84
Banff, 84, 143, 161; Castle 86; Duff House; market cross 85; seven-arched bridge 85
Banks, Joseph 198–9
Bannockburn, Battle of 107, 199, 201
Barcaldine Castle 86
Barra, Outer Hebrides 32, 86, 99; Castlebay 86; Kiessimul Castle 86
Barra Feis festival 86
Barrie, J. M. 98, 150
Barry Hill, Iron Age fort 72
Bass of Inverurie 143
Bathgate shale-oil industry 37
'Battle of the Braes', Skye 32–4
Bealach na Ba 74, 75, 190–1
Beauly 86–7
Beinn a'Ghlo 11
Beinn Alligin 205
Beinn Eighe National Nature Reserve 60, 87, 159, 205
Beinn na Caillich, Skye 195
Bell, Henry 139
Bell Rock, lighthouse 75
Bellamy, Dr David 60
Ben Arthur ('The Cobbler'); 62, 78
Benbecula, Outer Hebrides 87
Ben Cleuch 204
Ben Lawers 19, 87
Ben Ledi 98
Ben Lomond 159
Ben Lui National Nature Reserve 208
Ben MacDui 96
Ben Mor 163
Bennachie 72
Ben Nevis 63, 87, 134, 135
Ben Rinnes 70
Ben Vorlich 155
Ben Wyvis 202
Bernera Riot 31–2
Bettyhill 87
Bin Hill, Cullen 109
Birnam 119–20
Birnam Wood 119, 119
Black Isle 87–8, 88, 107, 134

Black Rock of Novar 128
Blackwater Reservoir 149
Black Wood of Rannoch 12
Blair Atholl 11, 88
Blair Castle 88
Blair Drummond Safari Park 113
Blairgowrie 88–9
Blairs College 177
Boat of Brig 197
Boat of Garten 89; station 89
Boath Dovecot, Auldearn 78, 79, 82
Bonar Bridge 89, 91
Bonawe 90, 91
Borve Castle, Benbecula 87
Bow Fiddle Rock, Portknockie 181
Bowmore, Islay, 144; Round Church 145
Boyne Castle 182
Braco, Roman Camp 77
Braemar 91
Braemar Castle 91
Braemar Games 42 91
Braes of Angus 72
Breacachadh Castle, Coll 102
Breadalbane 62
Brechin 91, 161; Cathedral 91; Round Tower 91
Brehon Laws 23, 127
Brei Holm, Shetlands 193
Brent Field, North Sea 36, 39
Bressay Island 192
Bridge of Allan 91–2
Broadford, Skye 195
Brodick 77, 78
Brodick Castle and gardens 9, 19, 77
Brodie Castle 57, 92, 93
Bronze Age sites 13, 72, 102, 103, 161, 189
Brora 92, 165
Broughty Castle 92
Broughty Ferry 92
Buchanan Castle 115
Buchlyvie 92
Buckie 92, 94, 129, 181; Cluny Harbour 92; Maritime Museum 94
Bullers of Buchan 94
Bullough, Sir John 182
Burghead 94, Burning of the Clavie 44, 49, 94
Burghead Well 94
Burns Robert, 43, 47, 49, 69, 116, 117, 131, 134, 138, 146–7
Burntisland 94
Bute island 94, 96

Cairngorms 19, 55, 56, 80–1, 82, 95, 96, 96, 97, 148
Caledonian Canal 96, 98, 134, 143
Caledonian Forest 54–5, 89
Callandar 98
Campbeltown 98–9
Cambuskenneth Abbey 201
Campbell, Clan 13, 21, 25, 76, 82, 141, 145, 170
Campbell, Colin, the Red Fox 82
Campbell, John Francis 146

Campbell, Dr John Lorne 99
Camster Cairns 161
Canna, Inner Hebrides 59, 99
Cape Wrath, lighthouse 99
Carinish, Trinity Temple 169
Carloway, Iron Age broch 152
Carnegie, Andrew 107, 119
Carnegie Dunfermline Trust 119
Carnoustie 99
Carrbridge 99
Carrick Castle, Cowal 104
Carsaig, Ross of Mull 163
Castlebay, Barra 86
Castle Grant 138–9
Castle Hill of Cullen 109
Castle Law Hill, Iron Age fort 72
Castle Menzies, Weem 69
Castle Stalker, 82
Castle Varrich, Tongue 205
Catterline 99
Cawdor Castle 99, 100–1, 102
Celts 13, 23, 45–6, 67, 87, 189, 193
Ceres 102
Chanonry Point and lighthouse 134
Charles Edward Stuart, Prince (Bonnie Prince Charlie) 16, 46, 88, 89, 109, 127, 138, 147, 148, 196, 197, 199
Charleston of Aberlour see Aberlour
Clachan Church 87
Clackmannan 102
clans Scottish 13, 16, 21–7
Clava Cairns 102
Claypotts Castle 92
Cleadale, Eigg, 123–4
Clickhimin Broch, Shetlands 189
Clo Mor cliffs, Cape Wrath 99
Clynelish Distillery, Brora 92
coalmining 104, 111, 165
Cochran, Robert mason builder 78
Coinneach Odhar, seer 96, 134
Coirechatachan, Skye 195
Colbost (Lewis), Black House 28
Coll island 102
Colliestone 102–3
Colonsay, Inner Hebrides 103; Kiloran Gardens 103
Colquhoun, Sir Alexander 139
Comhairle nan Eilean 152
Comrie 103; Museum of Scottish Tartans 103
Corrieyairack Pass 103–4, 169
Cowal Highland Gathering/Games 47, 104
Cowal peninsula 94, 104, 120
Cowdenbeath 104
Cowie 104
Craigellachie 104, 197
Craigellachie Bridge 104, 105
Craigievar Castle 72, 73
Craig Phadraig 143
Crail 104–5
Crail Capon (smoked haddock) 105
Crarae 105; Forest and Lodge Gardens 19, 105

Crathes Castle and Gardens 84, 84
Crathie Church, Balmoral 83
Crianlarich 62, 107
Crieff 72, 103, 107, 111, 169
Crinan Canal 77, 107
crofting 29–35, 51, 56, 86, 120, 127, 128, 152, 182, 184, 195
Crofting Holdings Act (1886), 29, 30, 34, 196, 204
Croick Church 107
Craighouse, Jura 146
Cromarty 87, 107–8; Fishertown 108; Hugh Miller's cottage 106, 108; Old Gaelic Chapel 108
Cruden Bay 39, 108
Cuillin Hills, Skye 51, 52–3, 195
Cul Beag, Inverpolly 143
Culbin Sands 60, 108, 128
Cullen 83, 108 9, 181
Cullen House 108
Culloden Moor 102, 109; Battle of (1746) 46, 84, 109, 131, 143, 147, 148, 176, 196; clan grave 20
Cul Mor, Inverpolly 143
Culross 109–11; Mercat Cross 110; Palace 109, 109; the Study 109, 110
Cupar 102, 111
Cutty Sark 116, 141

Dalgairn House Garden 111
Dallas Dhu 19
Dalwhinnie 103, 111
dancing, Scottish 42, 48, 91, 104
Davaar Island 99
Daviot 111, 143
Declaration of Arbroath (1320), 49, 75
Dee, river 72, 82, 84, 177
Deeside 82, 83, 96
Deirdre of the Sorrows 170
Dingwall 111–12, 202
Dochart, river 147
Dornoch 112
Dornoch Cathedral 112, 112
Dornoch Firth 89, 202
Douglas, Sir James 161, 163
Doune 112–13, 123
Doune Castle 113, 113, 114
Doune Motor Museum 113
Dounray atomic energy establishment, 113, 203
Drosten Stone, St Vigean's 184
Drumadoon, king's Caves 77
Drummond Castle, Muthill 165
Drumnadrochit 113
Drumochter Passs 103
Drymen 62, 115
Duart Castle, Mull 163
Dufftown 78, 115
Duffus Castle 115, 115–16
Duffus Church 116
Dull 116
Dumbarton, Dumbarton Castle 116
Dunbeath, Dunbeath Castle 116
Dunblane 116–17; Cathedral 116–17
Duncansby Head 117
Dundee 11, 93, 17–18; Harbour 117; oil supply bases 39; St Paul's Cathedral 118
Dun Eibhinn 103
Dunfermline 118–19
Dunfermline Abbey 118–19, 176

Dunkeld 11, 12, 12, 119, 120; Cathedral 119
Dunnet Head 120, 146
Dunollie Castle, Oban 170
Dunoon 104, 120
Dunottar Castle 201, 202
Dunrobin Castle 120
Dunstaffnage Castle 170
Dunvegan, Skye 196
Dunvegan Castle 196
Durness 33, 83, 121
Dysart 150; Stuart McDougall Museum 150

Eagle Stone, Ben Wyvis 202
East Aquhorthies stone circle 143
East Kilbride 41
Easter Ross 47, 87
East Neuk 104–5
Edinburgh 12, 21, 41, 104, 111; George IV's visit to 21–2; National Museums of Scotland 62, 129, 189, 193
Edward I, King 77, 84, 117, 155, 161, 184, 191
Edzell 121, 123
Edzell Castle 120–1, 123
Egilsay, Orkneys 173
Eigg, Inner Hebrides 59, 123
Eilean an Tighe, North Uist 169
Eilean Donan, Skye 195
Elcho Castle, near Perth 176, 177
Elephant Stone, Mortlach Church 115
Elfin Assynt church 205
Elgin 83, 115, 124–6, 159; Bishop's House 126; Cathedral 124–5, 125, 155; Old Mills 124, 126
Elgol, Skye 196
Elie 126
Ellon, Ellon Castle 126–7, 170
emigration from Highlands 26, 46, 77, 107, 120–1, 195
Eriskay, Outer Hebrides 127–8
Eriskay pony 127, 127–8
Evanton 128

Fair Isle 9, 128
Fair Isle knitting 128
Falkirk 103, 107, 111, 117, 169
Falkland 128
Falkland Palace 128, 184
Falls of Edinample 155
Falls of Foyers 134
Falls of Lora, Connel 170
Farr Stone, Clachan Churchyard 87
Faslane Naval Base 136
Fasque 122–3, 123
Fetlar, Shetlands 189; Brough Lodge Tower 189, Giant's Grave 189
Fettercairn 123
Fife Folk Museum 102
Findhorn 128
Findochty 128–9
Findon 129
Fingal's Cave, Staffa 199
Finlarig Castle, Killin 147
Firth of Clyde 77, 104, 139
Firth of Forth 148, 149, 150
Firth of Lorn 103, 163
Firth of Tay 92, 161
Five Sisters of Kintail 13
Flotta oil terminal 39, 175
Fochabers 58, 129, 197, Folk Museum 129; Gordon Castle 129

Forbes of Pitsligo, 4th Baron 182–3
Fordyce 129, 129
Fordyce Academy 129
Fordyce Castle 129, 130
Forestry Commission 13, 56, 108, 109, 182, 197
forests/woodlands 54–5, 60, 88, 95, 159
Forfar 131
Forfar Bridie 131
Forres 82, 92, 131, 155
Fort Augustus 103, 131, 134, 169; Benedictine Abbey and School 131
Fort George 16, 131, 134
Forth Bridge 142, 169
Forth, river/estuary 72, 102, 142, 148, 199
Forties Field 37, 39, 108
Fortingall 132–3, 134
Fortrose 87, 134
Fort William 16, 61, 63, 134, 135
Forvie Kirk 103
Foula, Shetlands 192
Fowlis Wester 107
Foyers 134
Fraserburgh 135, 143, 182
Free Church of Scotland 31, 78
Furnace 135
Fyvie 135–6
Fyvie Castle 135
Fyvie Church 136

Gaelic language/culture 27, 34, 45–7, 48, 75, 86, 99, 108, 120, 165, 170
Gairloch 87, 136, 181
Gairloch Heritage Museum 136
gardens 13, 16, 18, 19, 77, 84, 103, 105, 111, 123, 143, 165, 170, 178–9, 180, 203
Gardenstown ('Gamrie') 136; St John's Chapel 136
Garelochhead 136
Garmouth 136–7; 'Maggie Fair' 137
Gates of Negapatam, Evanton 128
Gaulcross silver hoard 129
George IV, king 21–2
Gigha 137; Achamore House 137
Gladstone, W. E. 123
Glamis 137; Angus Folk Museum 137
Glamis Castle 13, 137
Glascune Castle 89
Glasgow 41, 120, 139
Glencoe 16, 62–3, 103, 137, 137–8
Glencoe and North Lorn Folk Museum 138
Gleneagles 197
Glenelg, Wester Ross 13, 55
Glenfiddich Distillery 17
Glenfinnan 16, 138
Glenlivet whisky 204
Glenmore Lodge 197
Glen Orchy 90, 209
Glenrothes 138
Glen Roy parallel roads 197
Glenshee 66
Glen Spean 197
Goat Fell, Arran 9, 77
golf courses 99, 138, 169, 184
Gordon Castle, Fochabers 129
Gow, John, pirate 175
Grampians 51, 58, 60, 62, 197

Grangemouth oil refinery 39
Grantown-on-Spey 138, 155; Castle Grant 138–9
Great Glen 98, 197
'Groatie buckie' 146
Grulin, Mull 165

Haddo House, Old Meldrum 170, 171
Hadrian's Wall 43
Handa Island 139
Harlow, Battle of (1411) 67, 143
Harris 139
Harris tweed 152
Hawthorne, Nathaniel 62
Hebridean Small Isles 163
Hebrides see Inner and Outer Hebrides
Helensburgh 51, 139
Hell's Glen, Cowal 104
Helmsdale 139–40
herring industry 72, 77, 92, 94, 98, 102, 105, 139, 141, 159, 161, 163, 169, 177, 181, 182, 193, 203, 209, 210
Highland Boundary Fault 11, 51, 119
Highland Brigade 30–1
Highland Clearances 26, 27, 30, 77, 87
Highland Games/Gatherings 42, 48, 91, 104
Highland Line 72, 103, 165
Highland Railway 82, 89, 92, 154
Highland Wildlife Park, Kincraig 148
Hill o' Many Stanes, Lybster 161
Hill of Tarvit House 111
Historic Buildings and Monuments Directorate 12
Hogg, James 77, 98, 204
Holborn Head, Scrabster 189
Hopeman 140
Horlick, Sir James 137
Horne, Janet, burning of 112
Hoy, Orkneys 174; Dwarfie Stane 174; Old Man of Hoy 174
Huntingtower, Perth 177
Huntly 83, 140–1, 143
Huntly Castle 140, 140

Inchcailleoch, Loch Lomond 159
Inchmahome Augustinian Priory 150
Inchmurrin, Loch Lomond 159
Inchnadamph 54
Inchtuthill Roman Fort 77
Inner Hebrides 25, 29, 59, 169; Canna 59, 99; Colonsay 103; Eigg 59, 123; Gigha 137; Islay 13, 59–60, 144–6; Jura 146; Mull 50, 102, 144, 163–5, 166–7; Oronsay 103; Raasay 74, 182; Rhum 59, 59, 182; Scarba 146
Innerpeffray 141; Chapel 141; public library 141
Innes, Malcolm 22
Insh Church 148
Inveraray 141
Inveraray Castle 13, 16, 141; Combined Operations Museum 141
Inverarnan 62
Inverbervie 141
Inverewe Gardens, Poolewe 16, 18, 178–9, 180–1

Invergordon 141–2
Invergordon Mutiny (1931) 142
Inverkeithing 142
Inverlochy Castle 134
Inverness 10, 12, 76, 82, 88, 142–3; airport 41; Castle 143; Northern Meeting 47; St Andrew's Cathedral 142, 143
Inverpolly National Nature Reserve 64–5, 143
Inversnaid 62, 159
Inverurie 143–4, 170; Bass of 143; Keith Hall 143
Iona 9, 13, 144, 159, 163; Old Abbey and St Oran's Chapel 144, 144–5; Reilig Odhrain graveyard 144; St John's Cross and St Columba's shrine 9; Statutes of 26, 46
Iona community 144
Iron age sites 13, 72, 92, 103, 109, 113, 152, 165, 181, 192
Islay (Inner Hebrides) 144–6; Bowmore 144, 145; greylag goose habitats 59–60; Kildalton Cross 13, 145; Port Charlotte 144, 145–6; Port Ellen 144, 145; whisky distilleries 146

James VI of Scotland 19, 92, 135, 140, 165, 177, 184, 199
James of the Glens 82
Jarlshof, Shetland 13, 192
John O'Groats 146
Johnson, Dr Samuel 46, 86, 94, 102, 182, 195
Jura, Inner Hebrides 146

Keil Point, Mull of Kintyre 165
Keith 83, 146
Keith Festival 48
Keith Hall, Inverurie 143
Keith Inch 177
Kessock 88
Kelty 102
Kenmore 146–7
Keose seaweed-processing factory 152
Kerrera island 169
Kilchoar parish church 77
Kildalton Cross, Islay 13, 145
Kildrummy Castle 16
Killiecrankie, Pass of 11, 16, 103, 147; Battle of (1689) 88, 147; 'Soldier's Leap' 147, 147
Killin 147
Killin Church 147
Kilmahog 98
Kilmartin 13
Kilmoluaig 'cathedral', Lismore 154
Kilmuir Crofting Museum 31
Kiloran Gardens, Colonsay 103
Kilravock Castle 147–8
Kincardine 148
Kincraig 148; Highland Wildlife Park 148
Kingshouse inn, Loch Ba 62
Kingston 148; Dunfermline House 148
Kingussie 148; Highland Folk Museum 148; Ruthven Barracks 14–15, 16, 148
Kinlochbervie 148, 149
Kinlochleven 63, 148–9
Kinloss Abbey 131
Kinaird Head 135
Kinross 149
Kintore 149
Kirkcaldy 149–50; Museum and Art Gallery 150

Kirkwall 173, 174; Earl's Palace 174; Bishop's Palace 174; St Magnus Cathedral 173, 174; Tankerness House Museum 174
Kirriemuir 150
Kishorn 155
'Klondyker' ships 209
Knockfarrel fort 202
Knox, John 104, 176, 184
Kyle of Buate 94
Kyle of Lochalsh ferry 193, 194, 195
Kyle of Tongue 205

Lairg 150
Lairig Ghru pass 96
Lake of Menteith 150
Lamb Holm chapel 175
Lamlash, Arran 78
languages 45–7, 48
Largo, Upper and Lower 150, 151
Largs, Battle of (1263) 78, 174
Latheron 152
Leith Hall, Huntly 141
Leny House, Callandar 98
Lerwick 189, 192, 193; Fort Charlotte 192; Up Helly Aa Festival 45, 49, 192
Leverhulme, Lord 154
Lewis 13, 28, 32, 35, 139, 152, 154; Standing Stones of Callanish 13, 152; Stornoway 152, 154
Liathach mountain 205
Lindsay, Sir David 123
Lismore island 154
Loanhead Stone Circle, Daviot 143
Lochabar 63
Lochaline 154, 163
Lochaline House 153
Loch Assynt 158, 159
Loch Ba 62
Loch Broom 209, 210
Loch Campbelltown 98, 99
Loch Carron 74, 154–5, 155
Loch Carron village 154, 155–6
Loch Creran 86
Loch Druidibeg National Nature Reserve 197
Lochearnhead 155
Loch Eriboll 121
Loch Etive 75, 91, 170
Loch Faskally 180
Loch Fyne 19, 77, 98, 104, 105, 135, 141, 155, 203
Loch Garten 58, 89
Loch Gilp 77, 107, 155
Loch Gilphead 107, 155, 211
Loch Goil 104
Lochindorb Castle 155, 159
Loch Insh 148
Lochinver 159; Ardvreck Castle 158; 159
Loch Assynt 158, 159
Loch Katrine 205
Loch Kishorn 41
Loch Leven 11, 12, 148, 149
Loch Lochore see Castle 149
Loch Linnhe 82, 98, 134, 154
Loch Lomond 62, 78, 115, 159; Luss 159, 160; National Nature Reserve 115
Loch Long 78, 104
Loch Lubnaig, Trossachs 208
Lochmaddy, North Uist 169
Loch Maree 159, 160, 180
Loch Morar 159
Loch Morlich 80–1

Lochnagar 82
Loch nan Geireann 169
Loch nan Uamh 16
Loch Ness 98, 103, 113, 131, 134
Loch Ness Monster Exhibition 113
Loch Oich 98
Lochore Meadows 104
Loch Rannoch 12, 61
Loch Tay 19, 146, 147
Loch Torridon 74
Loch Tummel 11, 12, 180
Lockhard, J. G. 21
Lonach, the men of 24
Lorne Furnace 91
Lossiemouth 159–60
Lunardi, Vincenzo 102
Luss 159, 160
Luss Hills 62
Lybster 160–1

MacDonald, Alexander, Lord of the Isles 143
MacDonald, Clan 13, 22, 24, 25, 27, 32–3, 62–3, 124, 137–8, 145, 195, 196, 197
MacDonald, Sir Hector 111
Macdonald, Sir John Alexander 150
MacDonald, Ramsay 160
MacDougall, Clan 23–4, 170
Macduff 161
MacGregor, Clan 21–2, 62, 83, 115, 136, 159, 205
MacKelvie, Donald 'Tattie' 78
MacKenzie, Sir Alexander 152
MacKenzie, Colin 152
MacKenzie, Osgood 180–1
MacKinnon, Alexander 99
MacKinnon, Clan 24, 195
Mackintosh, Charles Rennie 139
MacLean, Clan 25, 137, 145, 163
MacLeod, Clan 21, 23, 124, 139, 144, 154, 159, 182, 195, 196
MacNab, Clan 21, 24, 147
MacNeill, Clan 86, 137
MacPherson, Clan 169
MacQuarrie, General Lachlan 165
Macrihanish 165
Maes Howe, Orkney 13, 174
Magnus, Jarl (Earl) 173, 174
Malcolm Canmore, King of Scots 43, 45, 67, 70, 91, 104, 131, 176, 208
Mallaig 16, 161, 162, 193
Margaret, Queen of Scots, 45, 74, 144, 176
Mary, Queen of Scots 11, 62, 72, 78, 128, 149
Maryculter 177
Matheson, Sir James 32, 154
Meadowbank clan gathering 25
Meigle Museum 13, 161
Methil, Fife 40
Mey Castle 161
Miller, Hugh 106, 108
Milngavie 61
Minard Castle, Crarae 105
Mingary 76
Mitchell, Donald, missionary 76
Monadhliath Mountains 99, 148, 197
Monck, General George 134, 199, 201
Moncrieffe, Sir Iain 22
Monifieth 161
Montrose, James Graham,

Marquis of 67
Montrose 39, 161, 163
Montrose Basin 12, 163
Moray Firth 40, 51, 67, 76, 87, 94, 98, 107, 108, 131, 136, 140, 161, 170, 173, 181, 182, 197
Mossmorran plant, Fife 39, 40
Mousa, Shetland 192; Iron Age brooch 13, 192
Muchalls, Muchalls Castle 163
Muck, Hebrides 163
Muckle Flugga, Shetlands 192
Mull 102, 144, 163–5; millstone on 164; red deer 50; Tobermory 163, 166–7
Mull of Kintyre 77, 98, 107, 137, 165
Munlochy 88, 88
Munro, Sir Hector 128
'Munroes' 62
music, Scottish 47–8, 48, 84
Muthill 165

Nairn 76, 78, 99, 147, 148, 165, 169
Napier Commission (1883) 31, 34
National Forest Parks 60
National Gaelic Mod 48
National Museums of Scotland, Edinburgh 62, 129, 189, 193
National Nature Reserves 13, 64–5, 87, 96, 103, 115, 143, 149, 159, 163, 197, 208
National Trust for Scotland 13, 19, 77, 87, 92, 99, 109, 128, 136, 138, 141, 144, 147, 170, 180, 201, 205
Nature Conservancy Council, 12–13, 59, 87, 182
Nature trails 87
Ness, spring digging 35
Newton Castle 89
Newtonmore 103, 169; Clan MacPherson Museum 169; tossing the caber 168
Nigg, oil industry in 142
Nigg Bay 40
Noltland Castle, Westray 175
Norn language 47, 189, 192
North Queensferry 169
North Ronaldsay 174
North Sea oil and gas 37–41, 67, 108, 135, 142, 155, 163, 175, 177, 189; map of oilfields 38
North Uist 87, 139, 169

Oban 54, 75, 86, 103, 163, 169–70; Dunollie Castle 170; McCaig's Folly 170
Ogilvie, John, missionary 146
Old Dumbarton Bridge 116
Old Man of Hoy 174
Old Man of Stoer 170
Old Meldrum 170
Ord of Caithness 170, 173
Orkney Islands 11, 13, 29, 47, 173–6; Egilsay 173; Flotta oil terminal 39, 175; Hoy 174; Kirkwall 173, 174; Maes Howe 13, 174; North Ronaldsay 174; Sanday 174; Scapa Flow 175; Skara Brae 13, 175; Stromness 175; Stronsay 175; Westray 175–6
Ormaclett Castle, South Uist 197
Oronsay, Inner Hebrides 103
Oronsay Priory 103
Outer Skerries, Shetlands 192–3

Outer Hebrides 13, 29, 169; Barra 32, 86; Benbecula 87; Eriskay 127–8; Harris 139; Lewis 13, 28, 32, 35, 139, 152, 154; North Uist 87, 139, 169; South Uist 59, 86, 87, 196–7

Pabay, Skye 195
Pannanich Lodge 82
Papa Stour, Shetlands 193; Kirstan's Hole 193
Paps of Jura 146
Pass of Drumochter 111
Pennan 176
Pentland Firth 98, 99, 117, 121, 173, 175, 189
Perth 11, 43, 54, 82, 176–7, 199; St John's Kirk 176
Peterculter 177
Peterhead 39, 177, 180; Arbuthnot Museum 180
Picts 69–70, 70, 72, 84, 89, 94, 105, 108, 116, 126, 129, 131, 137, 143, 149, 161, 184, 189, 193, 201, 202, 203, 208
Pilate, Pontius 134
pipes, pipe-band 27, 47, 104
Pipe Rock fossils 87
Pitlochry 11, 11, 180; Festival Theatre 11, 180
Pitmeddem Garden 170, 172
Pitsligo Castle, Rosehearty 182
Pittencrieff Glen and Estate 118, 119
Pittencrieff House Museum 119
Pittenweem 180; St Fillan's Cave 180
Playfair, William 203
Plockton 155, 155
Pluscarden Abbey 180
Poolewe, Inverewe Gardens 16, 18, 178–9, 180–1
Pornacroish 82
Port Charlotte, Islay 144, 145; Museum of Islay Life 145–6
Port Ellen, Islay 144, 145
Portessie 181
Portknockie 181
Port of Menteith 150
Portsoy 129, 181, 181–2
Portree, Skye 194, 195, 196
Pottinger, J. I. D. 22
Preston, Sir Henry 135
Pulteneytown, Wick 210

Queen Elizabeth Forest Park 159
Quoyness chambered tomb 174

Raasay, Inner Hebrides 74, 182
Raasay House, Clachan 182
railways 62, 82, 89, 92, 108, 134, 170, 208
Rait Castle 165
Ramsay, Andrew 183
Rannoch Door, Glencoe 12
Rannoch Moor 62
Rathven 94
Rhum, Inner Hebrides 59, 59, 182
Ring of Brogar 175
Robert Bruce, King 75, 77, 86, 102, 107, 108, 119, 127, 140, 143, 161, 163, 170
Rob Roy MacGregor 62, 83, 98, 115, 205
Rodel, Harris 139; St Clement's Church 139
Rogart 150
Rognvald, Earl 173, 174

Romans 43, 77, 98, 116, 131, 134, 177, 199
Rosehearty 182–3
Rosemarkie 87–8
Rothesay, Bute 94, 96
Rothesay Castle 94, 96
Rothiemurchus 19, 60
Rowandennan 159
Royal Scottish Country Dance Society 48
Royal Society for the Protection of Birds 13, 58, 148
Runciman, James and Walter 124

Saddell Abbey 165
St Andrew's 183–4; Castle 183; Cathedral 183; Royal and Ancient Golf Club 184; St Rule's 183; University 183
St Columba 143, 144, 163, 165
St Fergus 39
St Fillan's Chapel 62
St Kilda 9
St Maelrubha 74, 146, 159
St Monance 184
St Mungo 111
St Ninian's Isle 189, 193
St Ninian's Treasure 193
St Vigeans 184
Sanday, Orkneys 174
Sands of Forvie 60, 103
Scalasaig, Colonsay 103
Scalloway, Shetlands 193; Castle 193
Scapa Flow 175
Scarba Island 146
Schiehallion 183, 184
Scone 184; Moot Hill 184; Palace 184, 186–8; Stone of Destiny 75, 184, 185
Scotstarvit Tower 111
Scott, Sir Walter 21, 62, 69, 78, 83, 98, 177, 192, 202, 205
Scottish Fisheries Museum, Anstruther 74, 74
Scottish Wildlife Trust 13, 19
Scourie 139, 184
Scrabster 175, 189
Sea League 99
Sea Life Centre, Loch Creran 86
Selkirk, Alexander ('Robinson Crusoe') 150, 151
Sguer a'Ghlas Leathaid 54
Sheriffmuir 16, 117; Battle of (1715) 78, 91, 117
Shetland Islands 11, 13, 29, 47; 189–93; Brei Holm 193; Clickhimin Broch 189; Fetlar 189; fiddle music 48; Firths Voe 39; Foula 192; Jarlshof 13, 192; knitting 189; Lerwick 45, 49, 192, 193; Mainland 189, 192, 193; Mousa 13, 192; Muckle Flugga 192; Out Skerries 192–3; Papa Stour 193; St Ninian's Isle 189, 193; Scalloway 193; Sumburgh Airport 192; Unst 192, 193; Whalsay 193; Yell 193
Shetland ponies 192
Singing Sands, Eigg 124
Sites of Special Scientific Interest 13, 59
Skara Brae, Orkney 13, 175
Skinner, James Scott 84
Skye 32, 59, 136, 139, 182, 190–1, 193–6; Armadale 195; Armadale Castle 13, 16, 195; 'Battle of the Braes' 32–4; Broadford 195; Crofting

Museum, Kilmuir 31; Cuillin Hills 51, 52–3, 195; Dunvegan 196; Elgol 196; Portree 194, 195, 196
Slains Castle 108
Smoo Cave, Durness 121
Somerled, Lord of the Isles 77
Somerville, Mary 94
South Uist 86, 87, 196–7; Loch Druidibeg Nature Reserve 59, 197
Spean Bridge 197
Spey, river, Speyside 55, 58, 70, 89, 96, 99, 103, 104, 136, 138, 148, 169, 197, 198, 198–9
Spey Bay 197
Speyside Way 197–8
sporting estates 56, 58
Spynie, Spynie Palace 160
Stack of Handa 139
Stac Pollaidh, Inverpolly 143
Staffa 198–9; Fingal's Cave 199
Standing Stones of Callanish 13, 152
Standing Stones of Stenness 175
Statutes of Iona (1609) 26, 46
Stevenson, Robert Louis 82
Stewart, Earl Patrick 174, 193
Stirling 91, 199–201; Argyll Ludging, Castle Wynd 199; Castle 199; Mar's Wark 200, 201; pipe band 27; University 92
Stonefield Castle, Loch Fyne 203
Stonehaven 51, 201; fireball swinging ceremony 49, 201
Stone of Destiny 75, 184, 185
Stornoway, Lewis 152, 154
Strait of Corriebhreacan 146
Strathardle 12
Strathbogie 140
Strath Carron 107
Strathcona, Lord 103
Strath Conon 10, 54
Strath Fillan 62
Strathmore 72
Strathnaver Museum 87
Strath of Kildonan 201
Strathpeffer 201–2
Strathspey 136, 148
Strathspey Railway 89
Strathyre 202
Strome 154
Stromness, Orkneys 175
Stronsay, Orkneys 175
Strontian 202
Sueno's Stone, Forres 13, 131
Sullom Voe 39, 189

Tain 202–3; St Duthus Church and Chapel 203
Tamdhu distillery 197
Tarbert, Harris 139
Tarbert, Loch Fyne 203
Tarbet, Loch Lomond 159
Tarlair 161
Tarland 72
tartans 23, 103
Tarves church 170
Tay, river 11, 119, 120, 147, 177
Taylor, John, the 'Penniless Poet' 138
Taynuilt 91
Telford, Thomas 98, 104, 107, 120, 169, 177, 197, 210
Thomson, Robert William 201
Thornton, Colonel Thomas 58
Thurso 113, 203–4; Folk Museum 203; Old St Peter's Kirk 203

Tillicoutry 204
Tiree 204
Tobermory, Mull 163, 166–7
Tolquhon Castle 170
Tomintoul 204; The Five Sisters of Kintail 206–7
Tompitlac Pictish fortifications 89
Tongue, Tongue House 205
Torridon 54, 60, 87, 205, 205
tourism 56, 58, 60, 62, 82
Trossachs 60, 69, 98, 205, 208, 208
Tuguet 197
Tulliallan Castle 148
Tullibardine Chapel, Auchterarder 78, 79
Tullich 82
Tummel, river 11, 147, 180, 183
Tummel-Garry hydroelectric scheme 180
Turiff 208
Turiff Show 208
Tyndrum 208–9

Uamh Fhraing, Eigg 124
Ulbster Stone, Thurso 203
Ullapool 12, 143, 154, 209; Customs House Street 209
Ulva 165
Unst, Shetlands 37, 192, 193; Muness Castle 193
Urquhart, Sir Thomas 108
Urquhart Castle 113
Urquhart Priory, Kingston 148

Vatersay, Outer Hebrides 86
Vatersay Raiders 86
Victoria, Queen 82, 83, 91, 111, 138, 159, 204
Vikings 23, 77, 99, 111, 136, 144, 152, 169, 173, 176, 182, 189, 192, 195, 203, 204, 210

Wade, General George 69, 72, 103–4
Wallace, Sir William 117, 119, 201
Wallace Stone, Sheriffmuir 117
Wester Ross, 159, 205
West Highland Railway 134, 208
West Highland Way 61–3
Westray, Orkneys 175–6
whaling industry 92, 118, 175, 177
Whaligoe 210
Whalsay, Shetlands 193
whisky distilleries 17, 19, 60, 70, 92, 115, 134, 141, 146, 177, 195, 197, 203, 204, 210
Whisky Trail 19, 204
Whithorn 144, 159
Wick 210
wildlife reserves/habitats 12, 19, 58–60, 87, 143, 148, 149, 159, 163, 182, 197, 208
William the Lion, King 75, 118, 161, 177
Wine Tower, Fraserburgh 135
Wolf of Badenoch 124, 155
Wordsworth, Dorothy and William 62, 160

Yell, Shetlands 193; Old Haa of Burravoe 193
Young, Dr James 'Paraffin' 37
Younger Botanic Garden 104
Ythan, river 103, 126, 135

Zulu fishing boats 160